VIZ GRAPHIC NOVEL

INU-YASHA
A FEUDAL FAIRY TALE™

VOL. 3

STORY AND ART BY

RUMIKO TAKAHASHI

CONTENTS

This volume contains INU-YASHA #11
(second half) through INU-YASHA
PART 2 # 1 (first half) in their entirety.

STORY AND ART BY
RUMIKO TAKAHASHI

ENGLISH ADAPTATION BY
GERARD JONES

Translation/Mari Morimoto
Touch-Up Art & Lettering/Wayne Truman
Editor/Julie Davis
Assistant Editor/Bill Flanagan
Cover Design/Hidemi Sahara

V.P. of Sales & Marketing/Rick Bauer
V.P. of Editorial/Hyoe Narita
Publisher/Seiji Horibuchi

Printed in Canada

Published by Viz Communications, Inc.
P.O. Box 77010 • San Francisco, CA 94107

• get your own vizmail.net email account
• register for the weekly email newsletter
• sign up for your free catalog
• voice 1-800-394-3042 fax 415-384-8936
www.viz.com

10 9 8 7 6 5
First printing, December 1998
Fourth printing, April 2002
Fifth printing, October 2002

INU-YASHA GRAPHIC NOVELS TO DATE:
INU-YASHA VOL. 1
INU-YASHA VOL. 2
INU-YASHA VOL. 3
INU-YASHA VOL. 4
INU-YASHA VOL. 5
INU-YASHA VOL. 6
INU-YASHA VOL. 7
INU-YASHA VOL. 8
INU-YASHA VOL. 9
INU-YASHA VOL. 10
INU-YASHA VOL. 11
INU-YASHA VOL. 12

SCROLL ONE

THE DARK CASTLE

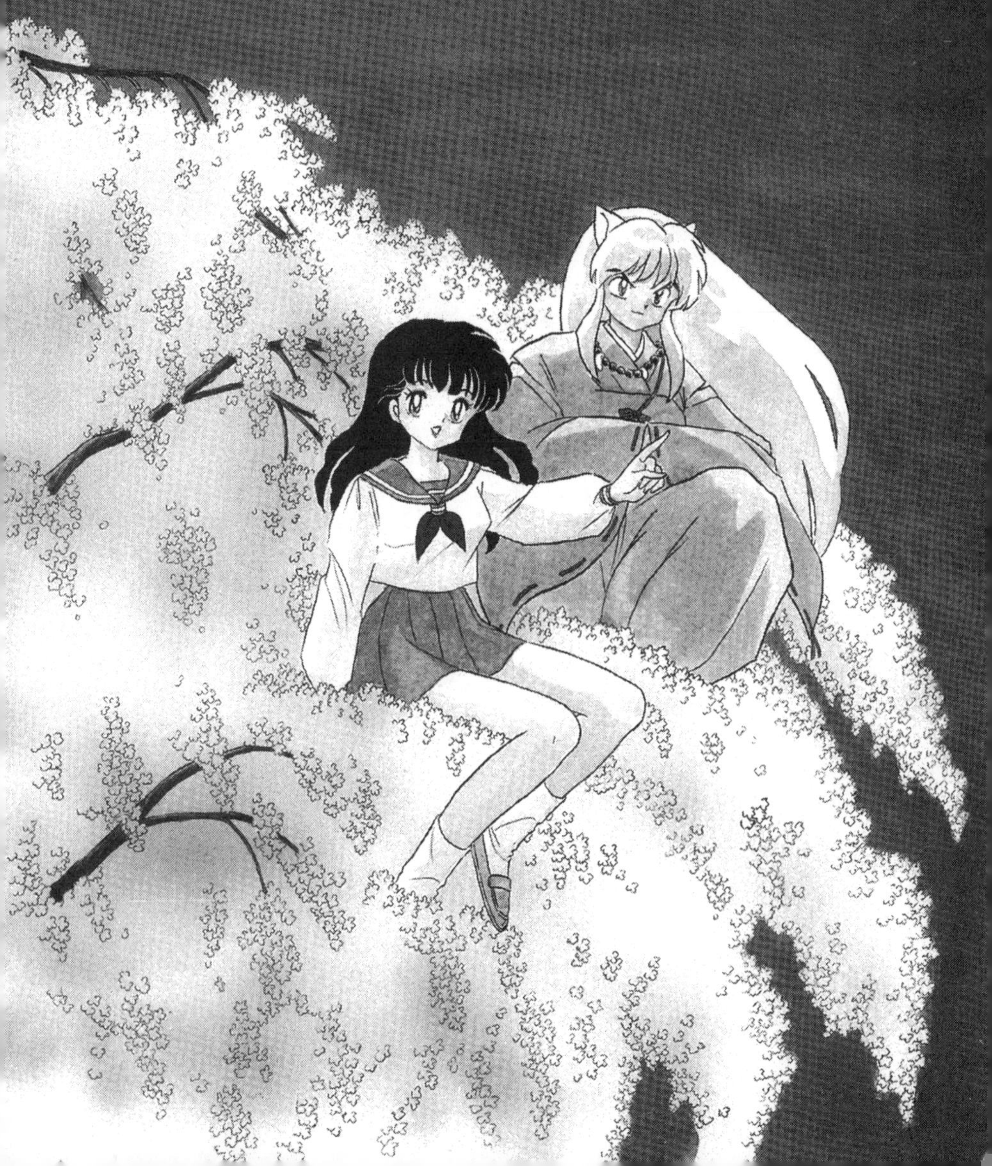

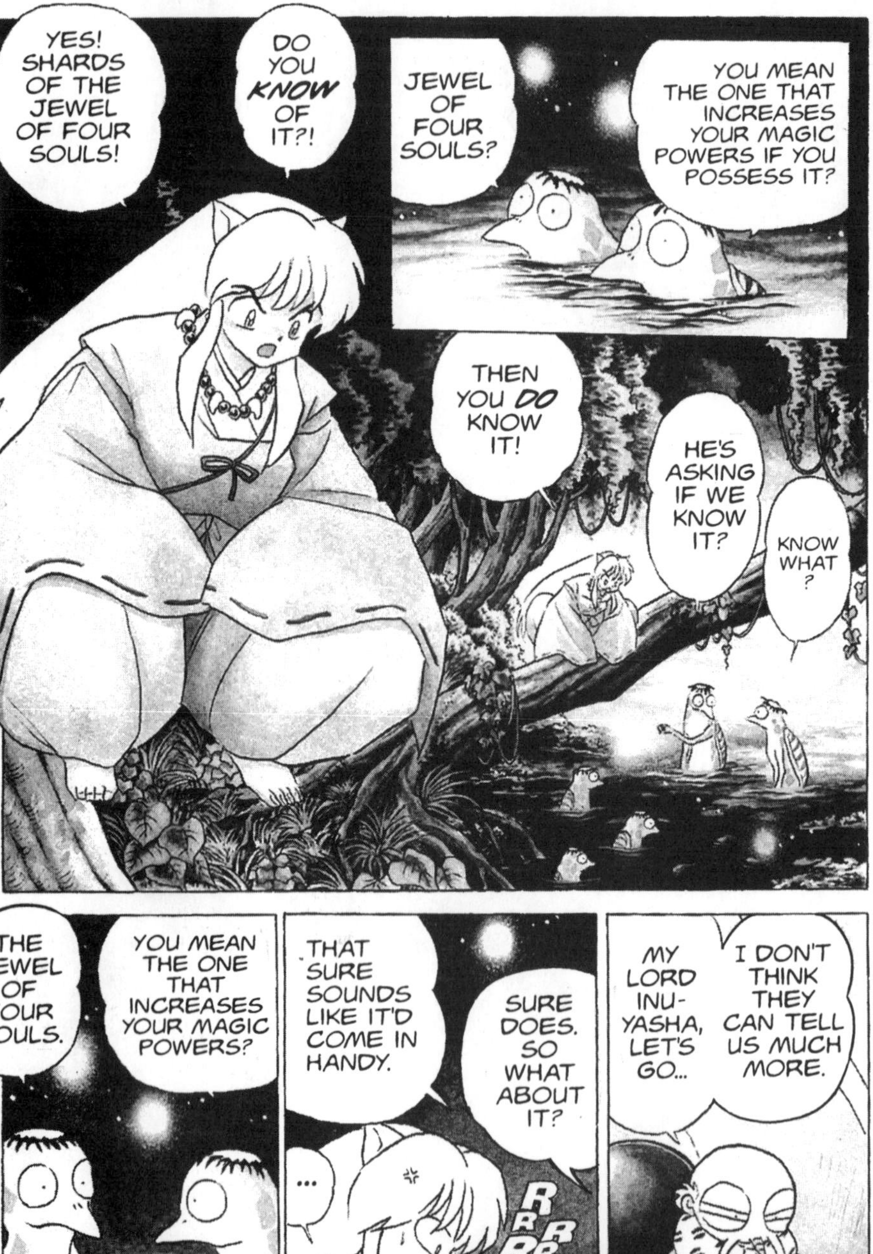
YES! SHARDS OF THE JEWEL OF FOUR SOULS!
DO YOU *KNOW* OF IT?!
JEWEL OF FOUR SOULS?
YOU MEAN THE ONE THAT INCREASES YOUR MAGIC POWERS IF YOU POSSESS IT?
THEN YOU *DO* KNOW IT!
HE'S ASKING IF WE KNOW IT?
KNOW WHAT?
THE JEWEL OF FOUR SOULS.
YOU MEAN THE ONE THAT INCREASES YOUR MAGIC POWERS?
THAT SURE SOUNDS LIKE IT'D COME IN HANDY.
SURE DOES. SO WHAT ABOUT IT?
...
RRRRRR
MY LORD INU-YASHA, LET'S GO...
I DON'T THINK THEY CAN TELL US MUCH MORE.

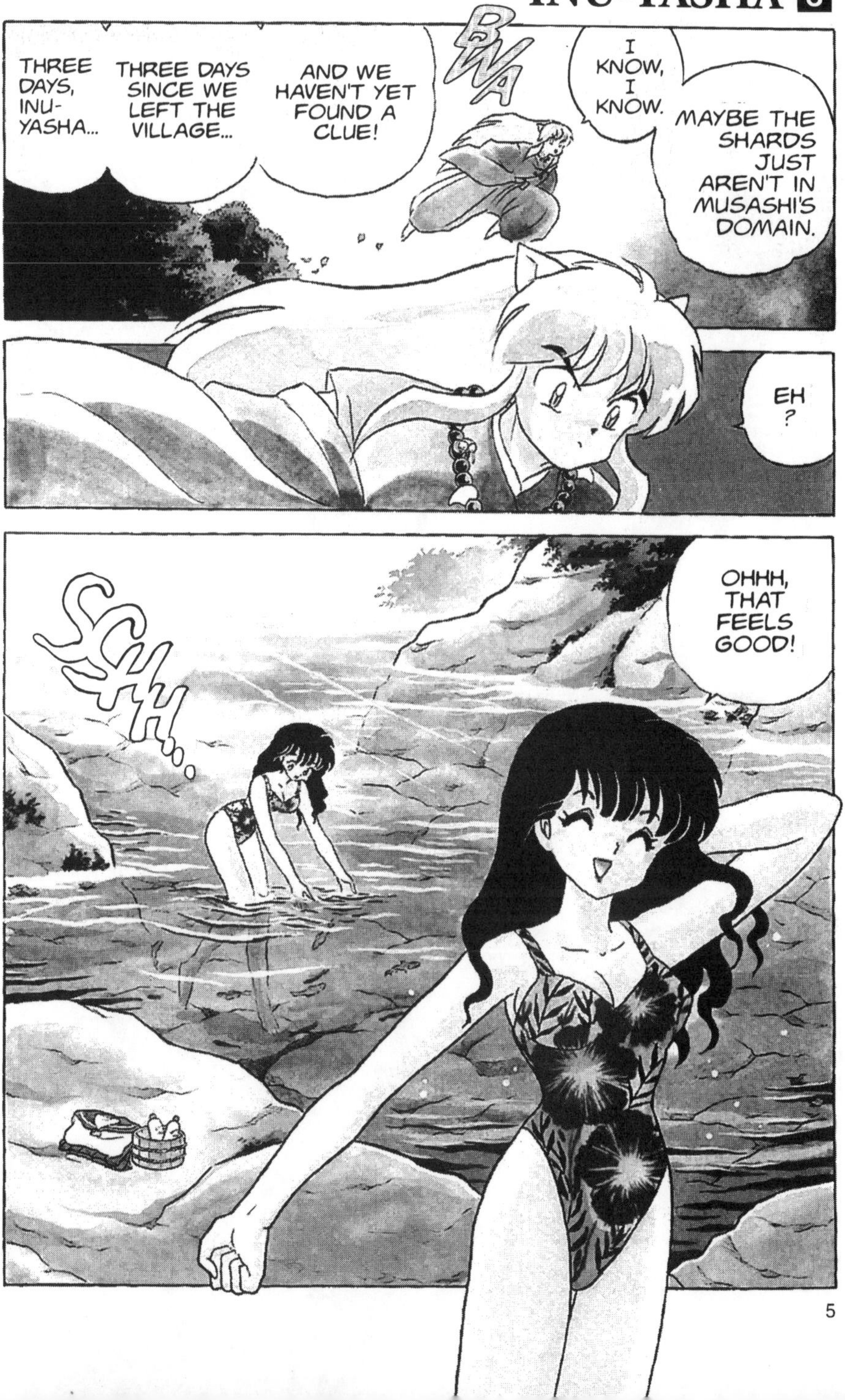
THREE DAYS, INU-YASHA...
THREE DAYS SINCE WE LEFT THE VILLAGE...
AND WE HAVEN'T YET FOUND A CLUE!
BWA
I KNOW, I KNOW.
MAYBE THE SHARDS JUST AREN'T IN MUSASHI'S DOMAIN.
EH?
SCHH...
OHHH, THAT FEELS GOOD!

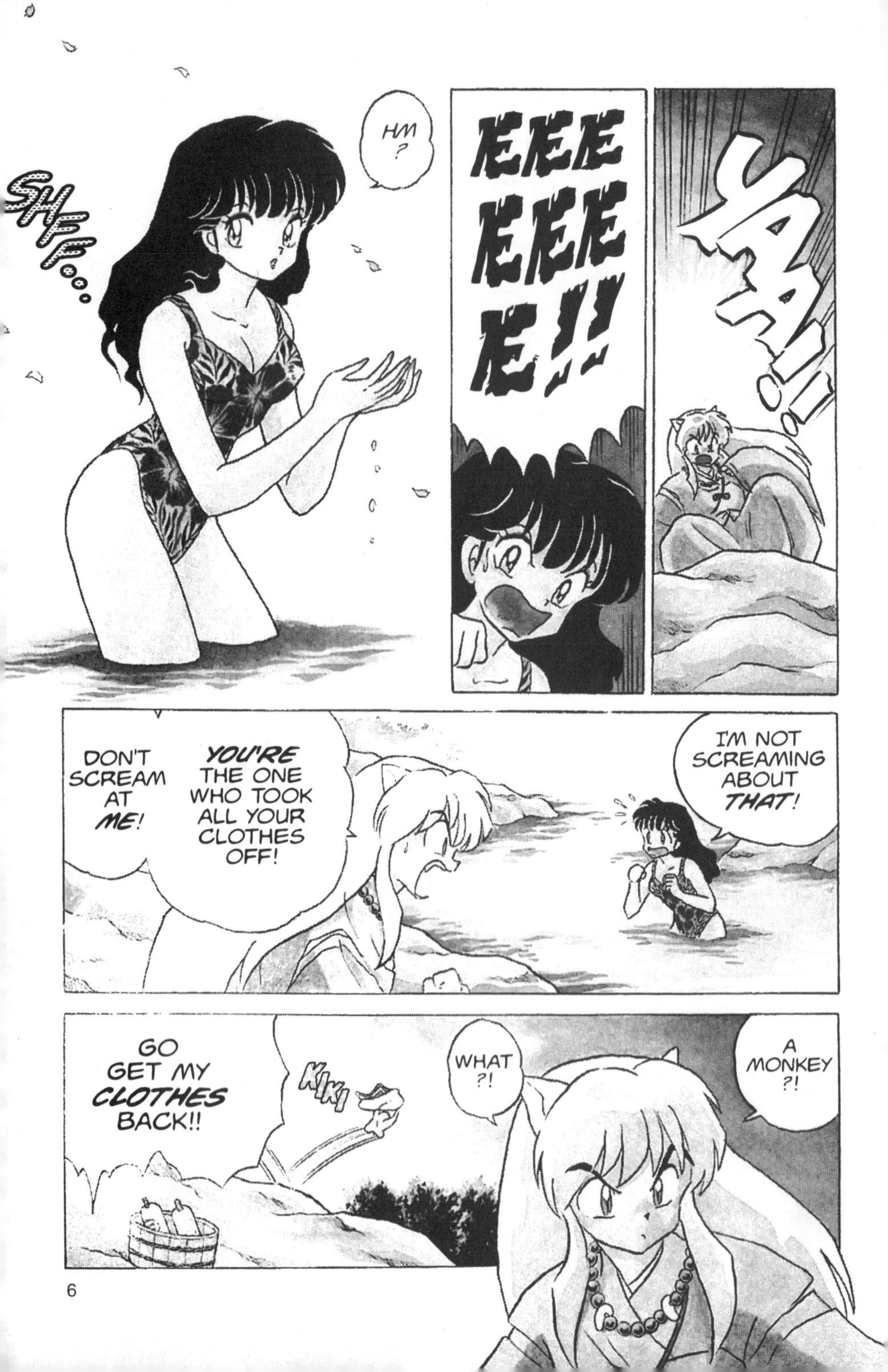
SHFF...
HM?
DON'T SCREAM AT ME!
YOU'RE THE ONE WHO TOOK ALL YOUR CLOTHES OFF!
I'M NOT SCREAMING ABOUT THAT!
GO GET MY CLOTHES BACK!!
KIKI
WHAT?!
A MONKEY?!

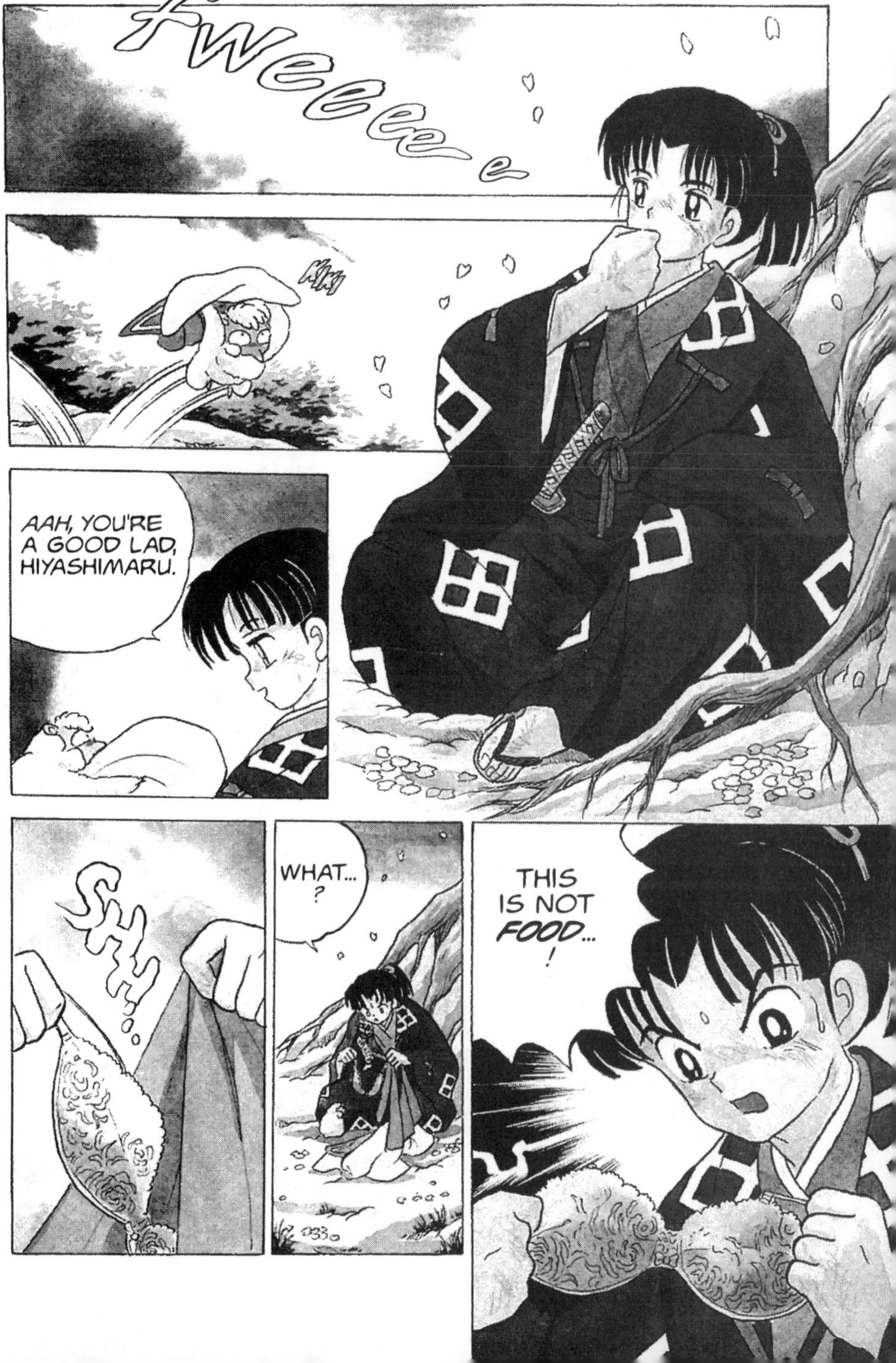
fweeeee
AAH, YOU'RE A GOOD LAD, HIYASHIMARU.
SHH
WHAT... ?
THIS IS NOT FOOD... !

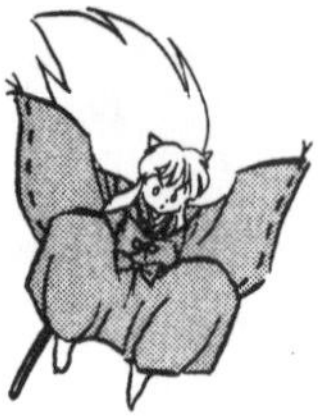

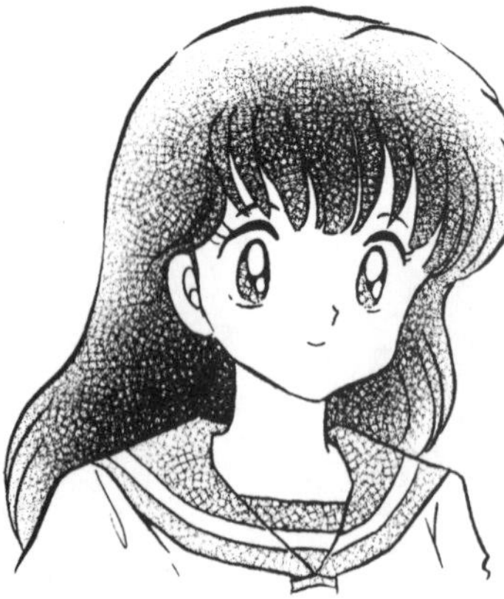

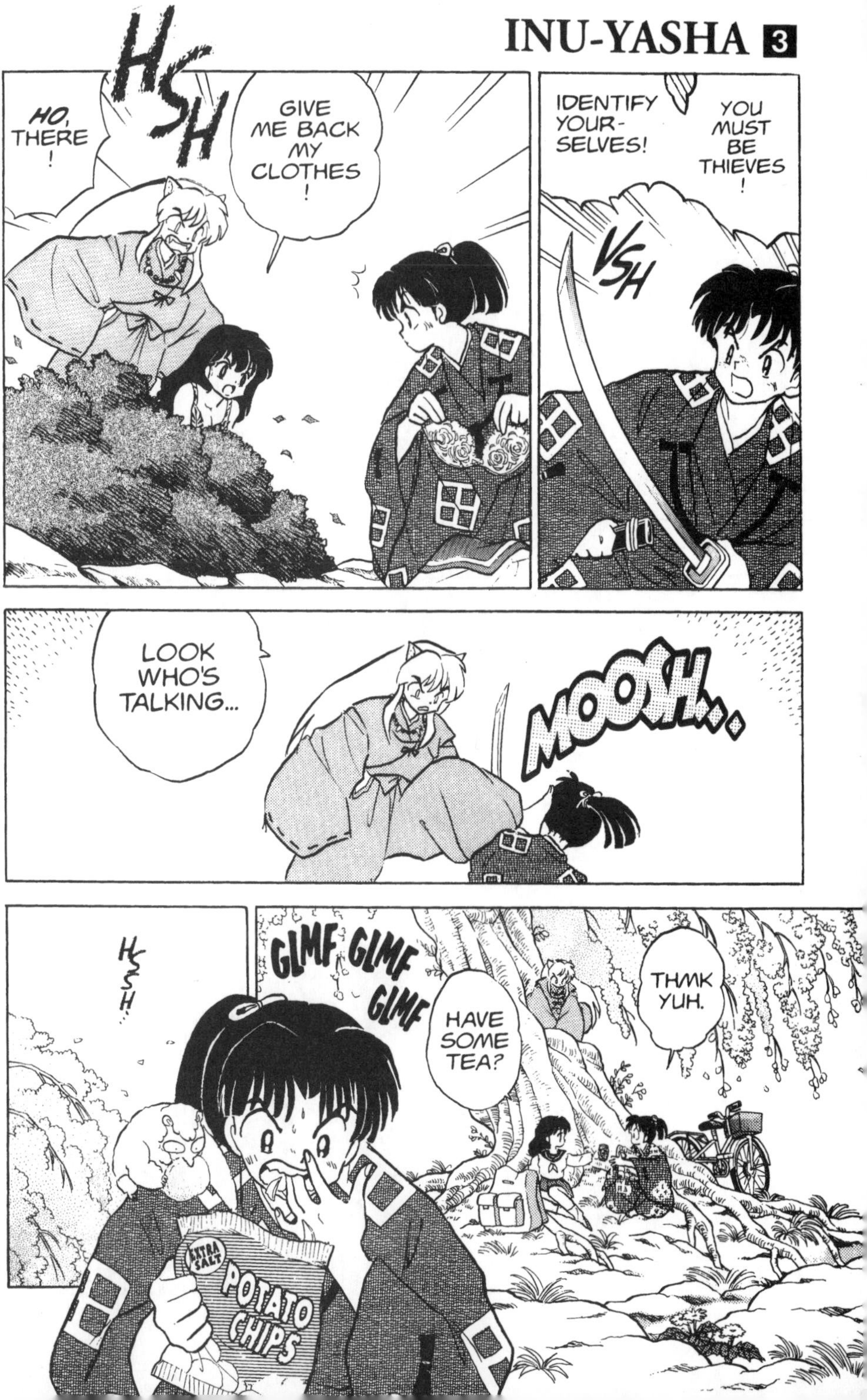
HSH
HO, THERE!
GIVE ME BACK MY CLOTHES!
IDENTIFY YOURSELVES!
YOU MUST BE THIEVES!
VSH
LOOK WHO'S TALKING...
MOOSH...
HSSH!
GLMF GLMF GLMF
HAVE SOME TEA?
THMK YUH.
EXTRA SALT
POTATO CHIPS

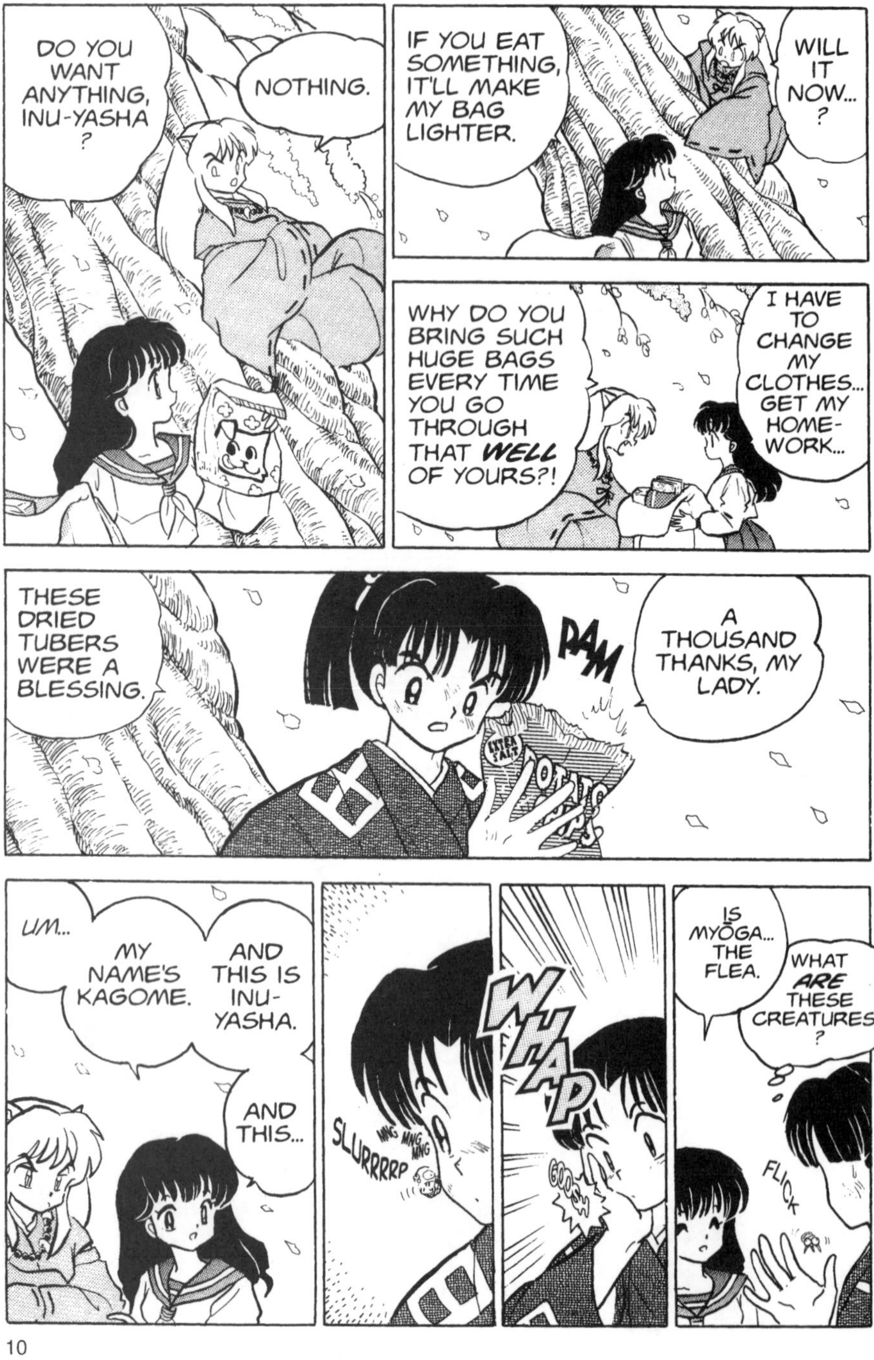
DO YOU WANT ANYTHING, INU-YASHA?
NOTHING.
IF YOU EAT SOMETHING, IT'LL MAKE MY BAG LIGHTER.
WILL IT NOW...?
WHY DO YOU BRING SUCH HUGE BAGS EVERY TIME YOU GO THROUGH THAT **WELL** OF YOURS?!
I HAVE TO CHANGE MY CLOTHES... GET MY HOMEWORK...
THESE DRIED TUBERS WERE A BLESSING.
RAM
A THOUSAND THANKS, MY LADY.
EXTRA SALT
UM...
MY NAME'S KAGOME.
AND THIS IS INU-YASHA.
AND THIS...
SLURRRRP
MNG MNG MNG
WHAP!
GOOSH
IS MYOGA... THE FLEA.
WHAT **ARE** THESE CREATURES...?
FLICK

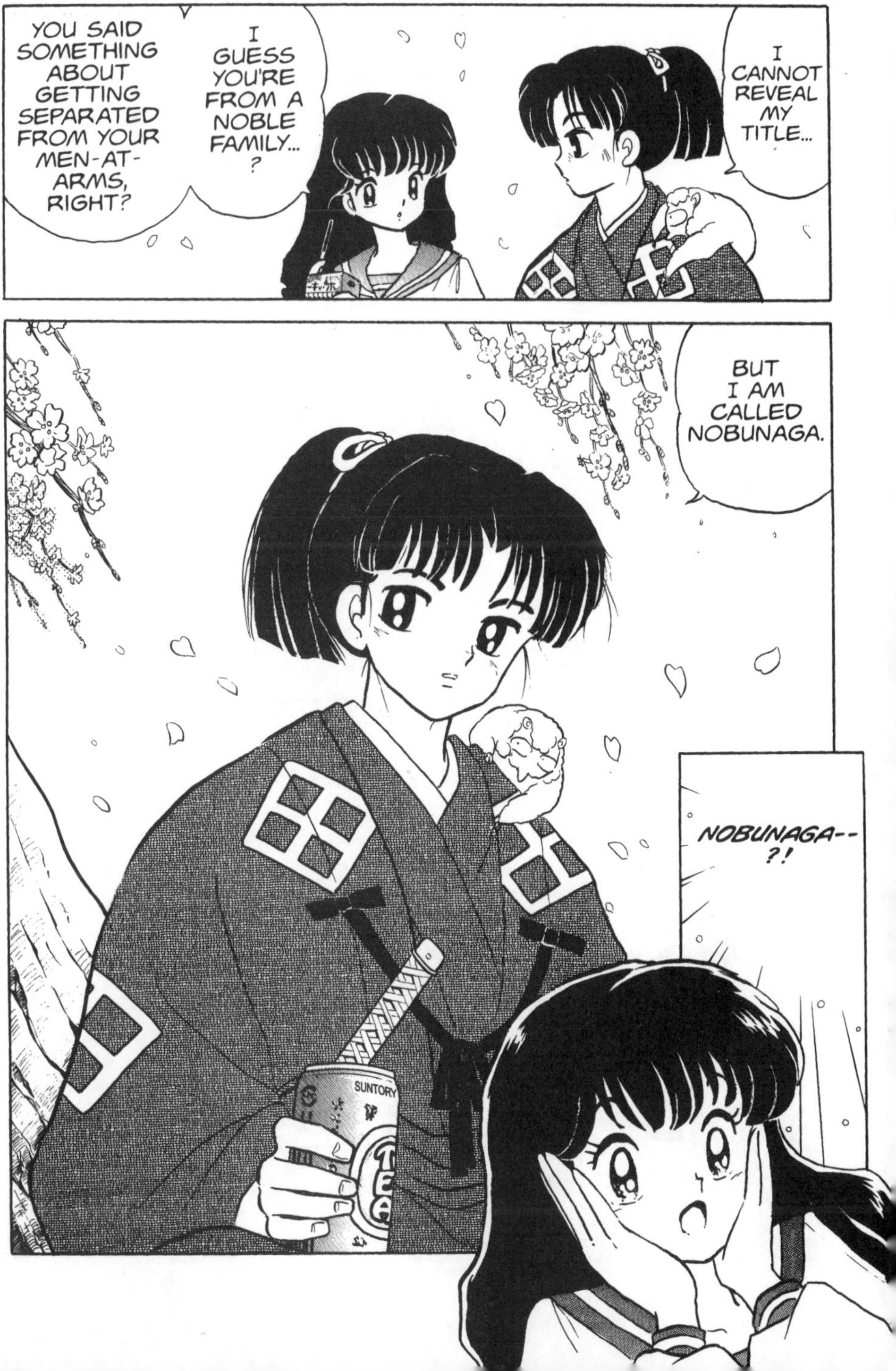
YOU SAID SOMETHING ABOUT GETTING SEPARATED FROM YOUR MEN-AT-ARMS, RIGHT?
I GUESS YOU'RE FROM A NOBLE FAMILY...?
I CANNOT REVEAL MY TITLE...
BUT I AM CALLED NOBUNAGA.
NOBUNAGA--?!
SUNTORY

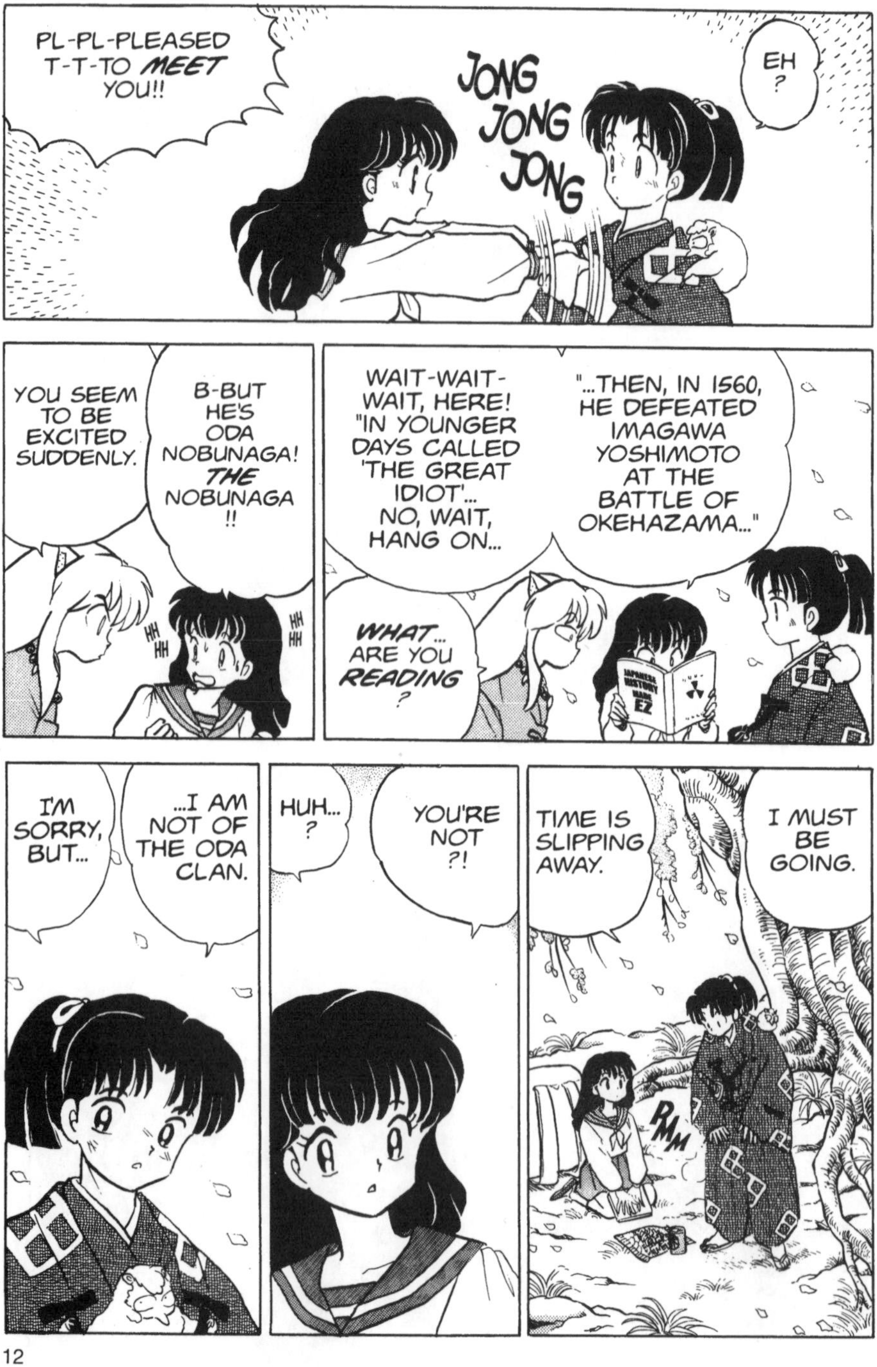
PL-PL-PLEASED T-T-TO MEET YOU!!
JONG JONG JONG
EH ?
YOU SEEM TO BE EXCITED SUDDENLY.
B-BUT HE'S ODA NOBUNAGA! THE NOBUNAGA !!
HH HH
HH HH
WAIT-WAIT-WAIT, HERE! "IN YOUNGER DAYS CALLED 'THE GREAT IDIOT'... NO, WAIT, HANG ON...
"...THEN, IN 1560, HE DEFEATED IMAGAWA YOSHIMOTO AT THE BATTLE OF OKEHAZAMA..."
WHAT... ARE YOU READING ?
I'M SORRY, BUT...
...I AM NOT OF THE ODA CLAN.
HUH... ?
YOU'RE NOT ?!
TIME IS SLIPPING AWAY.
I MUST BE GOING.
RMM

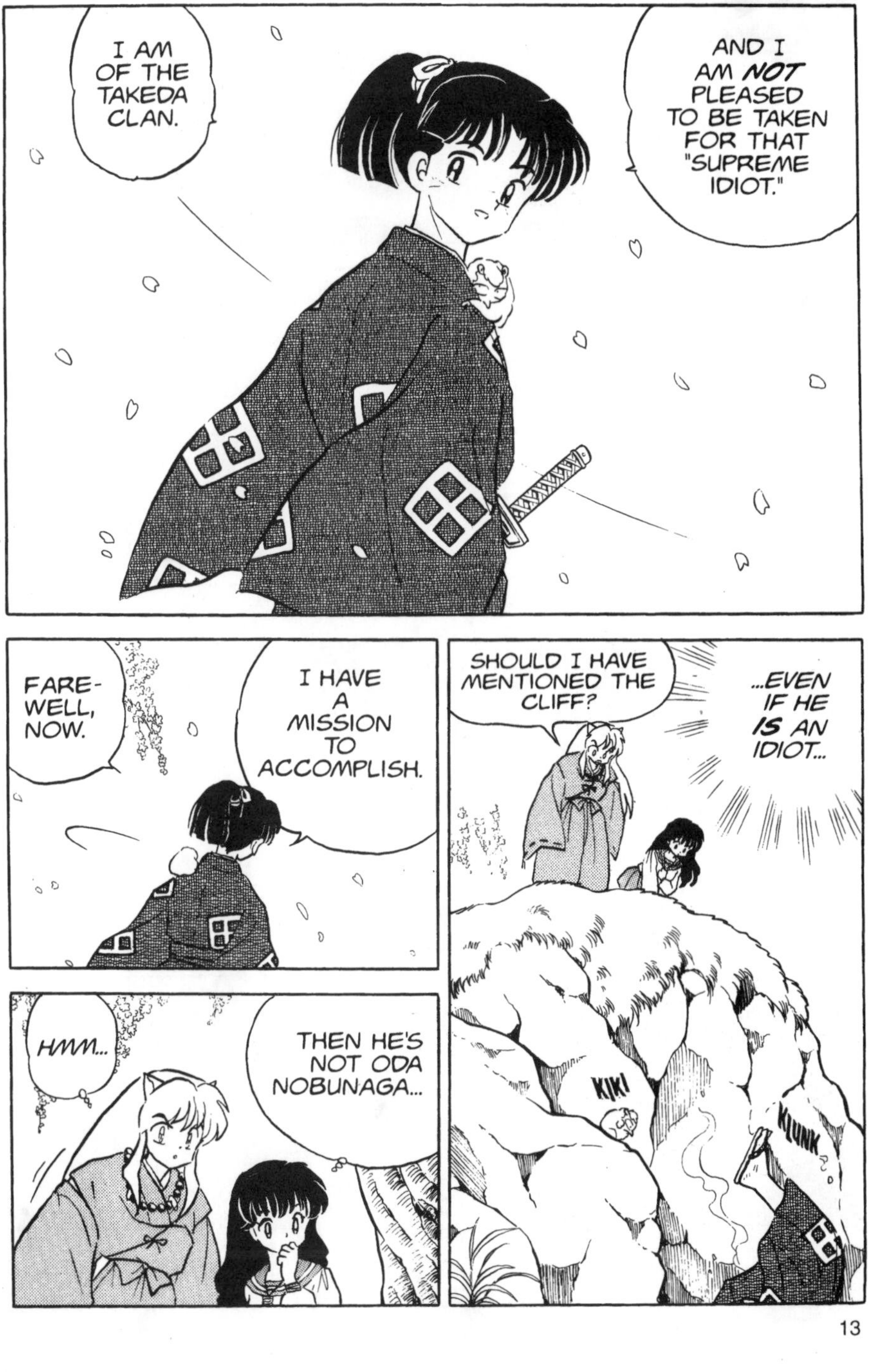
I AM OF THE TAKEDA CLAN.
AND I AM NOT PLEASED TO BE TAKEN FOR THAT "SUPREME IDIOT."
FARE-WELL, NOW.
I HAVE A MISSION TO ACCOMPLISH.
HMM...
THEN HE'S NOT ODA NOBUNAGA...
SHOULD I HAVE MENTIONED THE CLIFF?
...EVEN IF HE IS AN IDIOT...
KIKI
KLUNK

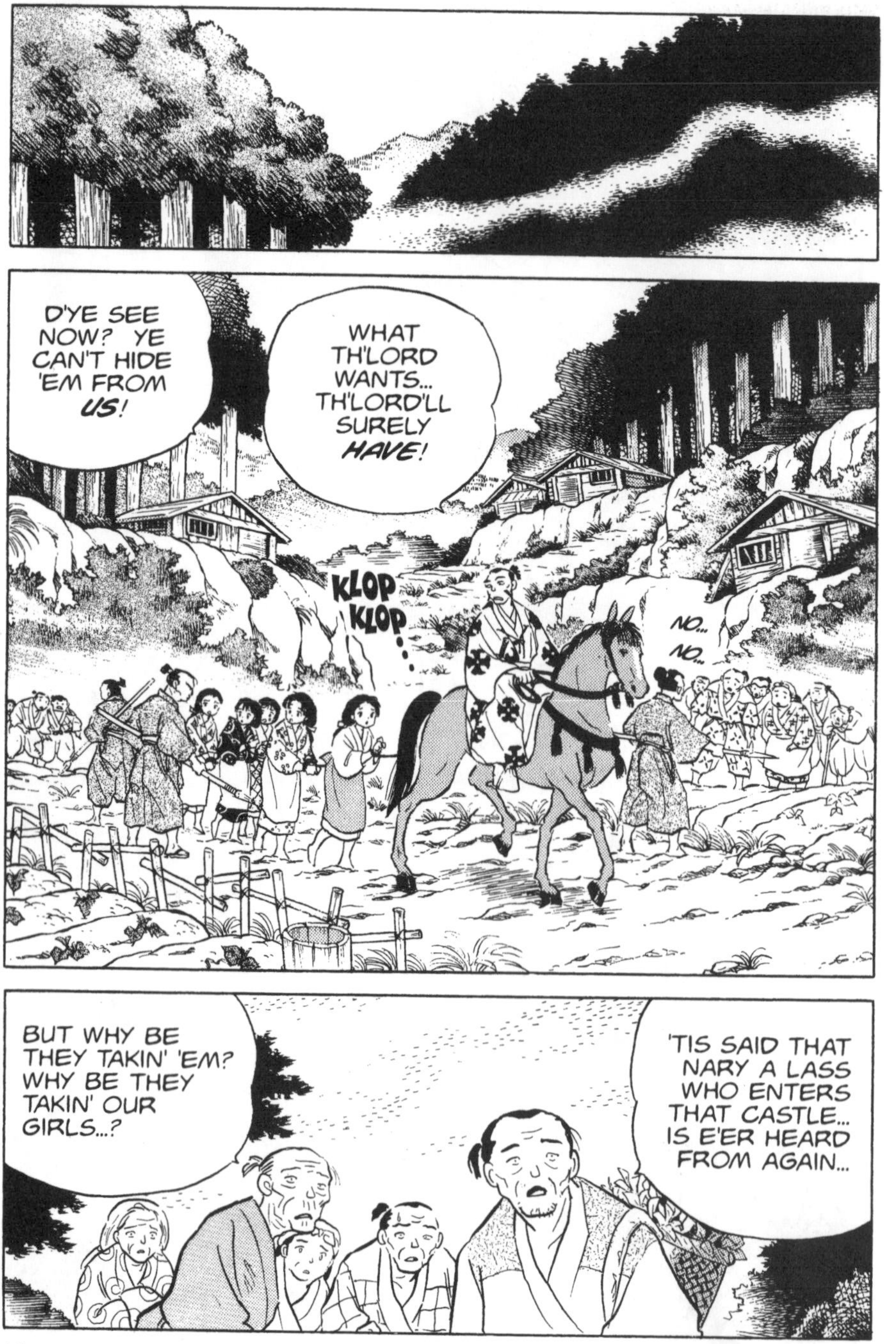
D'YE SEE NOW? YE CAN'T HIDE 'EM FROM *US*!
WHAT TH'LORD WANTS... TH'LORD'LL SURELY *HAVE*!
KLOP KLOP...
NO... NO...
BUT WHY BE THEY TAKIN' 'EM? WHY BE THEY TAKIN' OUR GIRLS...?
'TIS SAID THAT NARY A LASS WHO ENTERS THAT CASTLE... IS E'ER HEARD FROM AGAIN...

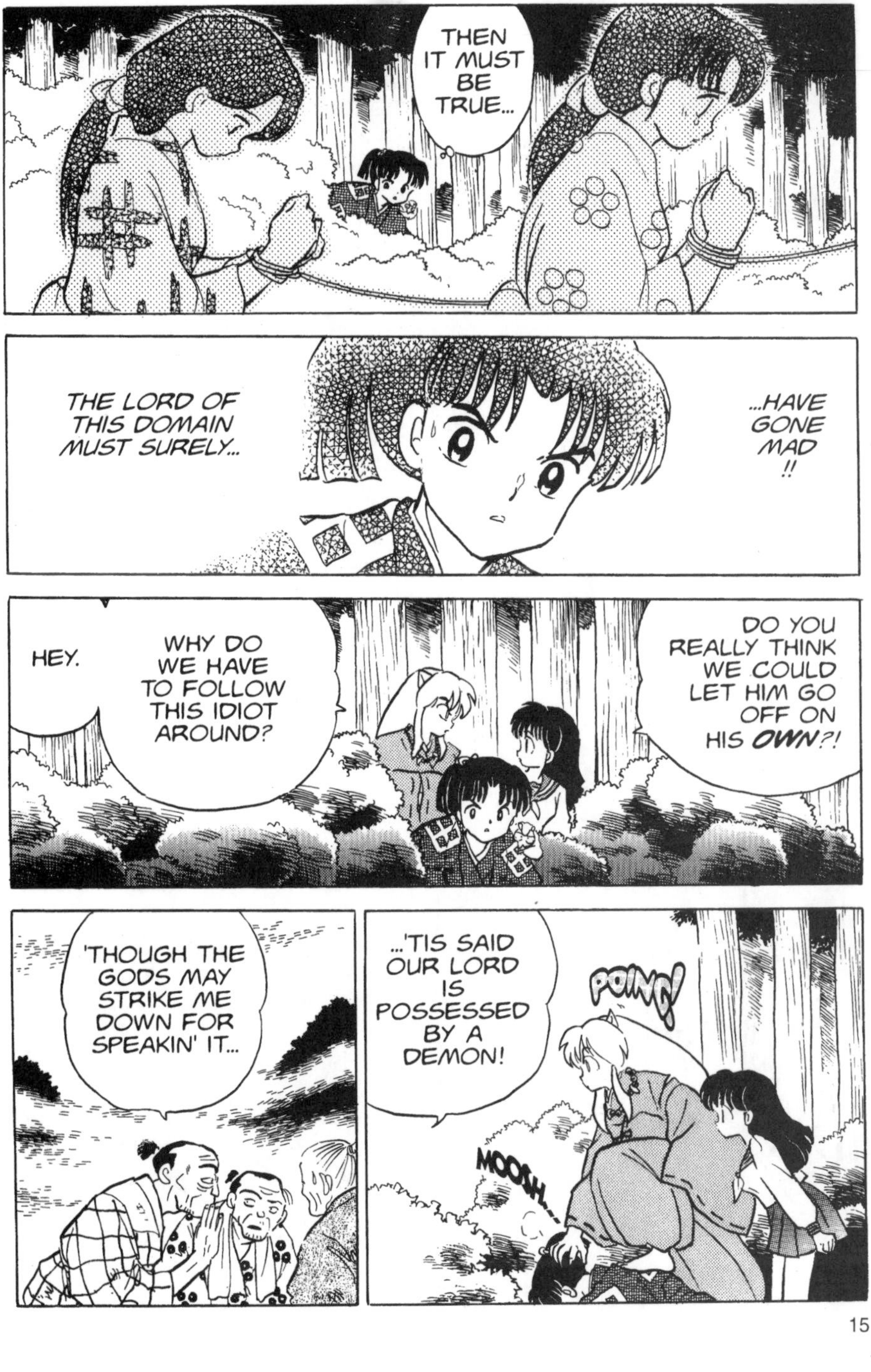
THEN IT MUST BE TRUE...
THE LORD OF THIS DOMAIN MUST SURELY...
...HAVE GONE MAD !!
HEY.
WHY DO WE HAVE TO FOLLOW THIS IDIOT AROUND?
DO YOU REALLY THINK WE COULD LET HIM GO OFF ON HIS OWN?!
'THOUGH THE GODS MAY STRIKE ME DOWN FOR SPEAKIN' IT...
...'TIS SAID OUR LORD IS POSSESSED BY A DEMON!
POING!
MOOSH...

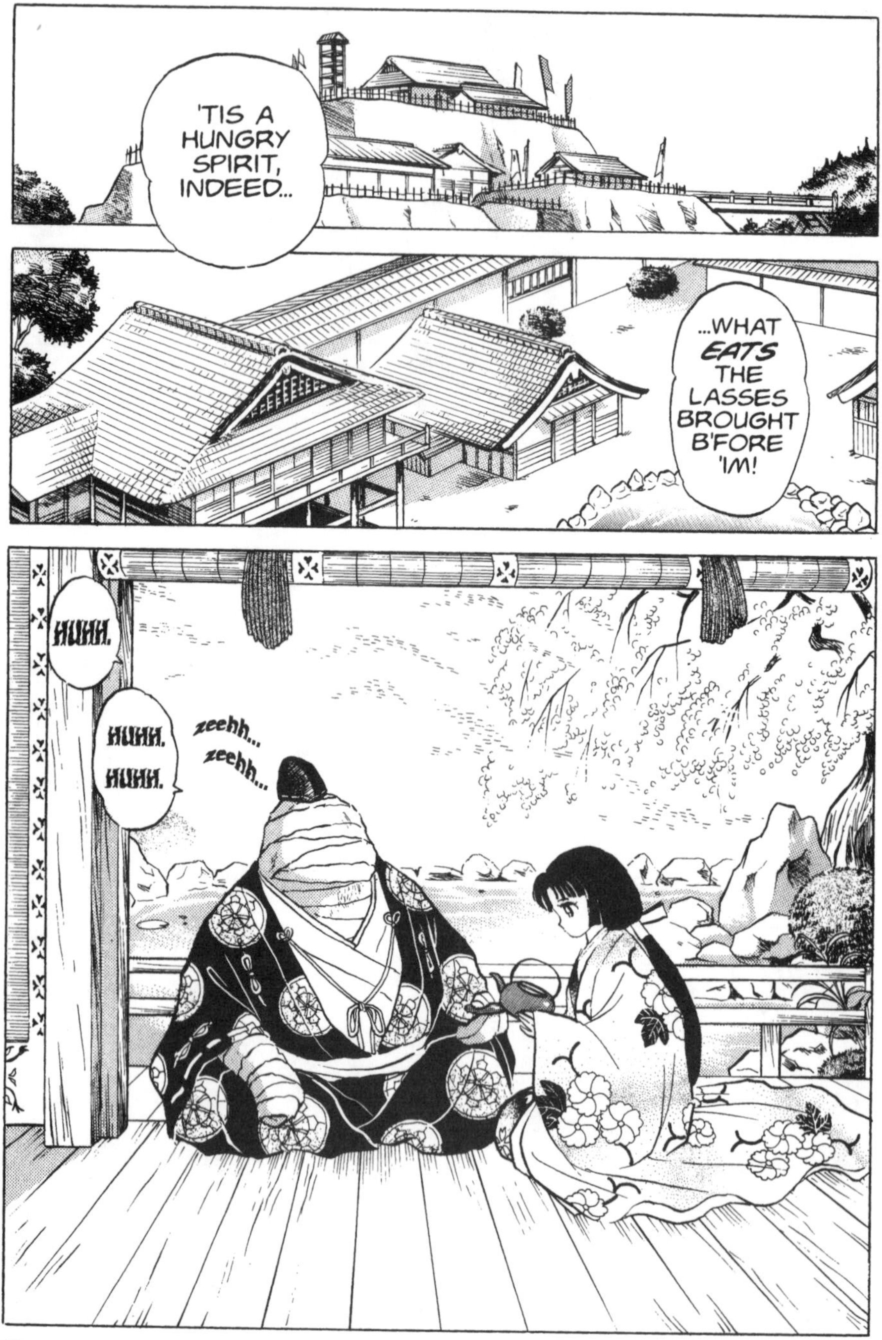
'TIS A HUNGRY SPIRIT, INDEED...
...WHAT EATS THE LASSES BROUGHT B'FORE 'IM!
HUHH.
HUHH. HUHH.
zeehh... zeehh...

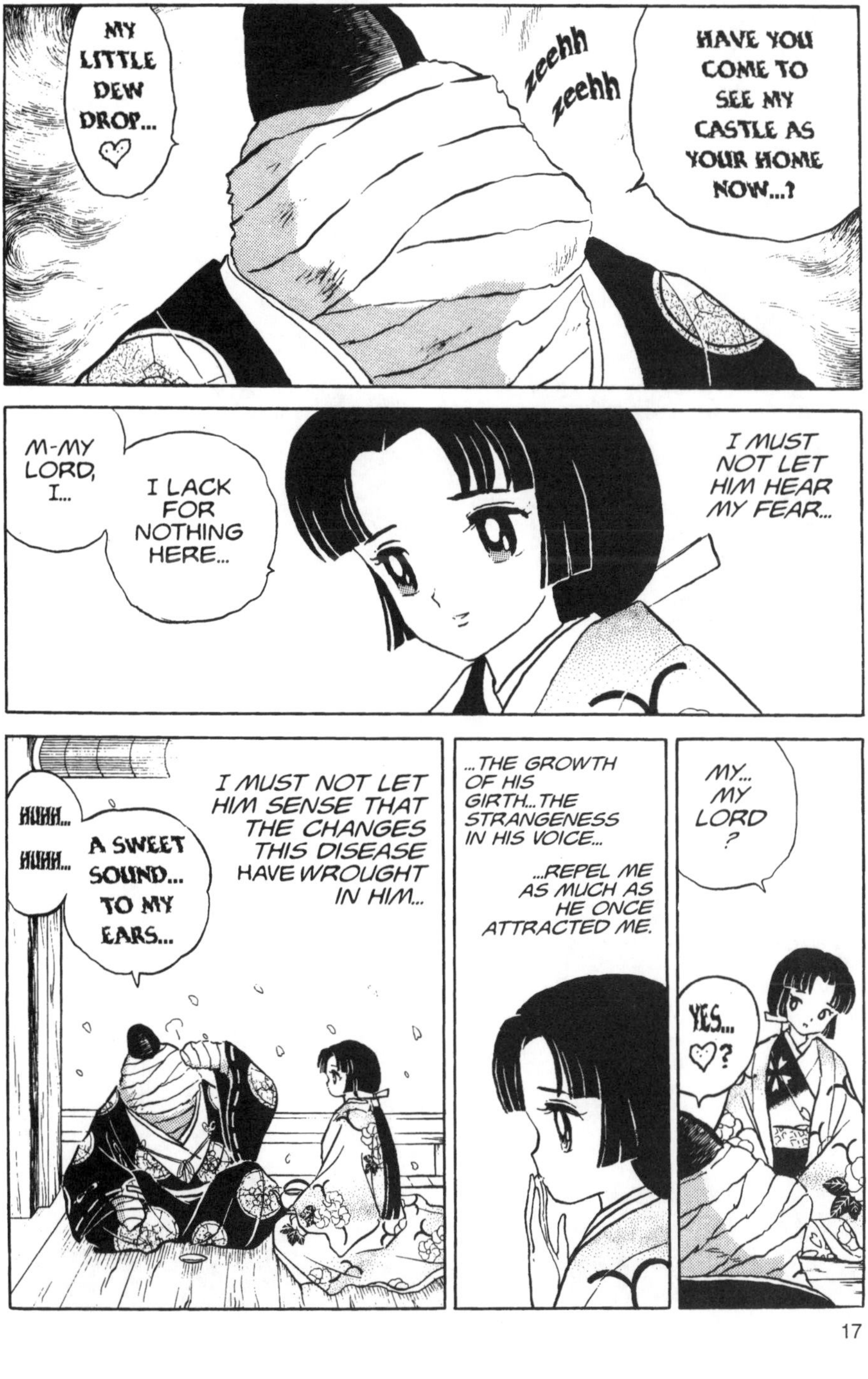
MY LITTLE DEW DROP... ♡
zeehh zeehh
HAVE YOU COME TO SEE MY CASTLE AS YOUR HOME NOW...?
M-MY LORD, I...
I LACK FOR NOTHING HERE...
I MUST NOT LET HIM HEAR MY FEAR...
HUHH... HUHH...
A SWEET SOUND... TO MY EARS...
I MUST NOT LET HIM SENSE THAT THE CHANGES THIS DISEASE HAVE WROUGHT IN HIM...
...THE GROWTH OF HIS GIRTH...THE STRANGENESS IN HIS VOICE...
...REPEL ME AS MUCH AS HE ONCE ATTRACTED ME.
MY... MY LORD ?
YES... ♡?

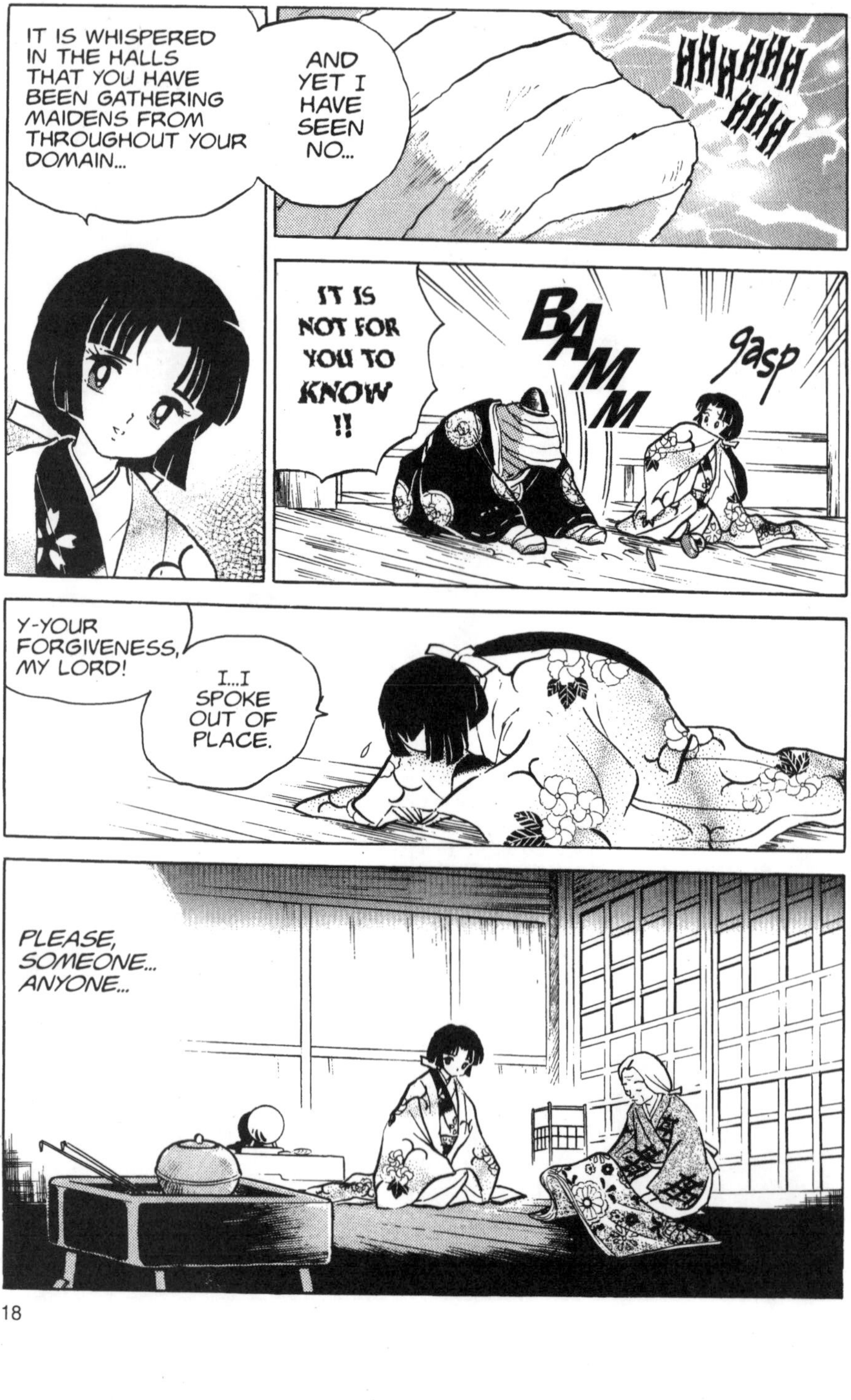
IT IS WHISPERED IN THE HALLS THAT YOU HAVE BEEN GATHERING MAIDENS FROM THROUGHOUT YOUR DOMAIN...
AND YET I HAVE SEEN NO...
HHHHHH HHH
IT IS NOT FOR YOU TO KNOW !!
BAMM
gasp
Y-YOUR FORGIVENESS, MY LORD!
I...I SPOKE OUT OF PLACE.
PLEASE, SOMEONE... ANYONE...

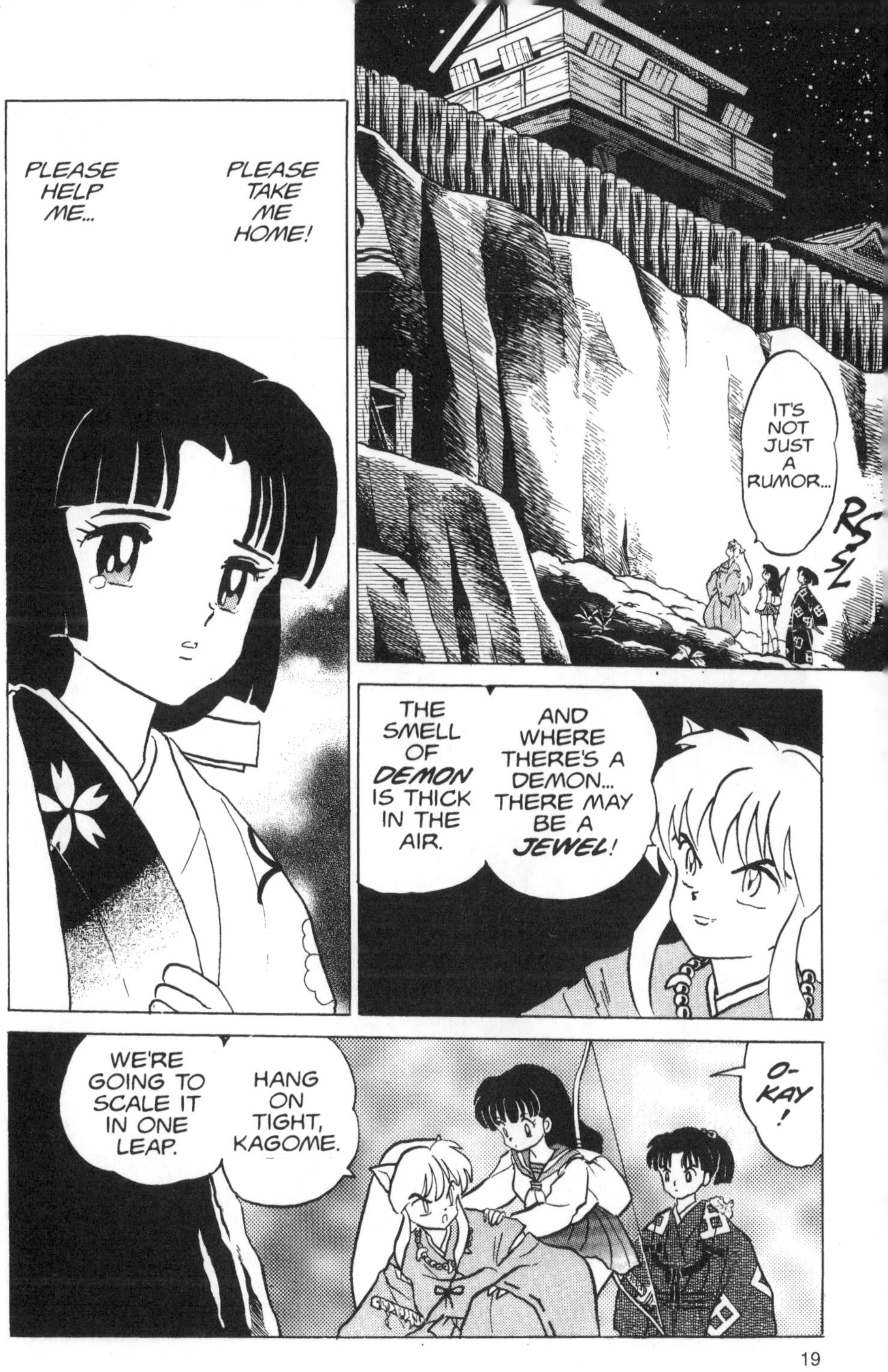

PLEASE HELP ME...
PLEASE TAKE ME HOME!
IT'S NOT JUST A RUMOR...
RSSL
THE SMELL OF DEMON IS THICK IN THE AIR.
AND WHERE THERE'S A DEMON... THERE MAY BE A JEWEL!
WE'RE GOING TO SCALE IT IN ONE LEAP.
HANG ON TIGHT, KAGOME.
O-KAY!

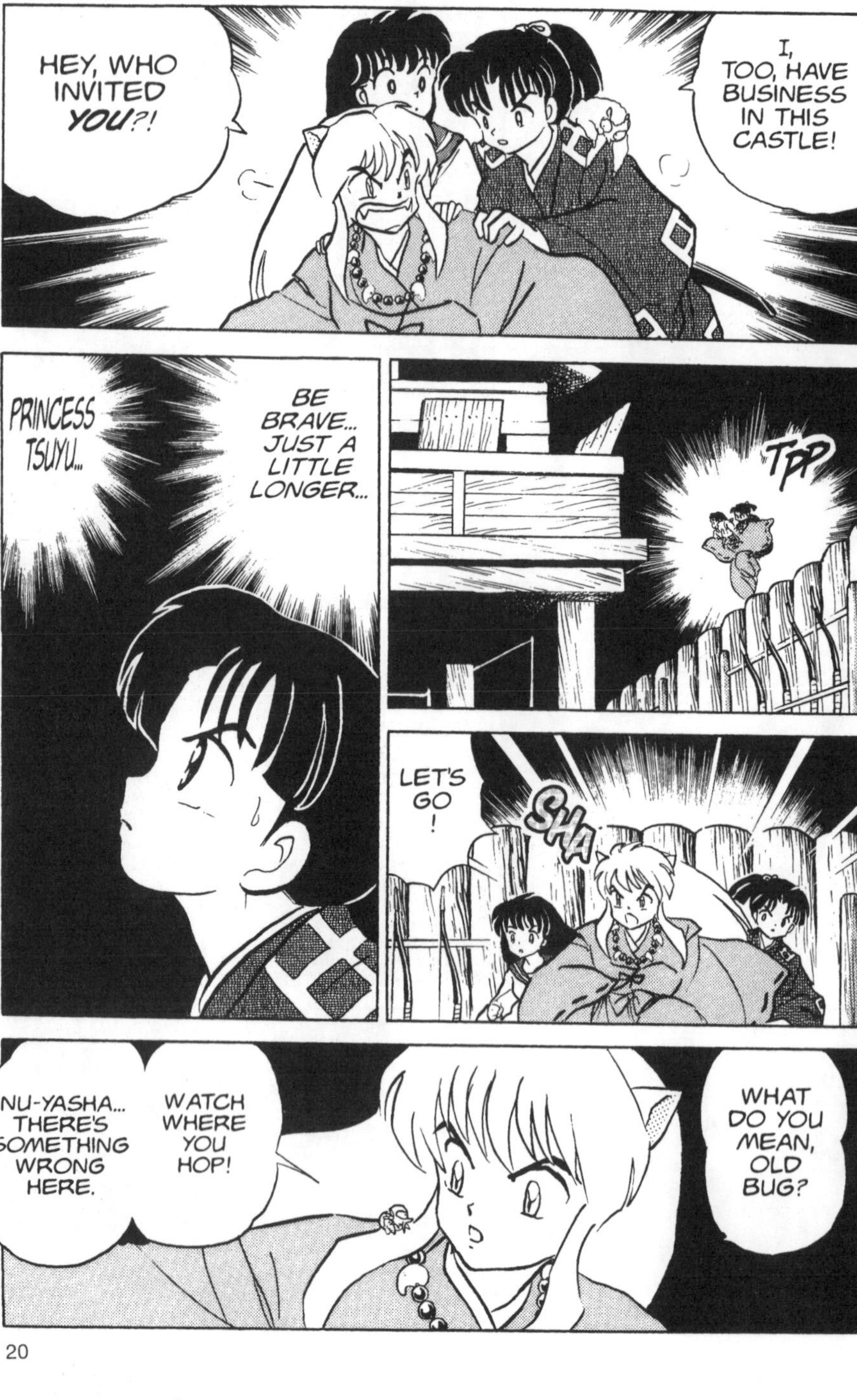
HEY, WHO INVITED YOU?!
I, TOO, HAVE BUSINESS IN THIS CASTLE!
PRINCESS TSUYU...
BE BRAVE... JUST A LITTLE LONGER...
TPP
LET'S GO!
SHA
INU-YASHA... THERE'S SOMETHING WRONG HERE.
WATCH WHERE YOU HOP!
WHAT DO YOU MEAN, OLD BUG?

A CASTLE OF THIS SIZE...

...AND NOT A SINGLE SENTRY IN SIGHT?!

'TIS STRANGE INDEED, BUT...

HUH ?

ASLEEP... ?

THIS LOOKS LIKE...

A SLEEPING SPELL !

THE WHOLE CASTLE RETINUE MUST BE AFFECTED...

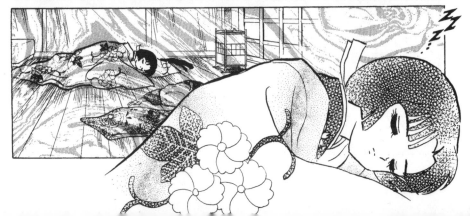

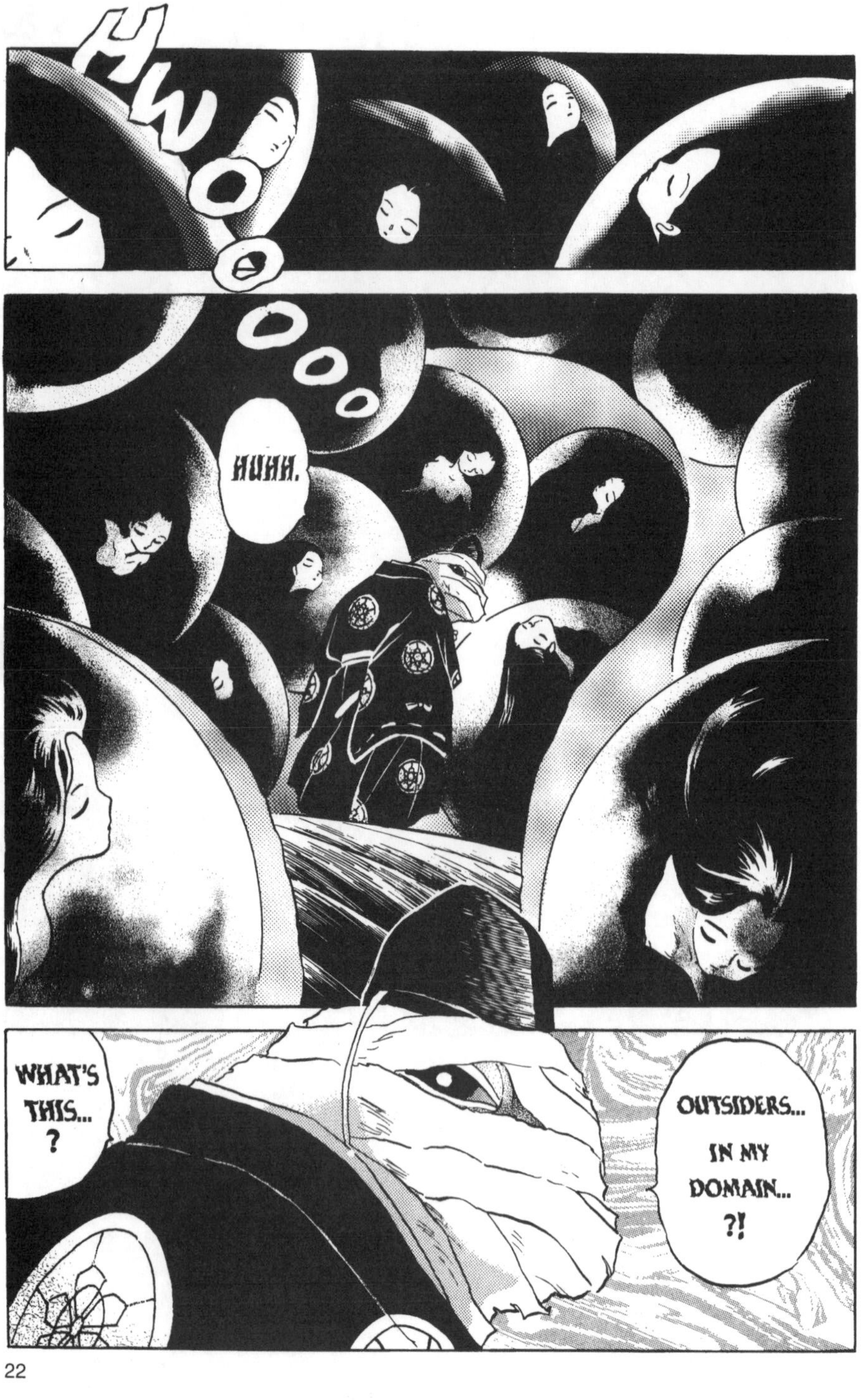
HWOOOOOOO
HUHH.
WHAT'S THIS... ?
OUTSIDERS... IN MY DOMAIN... ?!

SCROLL TWO
TSUKUMO NO GAMA

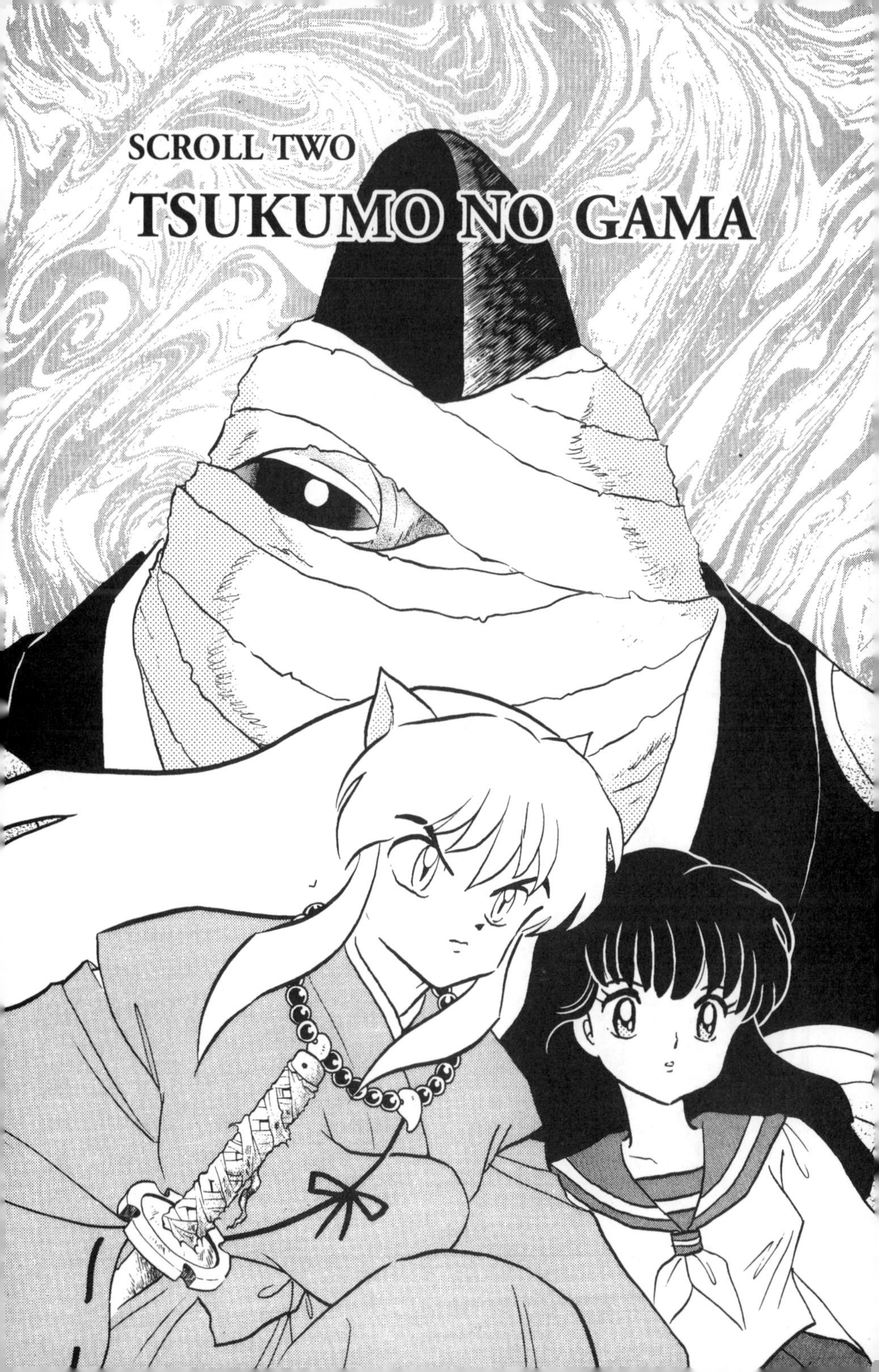

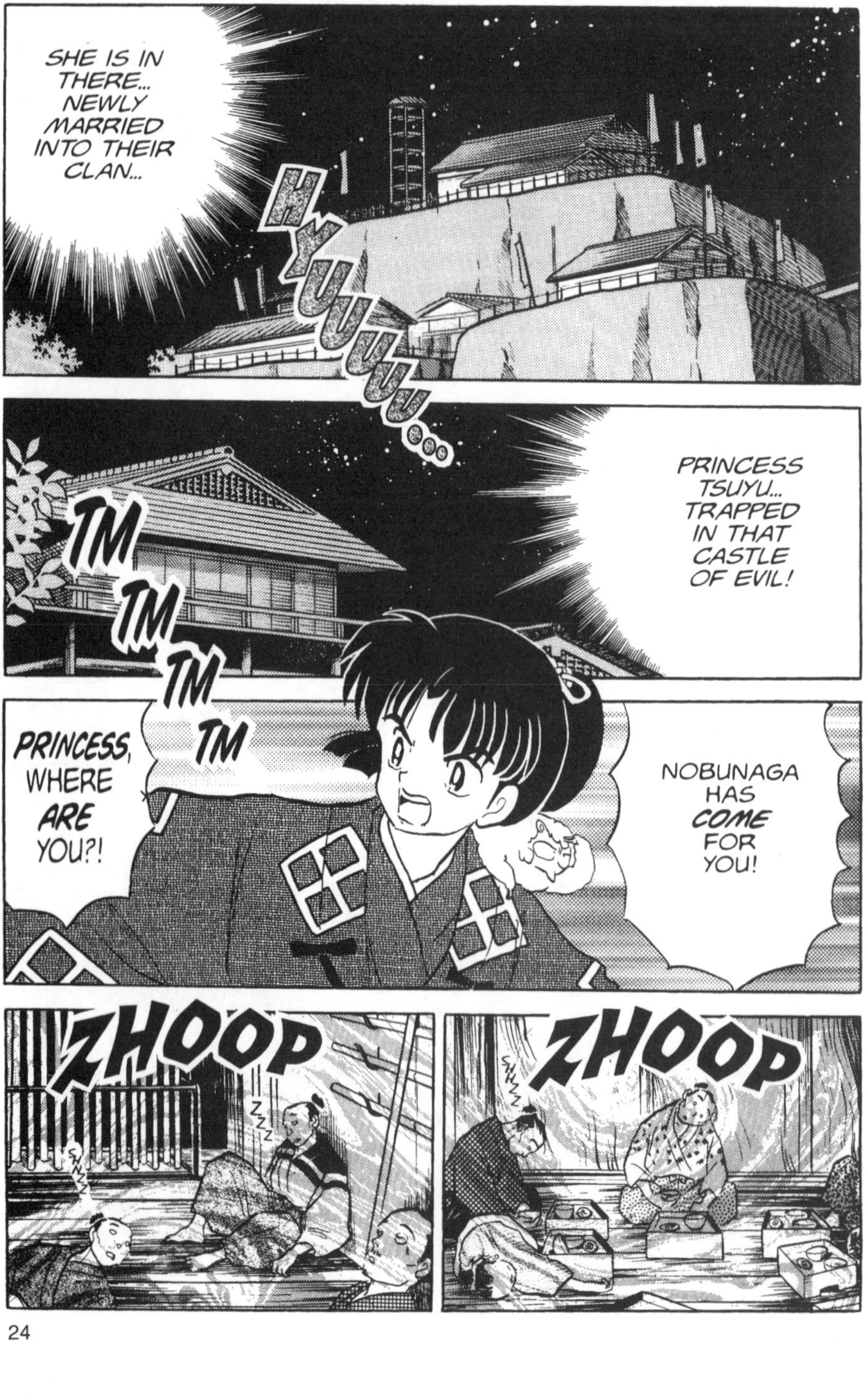
SHE IS IN THERE... NEWLY MARRIED INTO THEIR CLAN...
HYUUUUU...
TM TM TM TM
PRINCESS TSUYU... TRAPPED IN THAT CASTLE OF EVIL!
PRINCESS, WHERE ARE YOU?!
NOBUNAGA HAS COME FOR YOU!
ZHOOP
ZZZ
SHNZZ
SHNZZ
ZHOOP

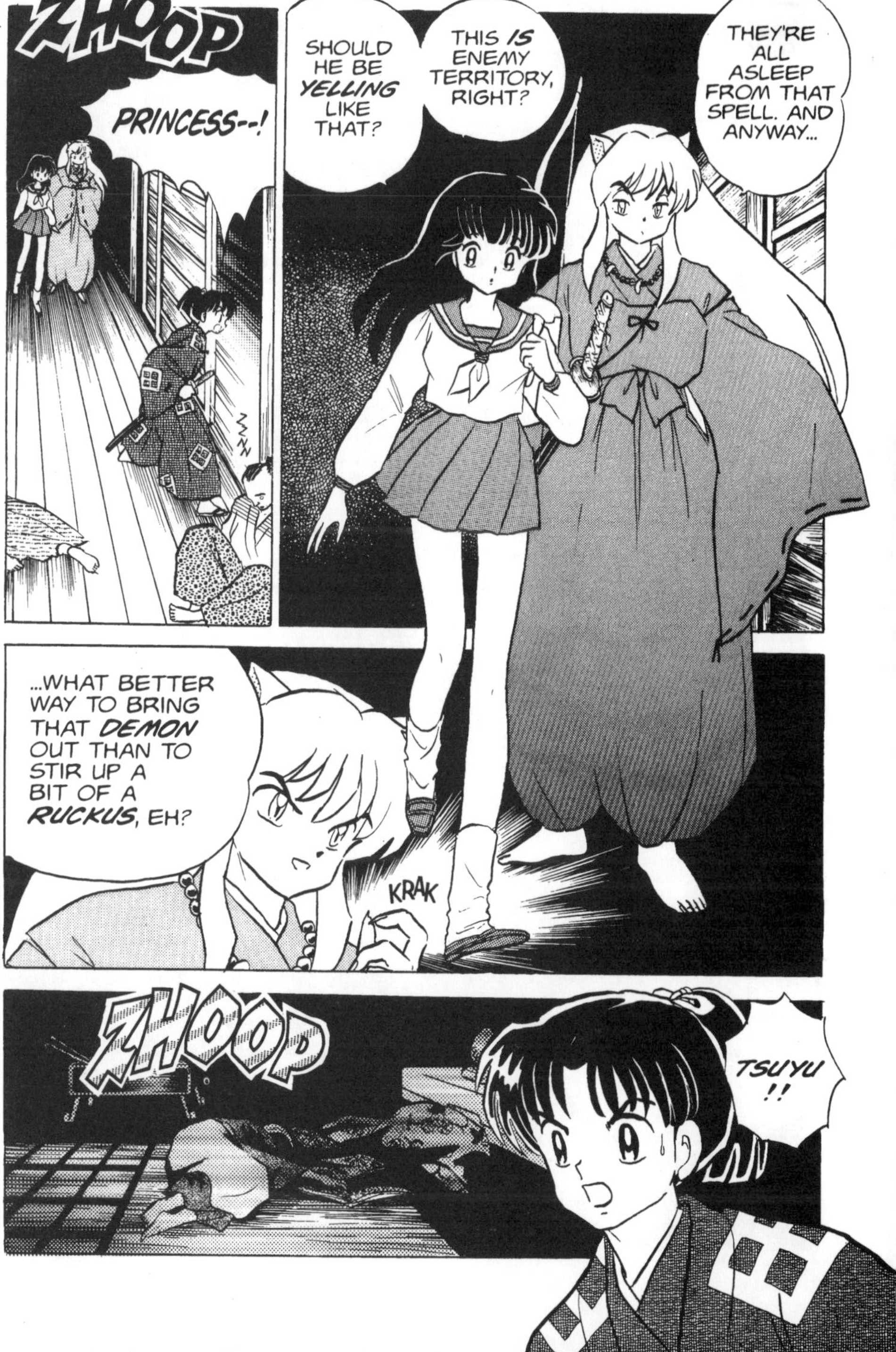
ZHOOP
PRINCESS--!
ZZNN
SHOULD HE BE YELLING LIKE THAT?
THIS IS ENEMY TERRITORY, RIGHT?
THEY'RE ALL ASLEEP FROM THAT SPELL. AND ANYWAY...
...WHAT BETTER WAY TO BRING THAT DEMON OUT THAN TO STIR UP A BIT OF A RUCKUS, EH?
KRAK
ZHOOP
TSUYU !!

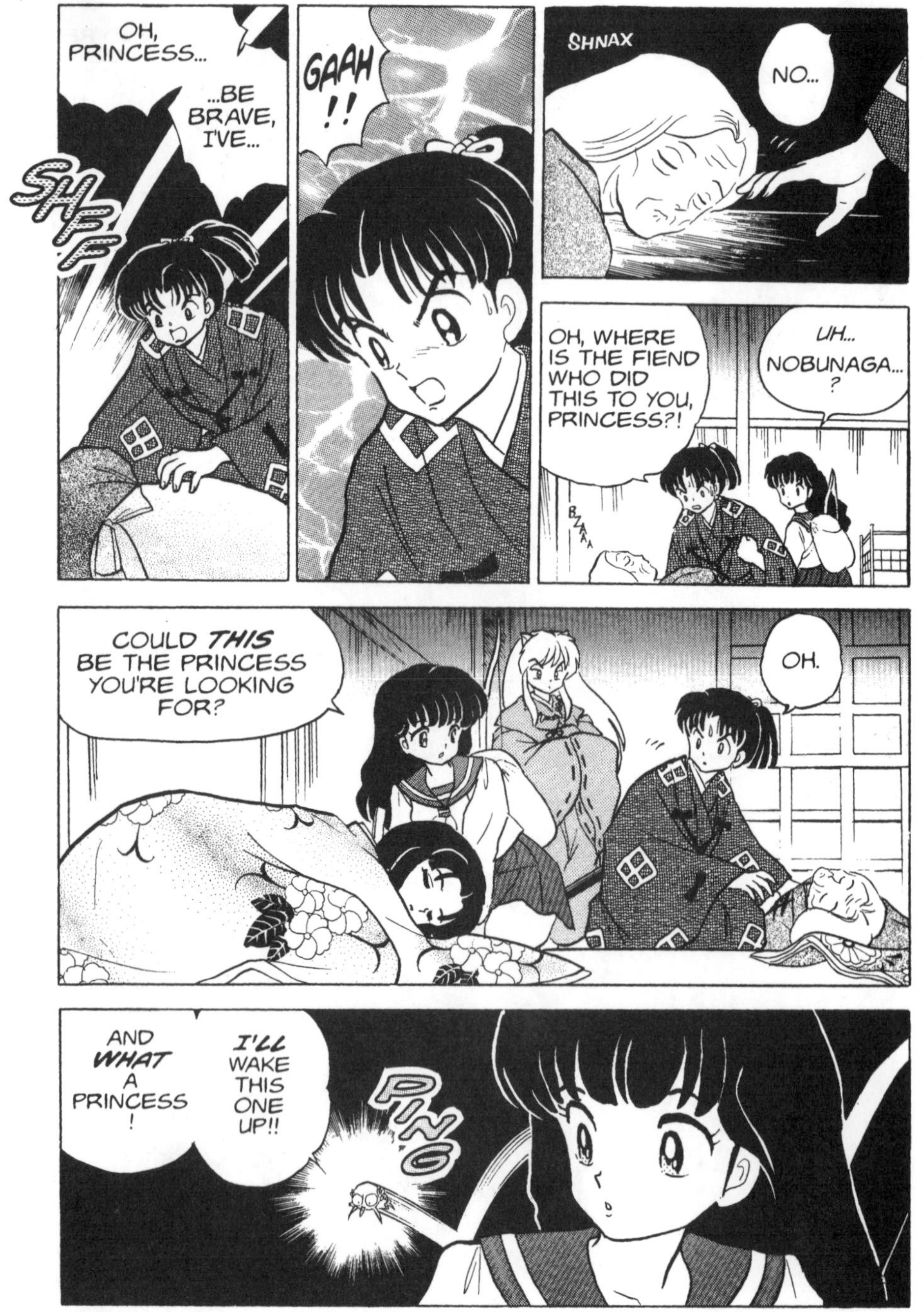

OH, PRINCESS...
...BE BRAVE, I'VE...
SHFF
GAAH!!
SHNAX
NO...
OH, WHERE IS THE FIEND WHO DID THIS TO YOU, PRINCESS?!
UH... NOBUNAGA...?
COULD THIS BE THE PRINCESS YOU'RE LOOKING FOR?
OH.
AND WHAT A PRINCESS!
I'LL WAKE THIS ONE UP!!
PING

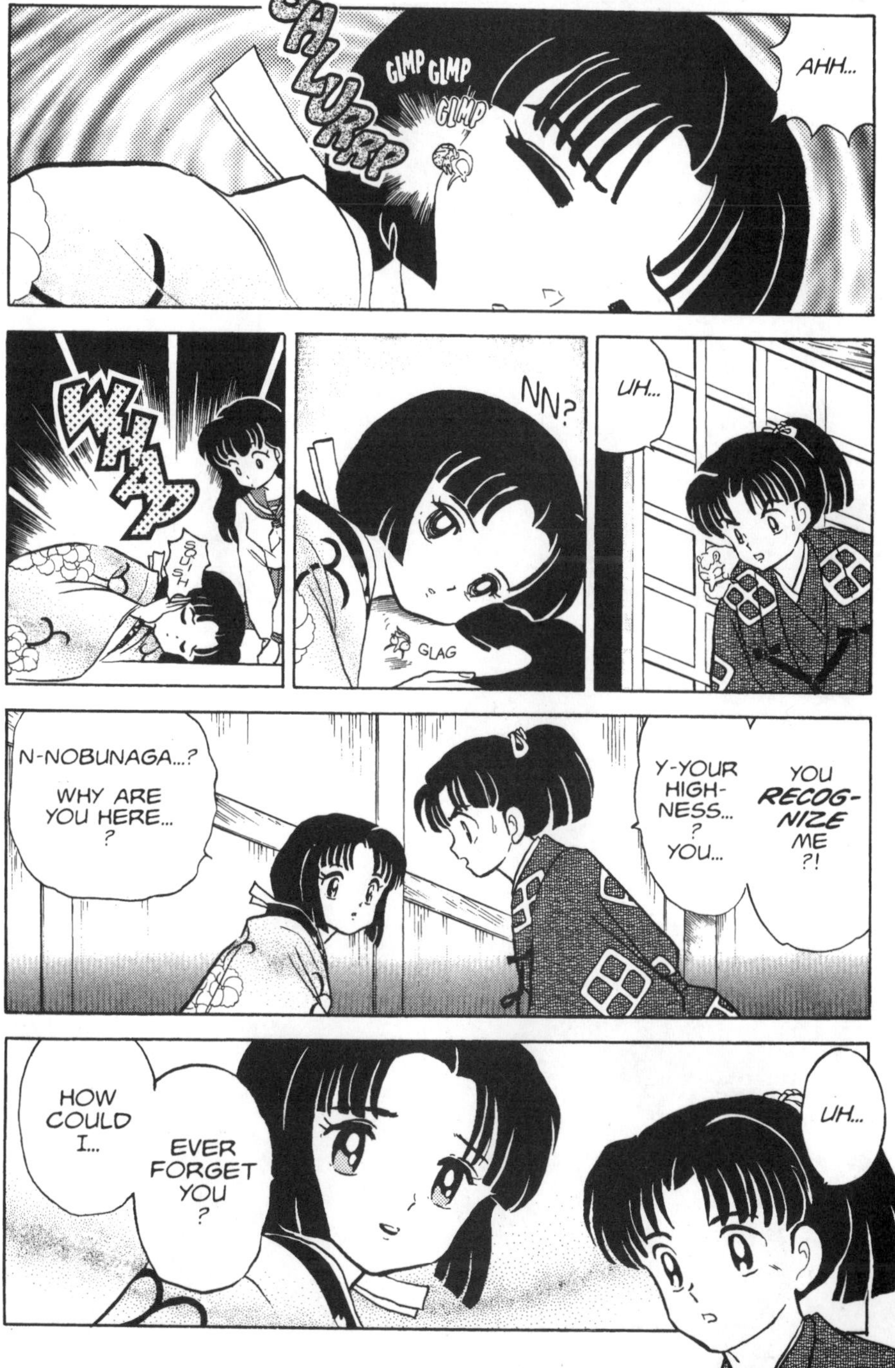
SHLURRP
GLMP GLMP
GLMP
AHH...
WHAP
SQUISH
NN?
GLAG
UH...
N-NOBUNAGA...?
WHY ARE YOU HERE...?
Y-YOUR HIGHNESS...? YOU...
YOU RECOGNIZE ME?!
HOW COULD I...
EVER FORGET YOU?
UH...

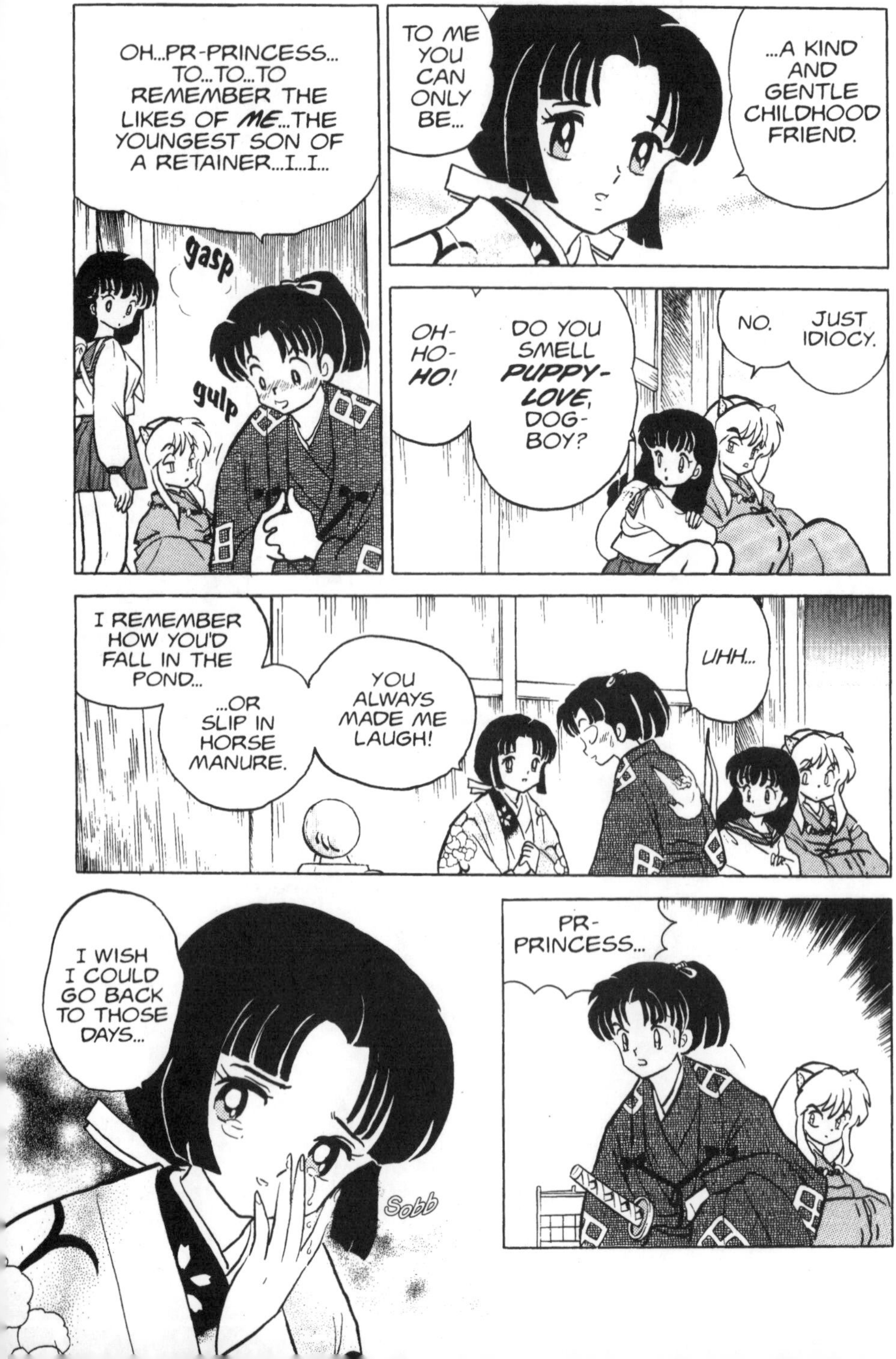
OH...PR-PRINCESS... TO...TO...TO REMEMBER THE LIKES OF *ME*...THE YOUNGEST SON OF A RETAINER...I...I...
gasp
gulp
TO ME YOU CAN ONLY BE...
...A KIND AND GENTLE CHILDHOOD FRIEND.
OH-HO-*HO*!
DO YOU SMELL *PUPPY-LOVE*, DOG-BOY?
NO.
JUST IDIOCY.
I REMEMBER HOW YOU'D FALL IN THE POND...
...OR SLIP IN HORSE MANURE.
YOU ALWAYS MADE ME LAUGH!
UHH...
I WISH I COULD GO BACK TO THOSE DAYS...
Sobb
PR-PRINCESS...

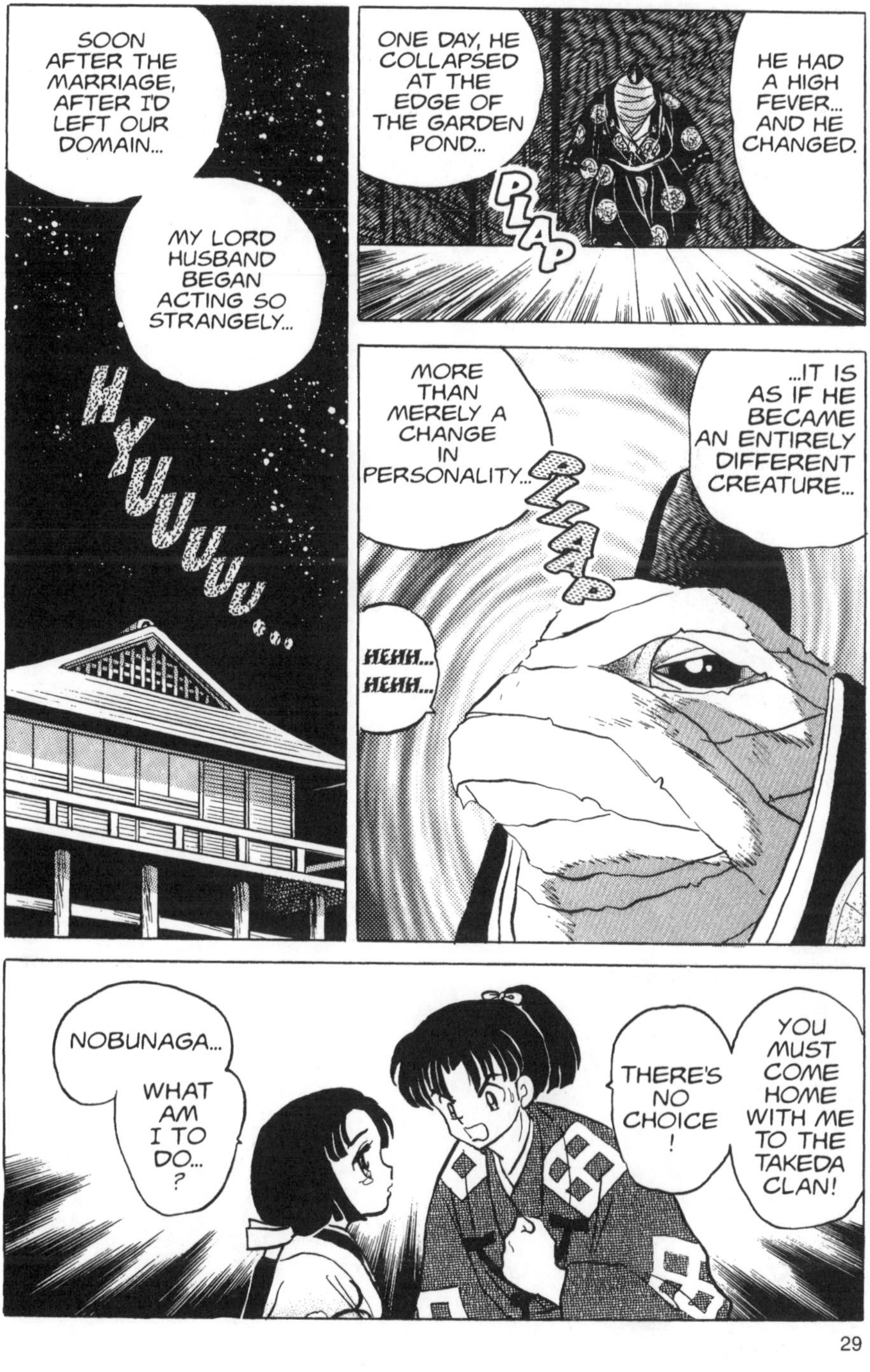
SOON AFTER THE MARRIAGE, AFTER I'D LEFT OUR DOMAIN...
MY LORD HUSBAND BEGAN ACTING SO STRANGELY...
HYUUUUU...
ONE DAY, HE COLLAPSED AT THE EDGE OF THE GARDEN POND...
PLAP
HE HAD A HIGH FEVER... AND HE CHANGED.
MORE THAN MERELY A CHANGE IN PERSONALITY...
PLAP
...IT IS AS IF HE BECAME AN ENTIRELY DIFFERENT CREATURE...
HEHH... HEHH...
NOBUNAGA...
WHAT AM I TO DO...?
THERE'S NO CHOICE!
YOU MUST COME HOME WITH ME TO THE TAKEDA CLAN!

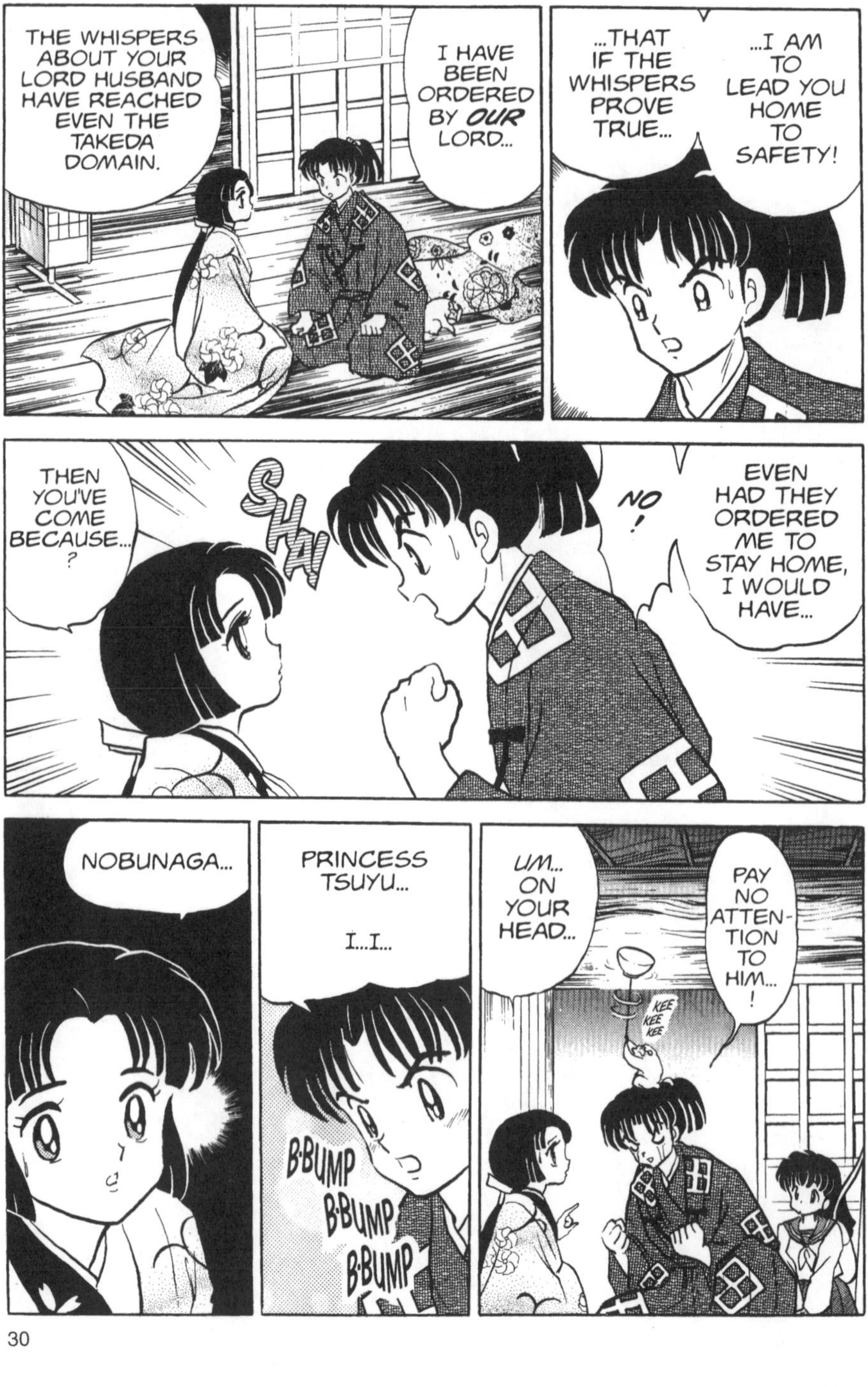
THE WHISPERS ABOUT YOUR LORD HUSBAND HAVE REACHED EVEN THE TAKEDA DOMAIN.
I HAVE BEEN ORDERED BY *OUR* LORD...
...THAT IF THE WHISPERS PROVE TRUE...
...I AM TO LEAD YOU HOME TO SAFETY!
THEN YOU'VE COME BECAUSE...?
SHA
NO!
EVEN HAD THEY ORDERED ME TO STAY HOME, I WOULD HAVE...
NOBUNAGA...
PRINCESS TSUYU...
I...I...
B-BUMP
B-BUMP
B-BUMP
UM... ON YOUR HEAD...
KEE KEE KEE
PAY NO ATTENTION TO HIM...!

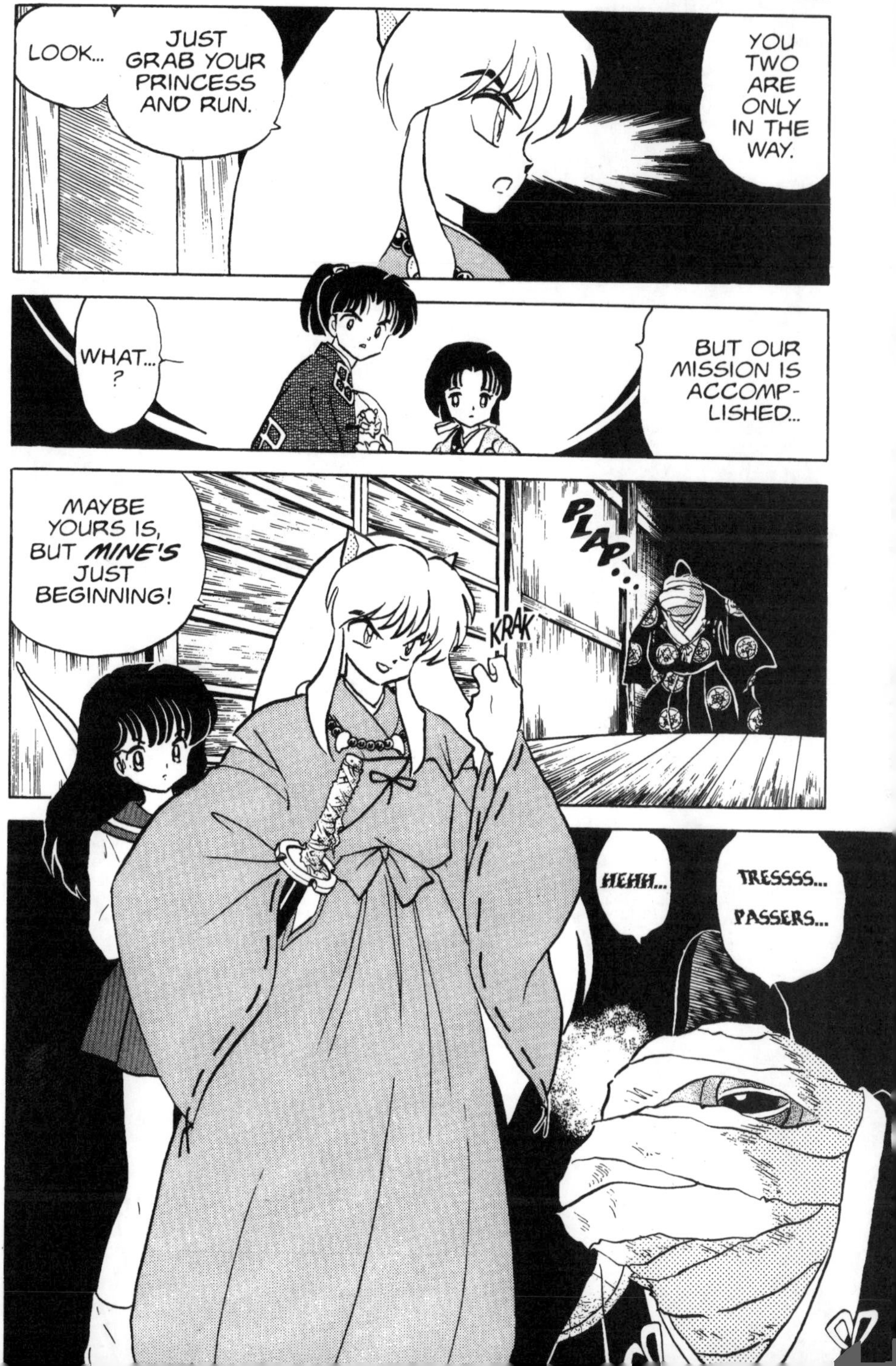
LOOK...
JUST GRAB YOUR PRINCESS AND RUN.
YOU TWO ARE ONLY IN THE WAY.
WHAT... ?
BUT OUR MISSION IS ACCOMPLISHED...
MAYBE YOURS IS, BUT *MINE'S* JUST BEGINNING!
PLAP...
KRAK
HEHH...
TRESSSS... PASSERS...

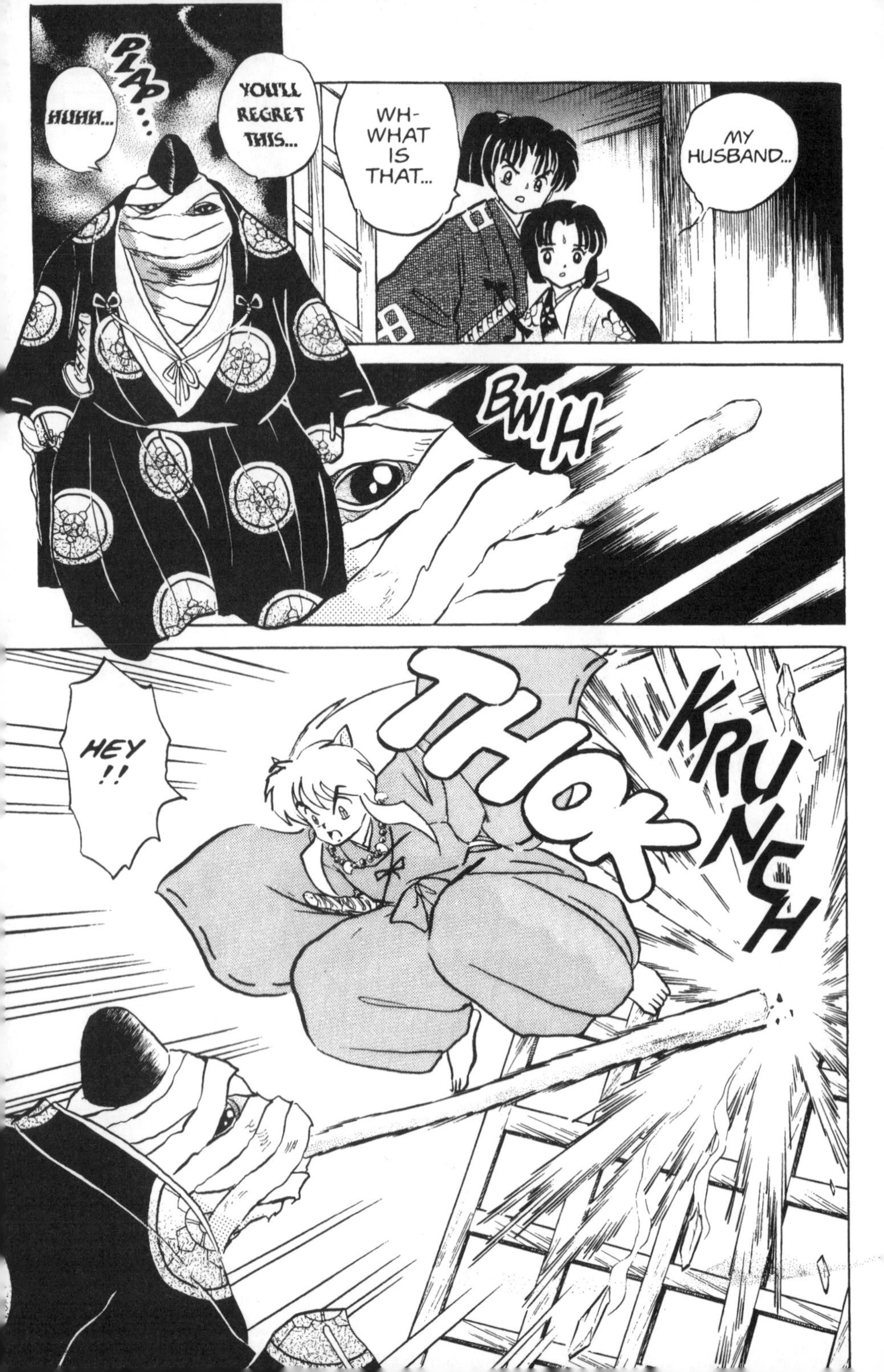
HUHH...
PLAP...
YOU'LL REGRET THIS...
WH-WHAT IS THAT...
MY HUSBAND...
BWIH
HEY !!
THOK
KRUNCH

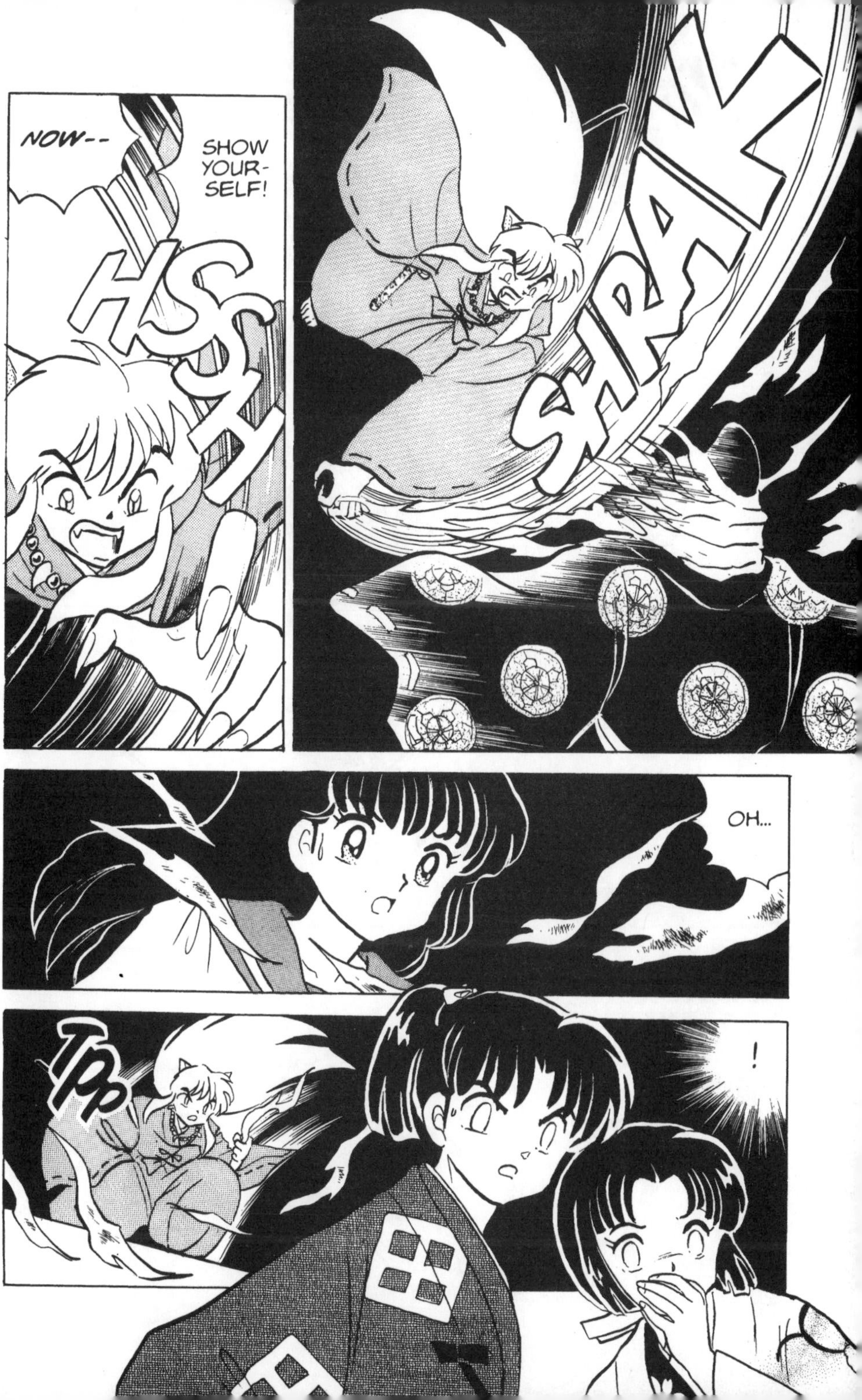
NOW--
SHOW YOUR-SELF!
HSSH
SHRAK
OH...
TPP
!

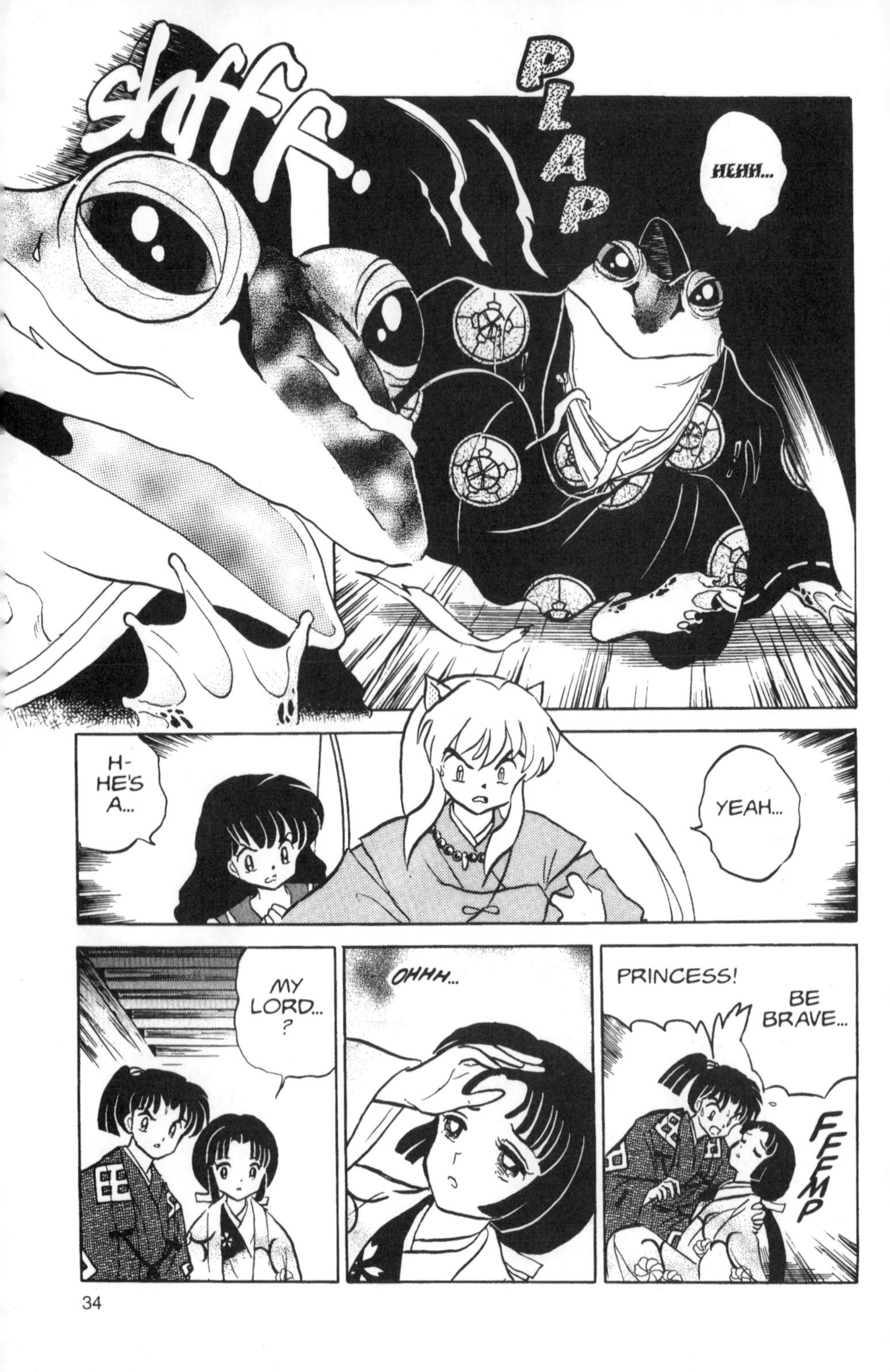
shfff...
PLAP
HEHH...
H-
HE'S
A...
YEAH...
MY
LORD...
?
OHHH...
PRINCESS!
BE
BRAVE...
FFEMP

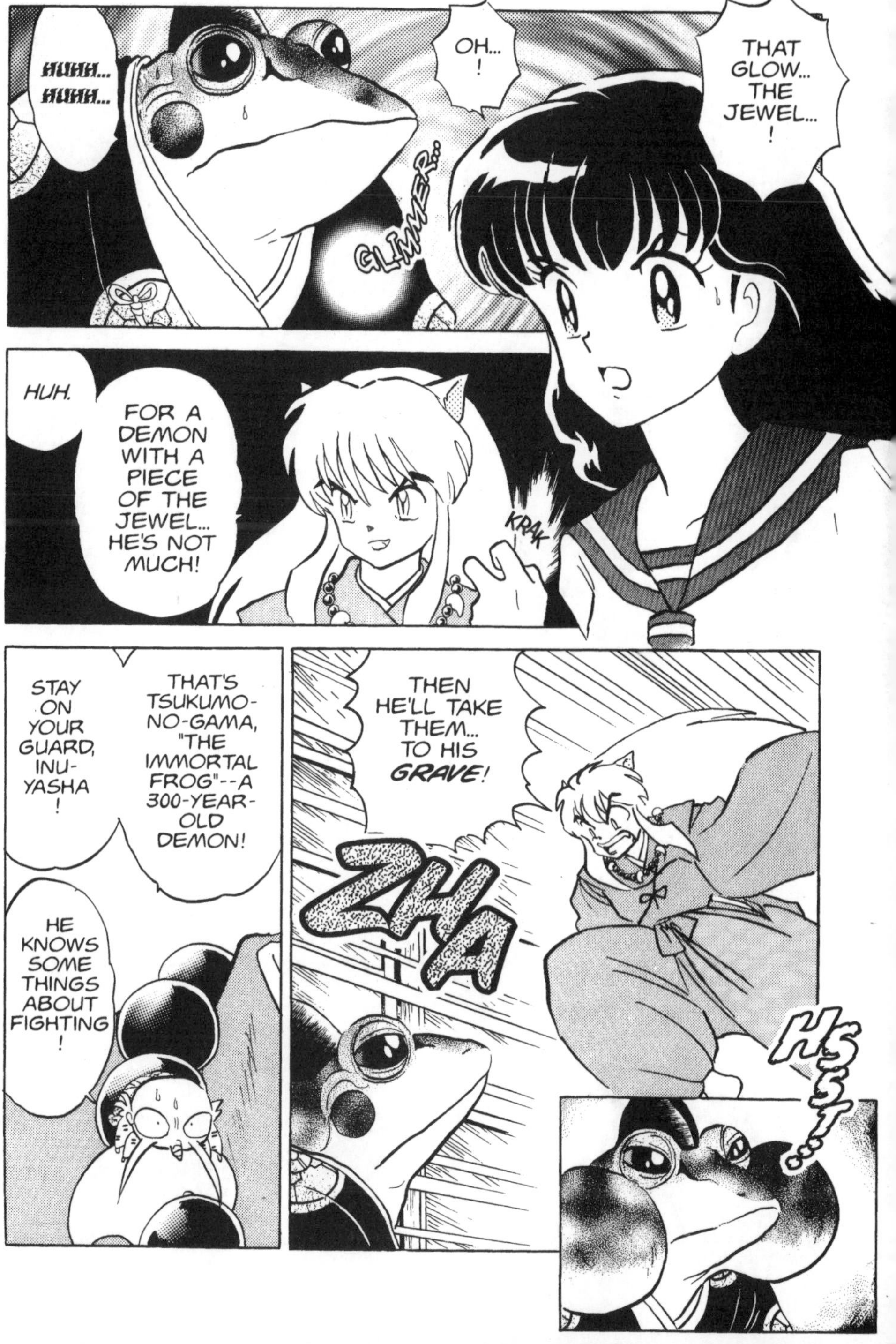
HUHH... HUHH...
GLIMMER...
OH...!
THAT GLOW... THE JEWEL...!
HUH.
FOR A DEMON WITH A PIECE OF THE JEWEL... HE'S NOT MUCH!
KRAK
STAY ON YOUR GUARD, INU-YASHA!
THAT'S TSUKUMO-NO-GAMA, "THE IMMORTAL FROG"--A 300-YEAR-OLD DEMON!
HE KNOWS SOME THINGS ABOUT FIGHTING!
THEN HE'LL TAKE THEM... TO HIS *GRAVE*!
ZHA
HSST...

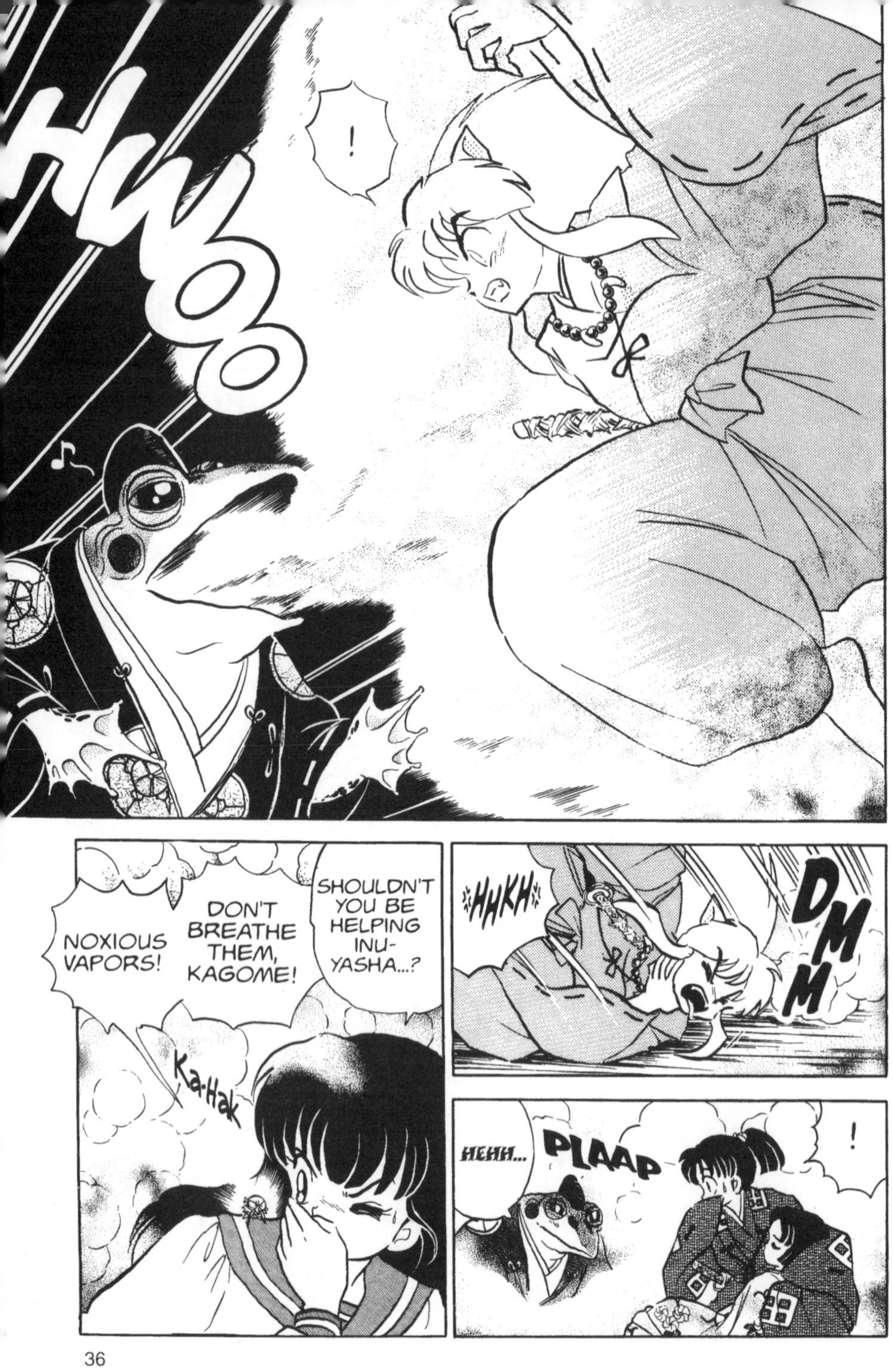

HYUOOO
!
♪
NOXIOUS VAPORS!
DON'T BREATHE THEM, KAGOME!
SHOULDN'T YOU BE HELPING INU-YASHA...?
Ka-Hak
HHKH
DMM
HEHH...
PLAAP
!

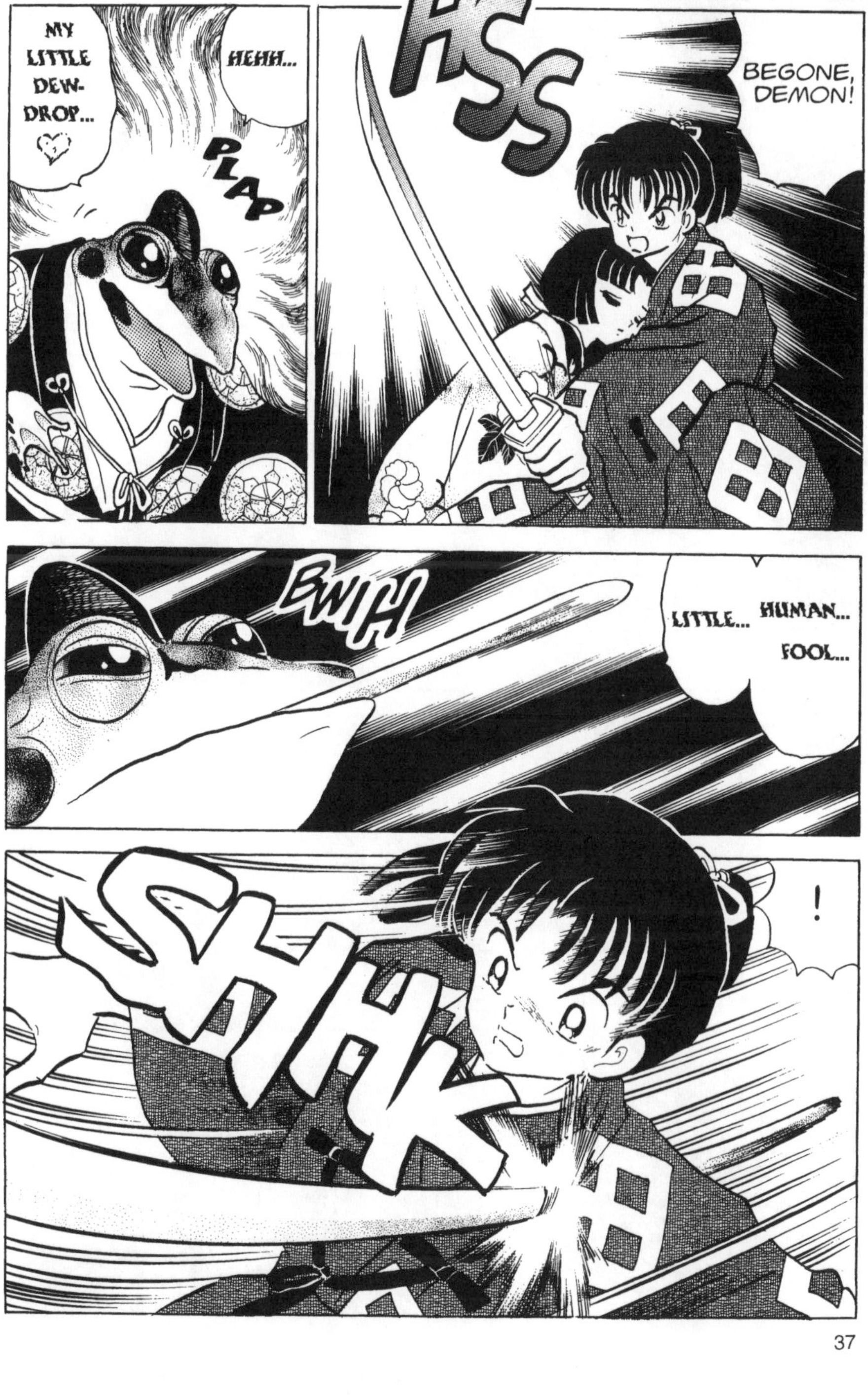
MY LITTLE DEW-DROP...
HEHH...
PLAP
HSS
BEGONE, DEMON!
BWISH
LITTLE... HUMAN... FOOL...
!
SHHK

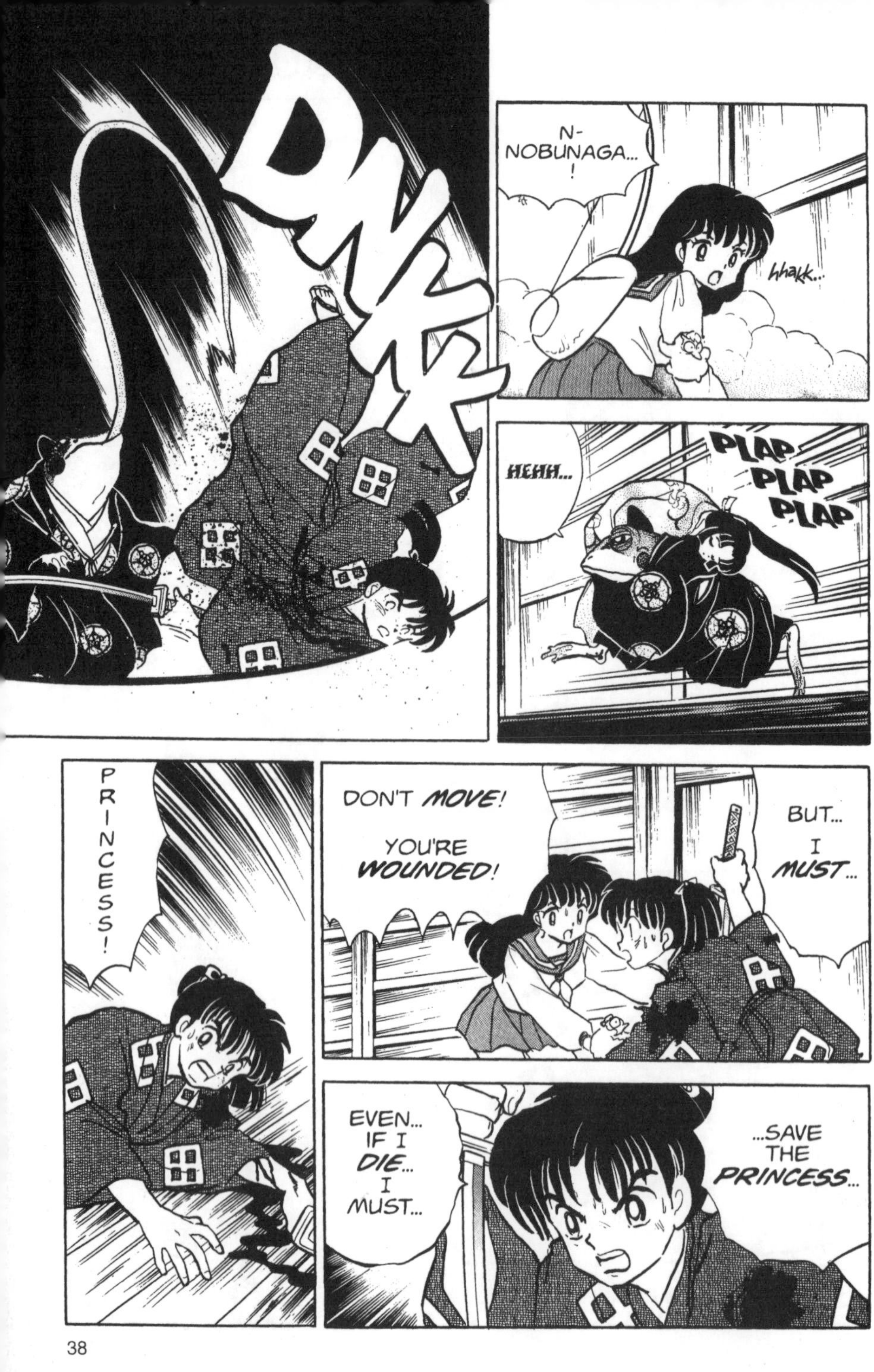
DNKK
N-NOBUNAGA...!
hhakk...
HEHH...
PLAP PLAP PLAP
PRINCESS!
DON'T *MOVE*!
YOU'RE *WOUNDED*!
BUT... I *MUST*...
EVEN... IF I *DIE*... I MUST...
...SAVE THE *PRINCESS*...

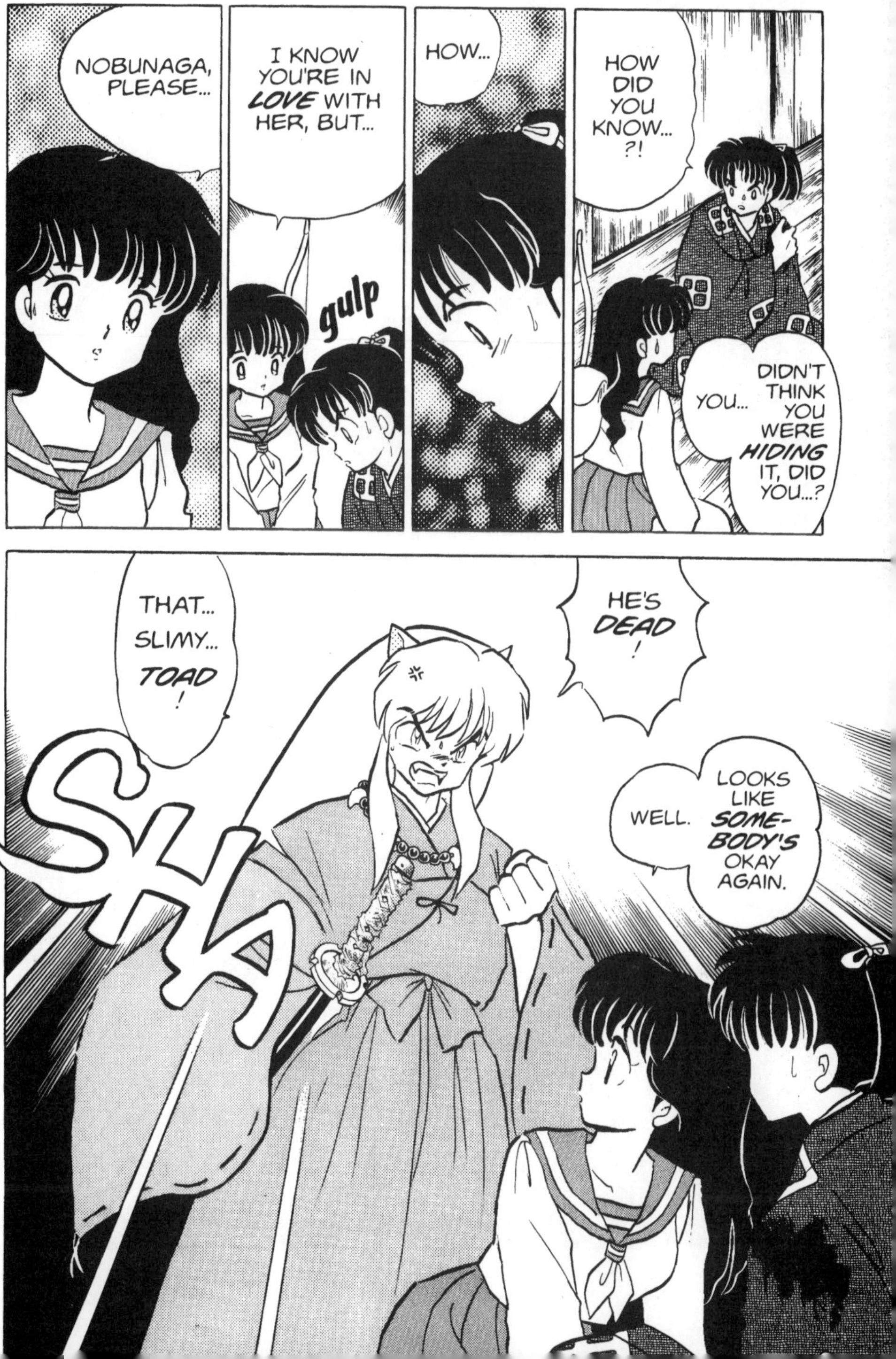
NOBUNAGA, PLEASE...
I KNOW YOU'RE IN LOVE WITH HER, BUT...
gulp
HOW...
HOW DID YOU KNOW... ?!
YOU...
DIDN'T THINK YOU WERE HIDING IT, DID YOU...?
SHA
THAT... SLIMY... TOAD!
HE'S DEAD!
WELL.
LOOKS LIKE SOMEBODY'S OKAY AGAIN.

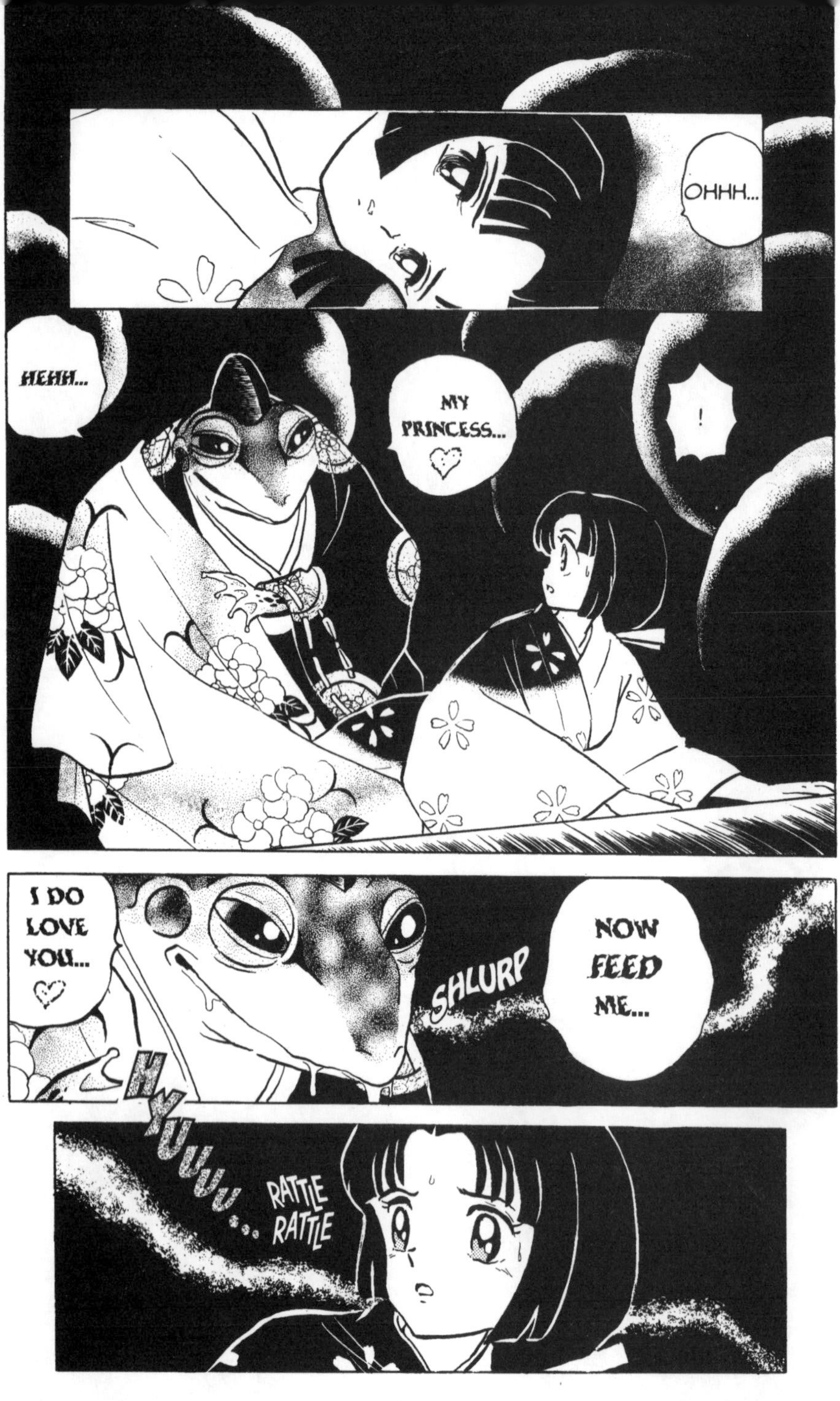
OHHH...
HEHH...
MY PRINCESS... ♡
!
I DO LOVE YOU... ♡
SHLURP
NOW FEED ME...
HYUUUU...
RATTLE RATTLE

SCROLL THREE

INHERITANCE OF SOULS

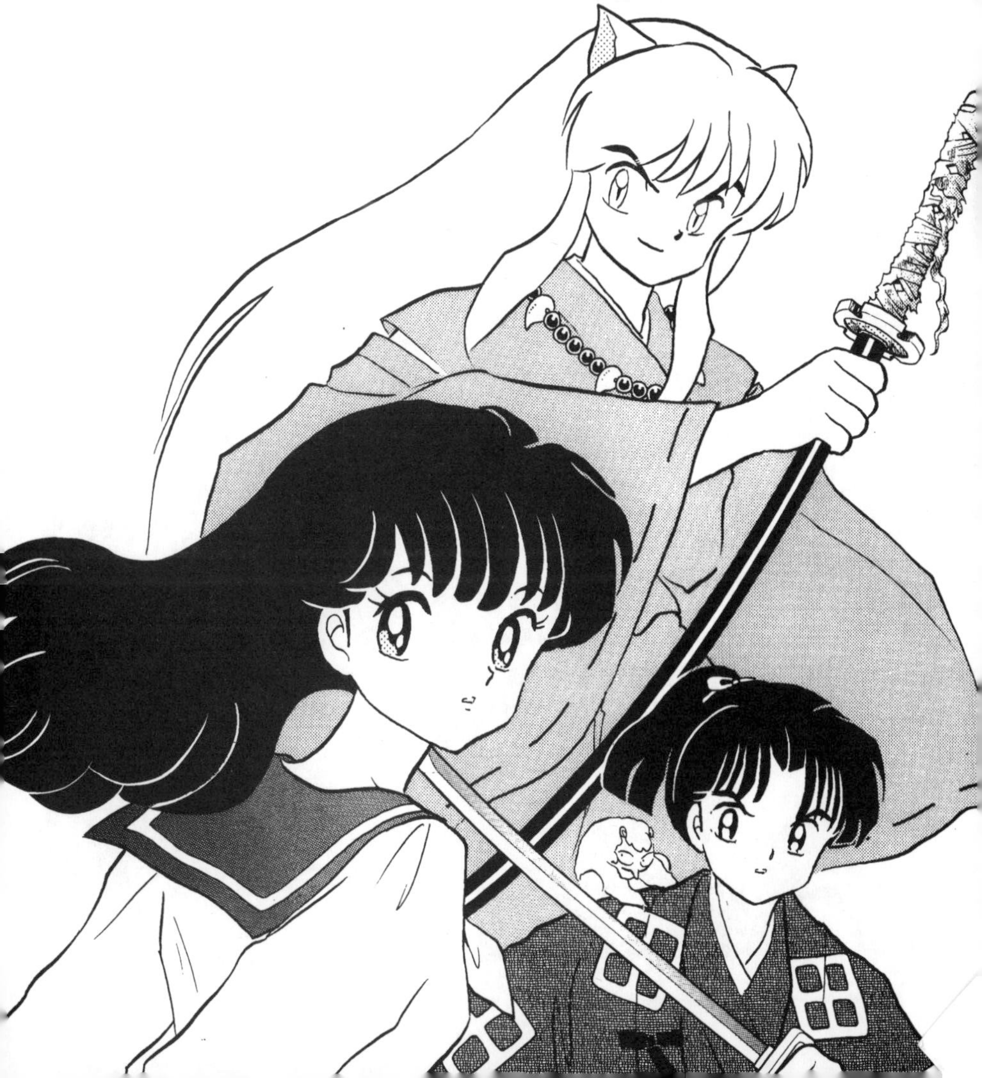

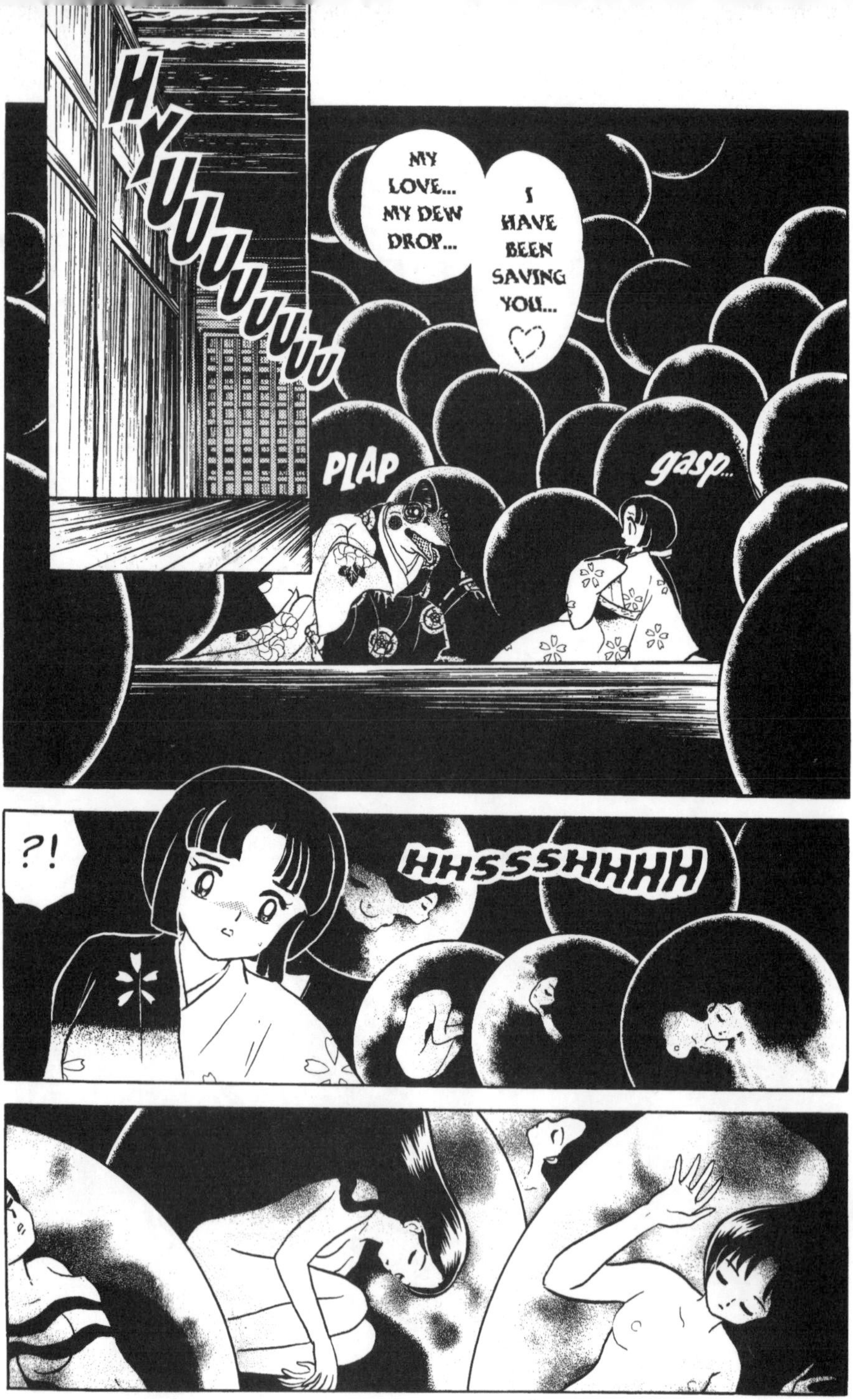
HYUUUUUUUUU
MY LOVE... MY DEW DROP...
I HAVE BEEN SAVING YOU... ♡
PLAP
gasp...
?!
HHSSSHHHH

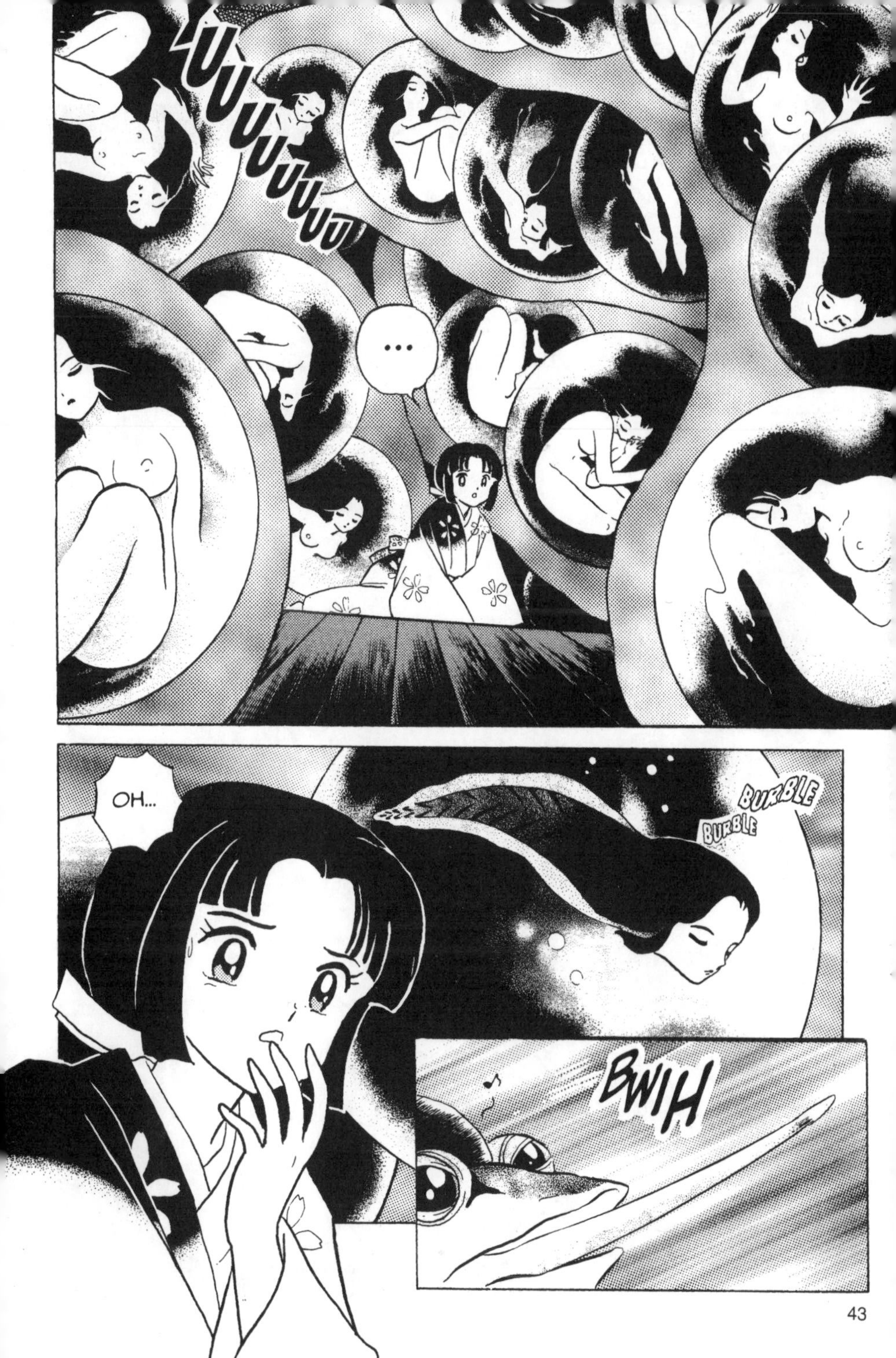
UUUUUUUU
...
OH...
BURBLE
BURBLE
BWIH

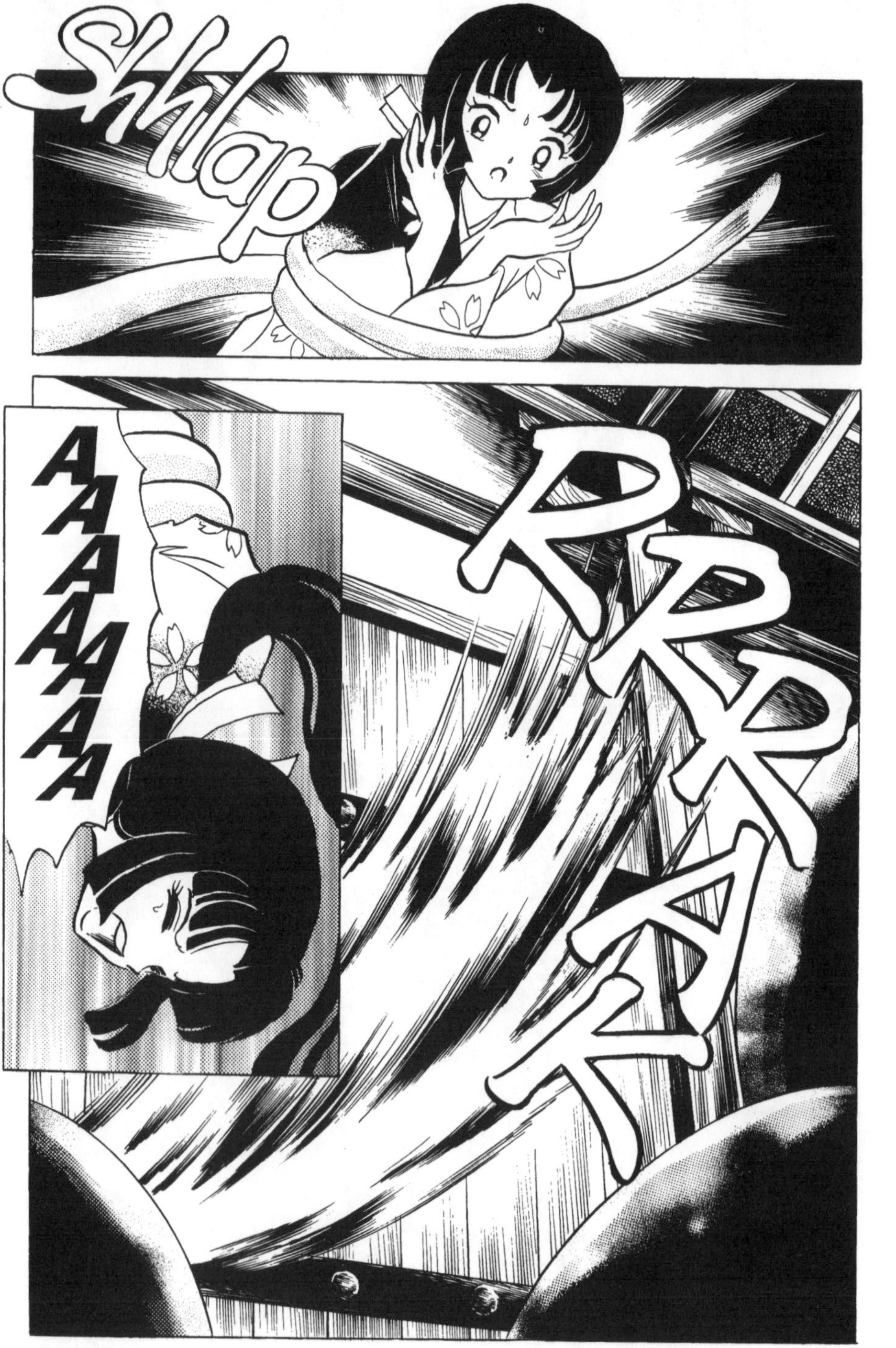
Shlap
AAAAAAAA
RRRAAK

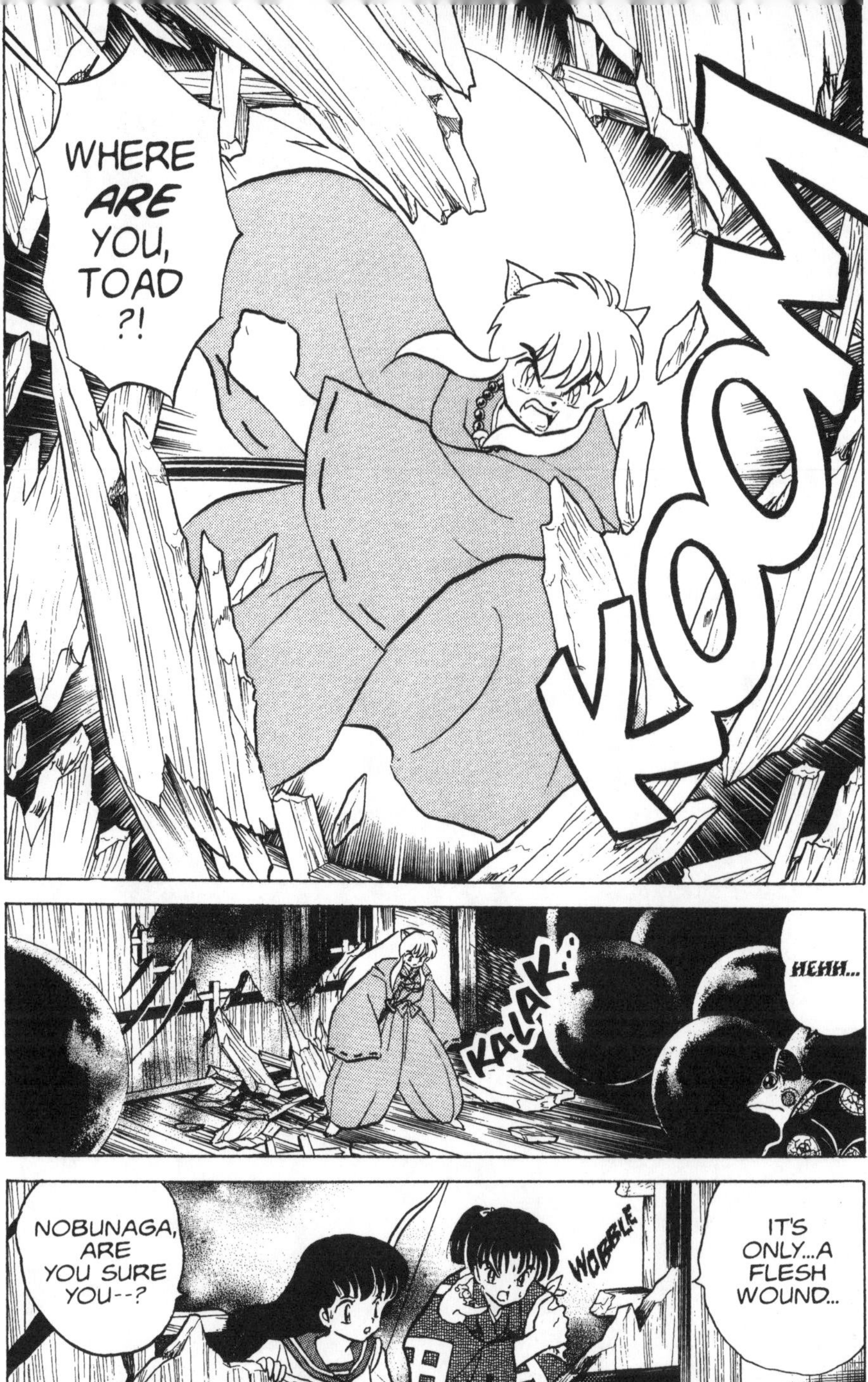
WHERE ARE YOU, TOAD ?!
KOOM
KA-LAK...
HEHH...
NOBUNAGA, ARE YOU SURE YOU--?
WOBBLE
IT'S ONLY...A FLESH WOUND...

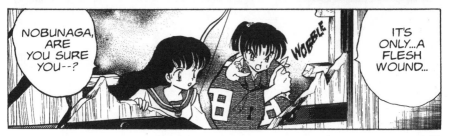

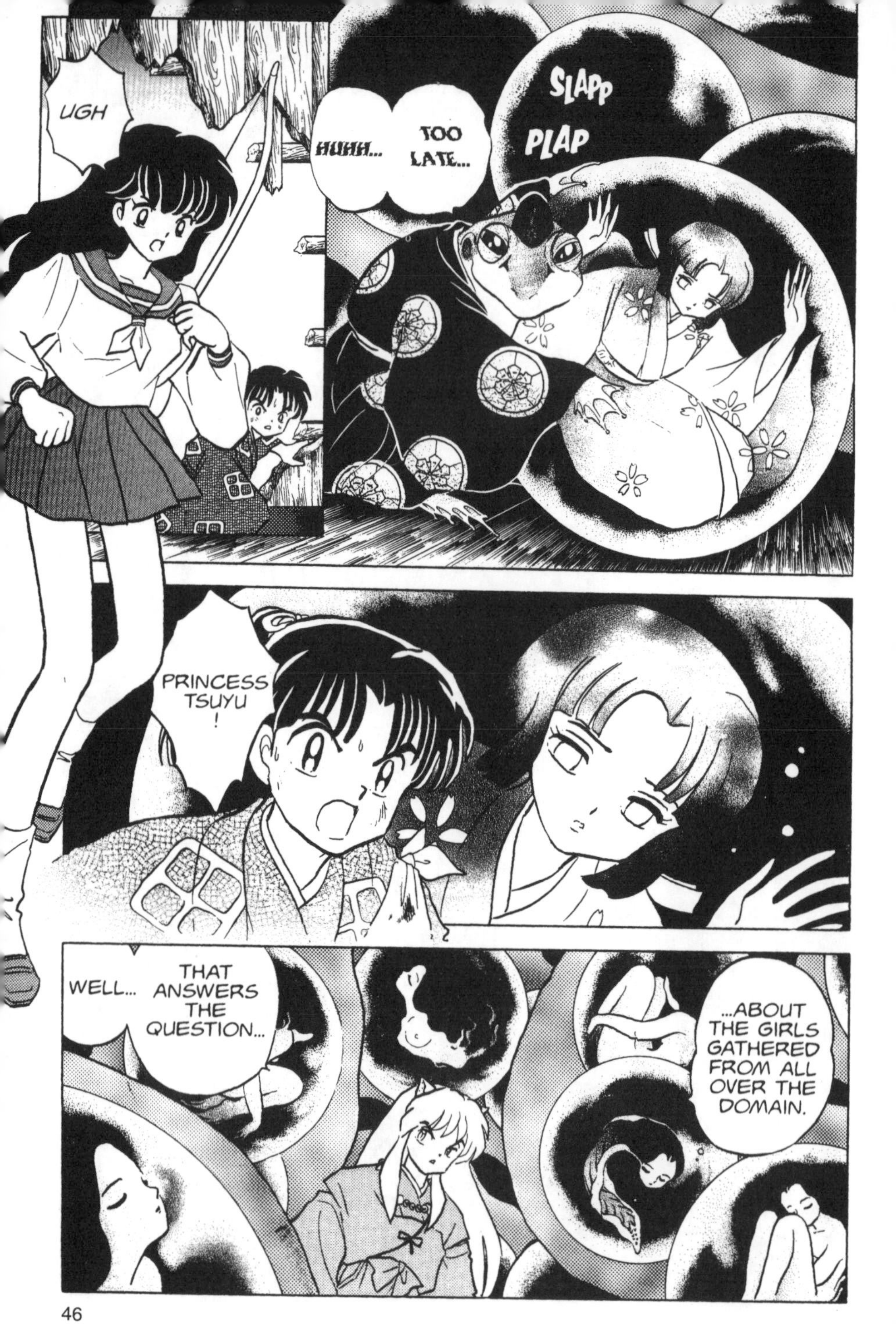

UGH
HUHH...
TOO LATE...
SLAPP
PLAP
PRINCESS TSUYU !
WELL...
THAT ANSWERS THE QUESTION...
...ABOUT THE GIRLS GATHERED FROM ALL OVER THE DOMAIN.

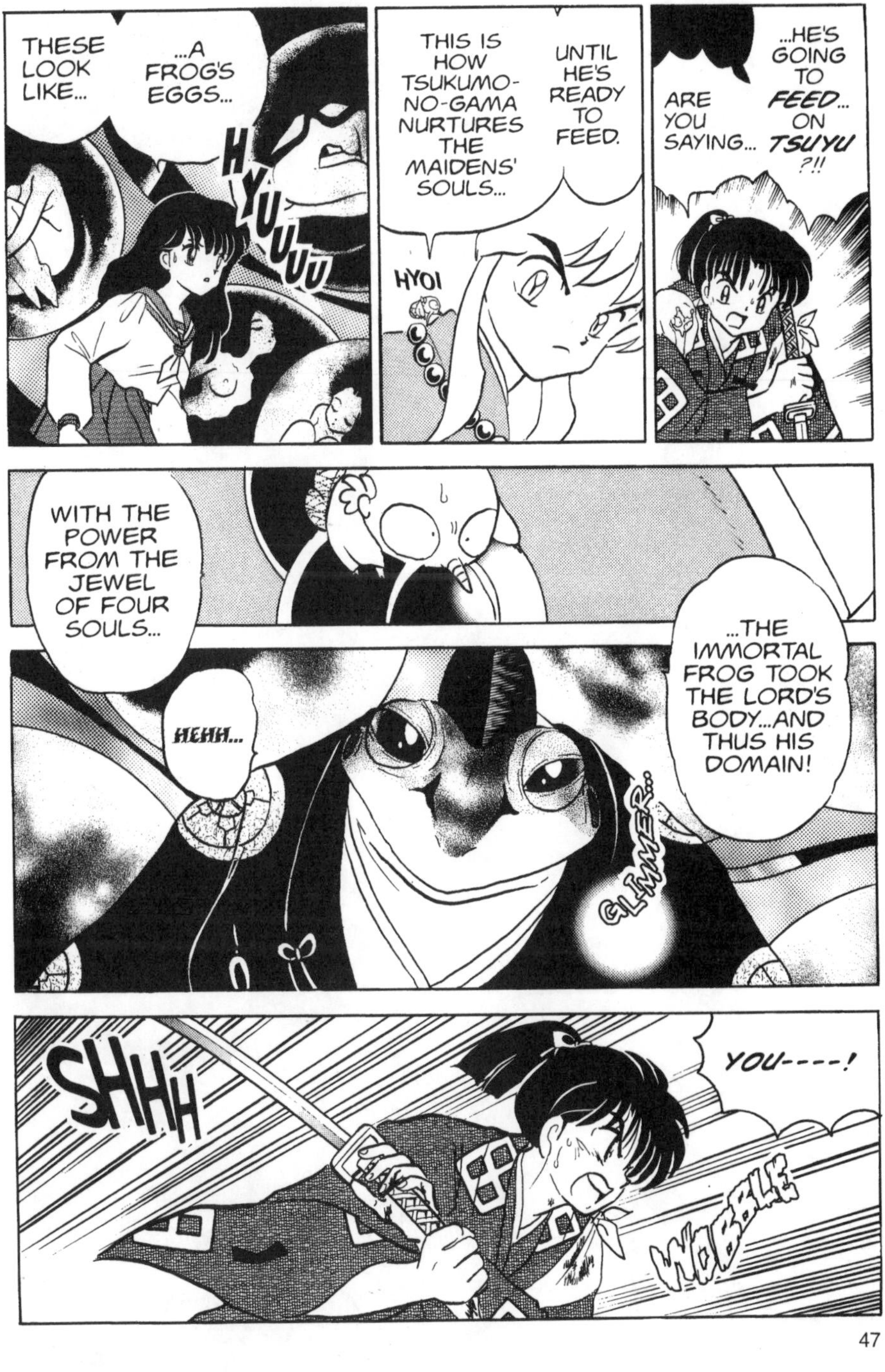
THESE LOOK LIKE...
...A FROG'S EGGS...
HYUUUUU
THIS IS HOW TSUKUMO-NO-GAMA NURTURES THE MAIDENS' SOULS...
UNTIL HE'S READY TO FEED.
HYOI
ARE YOU SAYING...
...HE'S GOING TO FEED... ON TSUYU ?!!
WITH THE POWER FROM THE JEWEL OF FOUR SOULS...
...THE IMMORTAL FROG TOOK THE LORD'S BODY...AND THUS HIS DOMAIN!
HEHH...
GLIMMER...
SHHH
YOU----!
WOBBLE

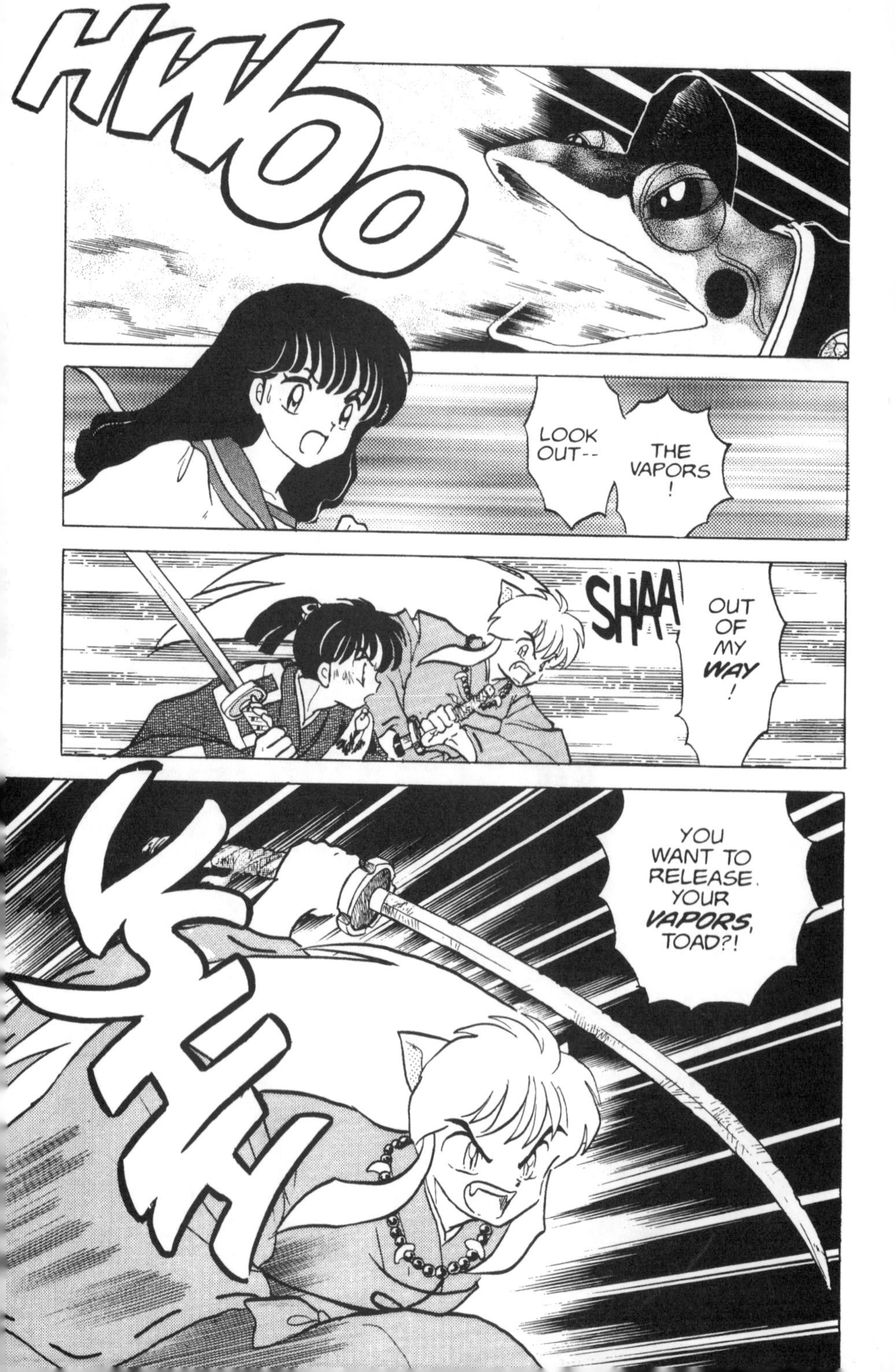
HWOO
LOOK OUT--
THE VAPORS!
SHAA
OUT OF MY WAY!
YOU WANT TO RELEASE YOUR VAPORS, TOAD?!

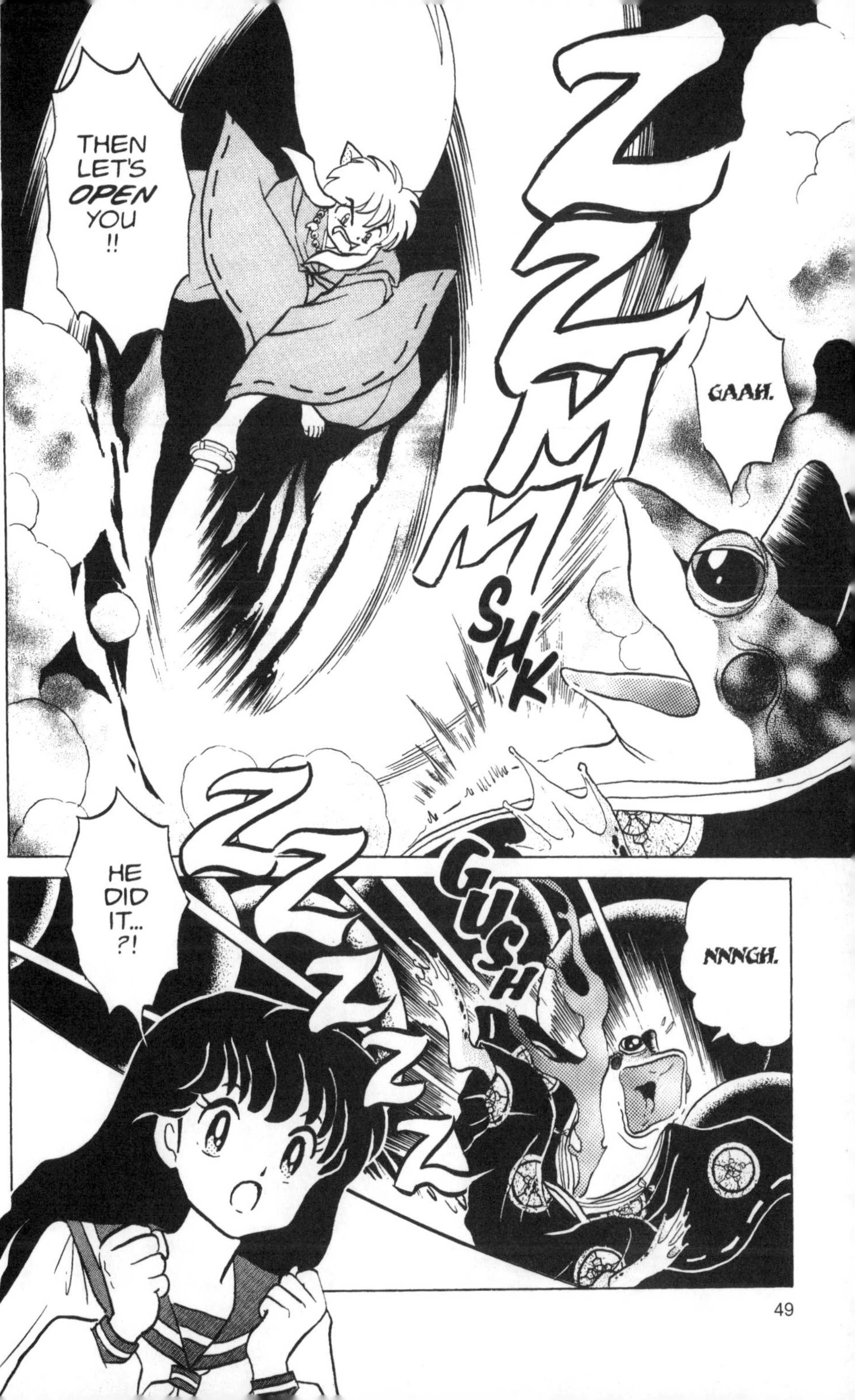
THEN LET'S *OPEN* YOU !!
SHK
GAAH.
HE DID IT... ?!
GUSH
NNNGH.

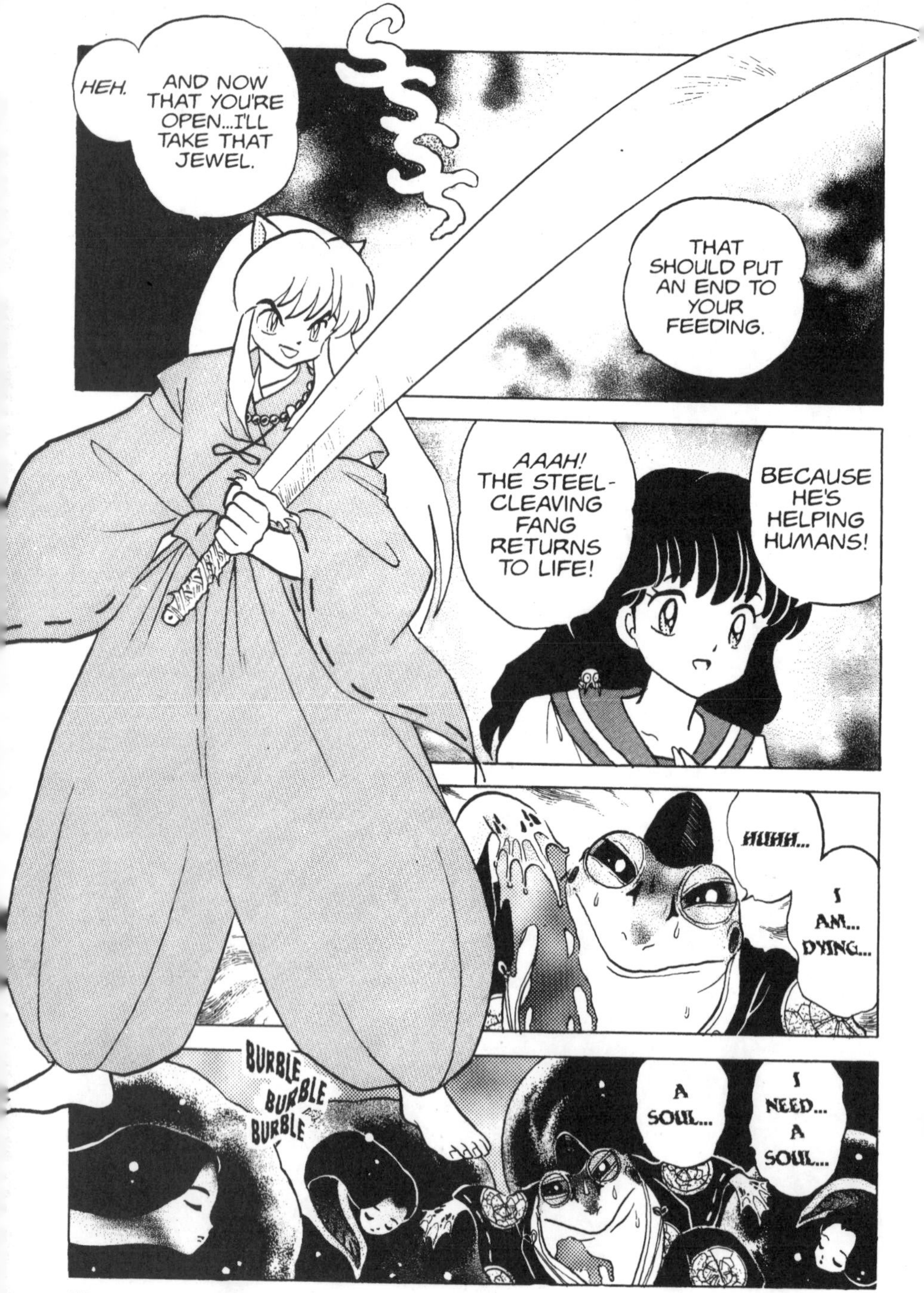
HEH.
AND NOW THAT YOU'RE OPEN...I'LL TAKE THAT JEWEL.
THAT SHOULD PUT AN END TO YOUR FEEDING.
AAAH! THE STEEL-CLEAVING FANG RETURNS TO LIFE!
BECAUSE HE'S HELPING HUMANS!
HUHH...
I AM... DYING...
BURBLE BURBLE BURBLE
A SOUL...
I NEED... A SOUL...

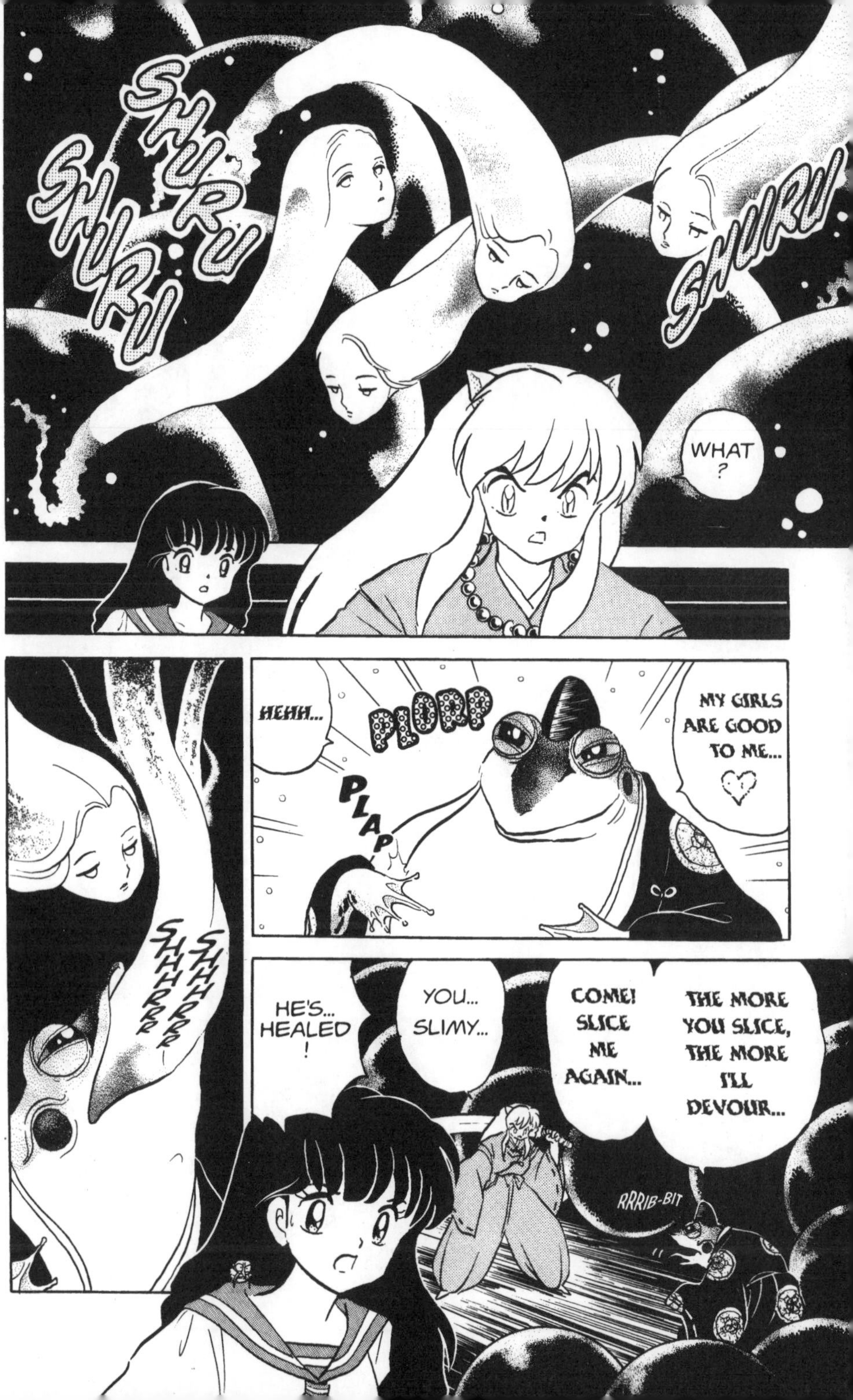
SHURU
SHURU
SHURU
WHAT?
SHHHRRR
SHHHRRR
HEHH...
PLORP
PLAP
MY GIRLS ARE GOOD TO ME... ♡
HE'S... HEALED!
YOU... SLIMY...
COME! SLICE ME AGAIN...
THE MORE YOU SLICE, THE MORE I'LL DEVOUR...
RRRIB-BIT

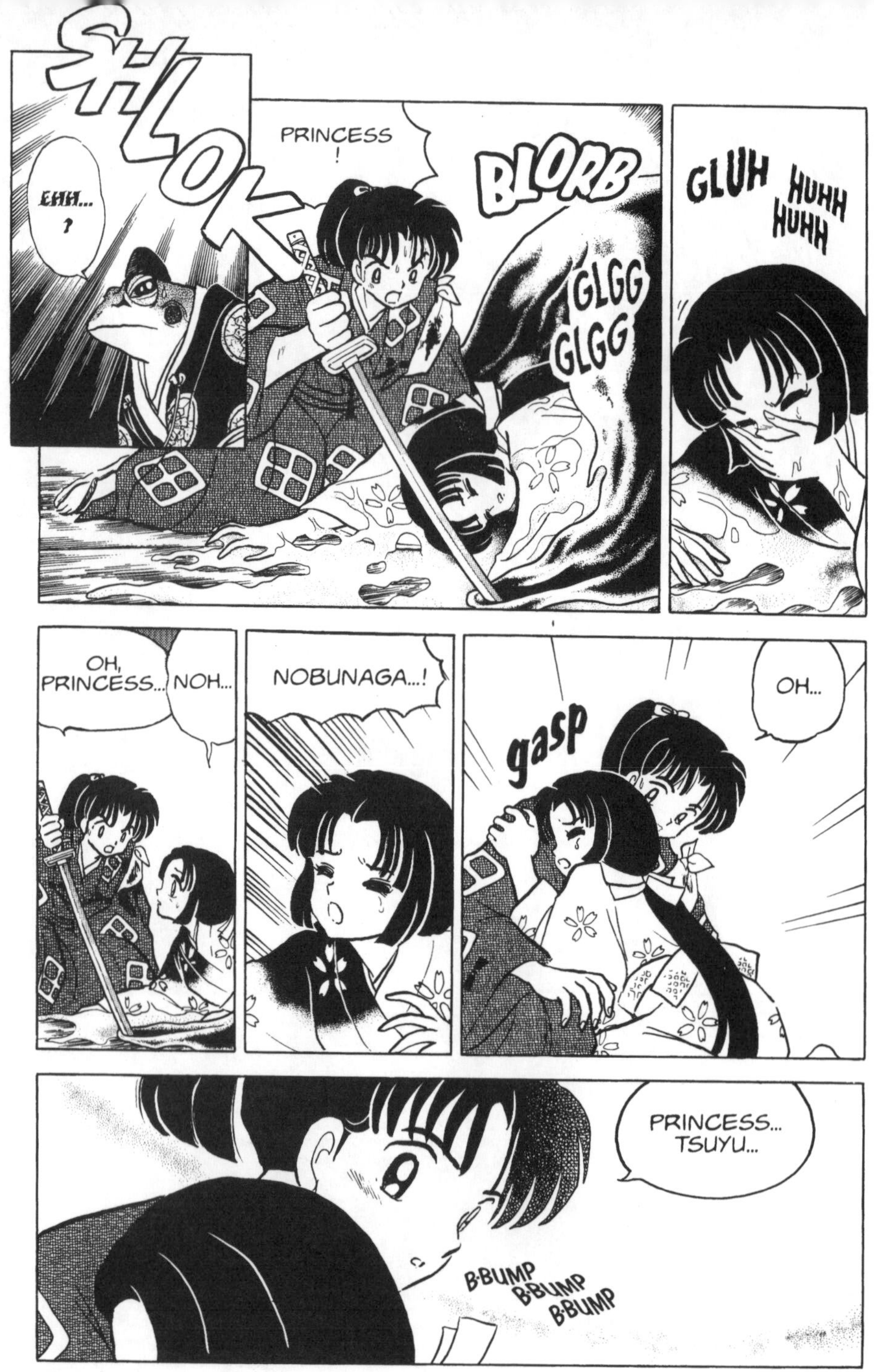
SHLOK
EHH... ?
PRINCESS !
BLORB
GLGG GLGG
GLUH
HUHH HUHH
OH, PRINCESS...
NOH...
NOBUNAGA...!
gasp
OH...
PRINCESS... TSUYU...
B-BUMP B-BUMP B-BUMP

NOW I CAN DIE HAPPY!
PERSON-ALLY, I'D RATHER NOT...
SOBB
TAKE YOUR HANDS OFF MY WIFE!
VWIH
SHH
I DON'T THINK SHE MINDS!
BUNG
GUH.
WOBBLE OBBLE
OBBLE
...
WHAT...?
WHO... WHO...?
PLAP
PLAP
MY...
PRINCESS...

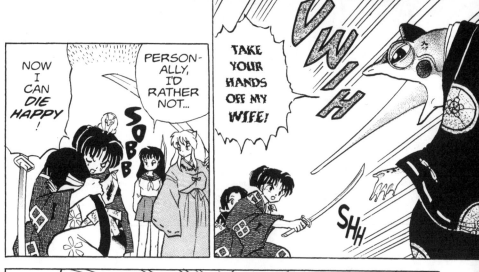

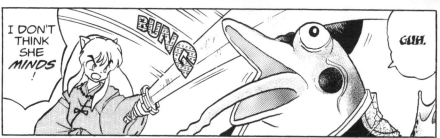

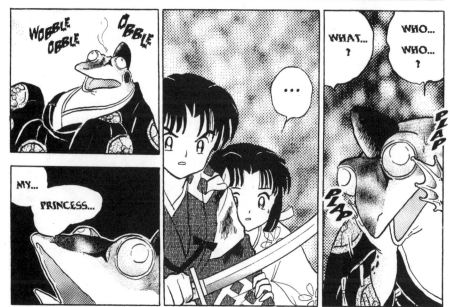

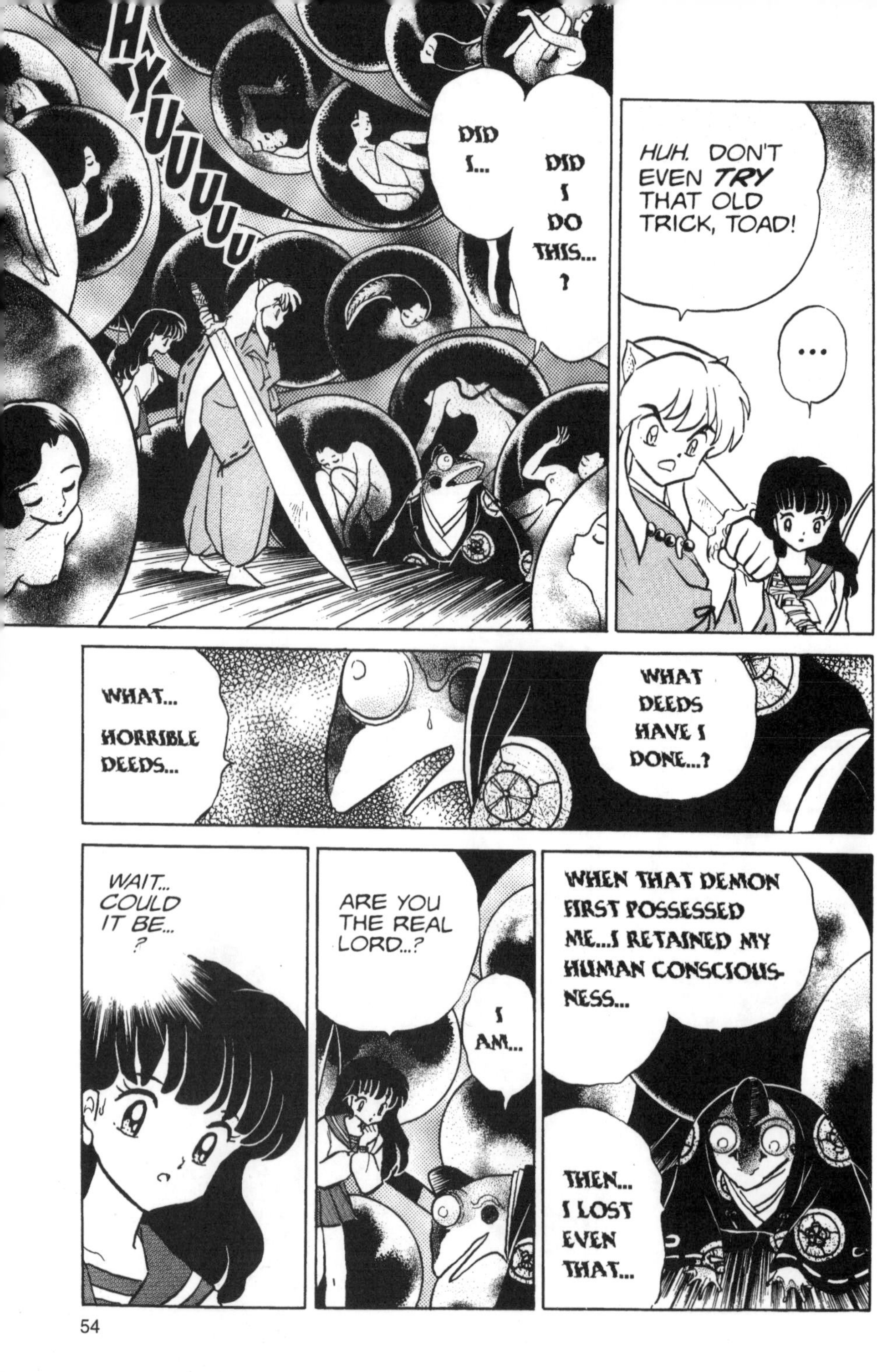
HYUUUUU
DID I...
DID I DO THIS...?
HUH. DON'T EVEN TRY THAT OLD TRICK, TOAD!
...
WHAT... HORRIBLE DEEDS...
WHAT DEEDS HAVE I DONE...?
WAIT... COULD IT BE...?
ARE YOU THE REAL LORD...?
I AM...
WHEN THAT DEMON FIRST POSSESSED ME...I RETAINED MY HUMAN CONSCIOUSNESS...
THEN... I LOST EVEN THAT...

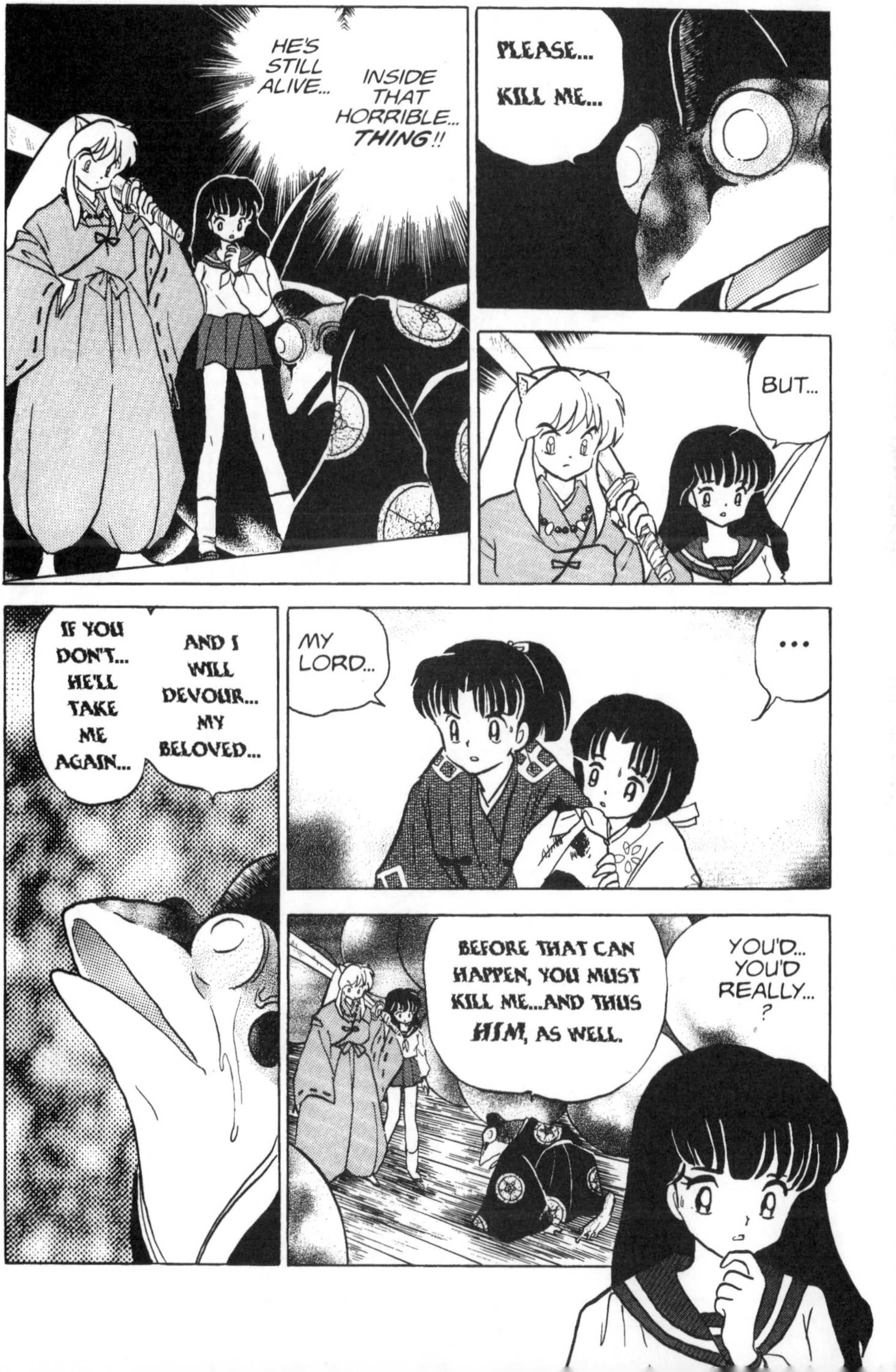
HE'S STILL ALIVE...
INSIDE THAT HORRIBLE... *THING*!!
PLEASE... KILL ME...
BUT...
IF YOU DON'T... HE'LL TAKE ME AGAIN...
AND I WILL DEVOUR... MY BELOVED...
MY LORD...
...
BEFORE THAT CAN HAPPEN, YOU MUST KILL ME...AND THUS *HIM*, AS WELL.
YOU'D... YOU'D REALLY... ?

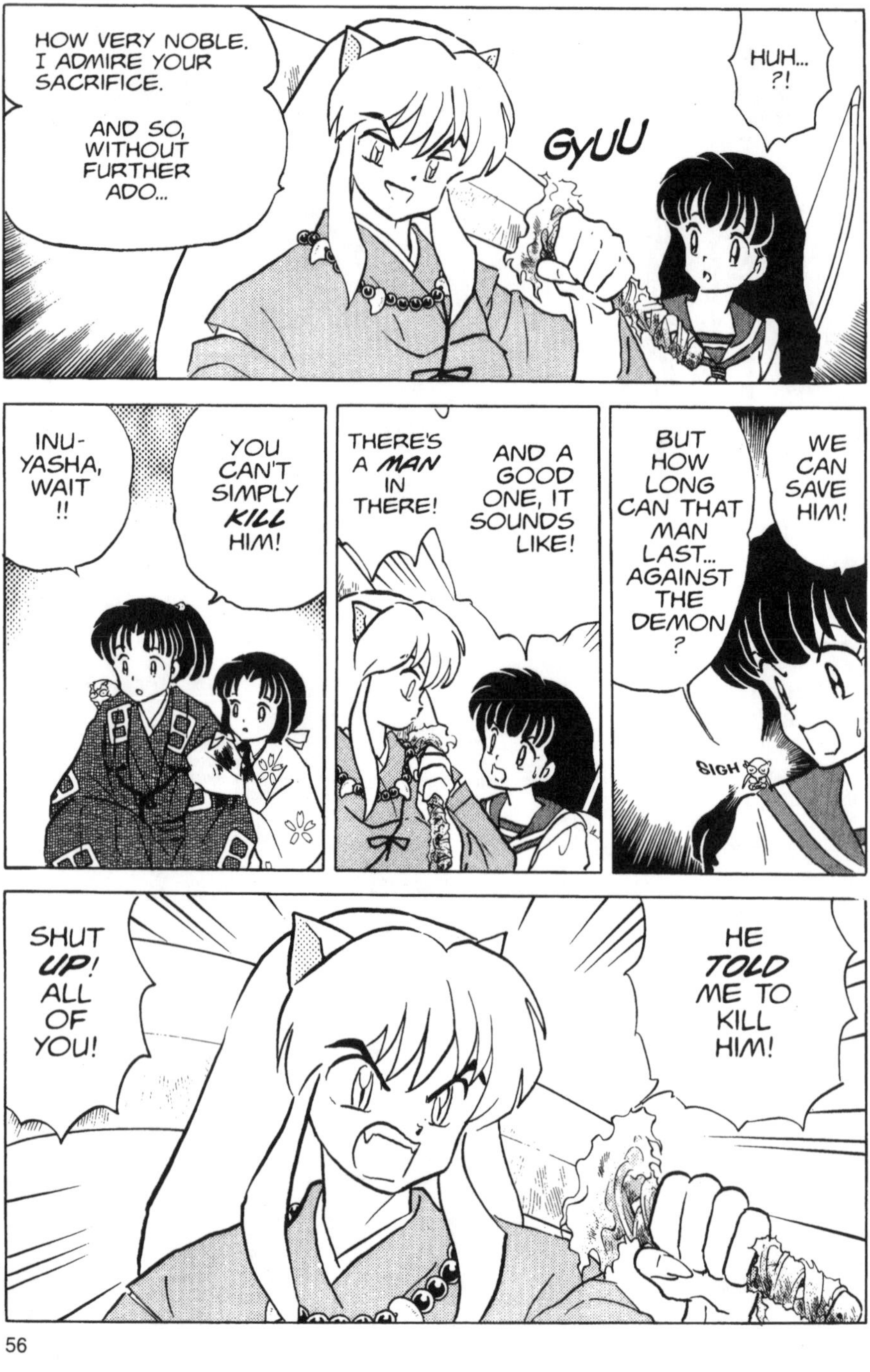
HOW VERY NOBLE. I ADMIRE YOUR SACRIFICE.
AND SO, WITHOUT FURTHER ADO...
GYUU
HUH... ?!
INU-YASHA, WAIT !!
YOU CAN'T SIMPLY KILL HIM!
THERE'S A MAN IN THERE!
AND A GOOD ONE, IT SOUNDS LIKE!
BUT HOW LONG CAN THAT MAN LAST... AGAINST THE DEMON ?
WE CAN SAVE HIM!
SIGH
SHUT UP! ALL OF YOU!
HE TOLD ME TO KILL HIM!

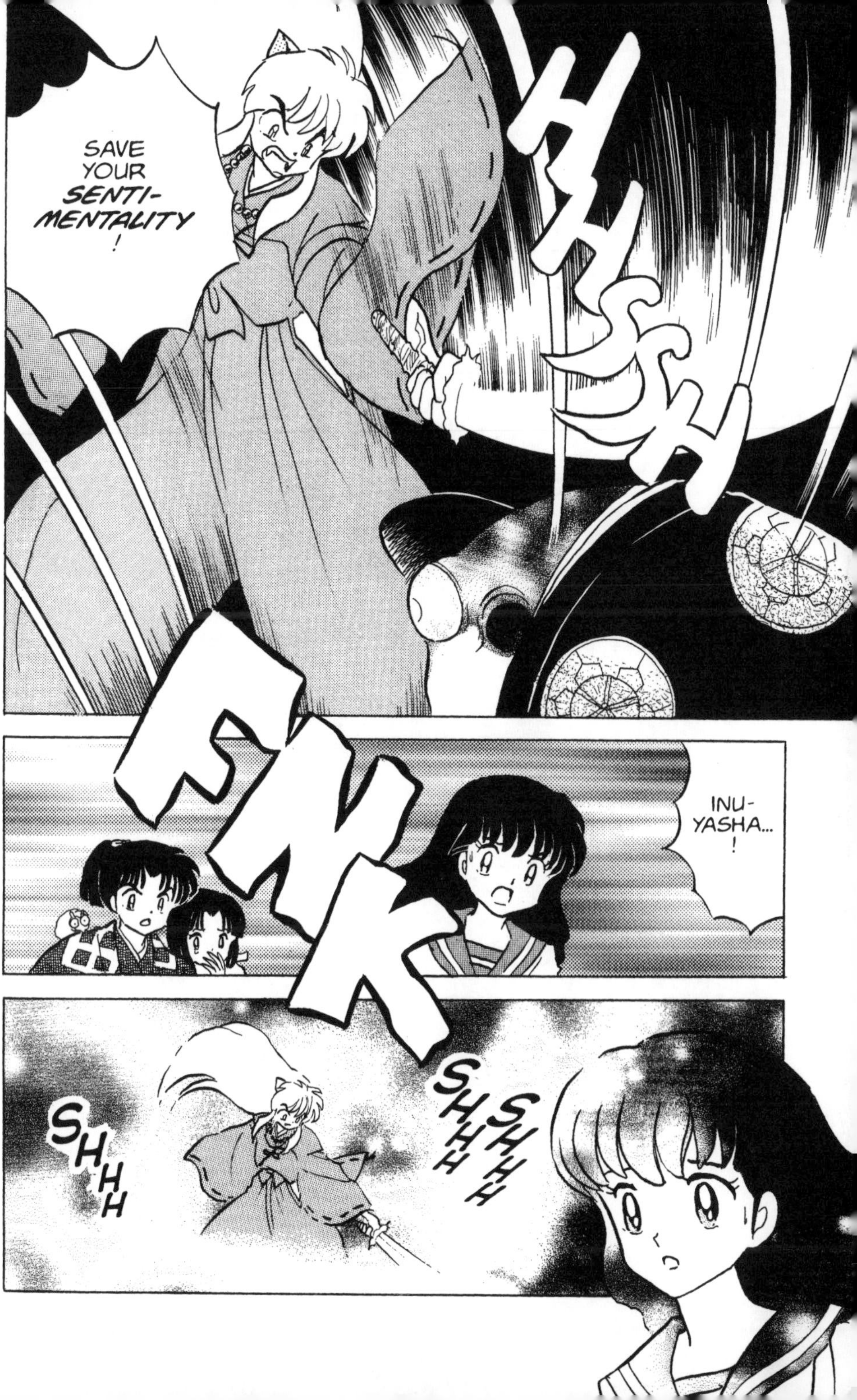
SAVE YOUR SENTI-MENTALITY!
SHHHSSHH
FINK
INU-YASHA...!
SHHH
SHHHH
SHHHH

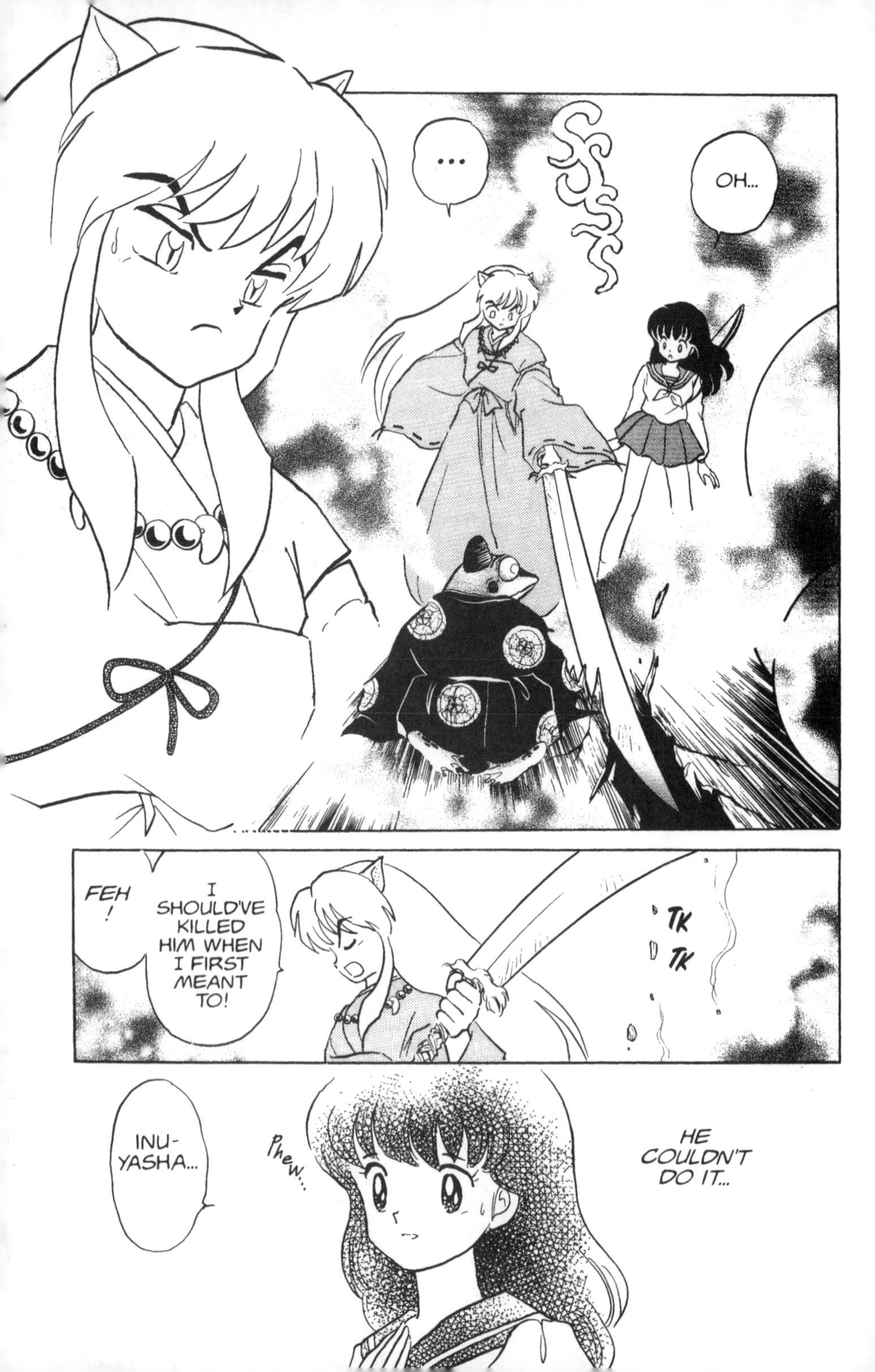
...
OH...
FEH!
I SHOULD'VE KILLED HIM WHEN I FIRST MEANT TO!
TK TK
INU-YASHA...
Phew...
HE COULDN'T DO IT...

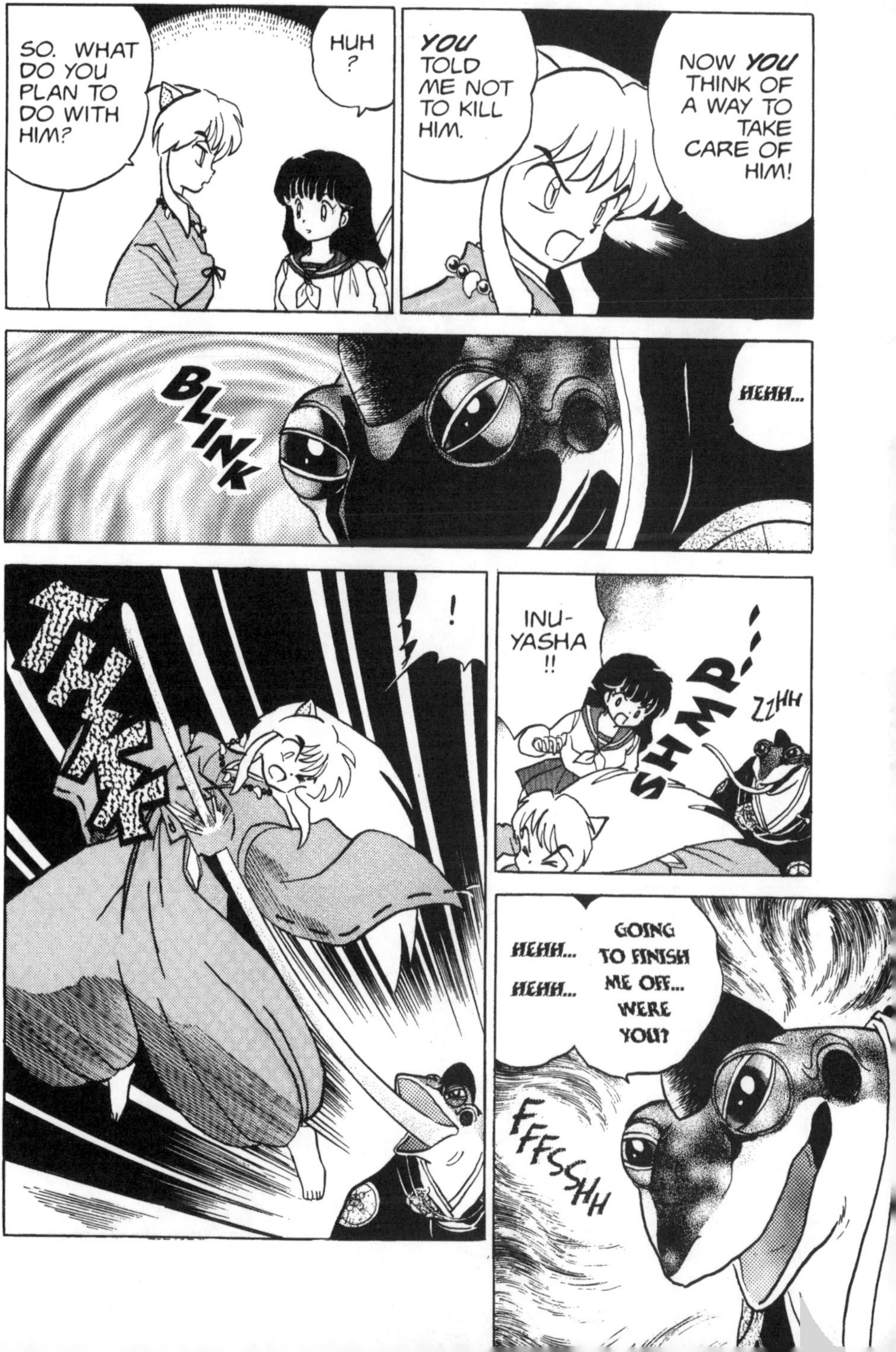
SO. WHAT DO YOU PLAN TO DO WITH HIM?
HUH ?
YOU TOLD ME NOT TO KILL HIM.
NOW YOU THINK OF A WAY TO TAKE CARE OF HIM!
BLINK
HEHH...
THWK
!
INU-YASHA !!
SHMP
ZZHH
HEHH... HEHH...
GOING TO FINISH ME OFF... WERE YOU?
FFFSSHH

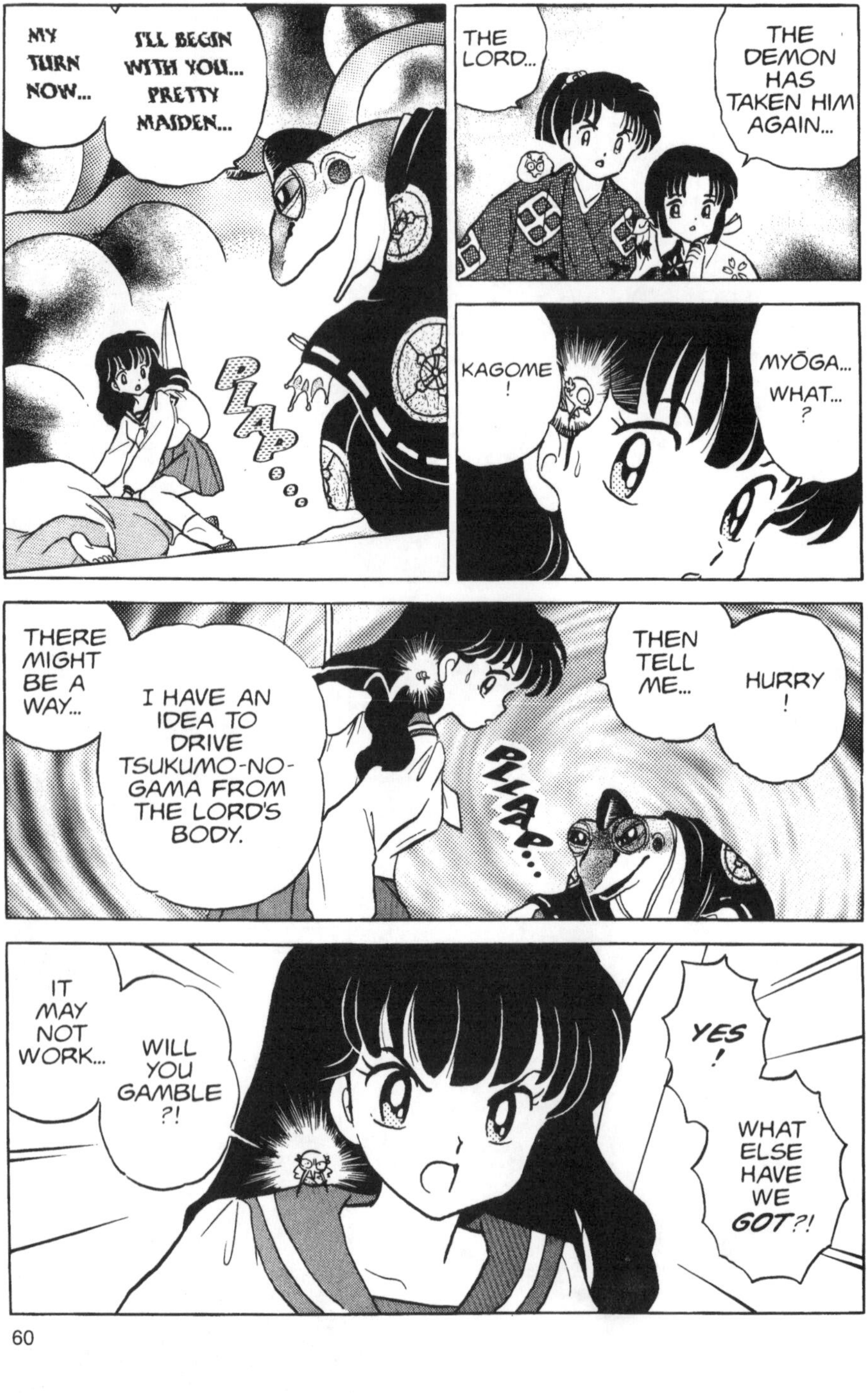
MY TURN NOW...
I'LL BEGIN WITH YOU... PRETTY MAIDEN...
PLAP...
THE LORD...
THE DEMON HAS TAKEN HIM AGAIN...
KAGOME!
MYŌGA... WHAT...?
THERE MIGHT BE A WAY...
I HAVE AN IDEA TO DRIVE TSUKUMO-NO-GAMA FROM THE LORD'S BODY.
THEN TELL ME...
HURRY!
PLAP...
IT MAY NOT WORK...
WILL YOU GAMBLE?!
YES!
WHAT ELSE HAVE WE ***GOT?!***

SCROLL FOUR

PLEA FOR MERCY

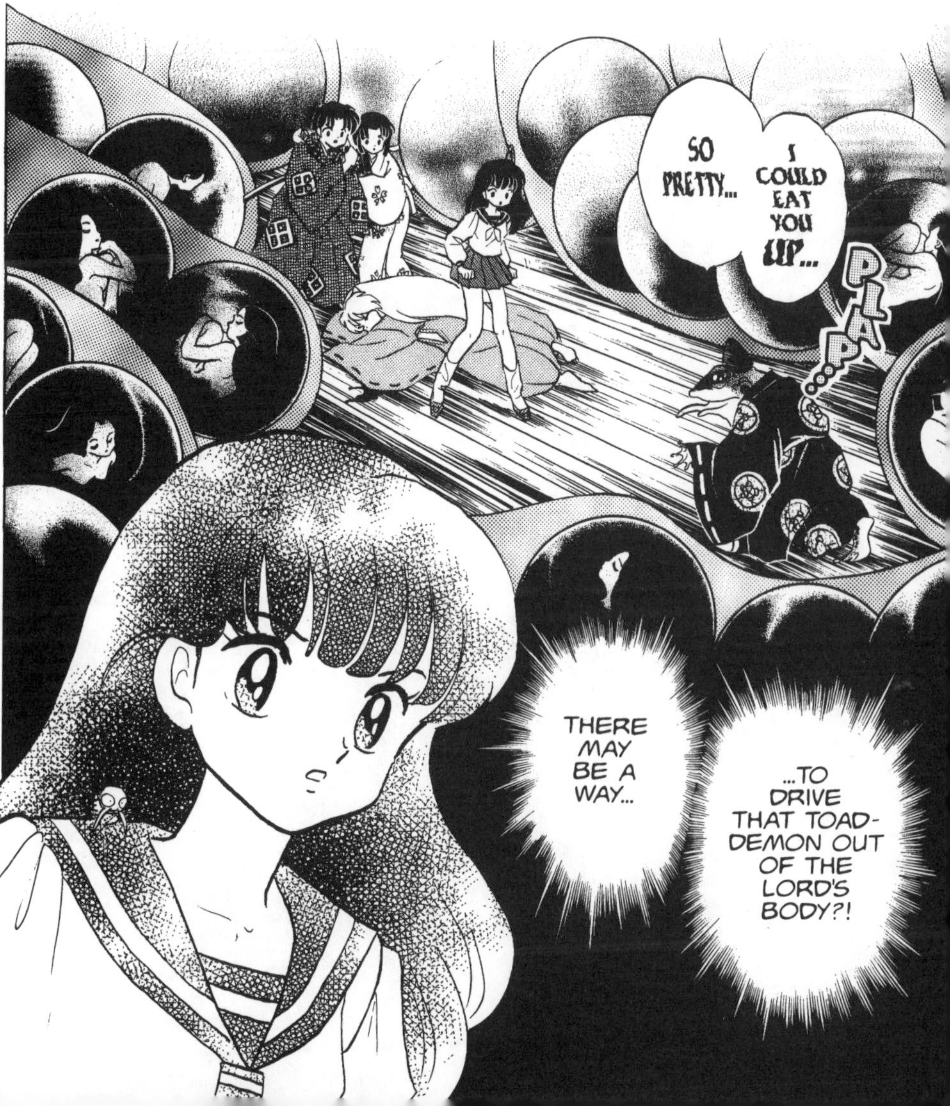
SO PRETTY...
I COULD EAT YOU UP...
PLAP...
THERE MAY BE A WAY...
...TO DRIVE THAT TOAD-DEMON OUT OF THE LORD'S BODY?!

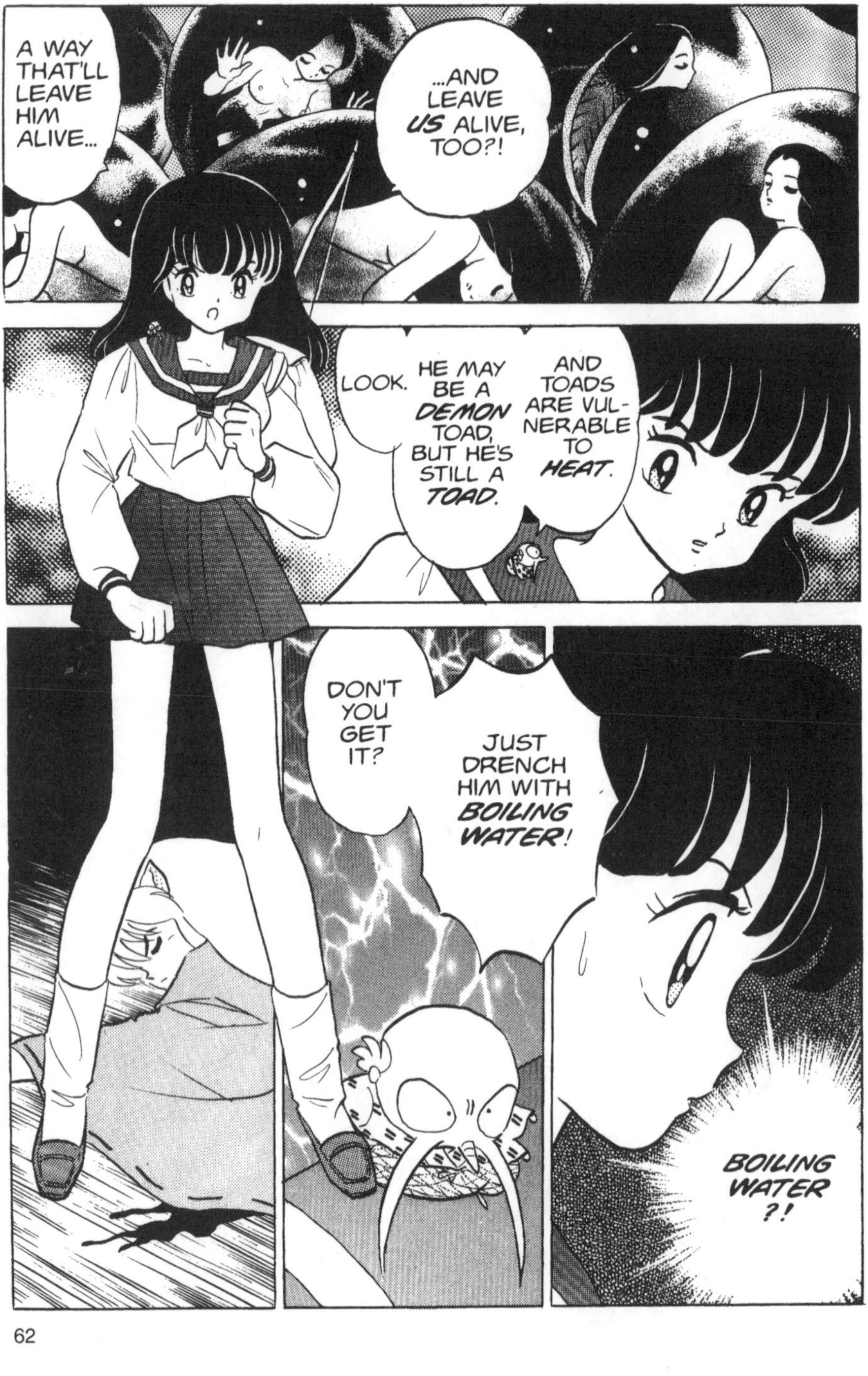
A WAY THAT'LL LEAVE HIM ALIVE...
...AND LEAVE US ALIVE, TOO?!
LOOK.
HE MAY BE A DEMON TOAD, BUT HE'S STILL A TOAD.
AND TOADS ARE VULNERABLE TO HEAT.
DON'T YOU GET IT?
JUST DRENCH HIM WITH BOILING WATER!
BOILING WATER?!

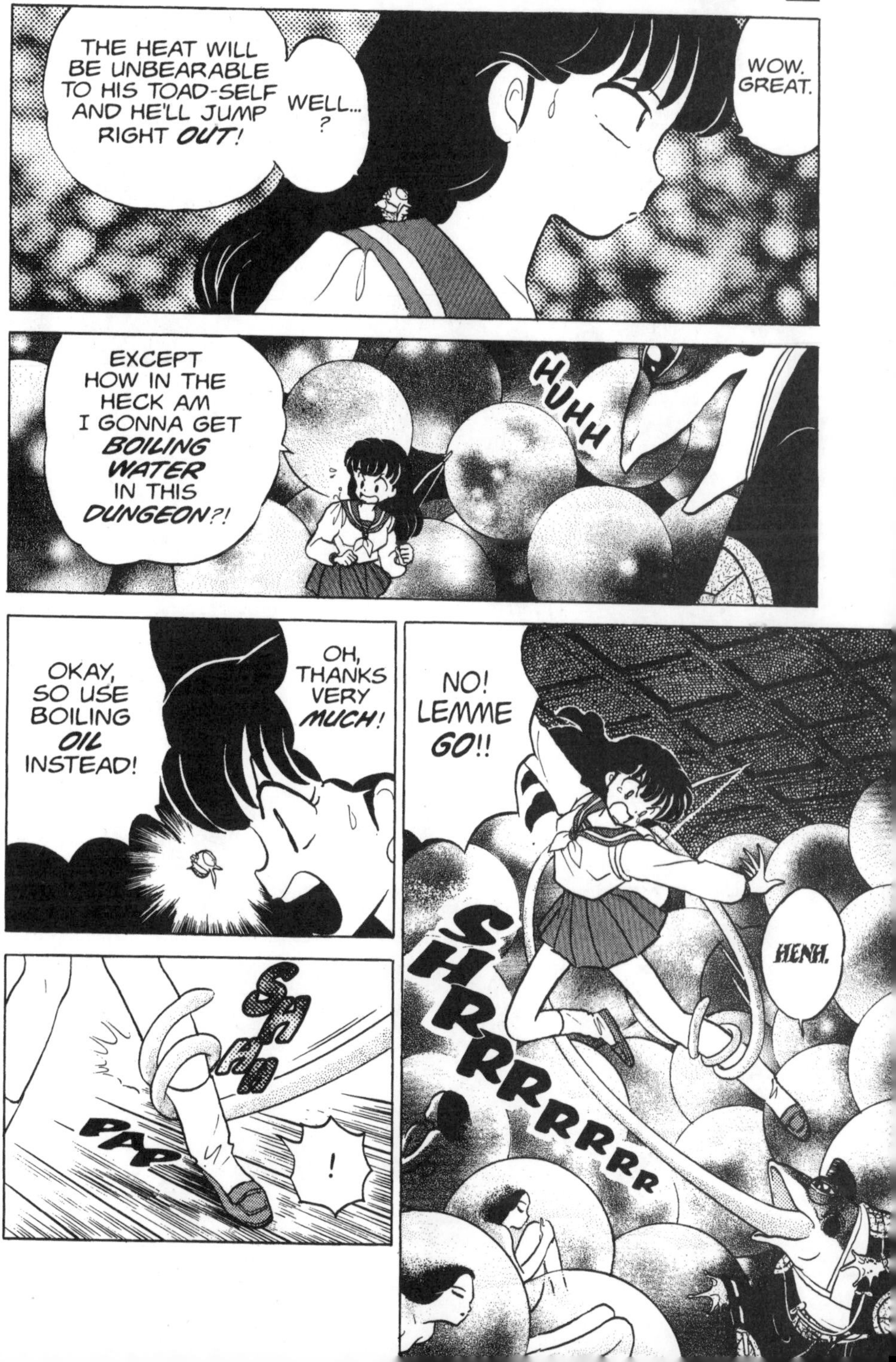
THE HEAT WILL BE UNBEARABLE TO HIS TOAD-SELF AND HE'LL JUMP RIGHT *OUT*!
WELL... ?
WOW. GREAT.
EXCEPT HOW IN THE HECK AM I GONNA GET *BOILING WATER* IN THIS *DUNGEON*?!
HUHH
OKAY, SO USE BOILING *OIL* INSTEAD!
OH, THANKS VERY *MUCH*!
SHHH
PAP
!
NO! LEMME *GO*!!
HENH.
SHRRRRRRRR

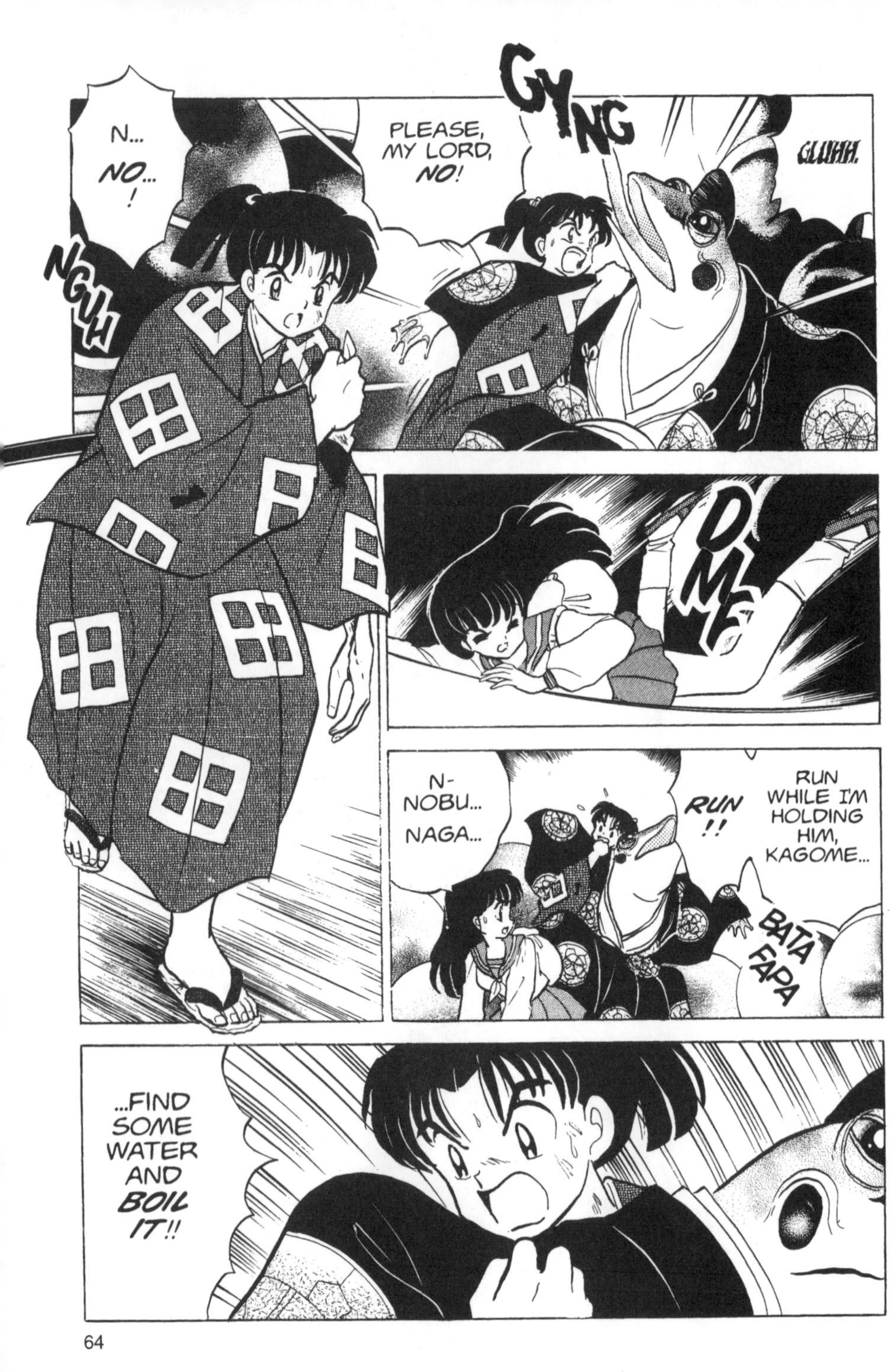

N... NO...!
NGUH
PLEASE, MY LORD, NO!
GYNG
GLUHH.
DMF
N- NOBU... NAGA...
RUN!!
RUN WHILE I'M HOLDING HIM, KAGOME...
BATA FAPA
...FIND SOME WATER AND BOIL IT!!

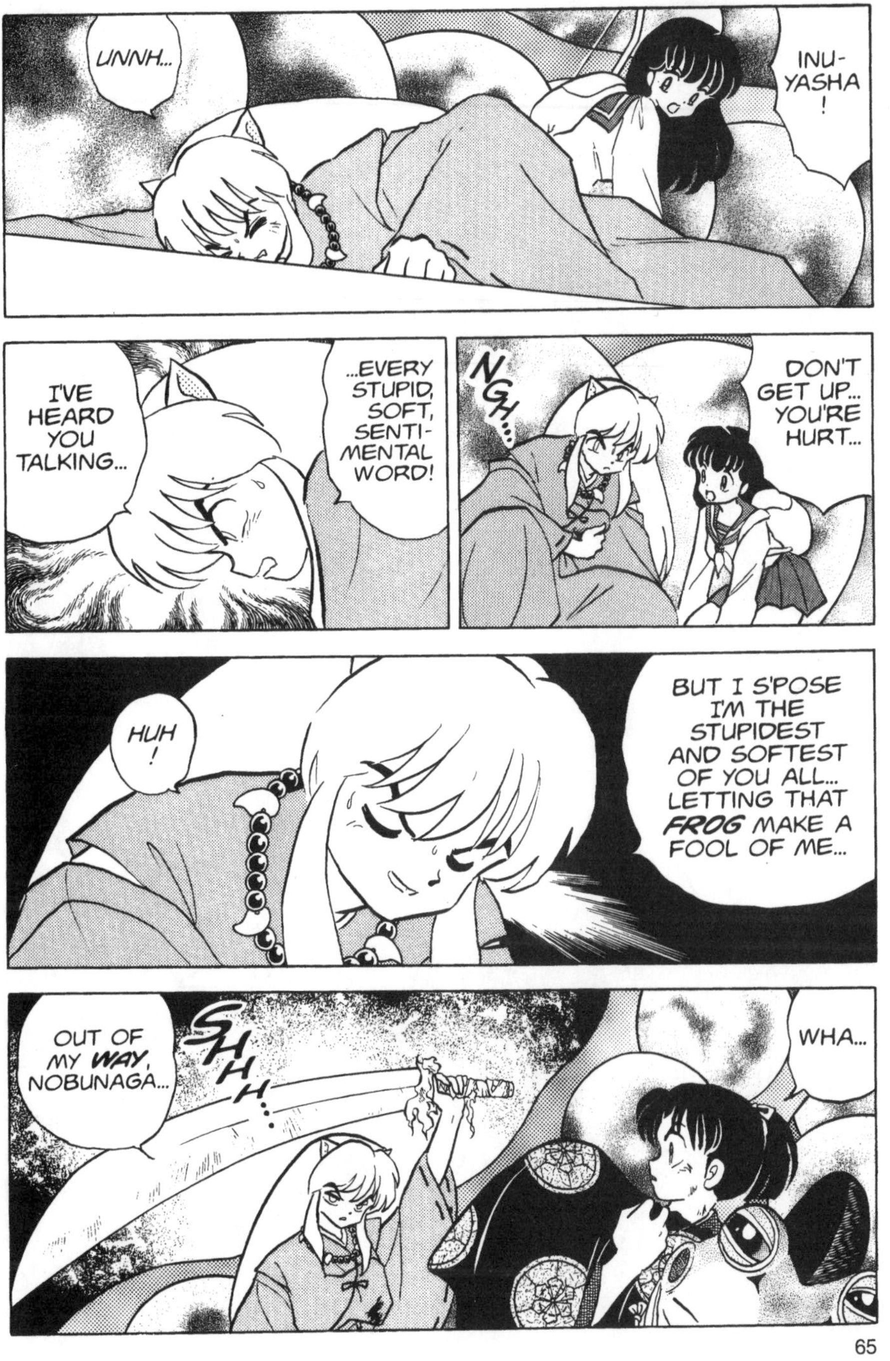
UNNH...
INU-YASHA!
I'VE HEARD YOU TALKING...
...EVERY STUPID, SOFT, SENTIMENTAL WORD!
NGH...
DON'T GET UP... YOU'RE HURT...
HUH!
BUT I S'POSE I'M THE STUPIDEST AND SOFTEST OF YOU ALL... LETTING THAT **FROG** MAKE A FOOL OF ME...
OUT OF MY **WAY**, NOBUNAGA...
SHHH...
WHA...

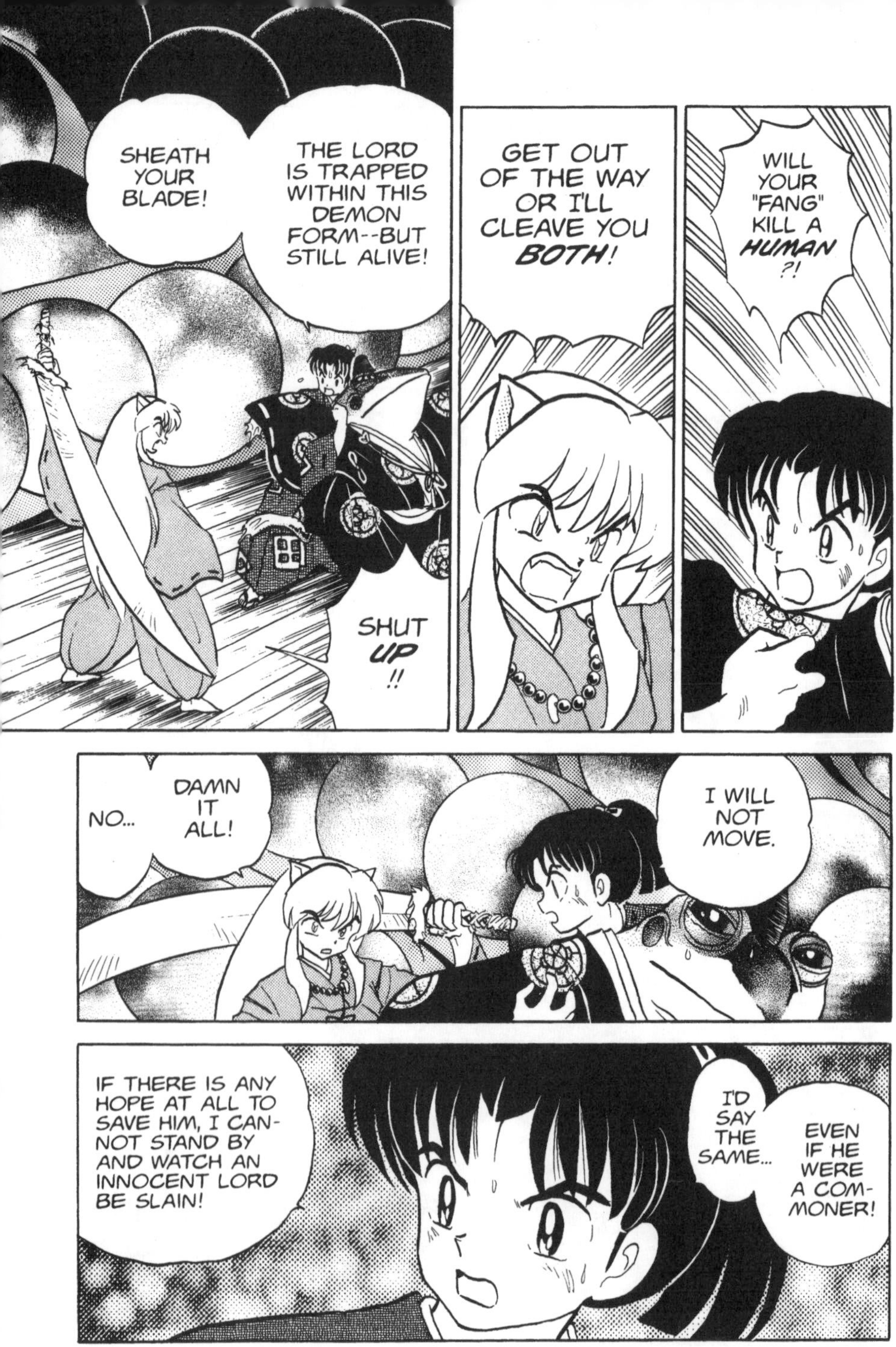
SHEATH YOUR BLADE!
THE LORD IS TRAPPED WITHIN THIS DEMON FORM--BUT STILL ALIVE!
SHUT UP!!
GET OUT OF THE WAY OR I'LL CLEAVE YOU BOTH!
WILL YOUR "FANG" KILL A HUMAN?!
NO...
DAMN IT ALL!
I WILL NOT MOVE.
IF THERE IS ANY HOPE AT ALL TO SAVE HIM, I CAN-NOT STAND BY AND WATCH AN INNOCENT LORD BE SLAIN!
I'D SAY THE SAME...
EVEN IF HE WERE A COM-MONER!

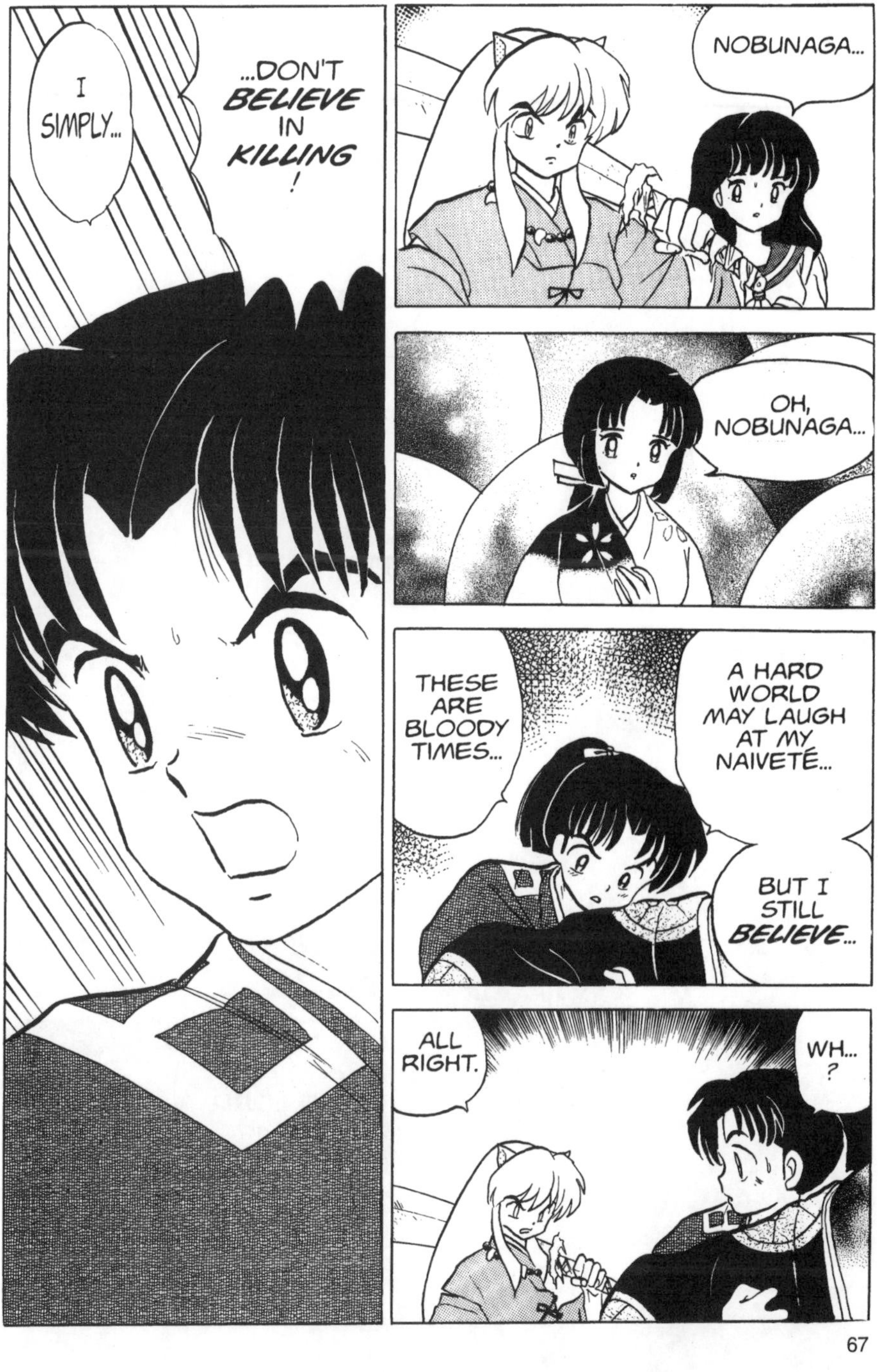
I SIMPLY...
...DON'T BELIEVE IN KILLING!
NOBUNAGA...
OH, NOBUNAGA...
THESE ARE BLOODY TIMES...
A HARD WORLD MAY LAUGH AT MY NAIVETÉ...
BUT I STILL BELIEVE...
ALL RIGHT.
WH...?

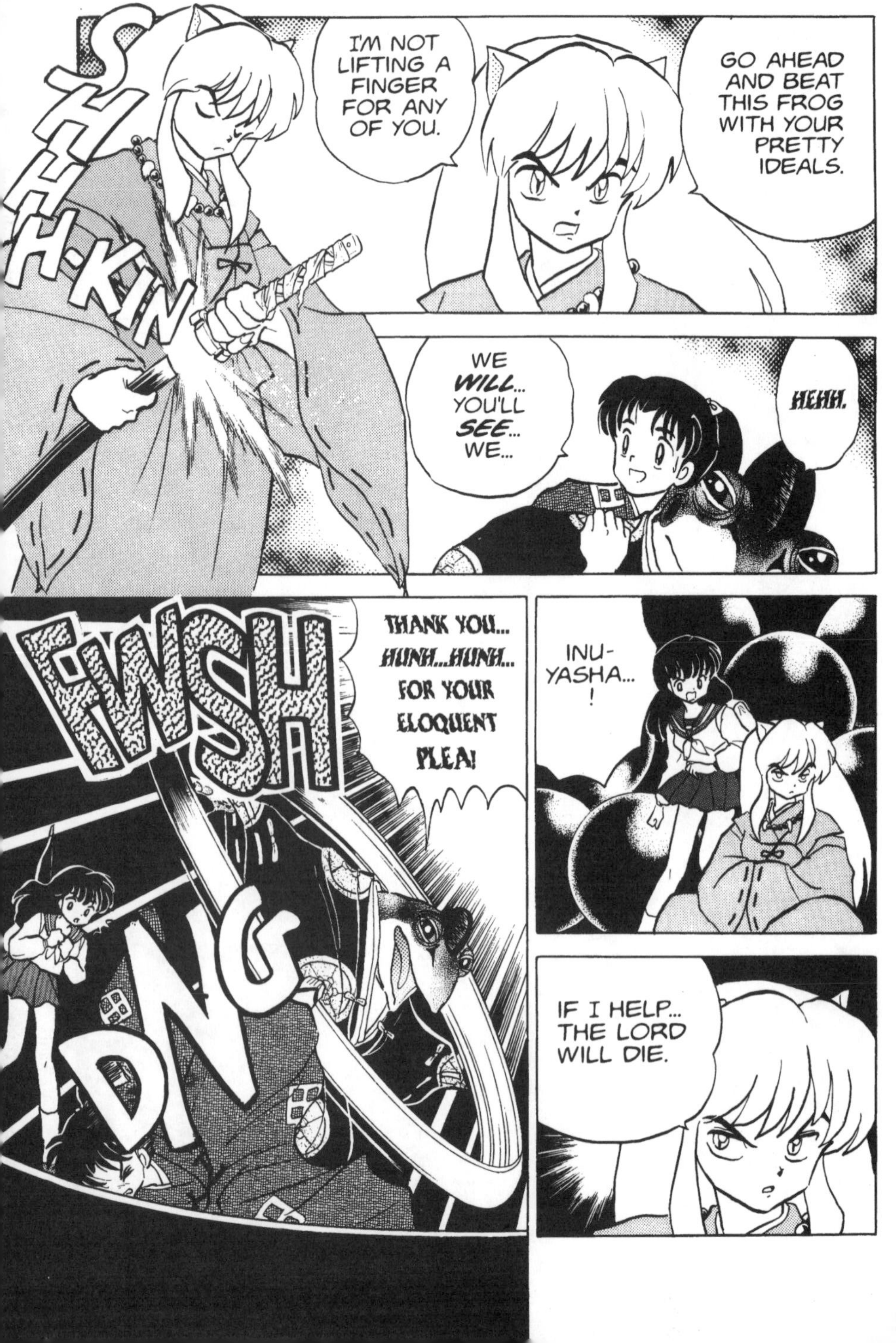
SHHHH-KIN
I'M NOT LIFTING A FINGER FOR ANY OF YOU.
GO AHEAD AND BEAT THIS FROG WITH YOUR PRETTY IDEALS.
WE *WILL*... YOU'LL *SEE*... WE...
HEHH.
F-WSH
THANK YOU... HUNH...HUNH... FOR YOUR ELOQUENT PLEA!
DNG
INU-YASHA... !
IF I HELP... THE LORD WILL DIE.

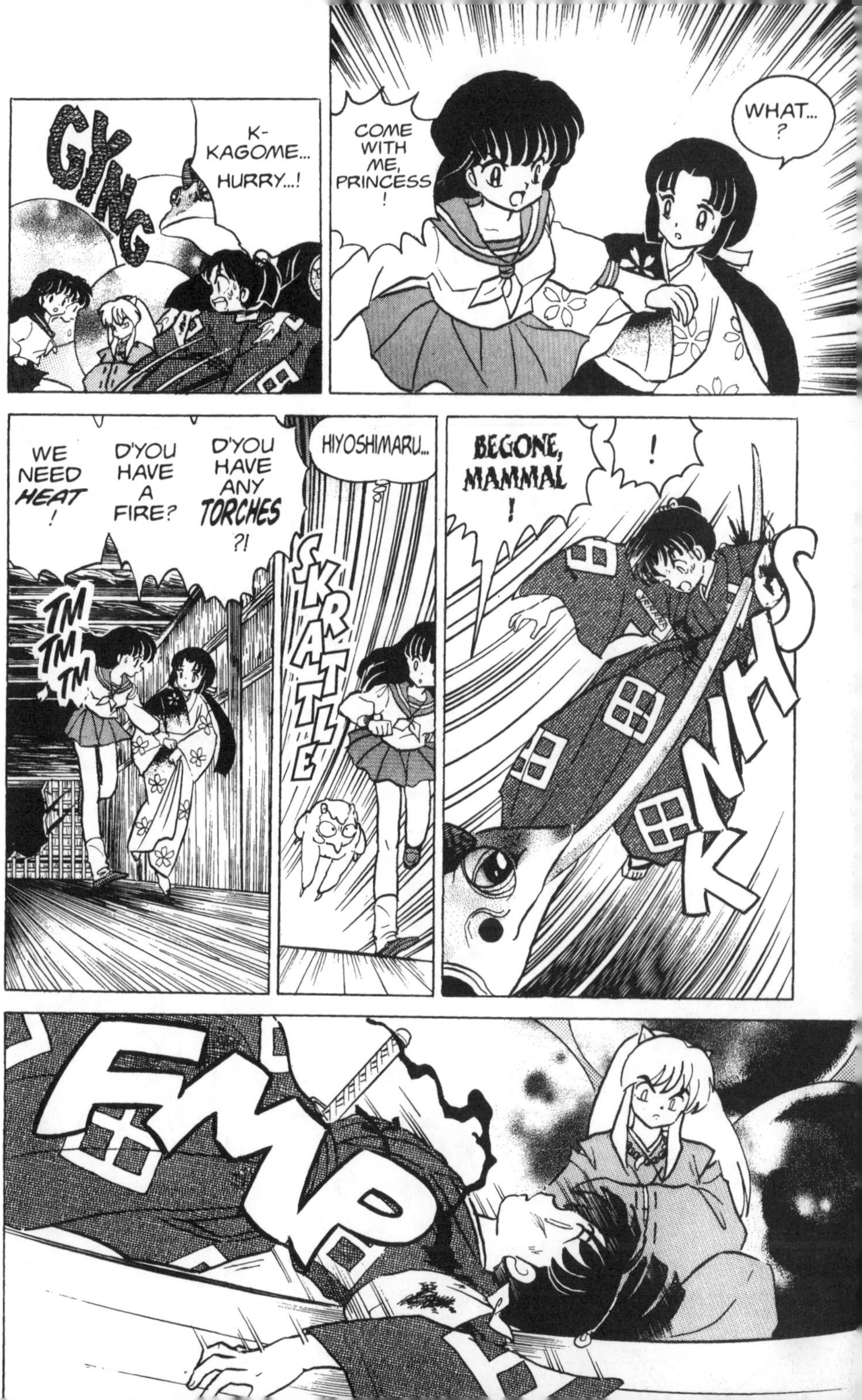
GYNG
K-KAGOME... HURRY...!
COME WITH ME, PRINCESS!
WHAT...?
WE NEED HEAT!
D'YOU HAVE A FIRE?
D'YOU HAVE ANY TORCHES?!
TM TM TM
HIYOSHIMARU...
SKRATTLE
BEGONE, MAMMAL!
!
SHNK
FMP

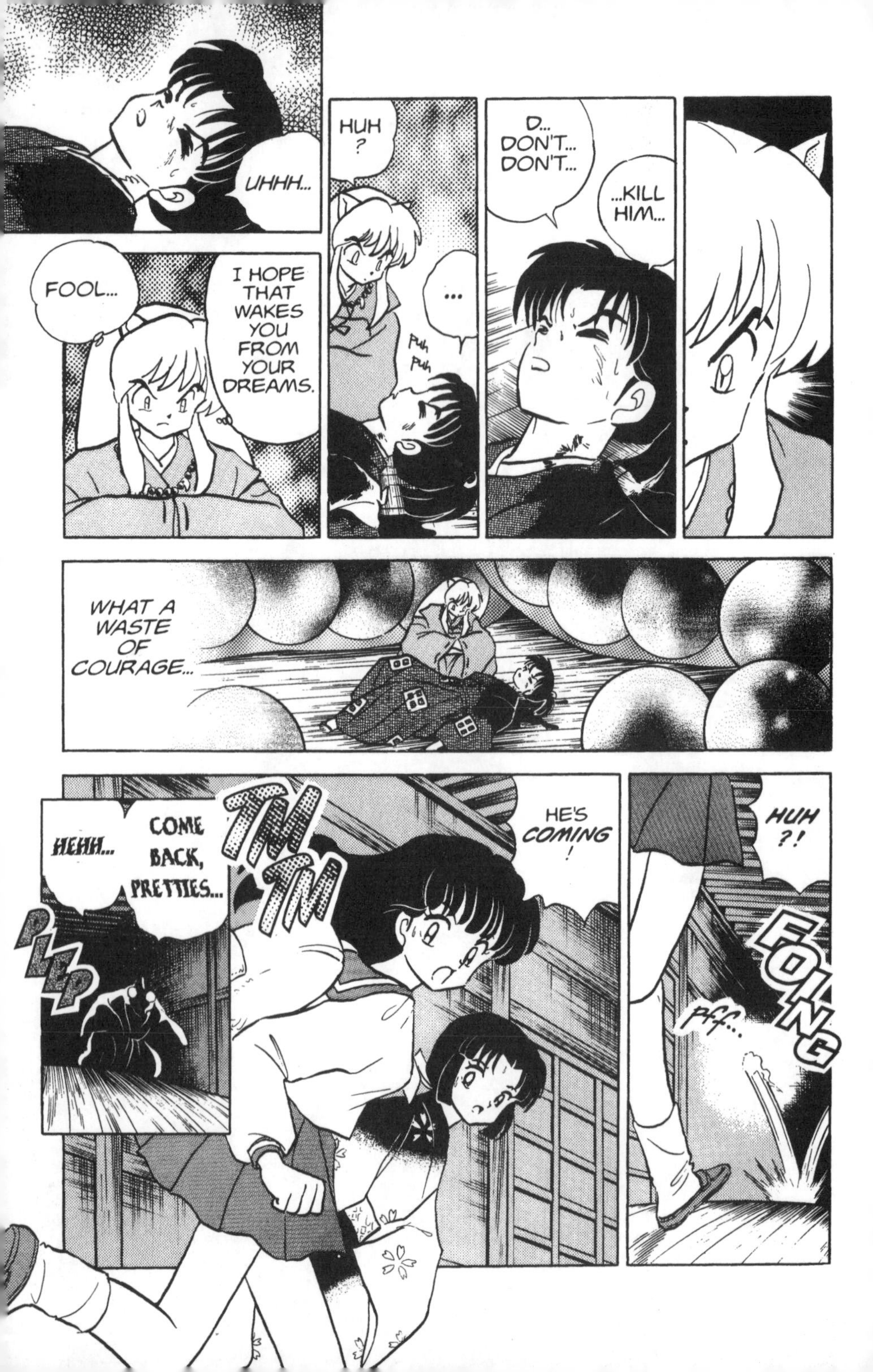
UHHH...
FOOL...
I HOPE THAT WAKES YOU FROM YOUR DREAMS.
HUH ?
...
Puh Puh
D... DON'T... DON'T...
...KILL HIM...
WHAT A WASTE OF COURAGE...
HEHHH...
COME BACK, PRETTIES...
PLOP
TM TM
HE'S COMING !
HUH ?!
FOING
pff...

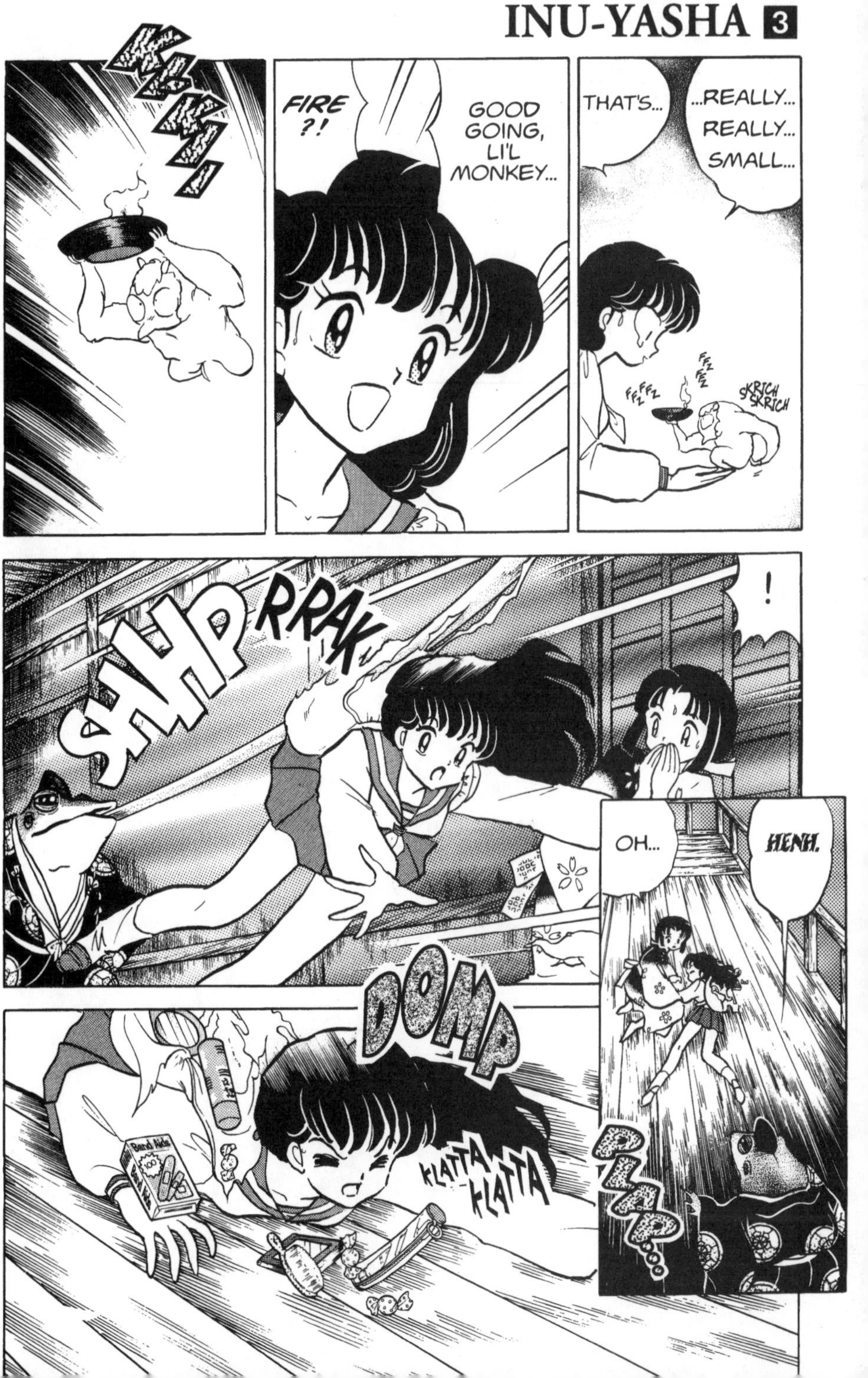

FIRE ?!
GOOD GOING, LI'L MONKEY...
THAT'S...
...REALLY... REALLY... SMALL...
FFZ FFZ
FFZ FFZ
SKRICH SKRICH
SHHP
RRAK
!
DOMP
KLATTA KLATTA
OH...
HENH.
PLAP...

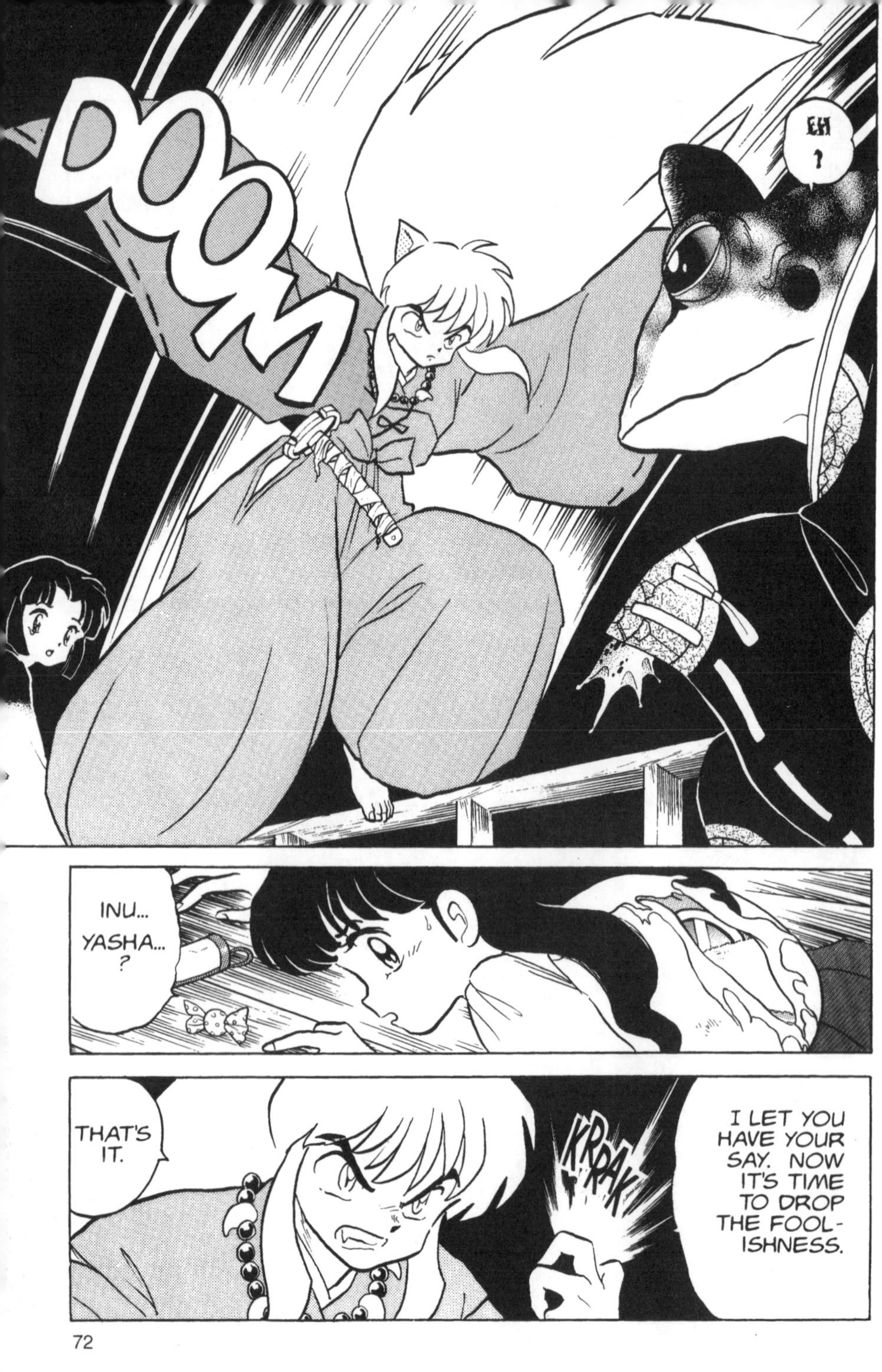
DOOM
EH?
INU... YASHA...?
THAT'S IT.
KRAK
I LET YOU HAVE YOUR SAY. NOW IT'S TIME TO DROP THE FOOL- ISHNESS.

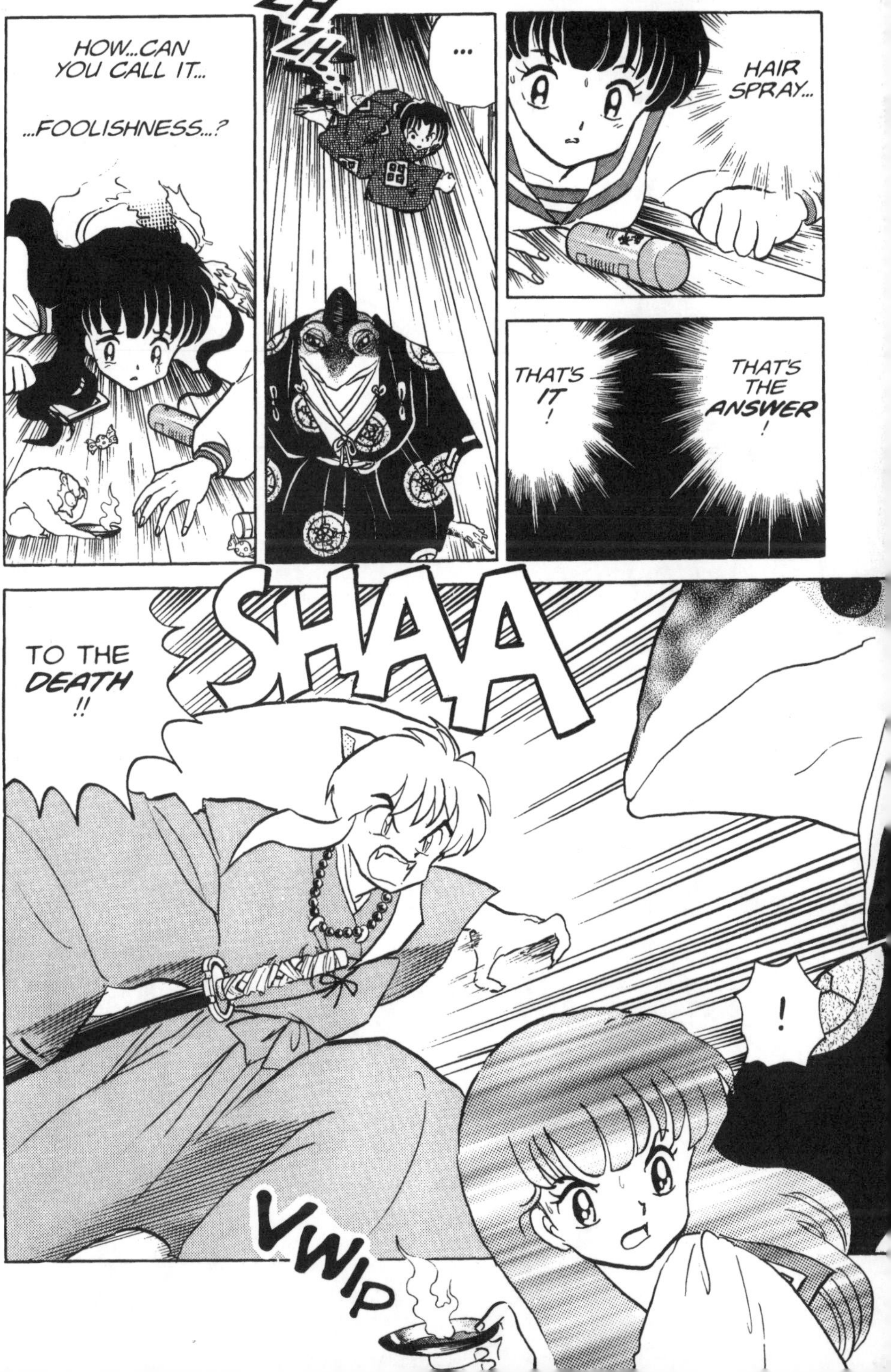
HOW...CAN YOU CALL IT...
...FOOLISHNESS...?
ZH ZH
...
HAIR SPRAY...
THAT'S IT!
THAT'S THE ANSWER!
TO THE DEATH!!
SHAA
!
VWIP

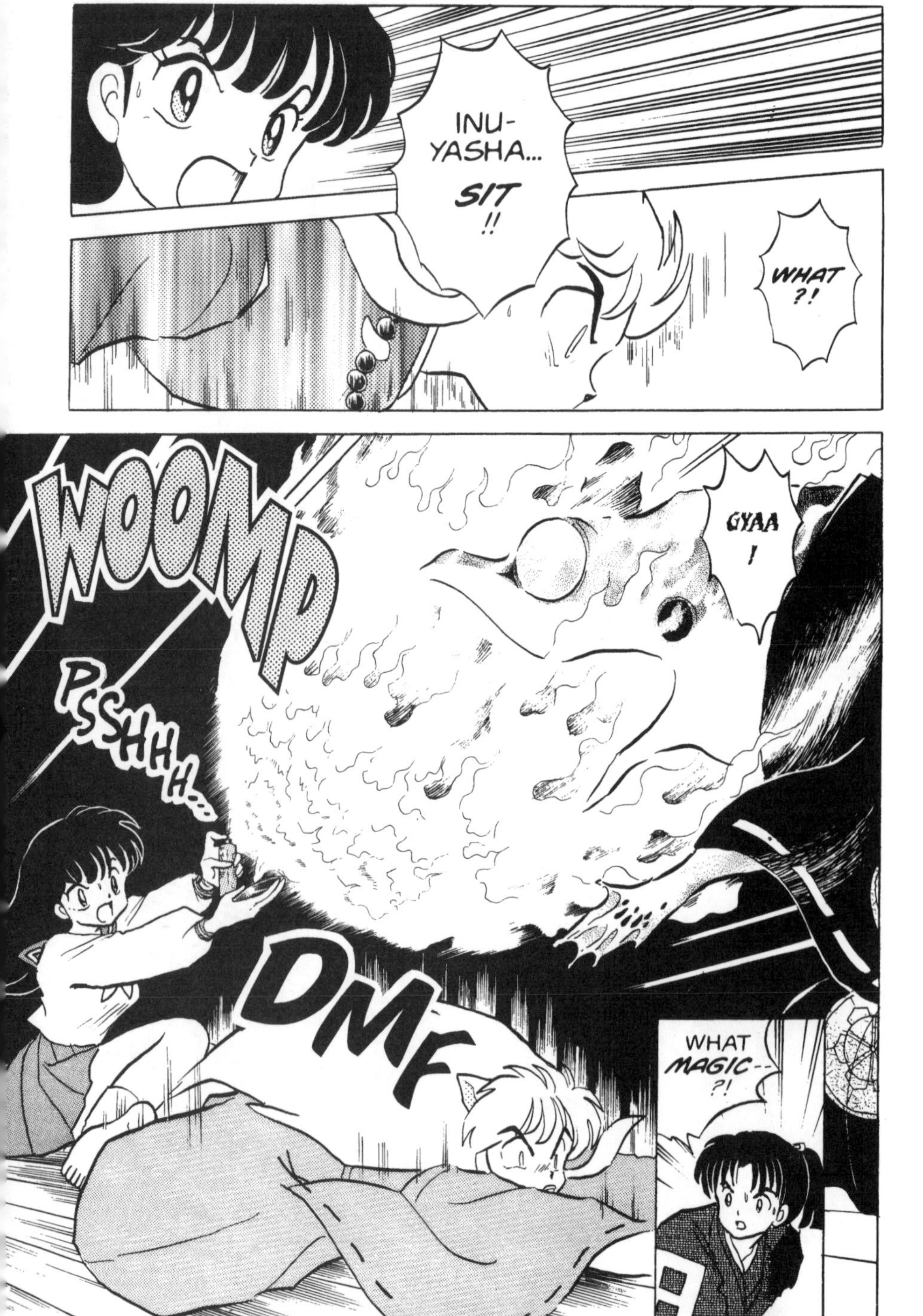
INU-YASHA... SIT!!
WHAT?!
WOOMP
PSSHHH...
GYAA!
DMF
WHAT MAGIC--?!

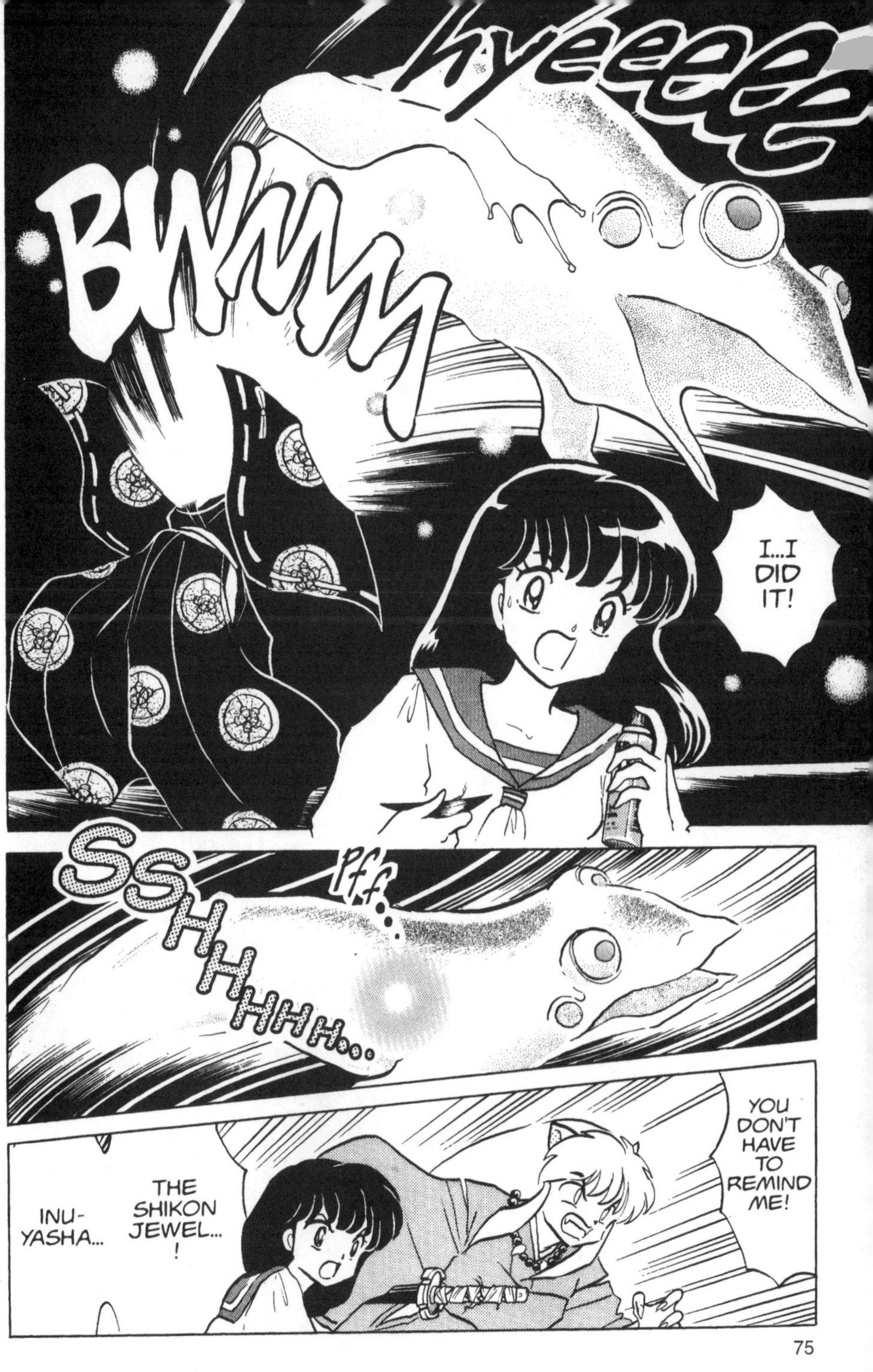
BWMM
hyeeeee
I...I DID IT!
SSHHHHHH...
Pff...
INU-YASHA...
THE SHIKON JEWEL...!
YOU DON'T HAVE TO REMIND ME!

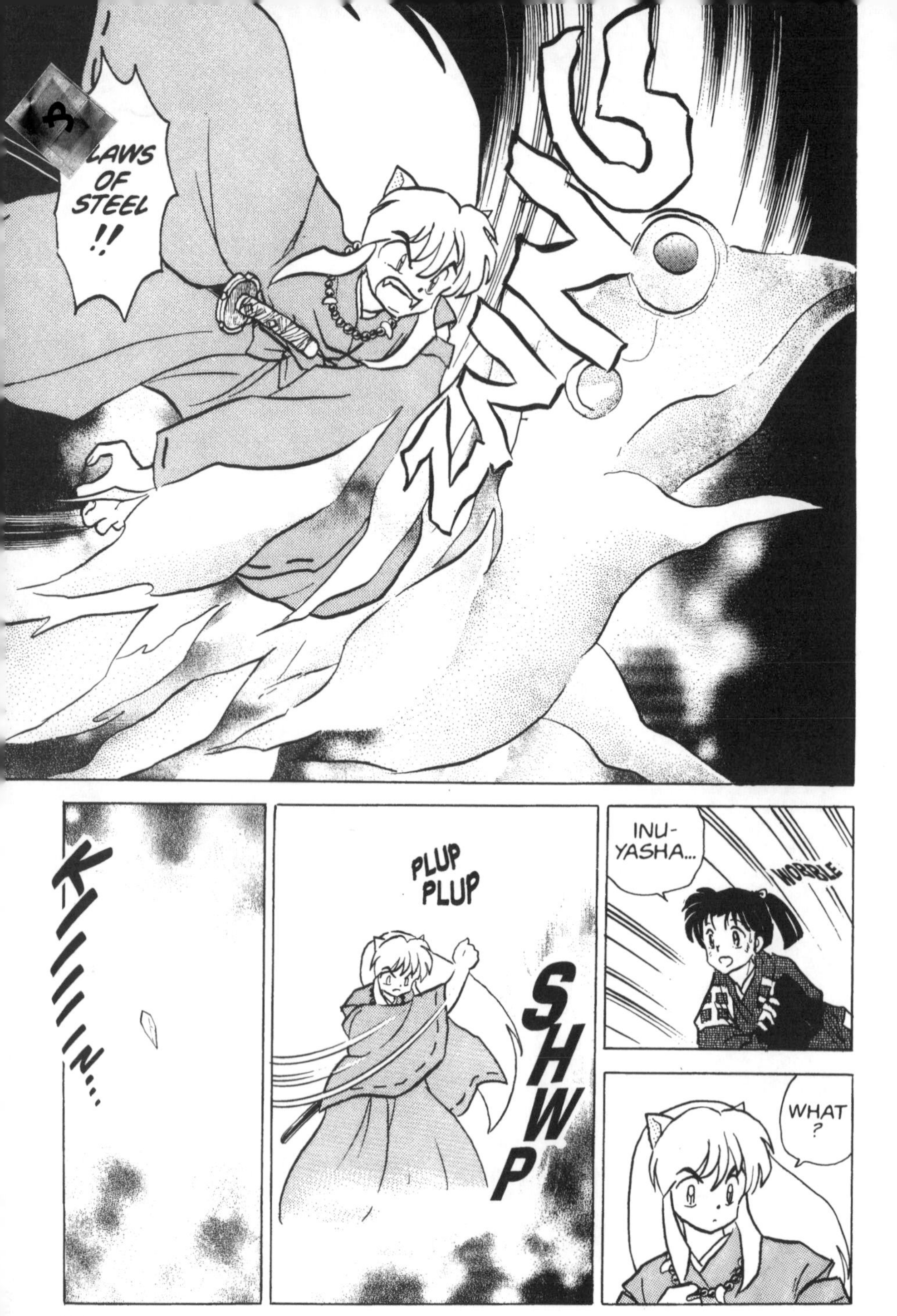

LAWS OF STEEL!!
KIIIIIN...
PLUP PLUP
SHWP
INU-YASHA...
WOBBLE
WHAT?

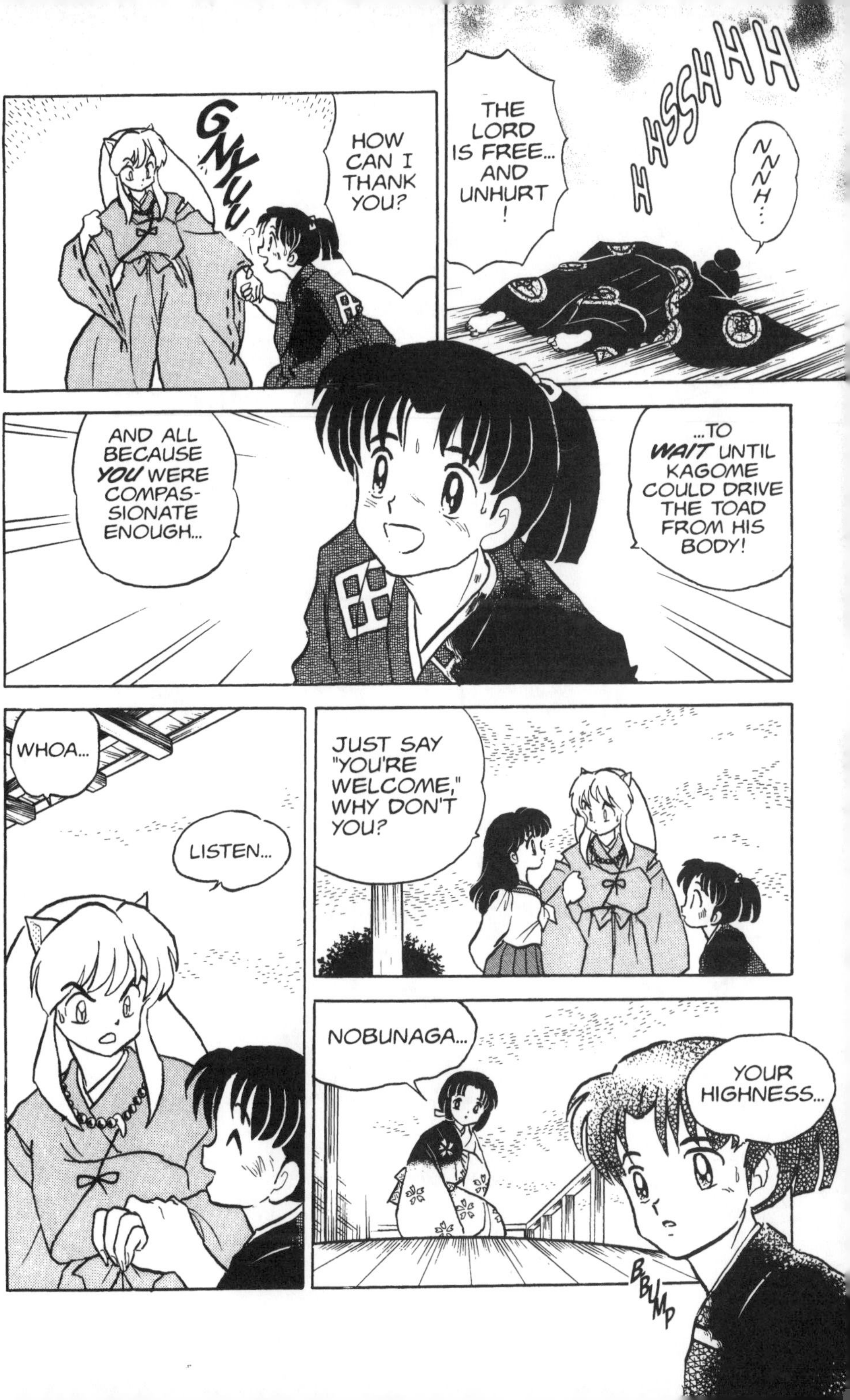
GNYUU
HOW CAN I THANK YOU?
THE LORD IS FREE... AND UNHURT!
HHSSHHHH
NNNH...
AND ALL BECAUSE YOU WERE COMPAS-SIONATE ENOUGH...
...TO WAIT UNTIL KAGOME COULD DRIVE THE TOAD FROM HIS BODY!
WHOA...
LISTEN...
JUST SAY "YOU'RE WELCOME," WHY DON'T YOU?
NOBUNAGA...
YOUR HIGHNESS...
BBUMP

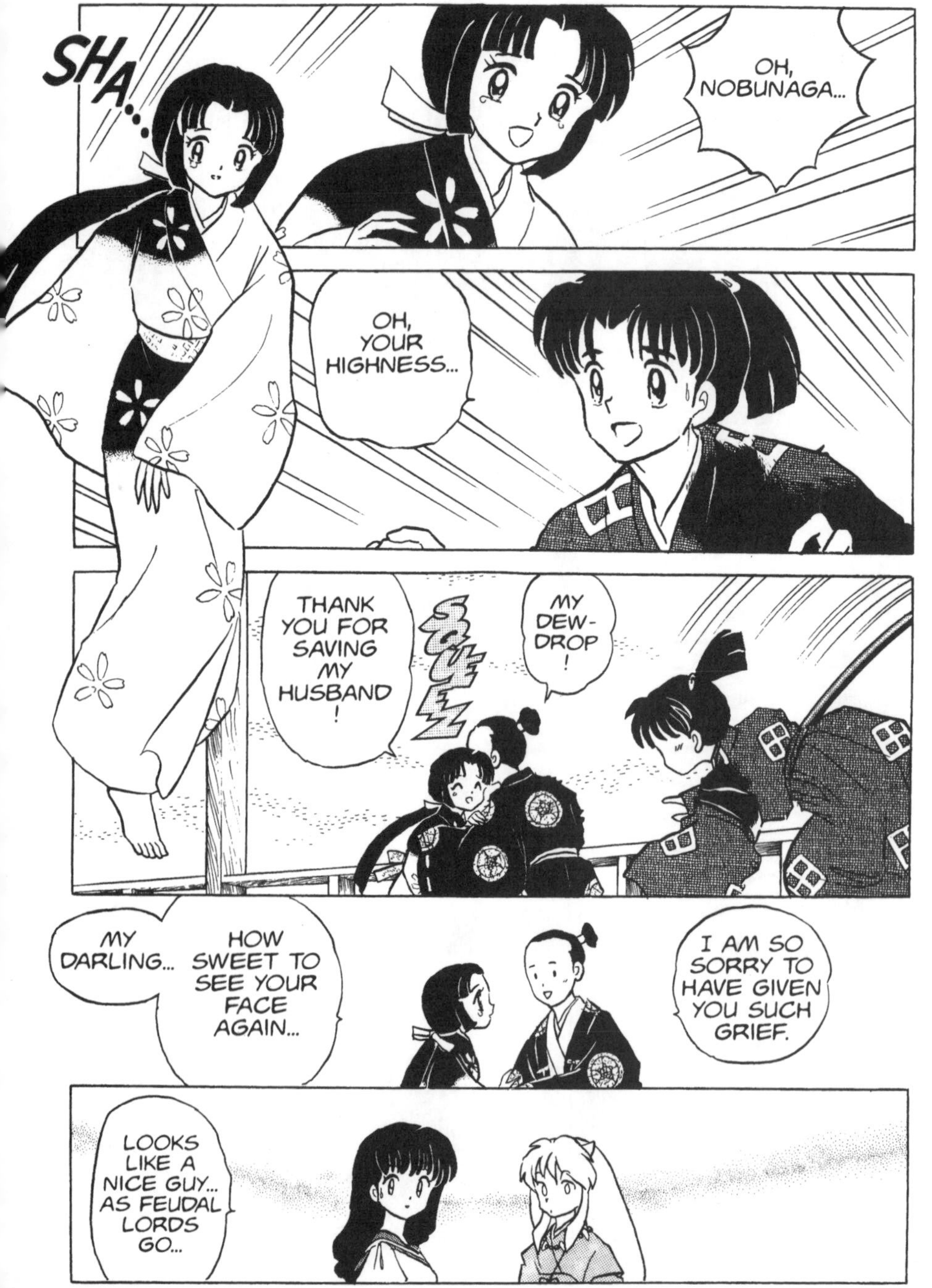

SHA...
OH, NOBUNAGA...
OH, YOUR HIGHNESS...
THANK YOU FOR SAVING MY HUSBAND!
MY DEW-DROP!
MY DARLING...
HOW SWEET TO SEE YOUR FACE AGAIN...
I AM SO SORRY TO HAVE GIVEN YOU SUCH GRIEF.
LOOKS LIKE A NICE GUY... AS FEUDAL LORDS GO...

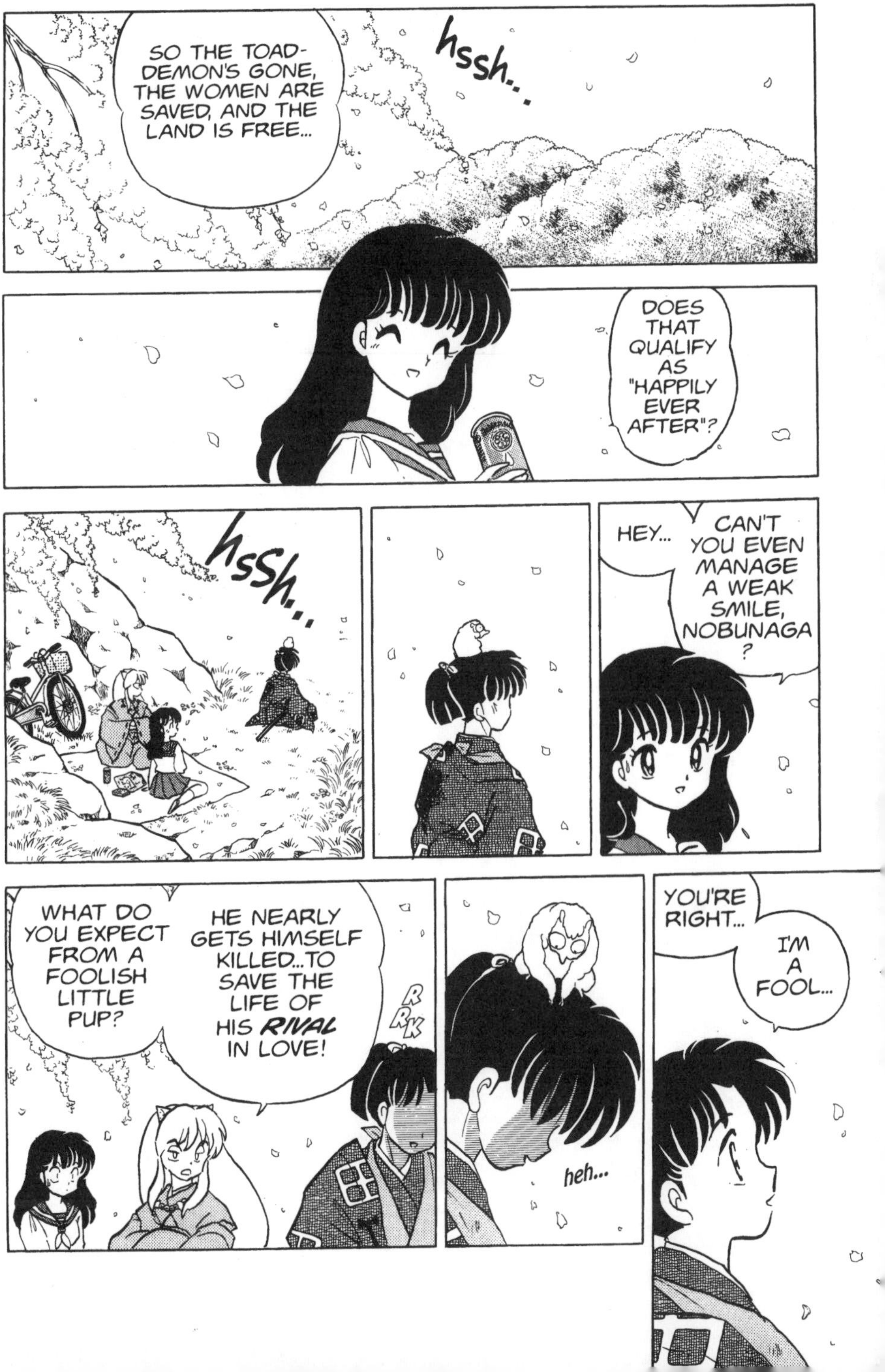
SO THE TOAD-DEMON'S GONE, THE WOMEN ARE SAVED, AND THE LAND IS FREE...
hssh...
DOES THAT QUALIFY AS "HAPPILY EVER AFTER"?
hssh...
HEY...
CAN'T YOU EVEN MANAGE A WEAK SMILE, NOBUNAGA?
WHAT DO YOU EXPECT FROM A FOOLISH LITTLE PUP?
HE NEARLY GETS HIMSELF KILLED...TO SAVE THE LIFE OF HIS RIVAL IN LOVE!
RRK
heh...
YOU'RE RIGHT...
I'M A FOOL...

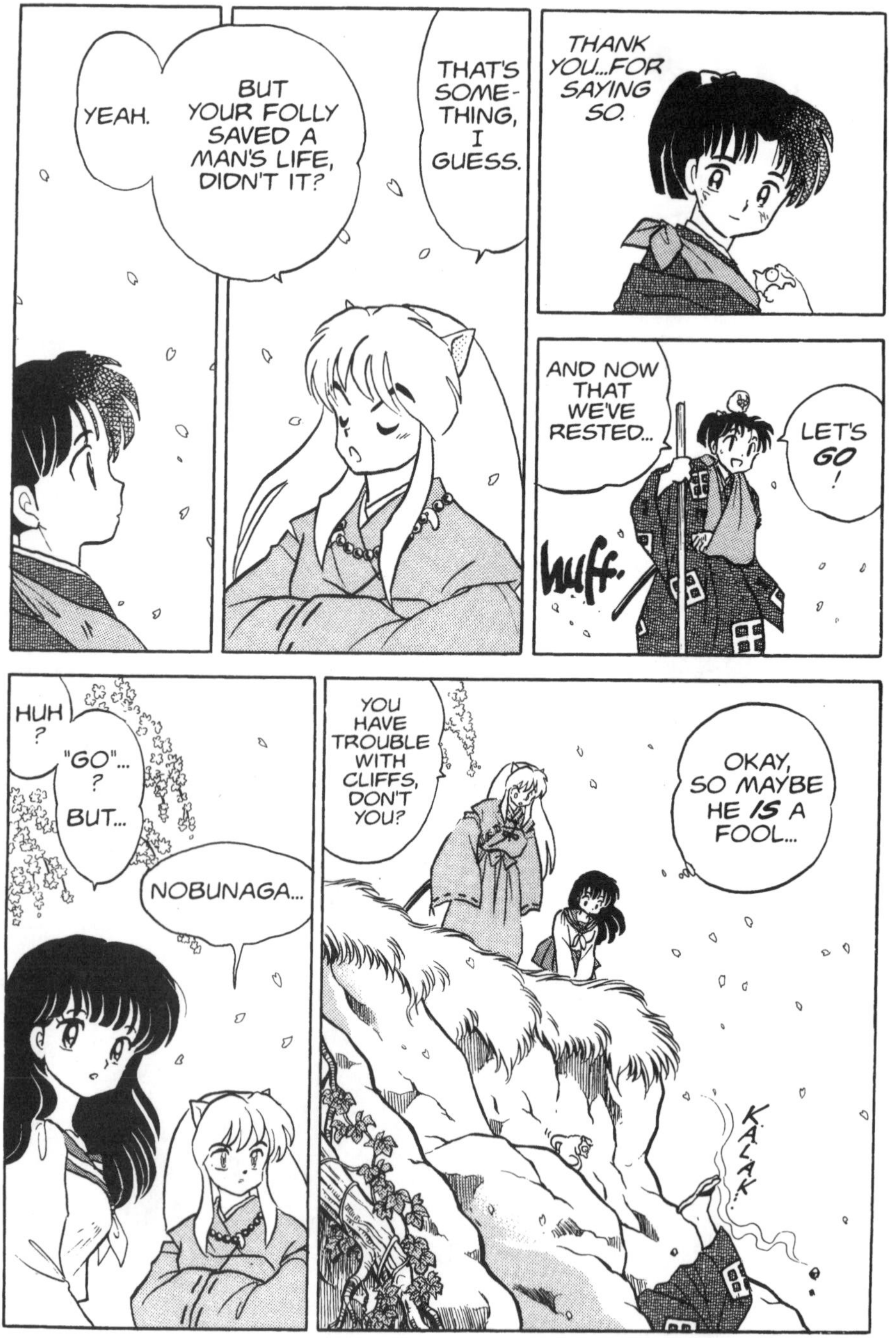
YEAH.
BUT YOUR FOLLY SAVED A MAN'S LIFE, DIDN'T IT?
THAT'S SOME-THING, I GUESS.
THANK YOU...FOR SAYING SO.
AND NOW THAT WE'VE RESTED...
huff.
LET'S *GO*!
HUH?
"GO"...? BUT...
NOBUNAGA...
YOU HAVE TROUBLE WITH CLIFFS, DON'T YOU?
OKAY, SO MAYBE HE *IS* A FOOL...
KALAK...

SCROLL FIVE

MASK OF FLESH

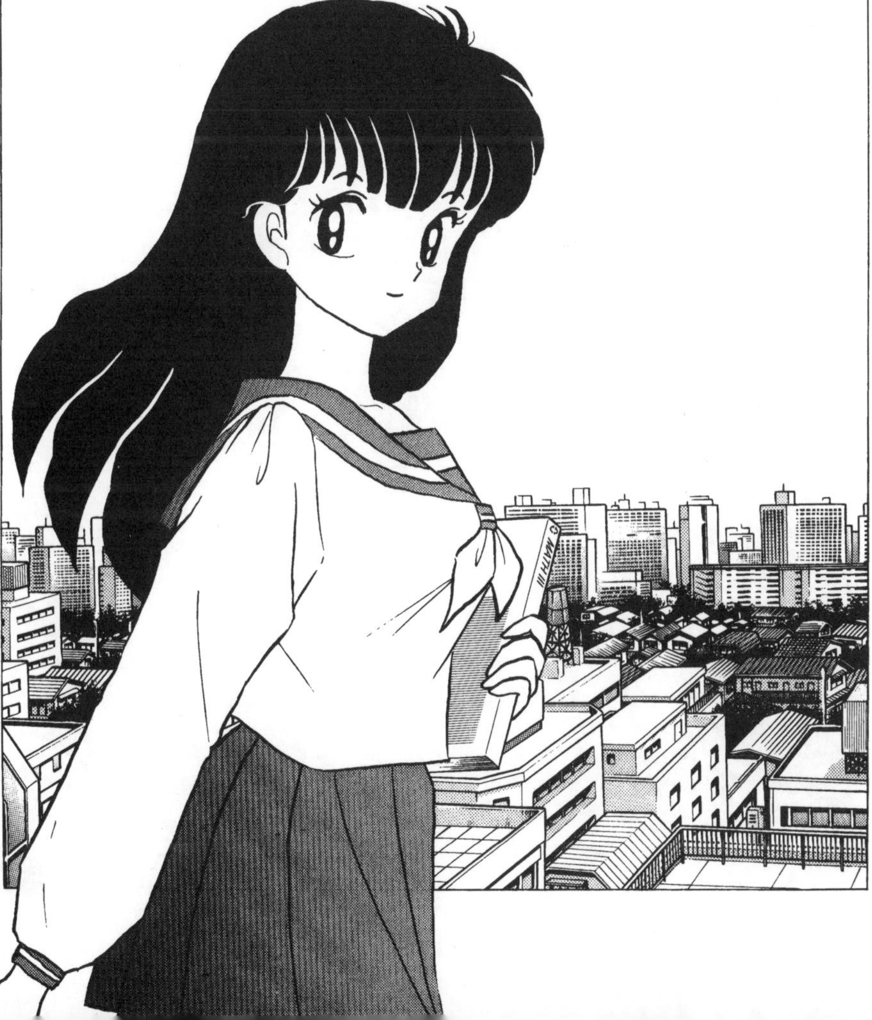

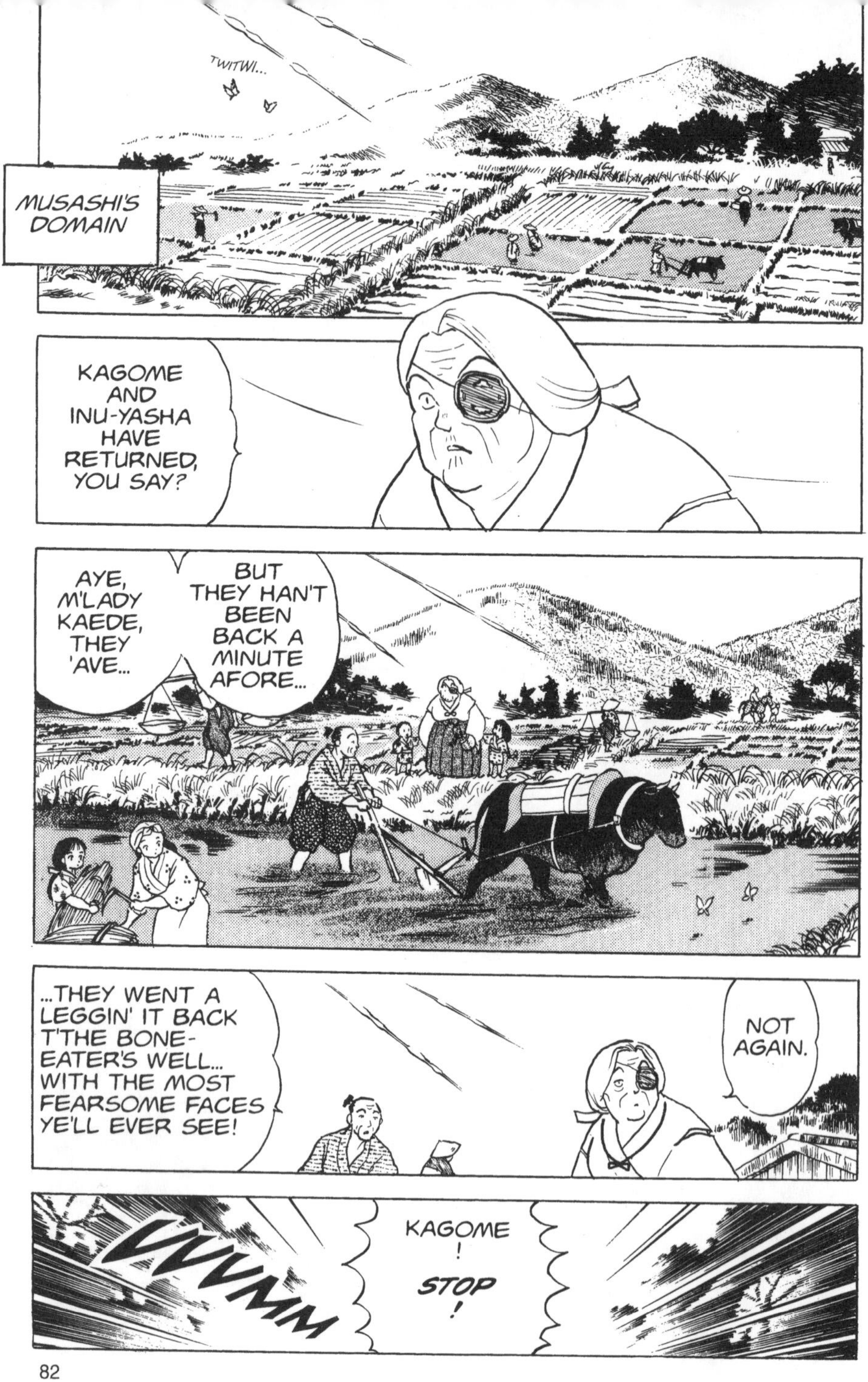
TWITWI...
MUSASHI'S DOMAIN
KAGOME AND INU-YASHA HAVE RETURNED, YOU SAY?
AYE, M'LADY KAEDE, THEY 'AVE...
BUT THEY HAN'T BEEN BACK A MINUTE AFORE...
...THEY WENT A LEGGIN' IT BACK T'THE BONE-EATER'S WELL... WITH THE MOST FEARSOME FACES YE'LL EVER SEE!
NOT AGAIN.
VVVMMM
KAGOME! STOP!

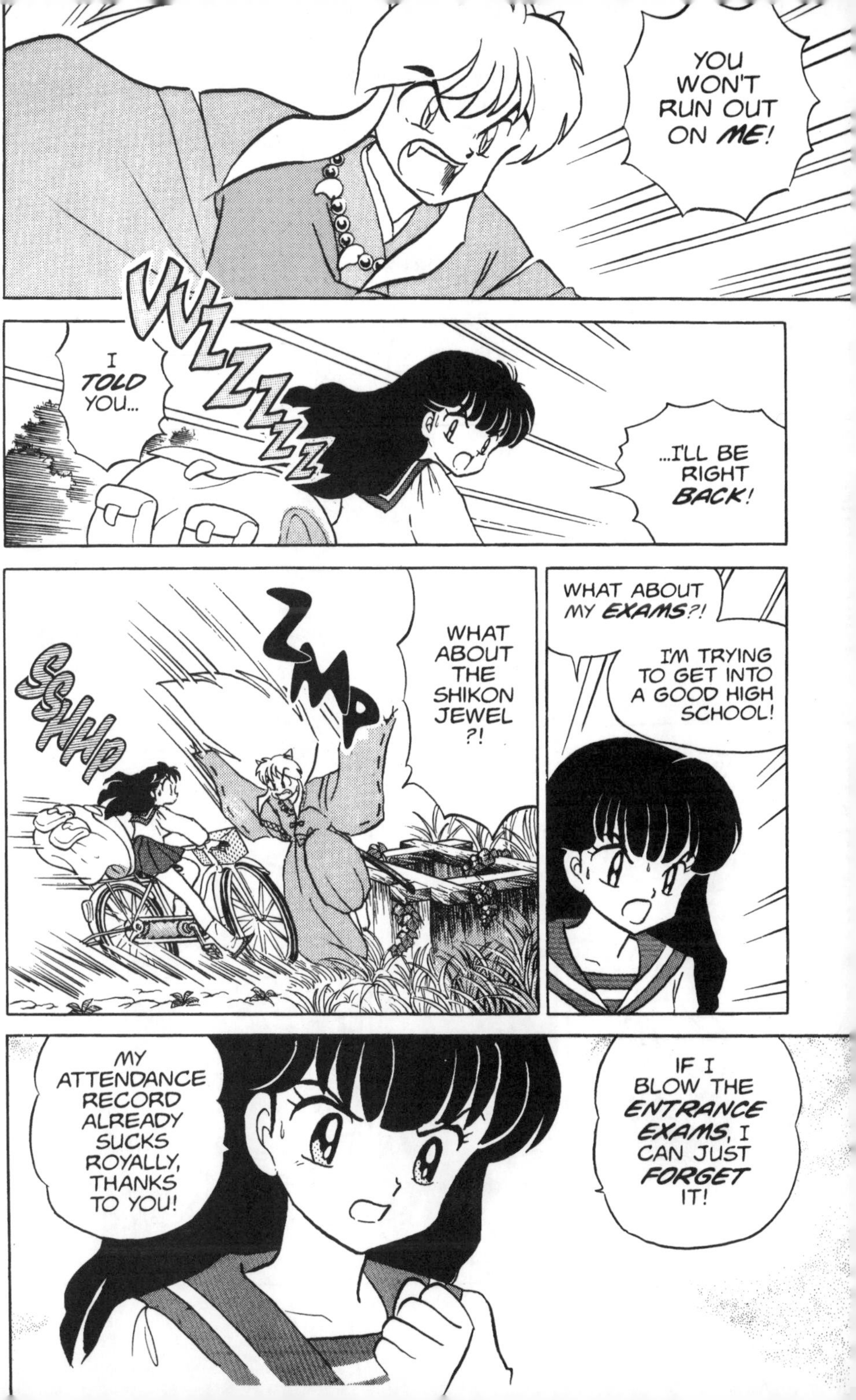
YOU WON'T RUN OUT ON ME!
VWZZZZZ
I TOLD YOU...
...I'LL BE RIGHT BACK!
SSHHP
ZMP
WHAT ABOUT THE SHIKON JEWEL ?!
WHAT ABOUT MY EXAMS?!
I'M TRYING TO GET INTO A GOOD HIGH SCHOOL!
MY ATTENDANCE RECORD ALREADY SUCKS ROYALLY, THANKS TO YOU!
IF I BLOW THE ENTRANCE EXAMS, I CAN JUST FORGET IT!

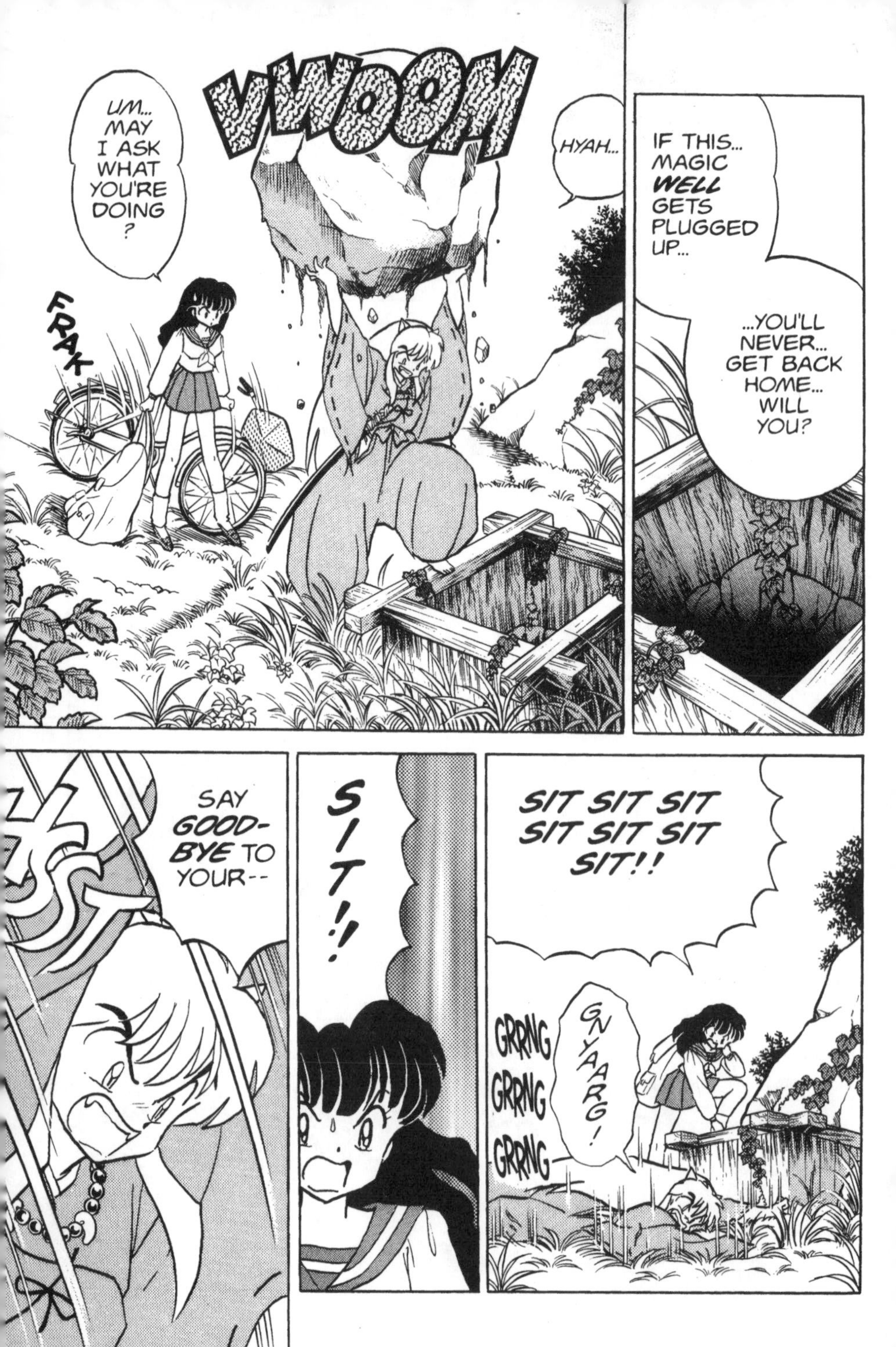
VWOOM
UM... MAY I ASK WHAT YOU'RE DOING?
FRAK
HYAH...
IF THIS... MAGIC WELL GETS PLUGGED UP...
...YOU'LL NEVER... GET BACK HOME... WILL YOU?
SAY GOOD-BYE TO YOUR--
SIT!!
SIT SIT SIT SIT SIT SIT SIT!!
GRRNG GRRNG GRRNG
GNYAARG!

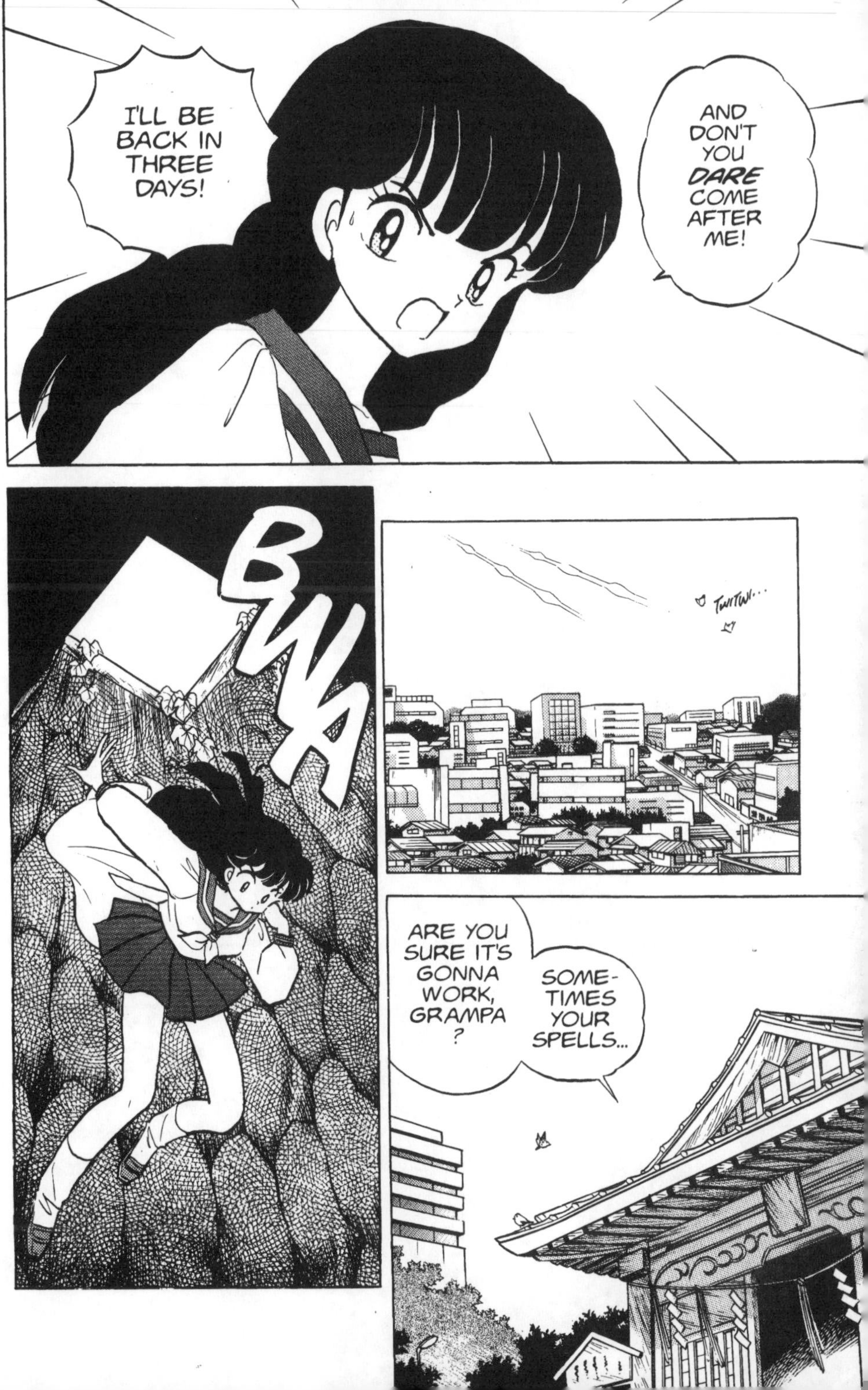
I'LL BE BACK IN THREE DAYS!
AND DON'T YOU DARE COME AFTER ME!
BWA
TWITWI...
ARE YOU SURE IT'S GONNA WORK, GRAMPA?
SOME-TIMES YOUR SPELLS...

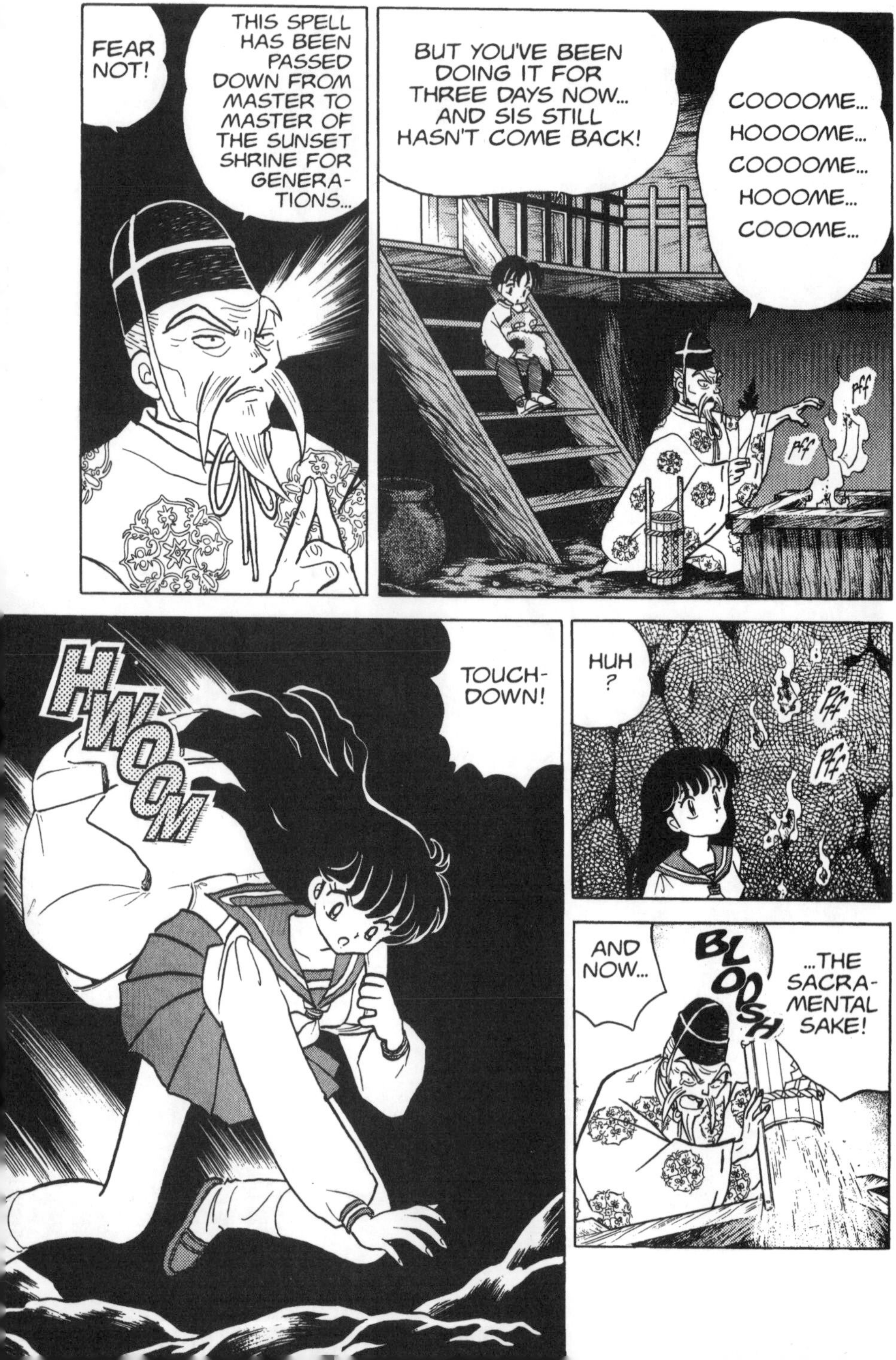
FEAR NOT!
THIS SPELL HAS BEEN PASSED DOWN FROM MASTER TO MASTER OF THE SUNSET SHRINE FOR GENERA- TIONS...
BUT YOU'VE BEEN DOING IT FOR THREE DAYS NOW... AND SIS STILL HASN'T COME BACK!
COOOOME... HOOOOME... COOOOME... HOOOME... COOOME...
pff
pff
HWOOM
TOUCH- DOWN!
HUH ?
pff
pff
AND NOW...
BLOOSH
...THE SACRA- MENTAL SAKE!

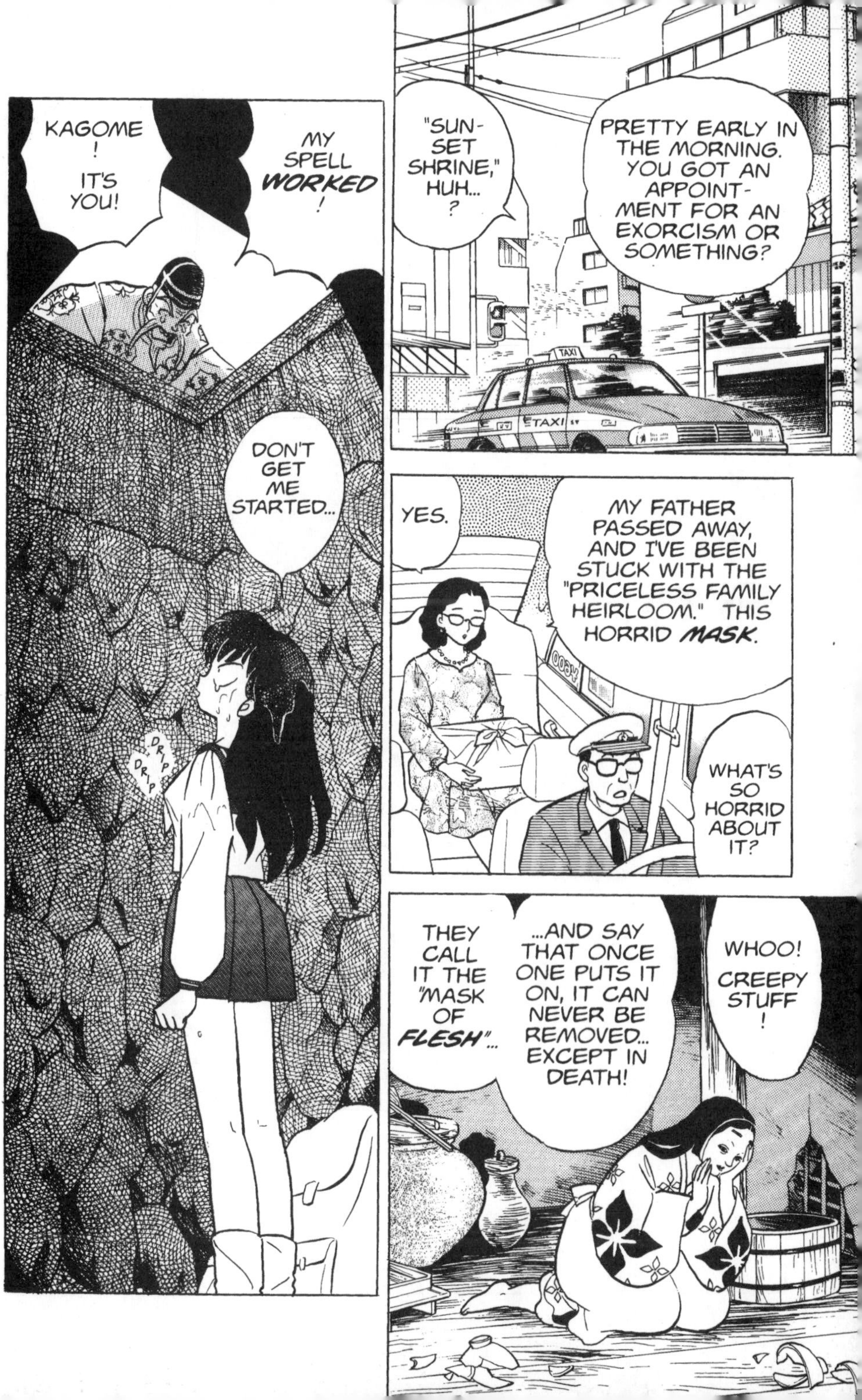
KAGOME! IT'S YOU!
MY SPELL WORKED!
DON'T GET ME STARTED...
DRIP DRIP
"SUN-SET SHRINE," HUH...?
PRETTY EARLY IN THE MORNING. YOU GOT AN APPOINTMENT FOR AN EXORCISM OR SOMETHING?
TAXI
TAXI
YES.
MY FATHER PASSED AWAY, AND I'VE BEEN STUCK WITH THE "PRICELESS FAMILY HEIRLOOM." THIS HORRID MASK.
WHAT'S SO HORRID ABOUT IT?
THEY CALL IT THE "MASK OF FLESH"...
...AND SAY THAT ONCE ONE PUTS IT ON, IT CAN NEVER BE REMOVED... EXCEPT IN DEATH!
WHOO! CREEPY STUFF!

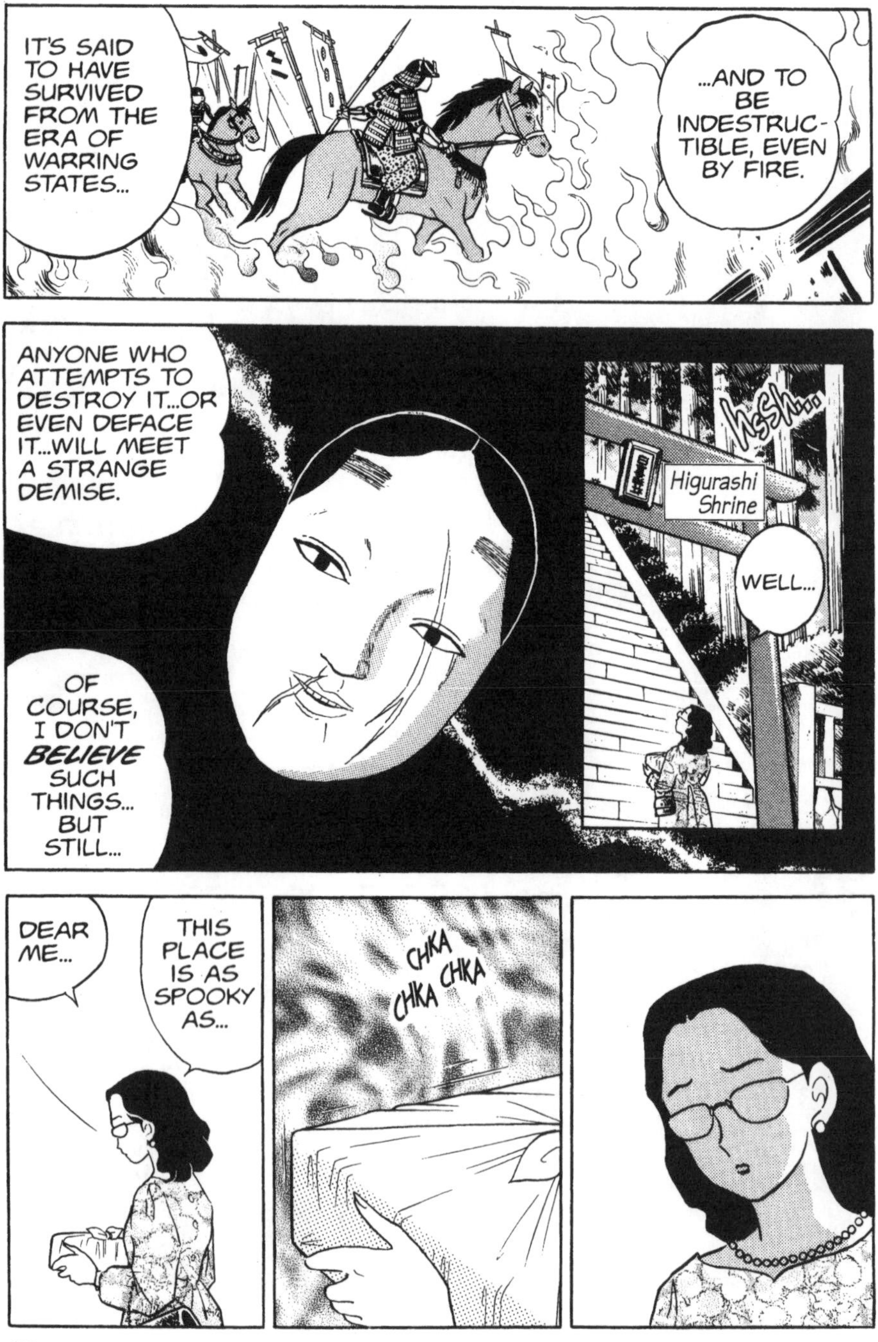
IT'S SAID TO HAVE SURVIVED FROM THE ERA OF WARRING STATES...
...AND TO BE INDESTRUCTIBLE, EVEN BY FIRE.
ANYONE WHO ATTEMPTS TO DESTROY IT...OR EVEN DEFACE IT...WILL MEET A STRANGE DEMISE.
OF COURSE, I DON'T BELIEVE SUCH THINGS... BUT STILL...
hssh...
Higurashi Shrine
WELL...
DEAR ME...
THIS PLACE IS AS SPOOKY AS...
CHKA CHKA CHKA

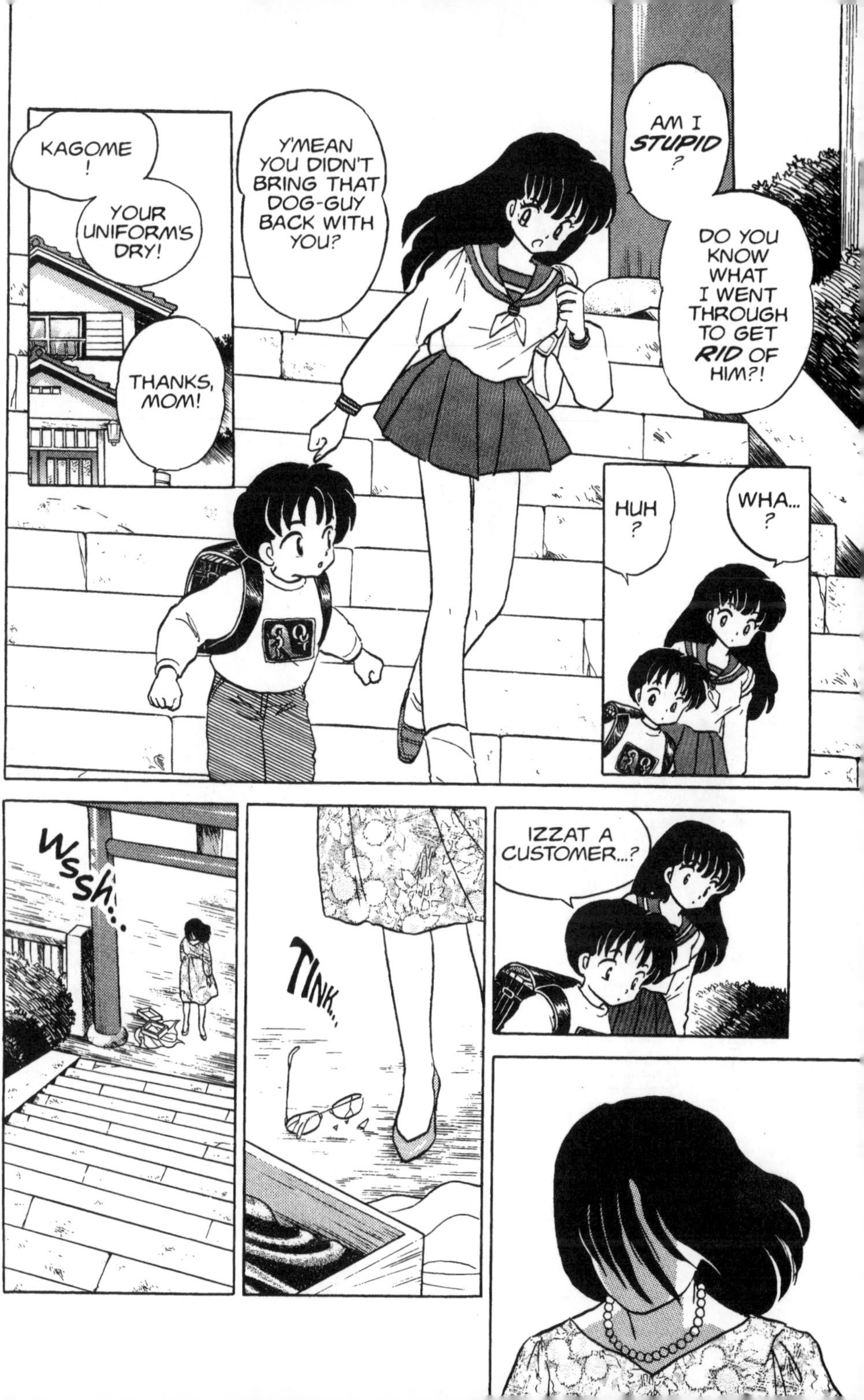
KAGOME!
YOUR UNIFORM'S DRY!
THANKS, MOM!
Y'MEAN YOU DIDN'T BRING THAT DOG-GUY BACK WITH YOU?
AM I STUPID?
DO YOU KNOW WHAT I WENT THROUGH TO GET RID OF HIM?!
HUH?
WHA...?
WSSH...
TINK...
IZZAT A CUSTOMER...?

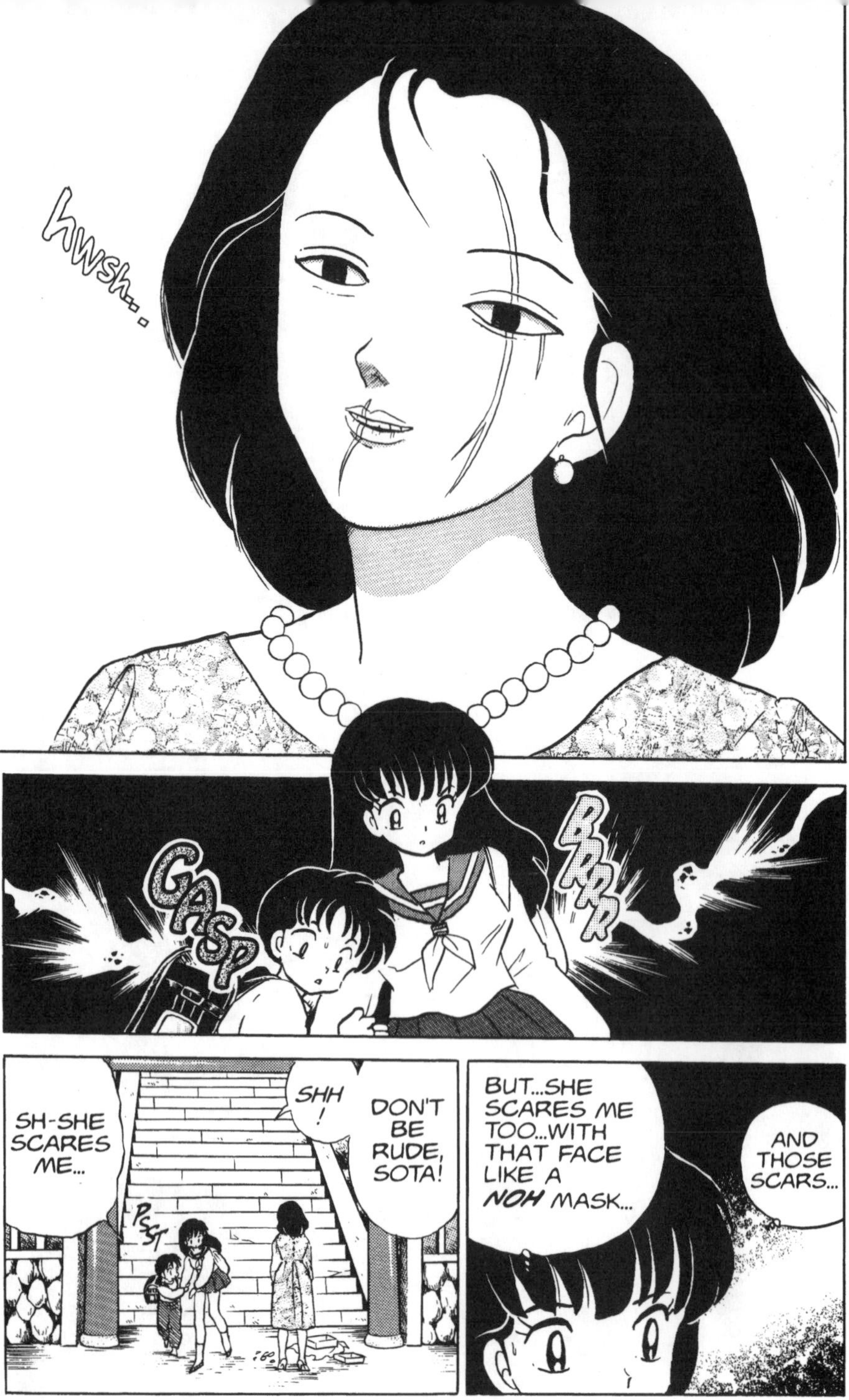
hwsh...
GASP
BRRR
SH-SHE SCARES ME...
SHH!
DON'T BE RUDE, SOTA!
PSST
BUT...SHE SCARES ME TOO...WITH THAT FACE LIKE A NOH MASK...
AND THOSE SCARS...

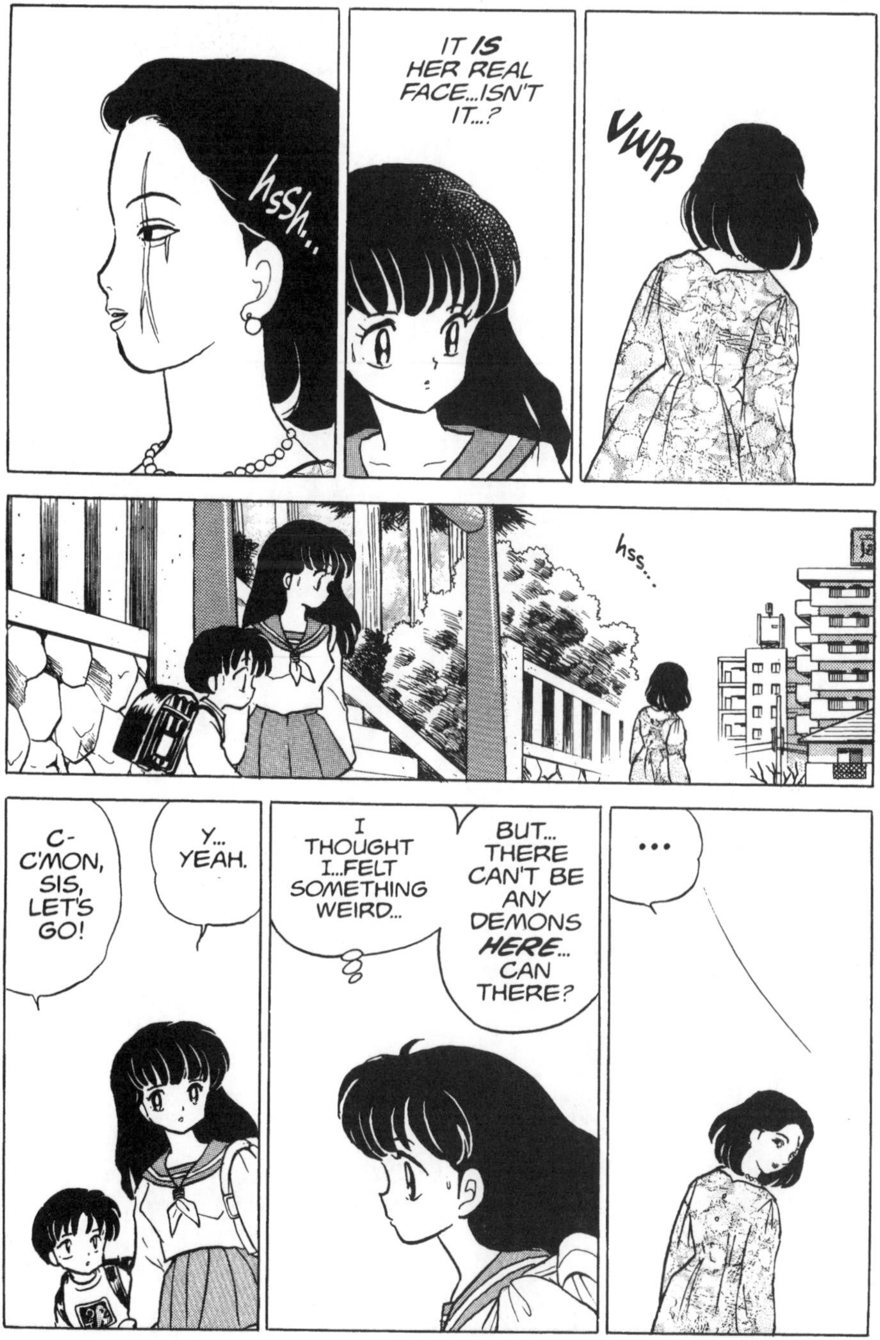
hsSh...
IT IS HER REAL FACE...ISN'T IT...?
VWPP
hss...
C-C'MON, SIS, LET'S GO!
Y... YEAH.
I THOUGHT I...FELT SOMETHING WEIRD...
BUT... THERE CAN'T BE ANY DEMONS HERE... CAN THERE?
...

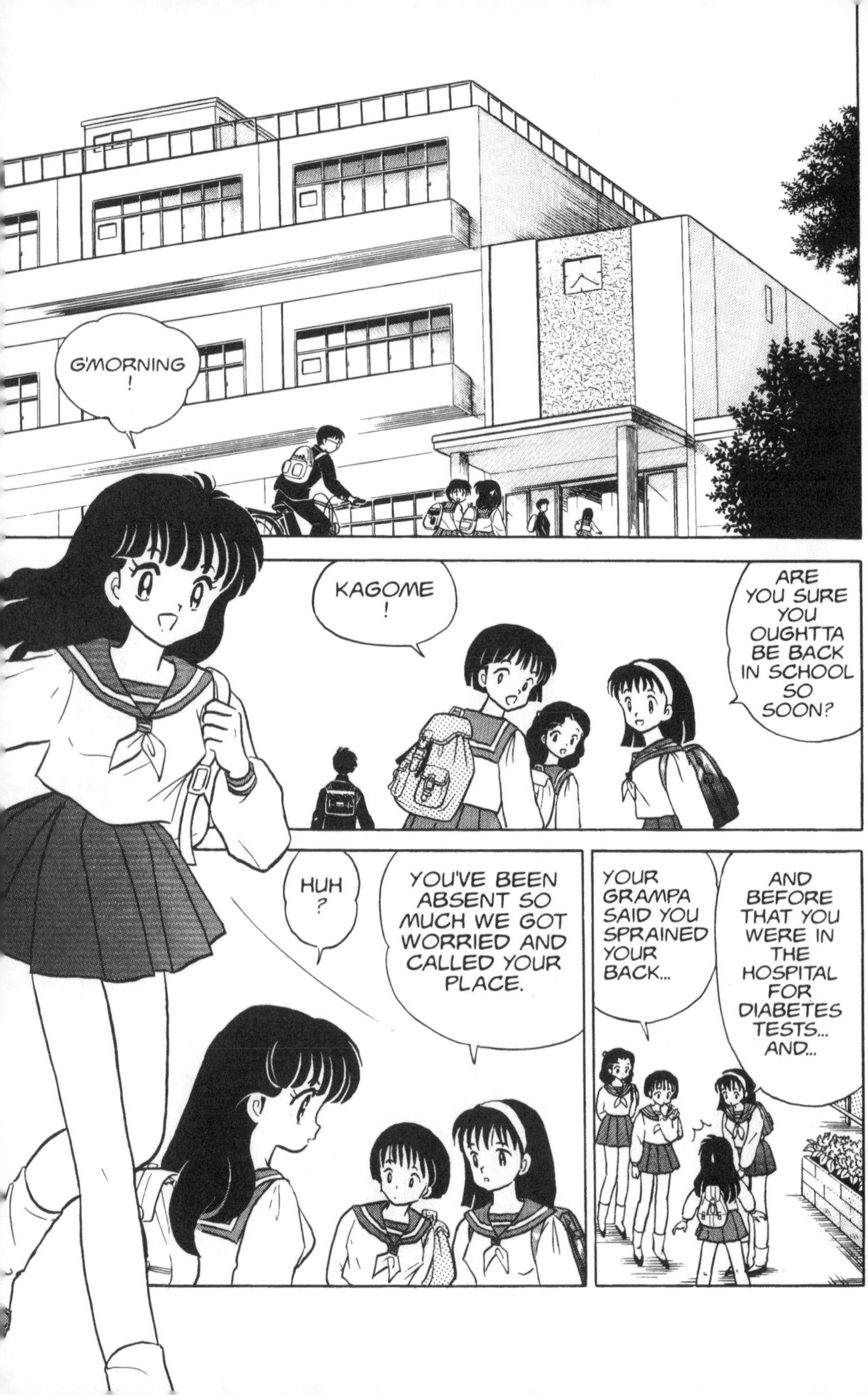

G'MORNING !
KAGOME !
ARE YOU SURE YOU OUGHTTA BE BACK IN SCHOOL SO SOON?
HUH ?
YOU'VE BEEN ABSENT SO MUCH WE GOT WORRIED AND CALLED YOUR PLACE.
YOUR GRAMPA SAID YOU SPRAINED YOUR BACK...
AND BEFORE THAT YOU WERE IN THE HOSPITAL FOR DIABETES TESTS... AND...

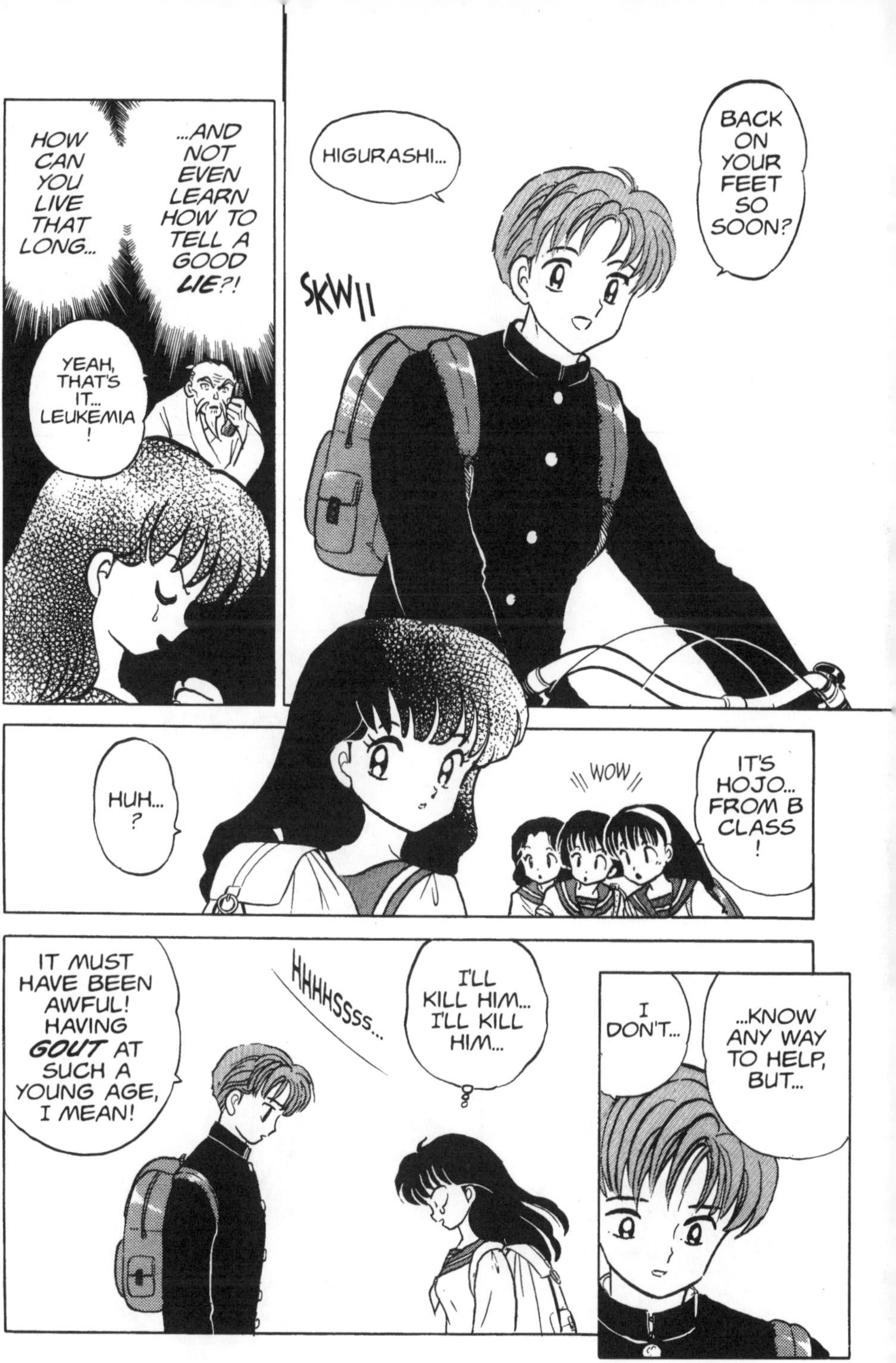
HOW CAN YOU LIVE THAT LONG...
...AND NOT EVEN LEARN HOW TO TELL A GOOD **LIE**?!
YEAH, THAT'S IT... LEUKEMIA!
HIGURASHI...
SKW
BACK ON YOUR FEET SO SOON?
HUH...?
WOW
IT'S HOJO... FROM B CLASS!
IT MUST HAVE BEEN AWFUL! HAVING ***GOUT*** AT SUCH A YOUNG AGE, I MEAN!
HHHHSSSS...
I'LL KILL HIM... I'LL KILL HIM...
I DON'T...
...KNOW ANY WAY TO HELP, BUT...

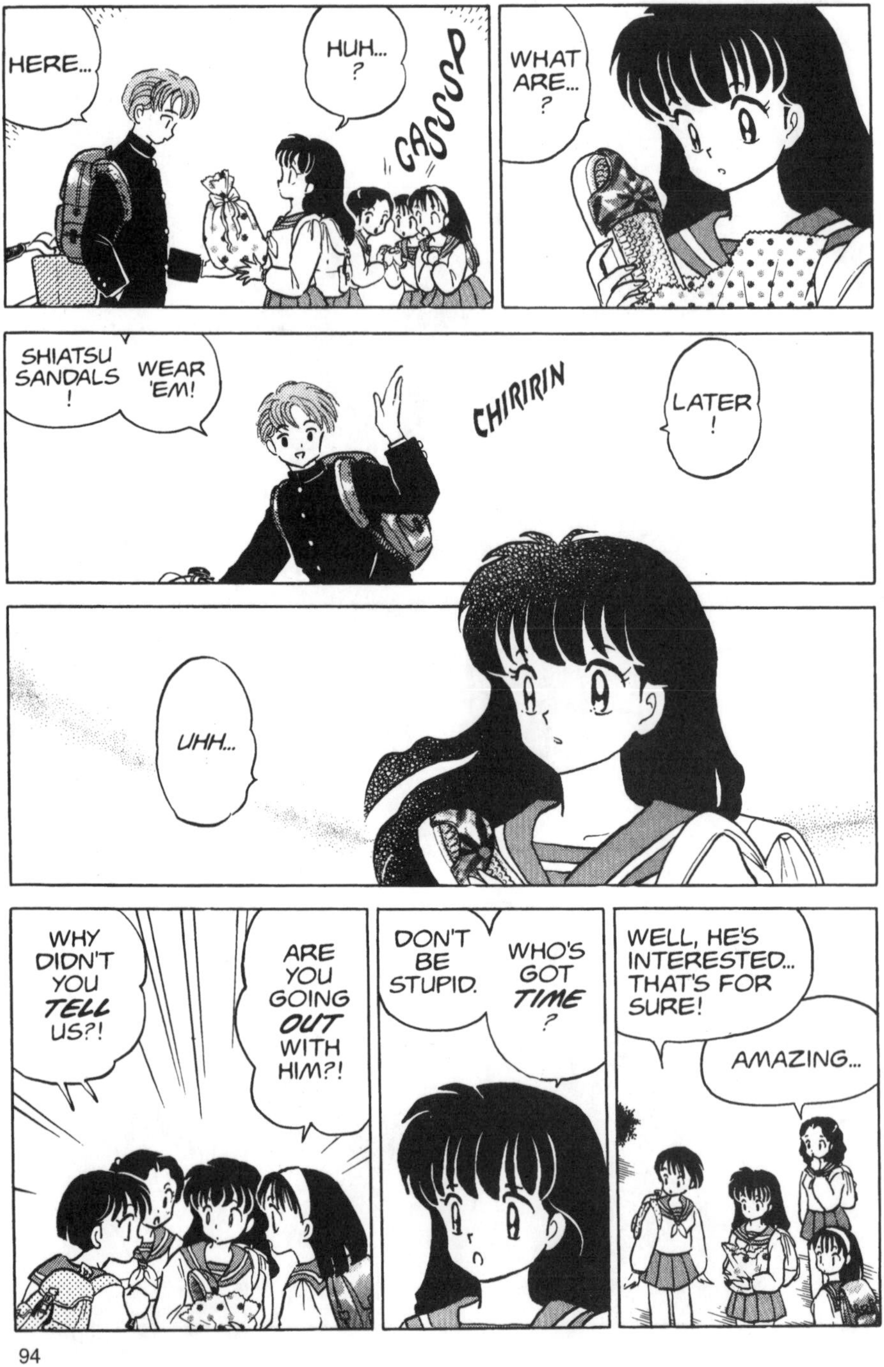
HERE...
HUH... ?
GASSSP
WHAT ARE... ?
SHIATSU SANDALS !
WEAR 'EM!
CHIRIRIN
LATER !
UHH...
WHY DIDN'T YOU *TELL* US?!
ARE YOU GOING *OUT* WITH HIM?!
DON'T BE STUPID.
WHO'S GOT *TIME* ?
WELL, HE'S INTERESTED... THAT'S FOR SURE!
AMAZING...

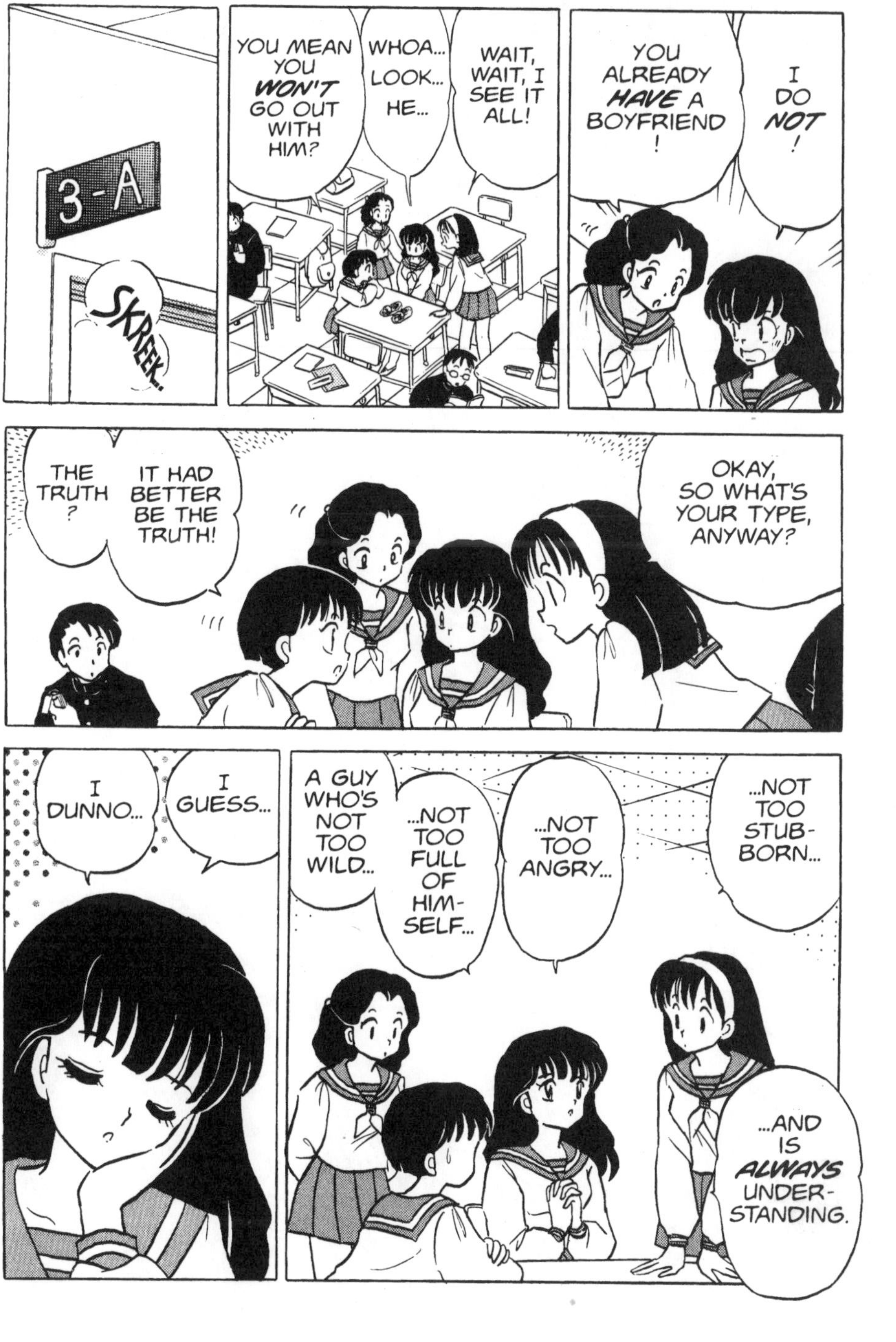
3-A
SKREEK...
YOU MEAN YOU *WON'T* GO OUT WITH HIM?
WHOA... LOOK... HE...
WAIT, WAIT, I SEE IT ALL!
YOU ALREADY *HAVE* A BOYFRIEND!
I DO *NOT*!
THE TRUTH?
IT HAD BETTER BE THE TRUTH!
OKAY, SO WHAT'S YOUR TYPE, ANYWAY?
I DUNNO...
I GUESS...
A GUY WHO'S NOT TOO WILD...
...NOT TOO FULL OF HIM-SELF...
...NOT TOO ANGRY...
...NOT TOO STUB-BORN...
...AND IS *ALWAYS* UNDER-STANDING.

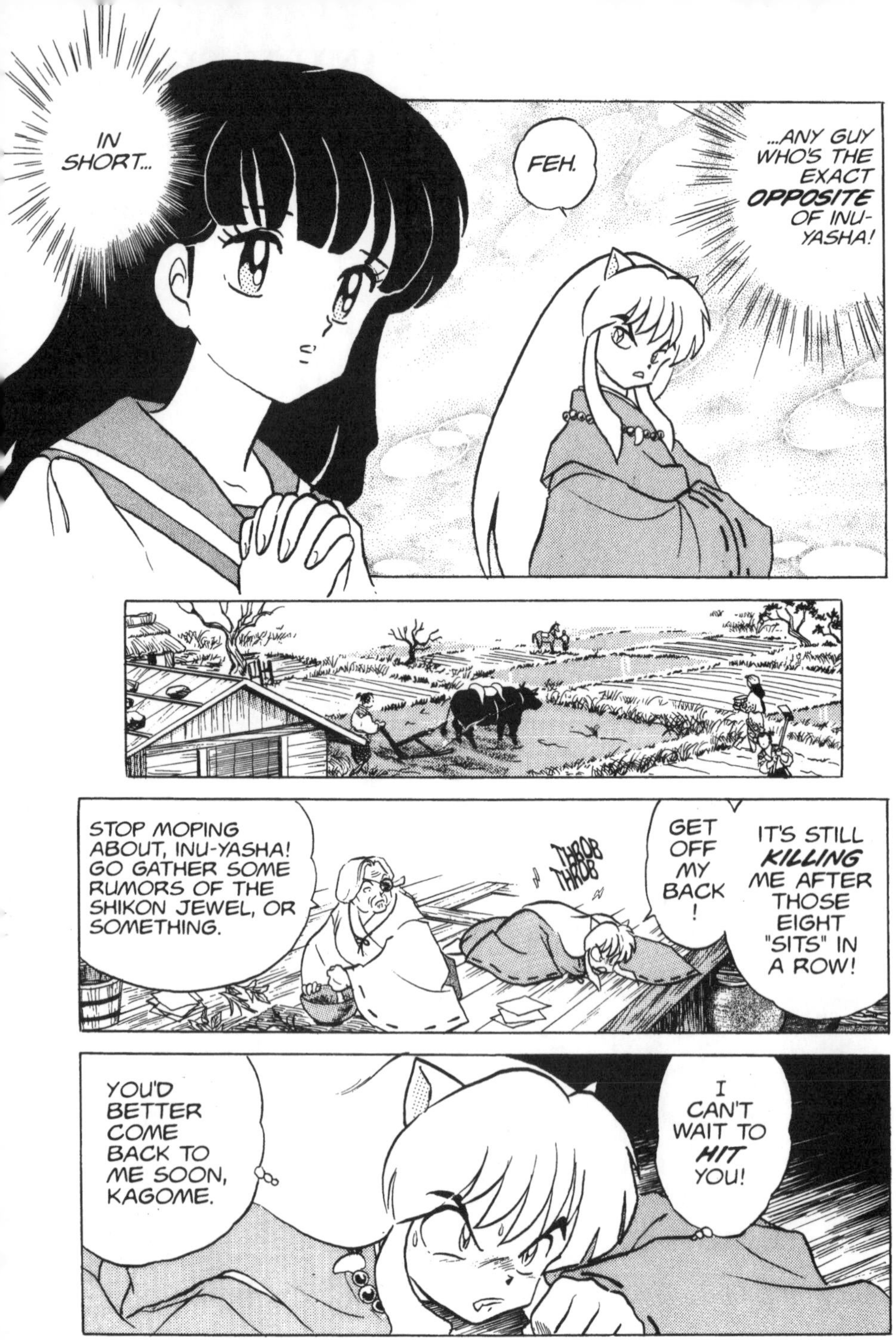
IN SHORT...
FEH.
...ANY GUY WHO'S THE EXACT OPPOSITE OF INU-YASHA!
STOP MOPING ABOUT, INU-YASHA! GO GATHER SOME RUMORS OF THE SHIKON JEWEL, OR SOMETHING.
THROB THROB
GET OFF MY BACK!
IT'S STILL KILLING ME AFTER THOSE EIGHT "SITS" IN A ROW!
YOU'D BETTER COME BACK TO ME SOON, KAGOME.
I CAN'T WAIT TO HIT YOU!

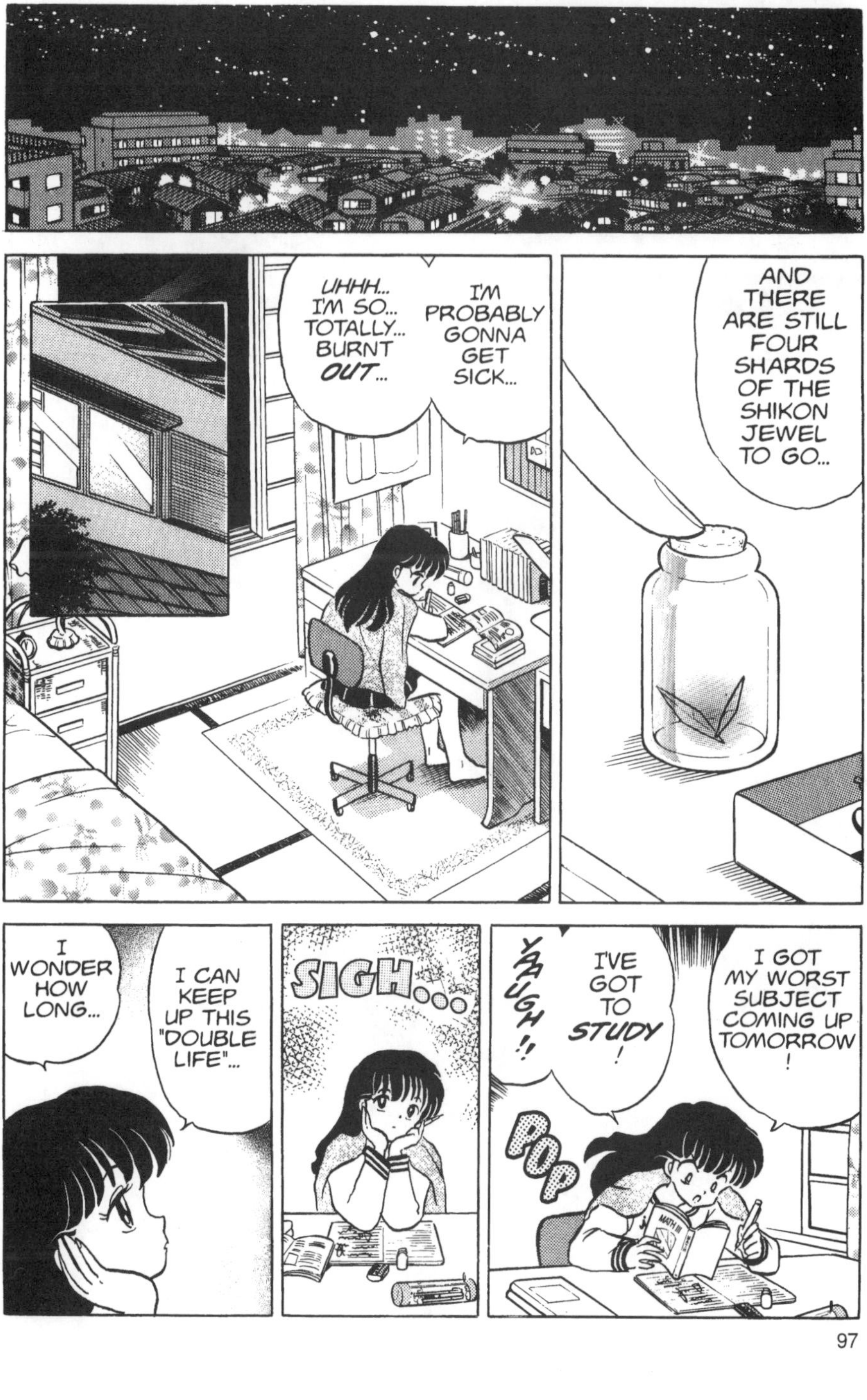
UHHH... I'M SO... TOTALLY... BURNT OUT...
I'M PROBABLY GONNA GET SICK...
AND THERE ARE STILL FOUR SHARDS OF THE SHIKON JEWEL TO GO...
I WONDER HOW LONG...
I CAN KEEP UP THIS "DOUBLE LIFE"...
SIGH...
YAAUGH!!
I'VE GOT TO STUDY!
I GOT MY WORST SUBJECT COMING UP TOMORROW!
POP
MATH III

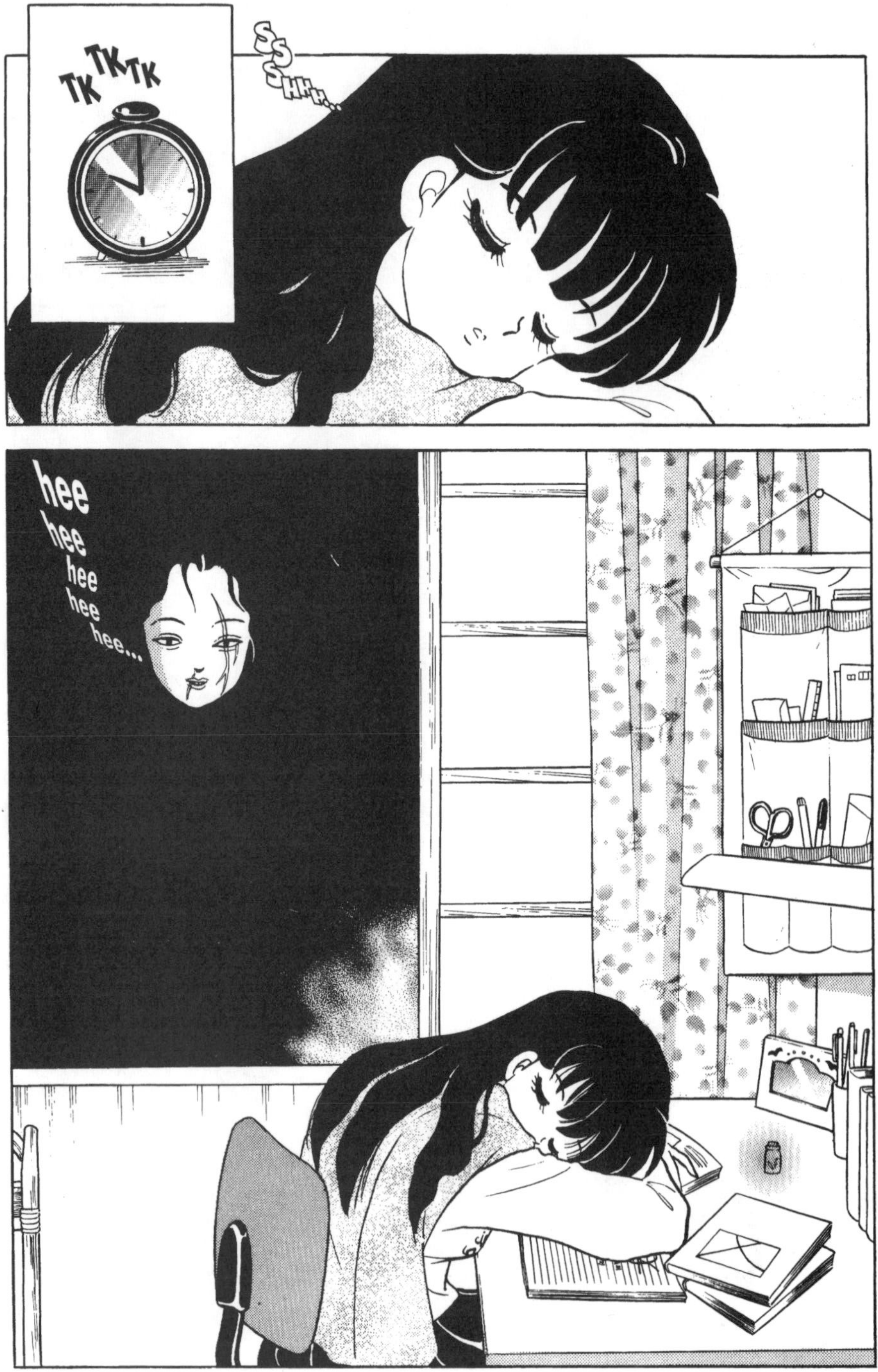
TK TK TK TK
SSSHHH...
hee hee hee hee hee...

SCROLL SIX

THE BROKEN BODY

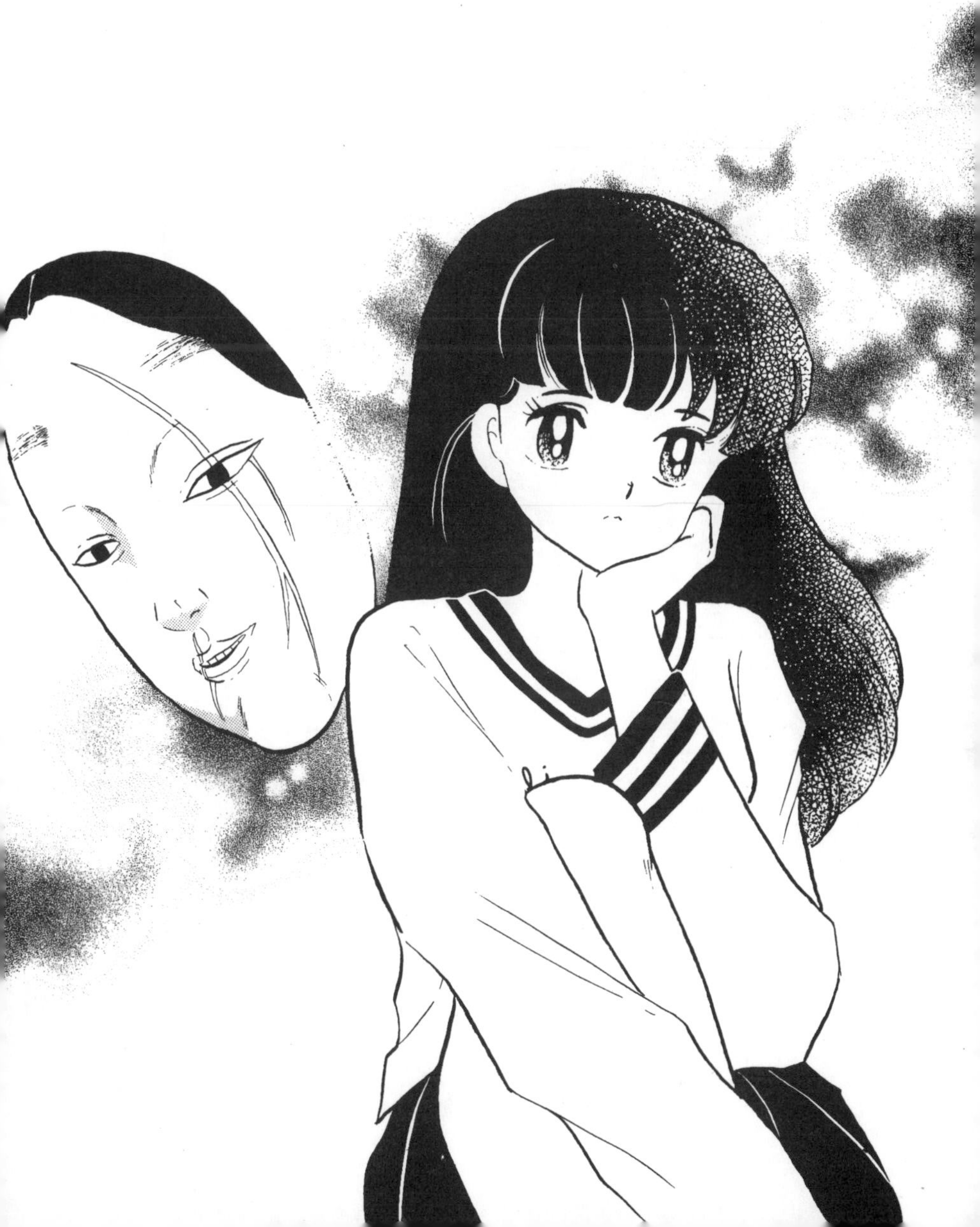

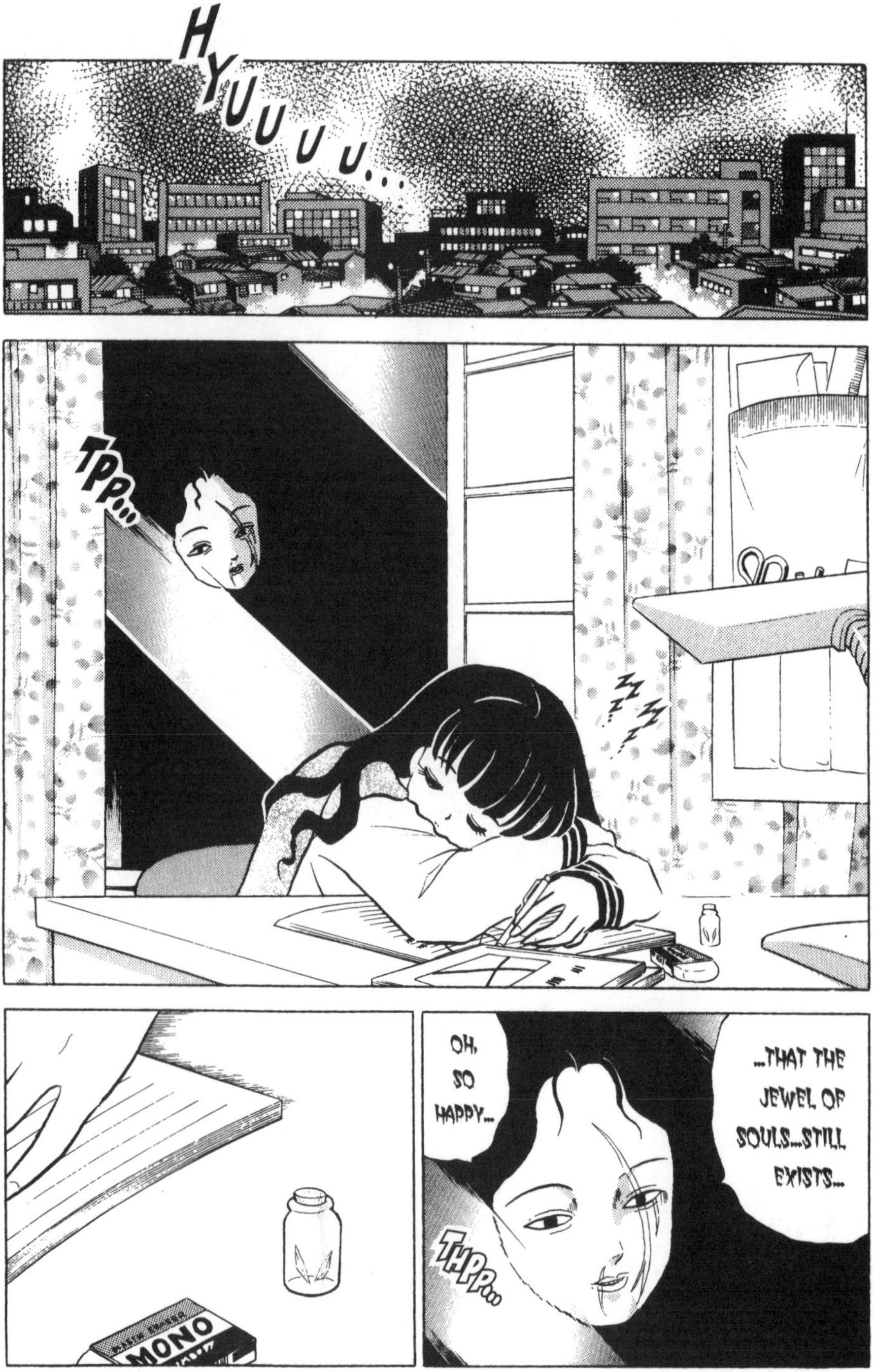

HYUUUUU...
TPP...
MONO
OH, SO HAPPY...
...THAT THE JEWEL OF SOULS...STILL EXISTS...
THPP...

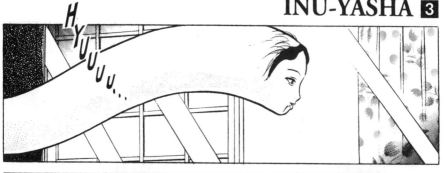

HYUUUU...

UMAO...I DON'T KNOW WHY... BUT THIS PLACE GIVES ME THE CREEPS...

UMMMM

STRANGE THINGS HAPPEN IN THIS NEIGH-BORHOOD, SHIKAKO...

LIKE THE GHOST OF THAT WOMAN WHO DIED IN THAT HIT-AND-RUN...

AAA, DON'T *TELL* ME!

COME ON, I'M JUST KIDDING!

OH, YOU'RE TERRIBLE!

HWOOOOOOO

HUH ?!

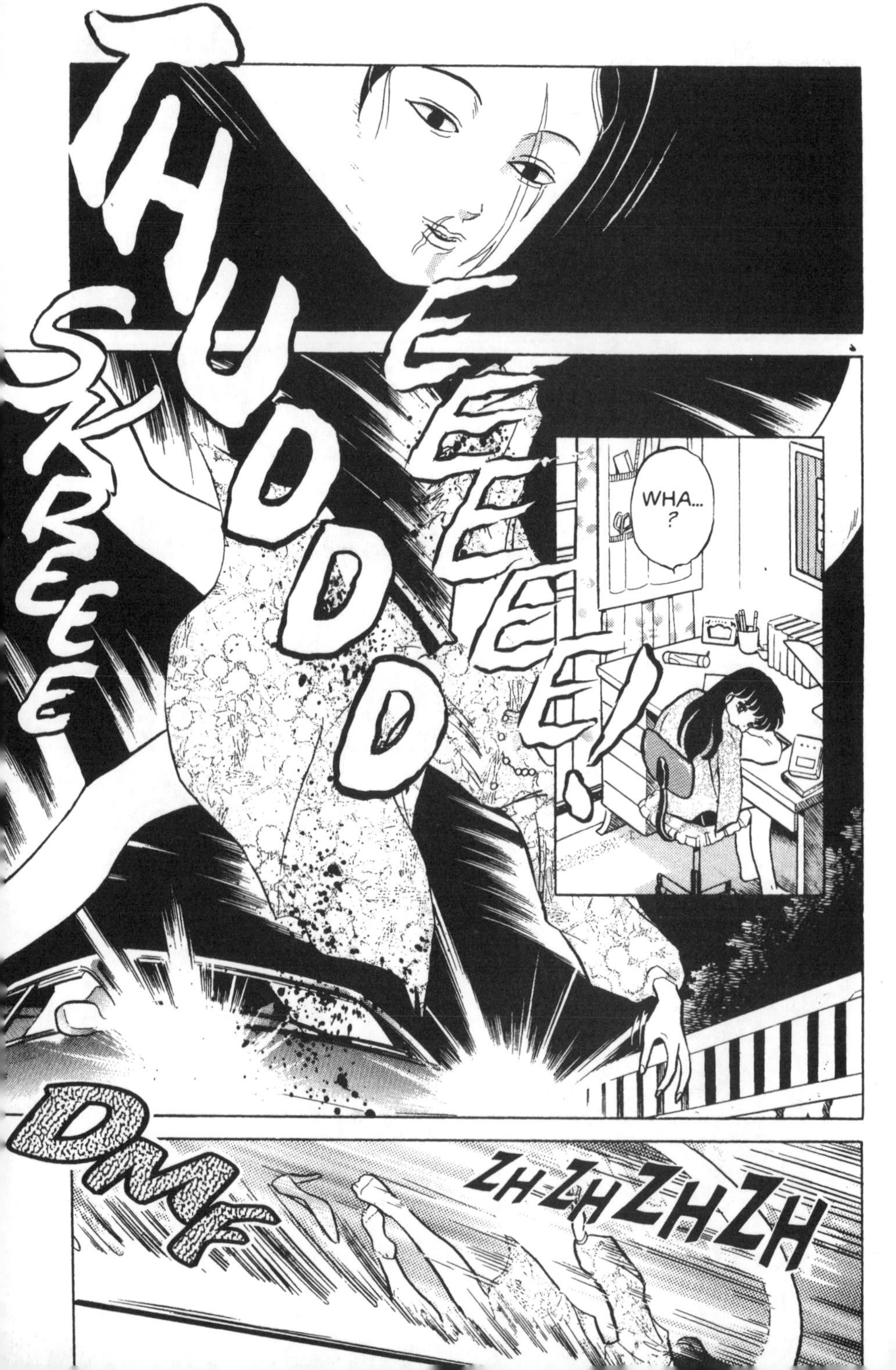
THUDDD
SKREEEE
EEEEE!
WHA...?
DMF
ZH ZH ZHZHZH

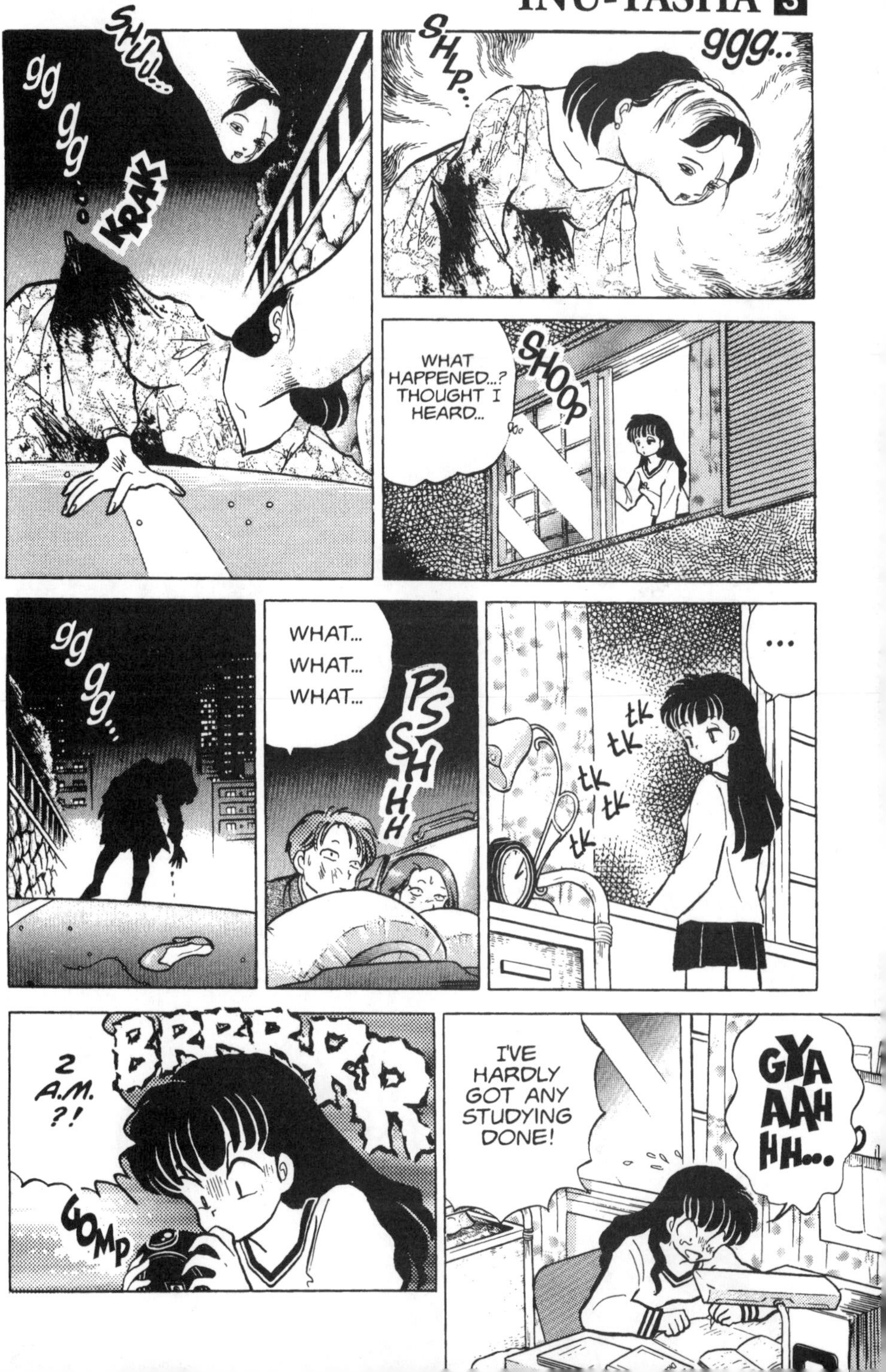
SHUU...
gg gg...
KRAK
SHLP...
ggg...
WHAT HAPPENED...? THOUGHT I HEARD...
SHOOP
gg gg...
WHAT... WHAT... WHAT...
PSSHHH
...
tk tk tk tk tk
BRRRRRR
2 A.M. ?!
GOMP
I'VE HARDLY GOT ANY STUDYING DONE!
GYAAAHHH...

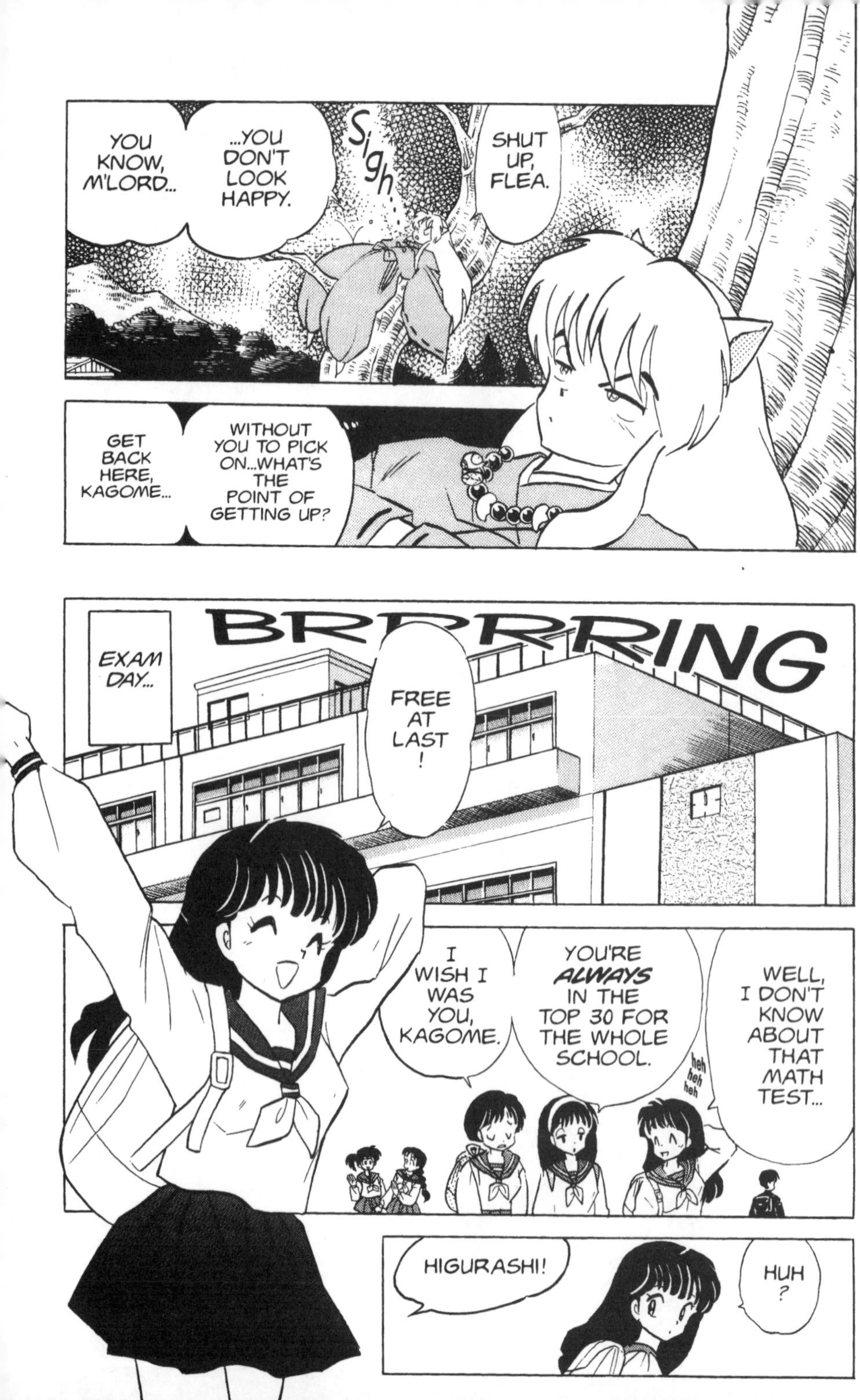
YOU KNOW, M'LORD...
...YOU DON'T LOOK HAPPY.
Sigh
SHUT UP, FLEA.
GET BACK HERE, KAGOME...
WITHOUT YOU TO PICK ON...WHAT'S THE POINT OF GETTING UP?
EXAM DAY...
BRRRRING
FREE AT LAST!
I WISH I WAS YOU, KAGOME.
YOU'RE ALWAYS IN THE TOP 30 FOR THE WHOLE SCHOOL.
heh heh heh
WELL, I DON'T KNOW ABOUT THAT MATH TEST...
HIGURASHI!
HUH?

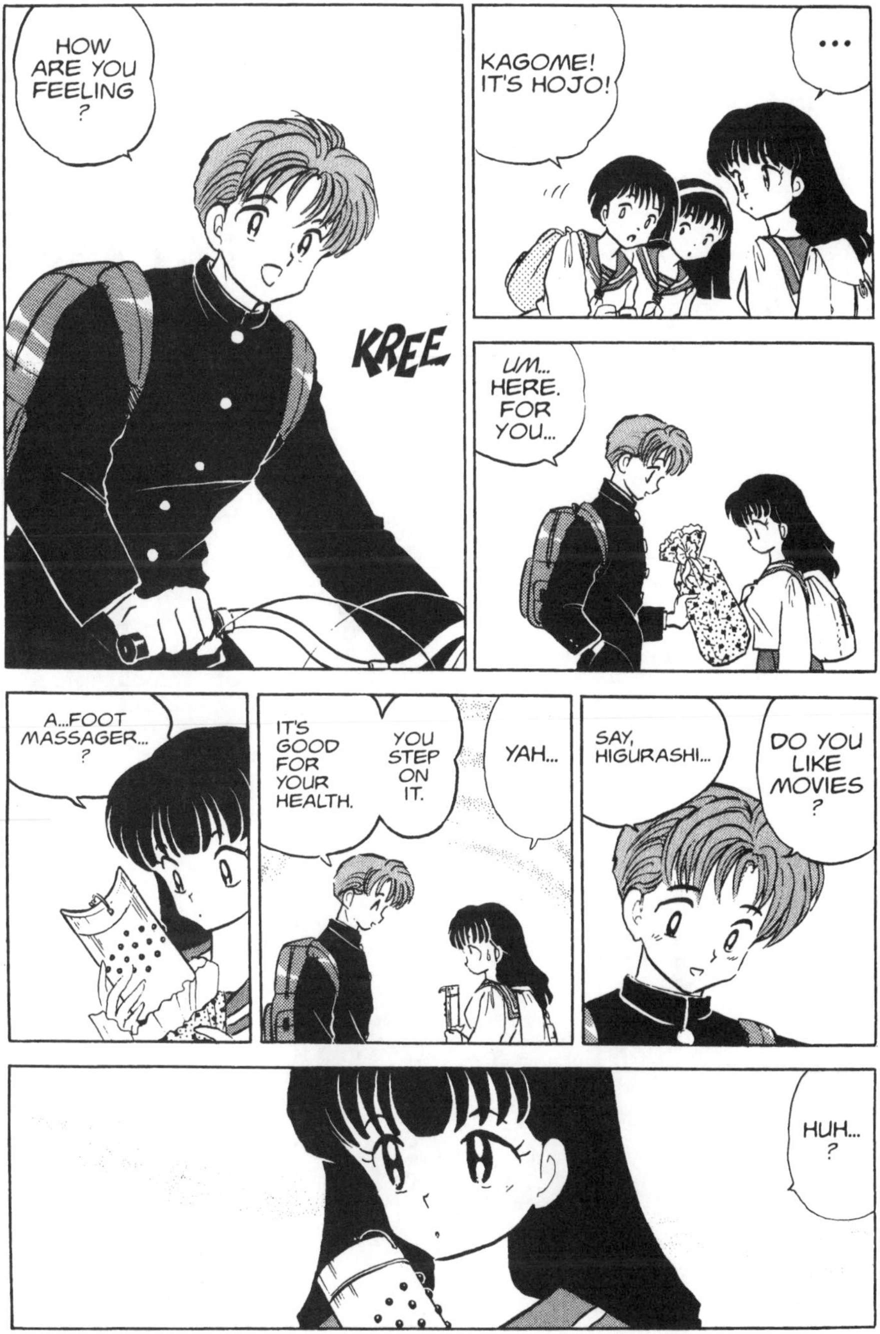
HOW ARE YOU FEELING ?
KREE
KAGOME! IT'S HOJO!
...
UM... HERE. FOR YOU...
A...FOOT MASSAGER... ?
IT'S GOOD FOR YOUR HEALTH.
YOU STEP ON IT.
YAH...
SAY, HIGURASHI...
DO YOU LIKE MOVIES ?
HUH... ?

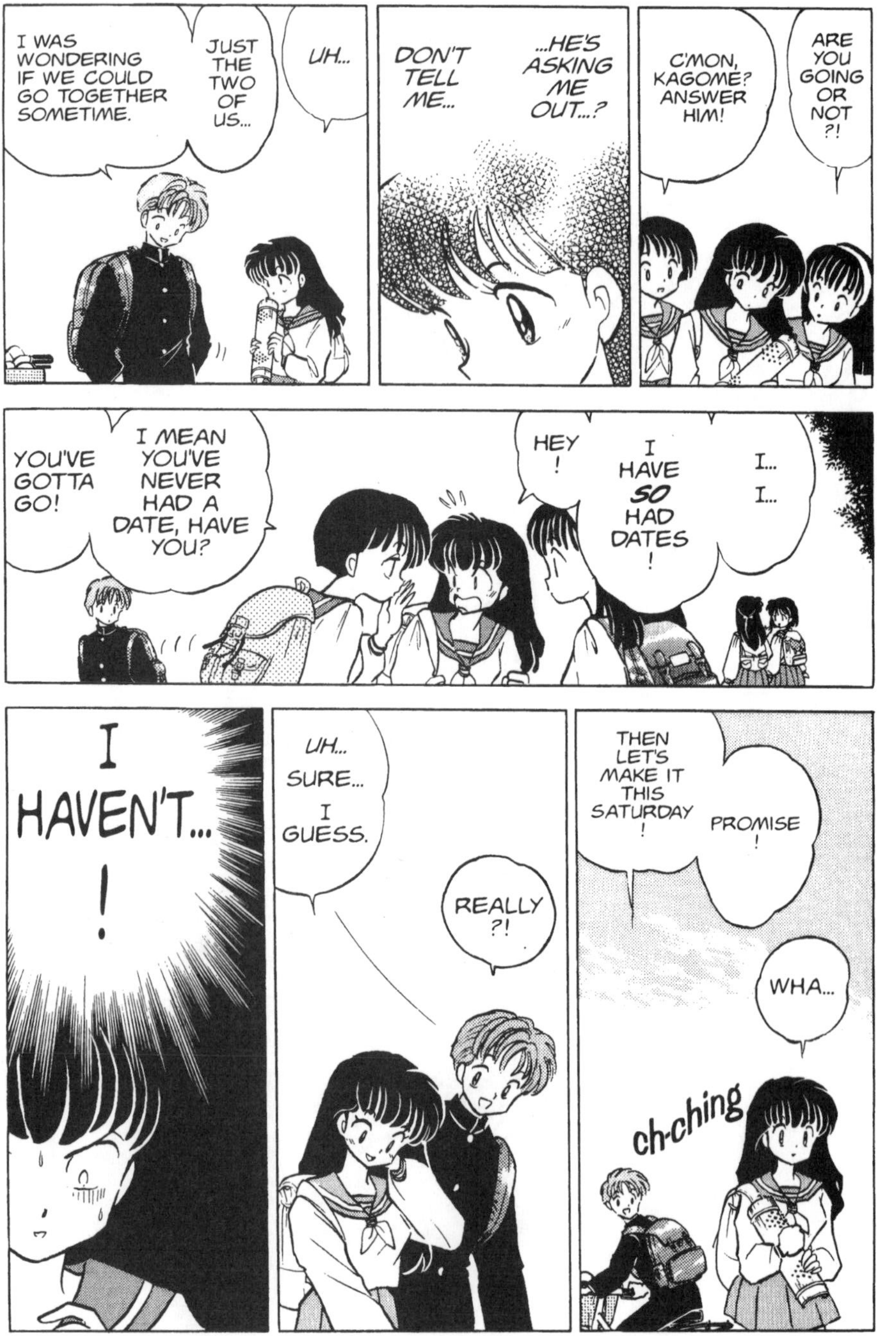
I WAS WONDERING IF WE COULD GO TOGETHER SOMETIME.
JUST THE TWO OF US...
UH...
DON'T TELL ME...
...HE'S ASKING ME OUT...?
C'MON, KAGOME? ANSWER HIM!
ARE YOU GOING OR NOT ?!
YOU'VE GOTTA GO!
I MEAN YOU'VE NEVER HAD A DATE, HAVE YOU?
HEY !
I HAVE SO HAD DATES !
I... I...
I HAVEN'T... !
UH... SURE... I GUESS.
REALLY ?!
THEN LET'S MAKE IT THIS SATURDAY !
PROMISE !
WHA...
ch-ching

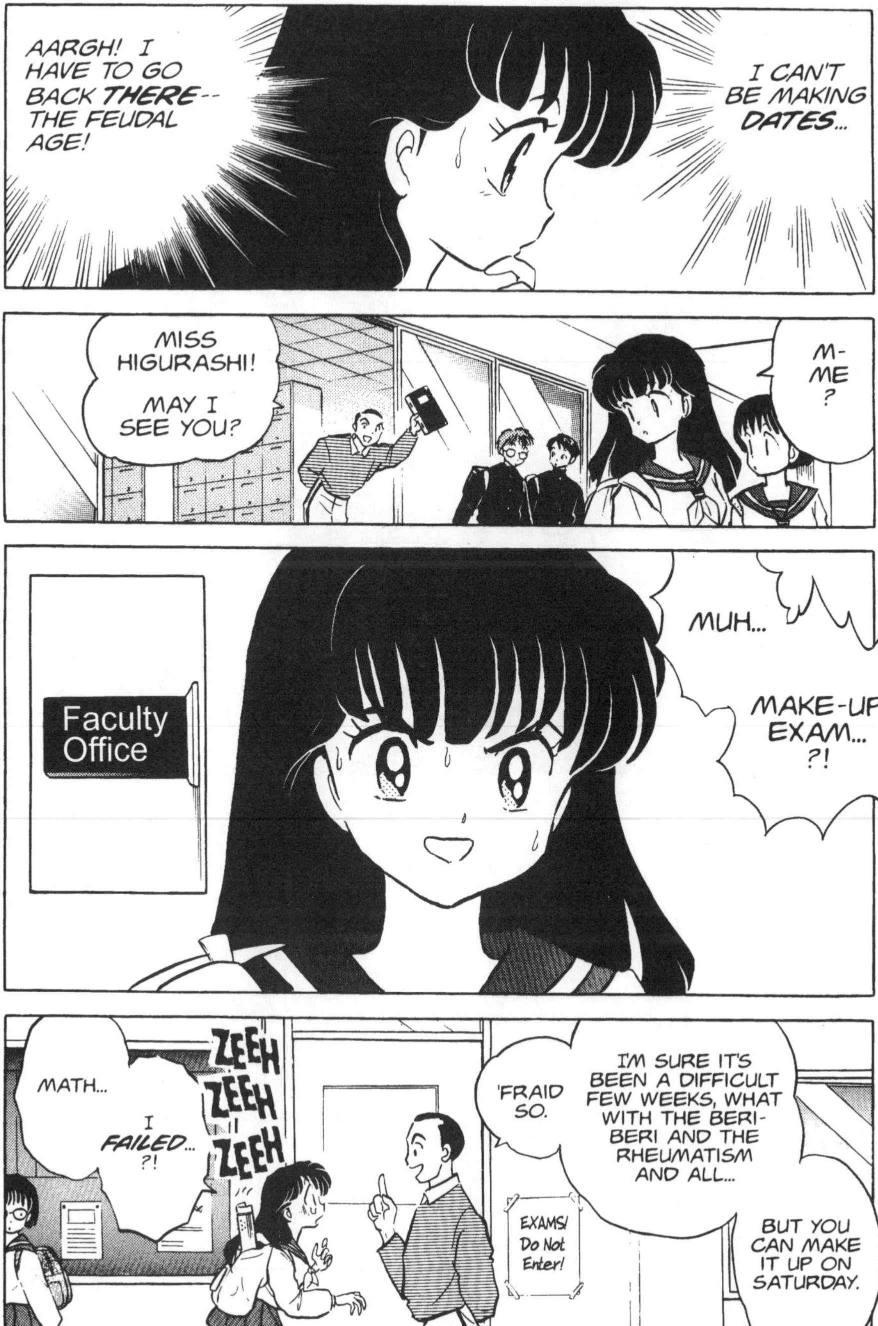
AARGH! I HAVE TO GO BACK **THERE**-- THE FEUDAL AGE!
I CAN'T BE MAKING **DATES**...
MISS HIGURASHI!
MAY I SEE YOU?
M-ME?
Faculty Office
MUH...
MAKE-UP EXAM...?!
MATH...
I **FAILED**...?!
ZEEH ZEEH ZEEH
'FRAID SO.
I'M SURE IT'S BEEN A DIFFICULT FEW WEEKS, WHAT WITH THE BERI-BERI AND THE RHEUMATISM AND ALL...
EXAMS! Do Not Enter!
BUT YOU CAN MAKE IT UP ON SATURDAY.

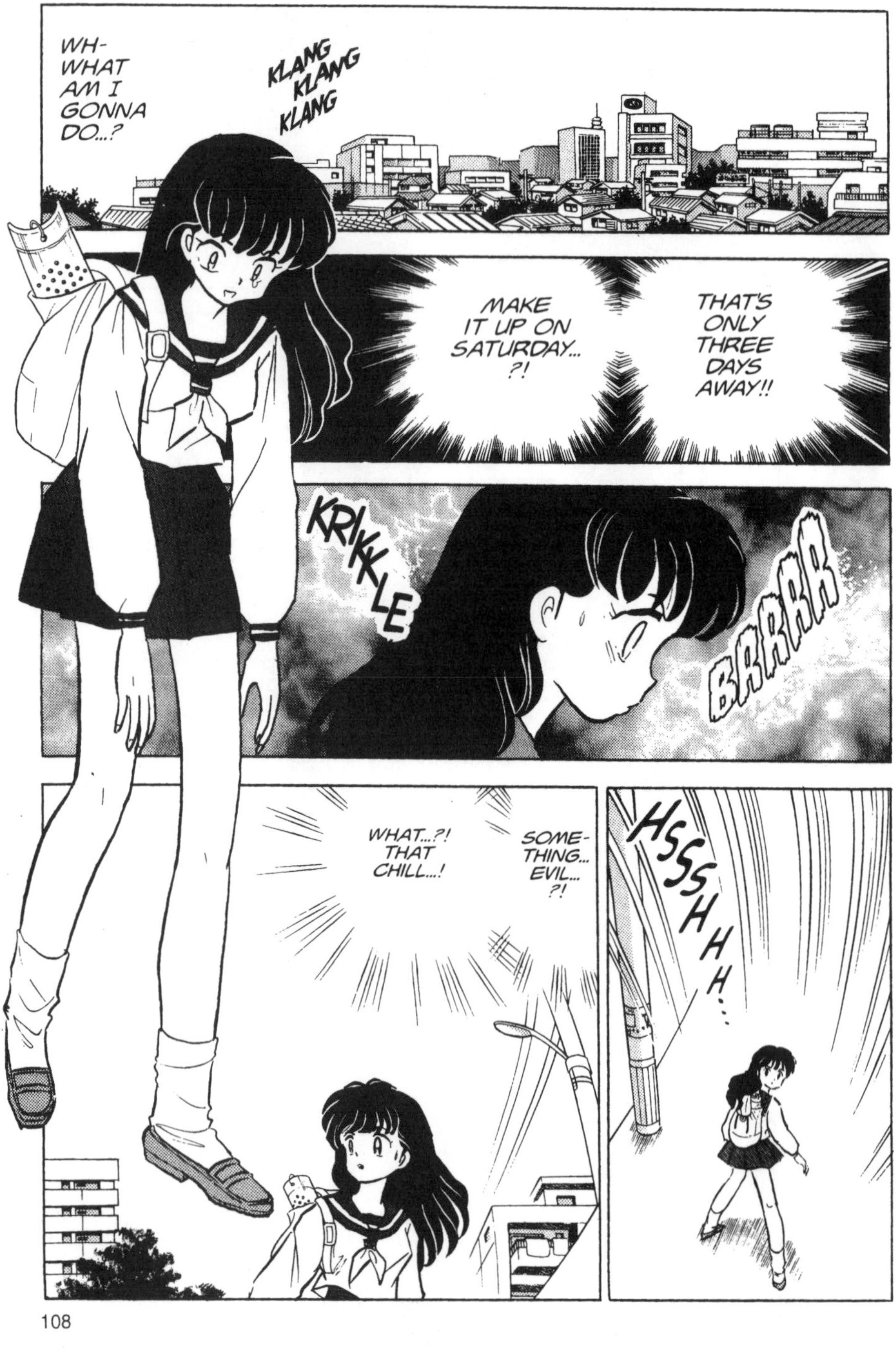
WH- WHAT AM I GONNA DO...?
KLANG KLANG KLANG
MAKE IT UP ON SATURDAY... ?!
THAT'S ONLY THREE DAYS AWAY!!
KRIKKLE
BRRRRR
WHAT...?! THAT CHILL...!
SOME- THING... EVIL... ?!
HSSSHHH...

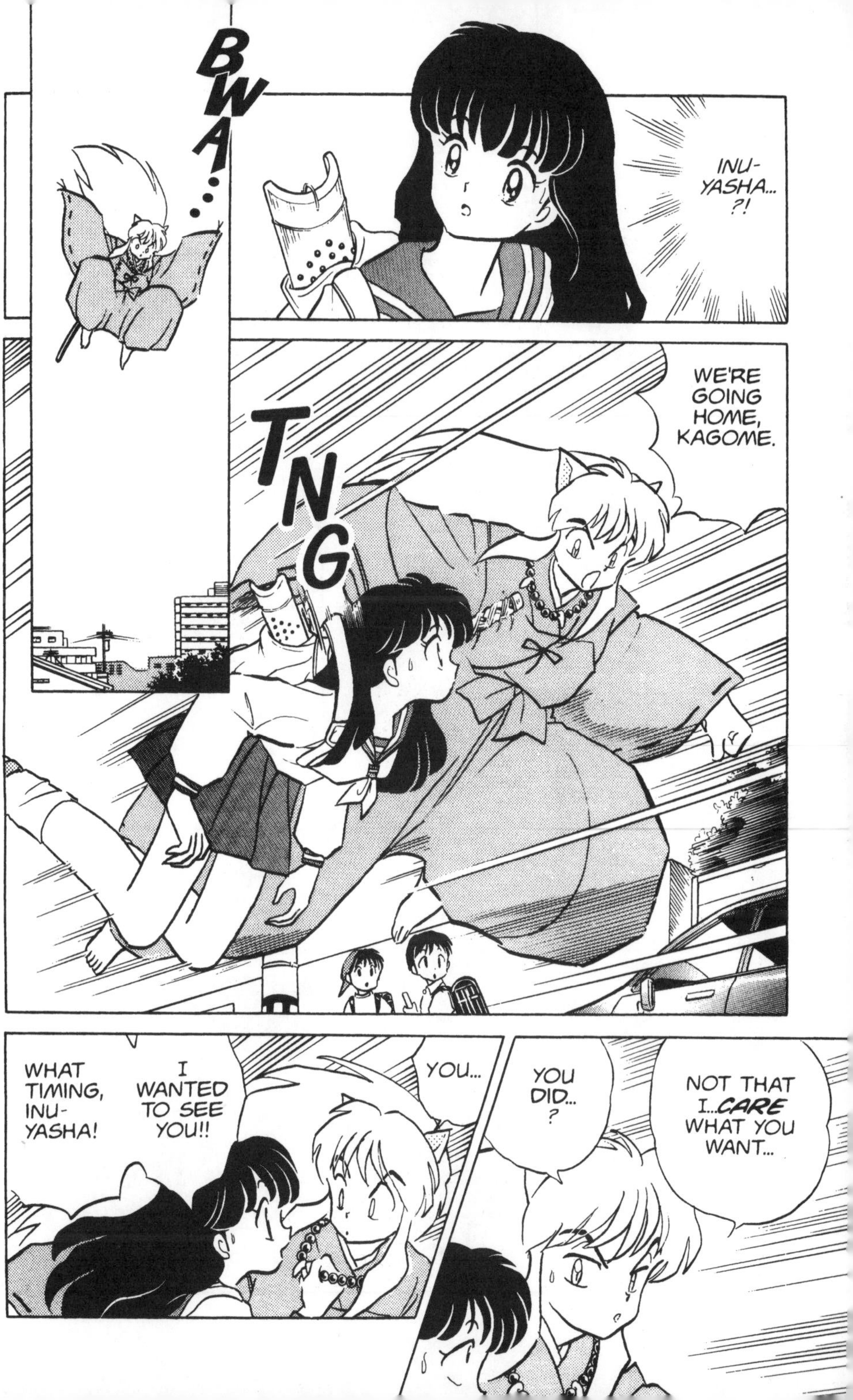
BWA...
INU-YASHA...?!
TNG
WE'RE GOING HOME, KAGOME.
WHAT TIMING, INU-YASHA!
I WANTED TO SEE YOU!!
YOU...
YOU DID...?
NOT THAT I...CARE WHAT YOU WANT...

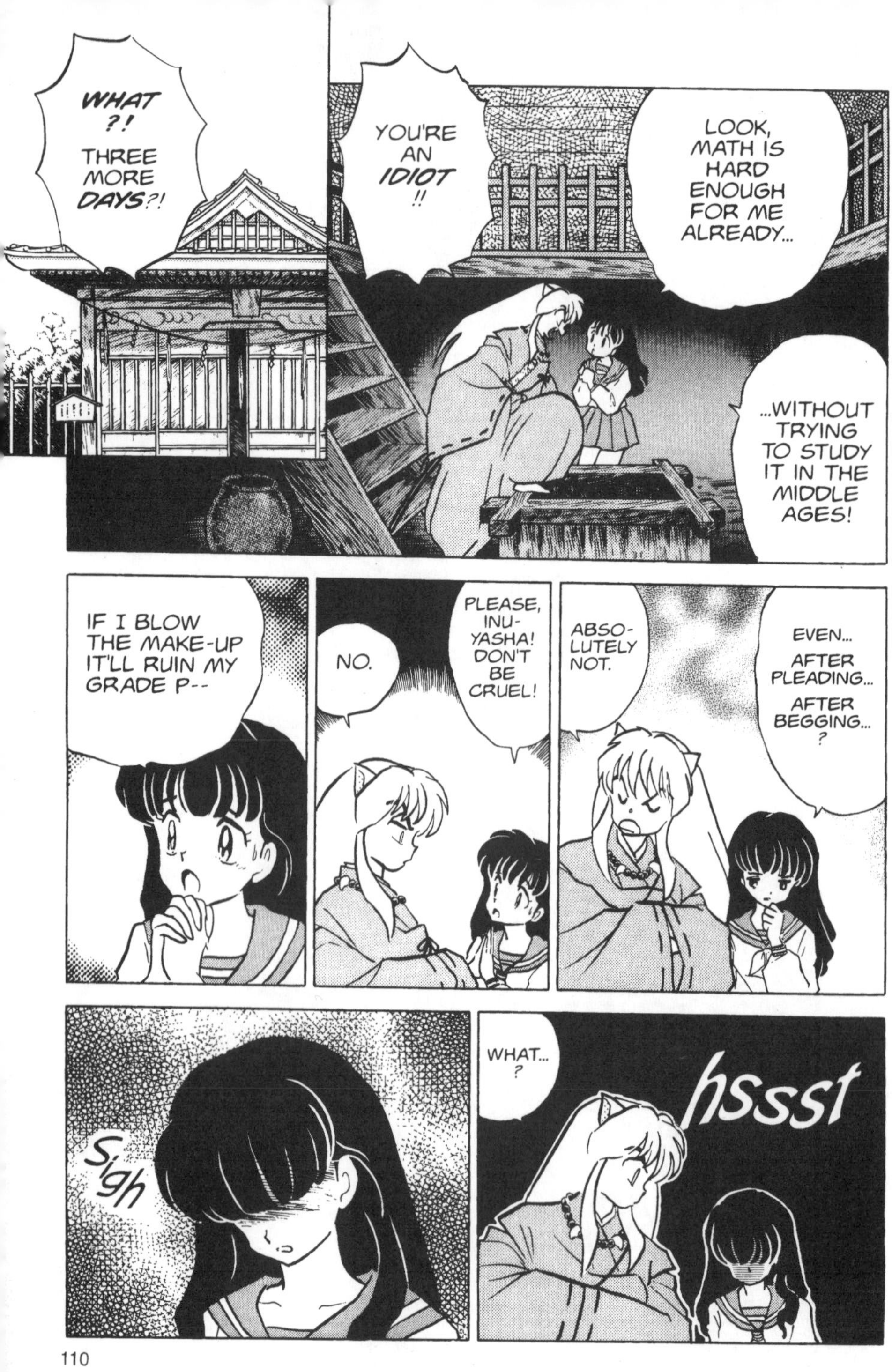
WHAT?! THREE MORE DAYS?!
YOU'RE AN IDIOT!!
LOOK, MATH IS HARD ENOUGH FOR ME ALREADY...
...WITHOUT TRYING TO STUDY IT IN THE MIDDLE AGES!
IF I BLOW THE MAKE-UP IT'LL RUIN MY GRADE P--
NO.
PLEASE, INU-YASHA! DON'T BE CRUEL!
ABSO-LUTELY NOT.
EVEN... AFTER PLEADING... AFTER BEGGING...?
Sigh
WHAT...?
hssst

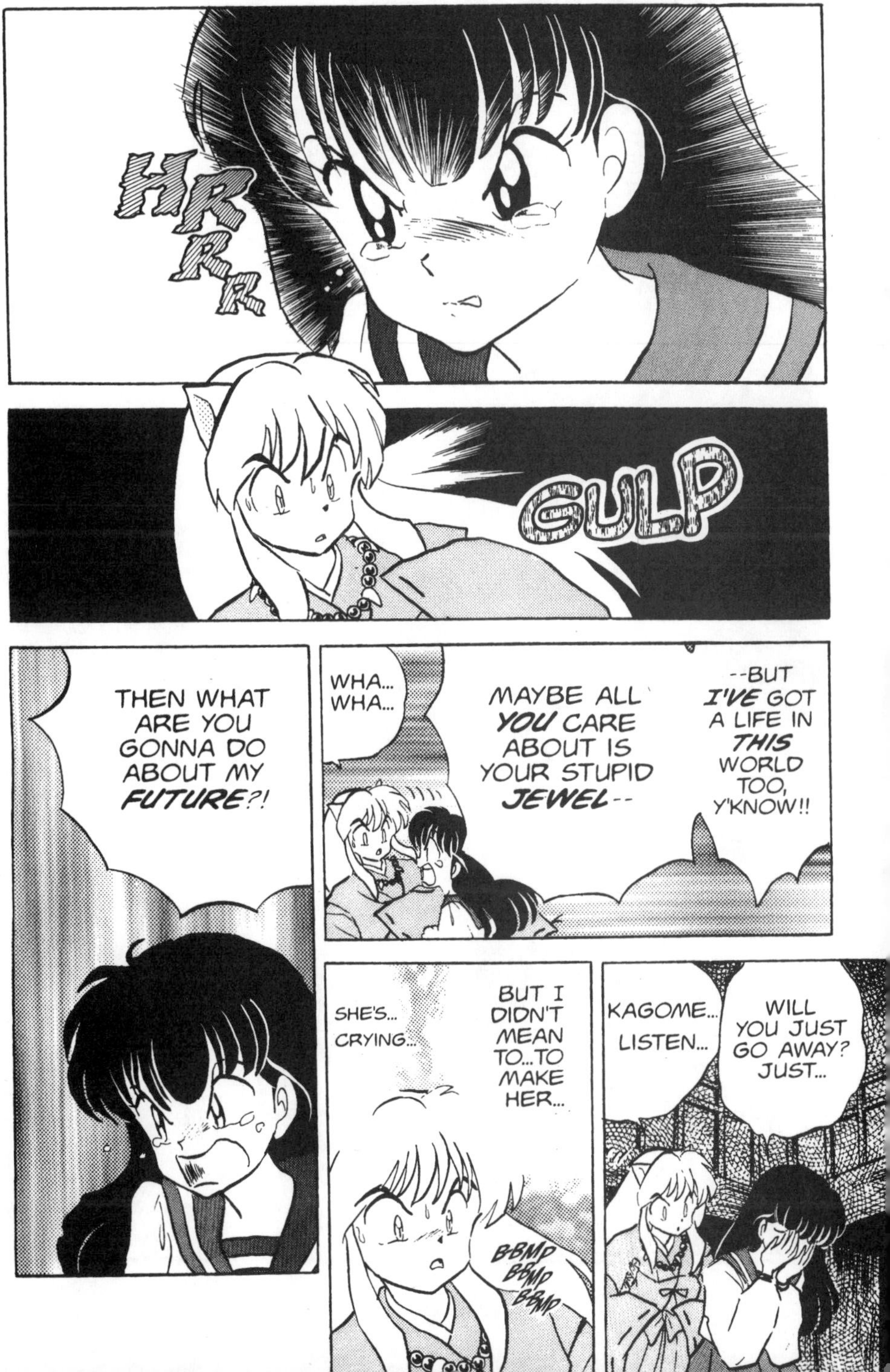
HRRR
GULP
THEN WHAT ARE YOU GONNA DO ABOUT MY FUTURE?!
WHA... WHA...
MAYBE ALL YOU CARE ABOUT IS YOUR STUPID JEWEL--
--BUT I'VE GOT A LIFE IN THIS WORLD TOO, Y'KNOW!!
SHE'S... CRYING...
BUT I DIDN'T MEAN TO...TO MAKE HER...
B-BMP B-BMP B-BMP
KAGOME... LISTEN...
WILL YOU JUST GO AWAY? JUST...

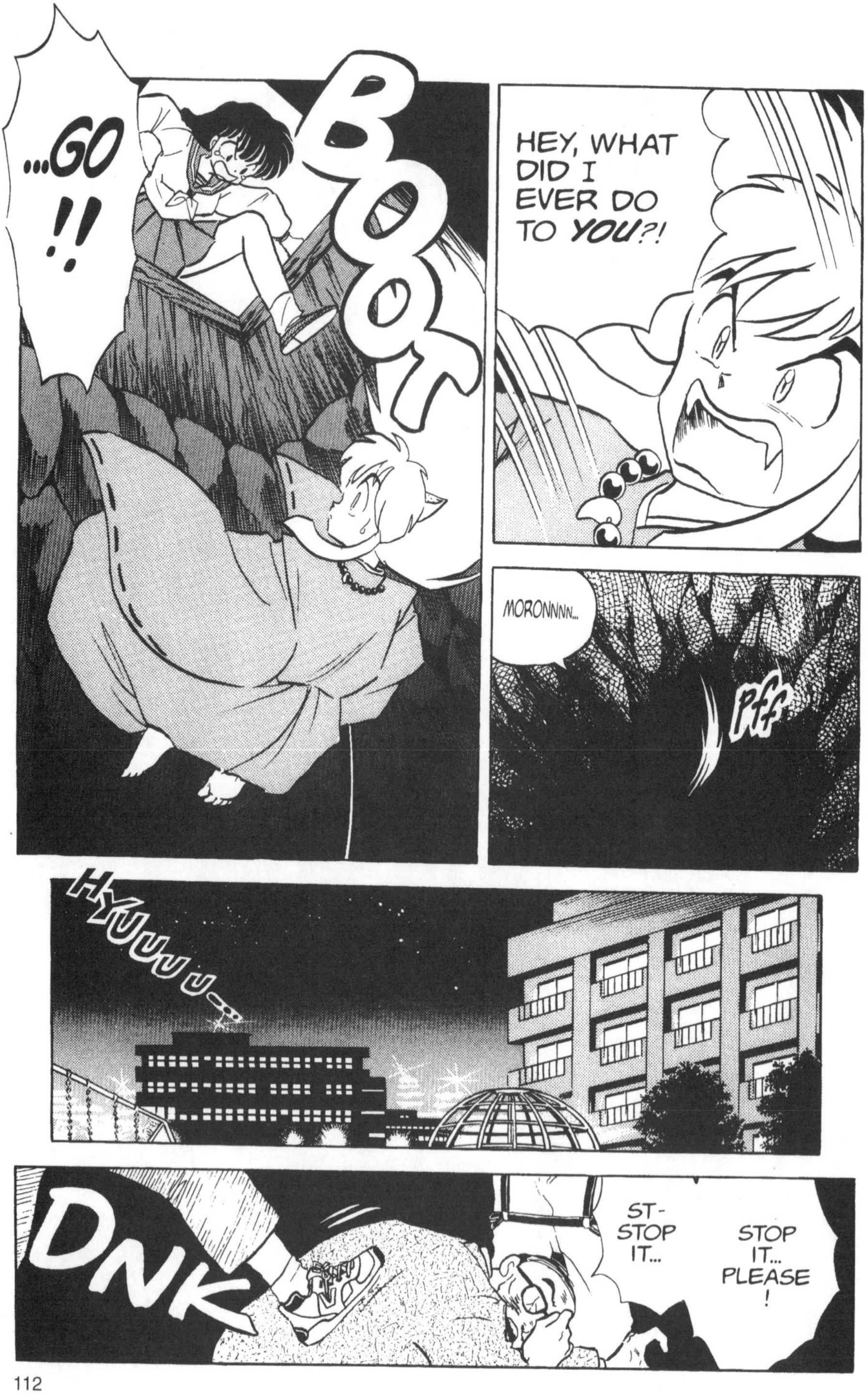
...GO!!
BOOT
HEY, WHAT DID I EVER DO TO *YOU*?!
MORONNNN...
Pff
HYUUUUU-
DNK
ST-STOP IT...
STOP IT... PLEASE!

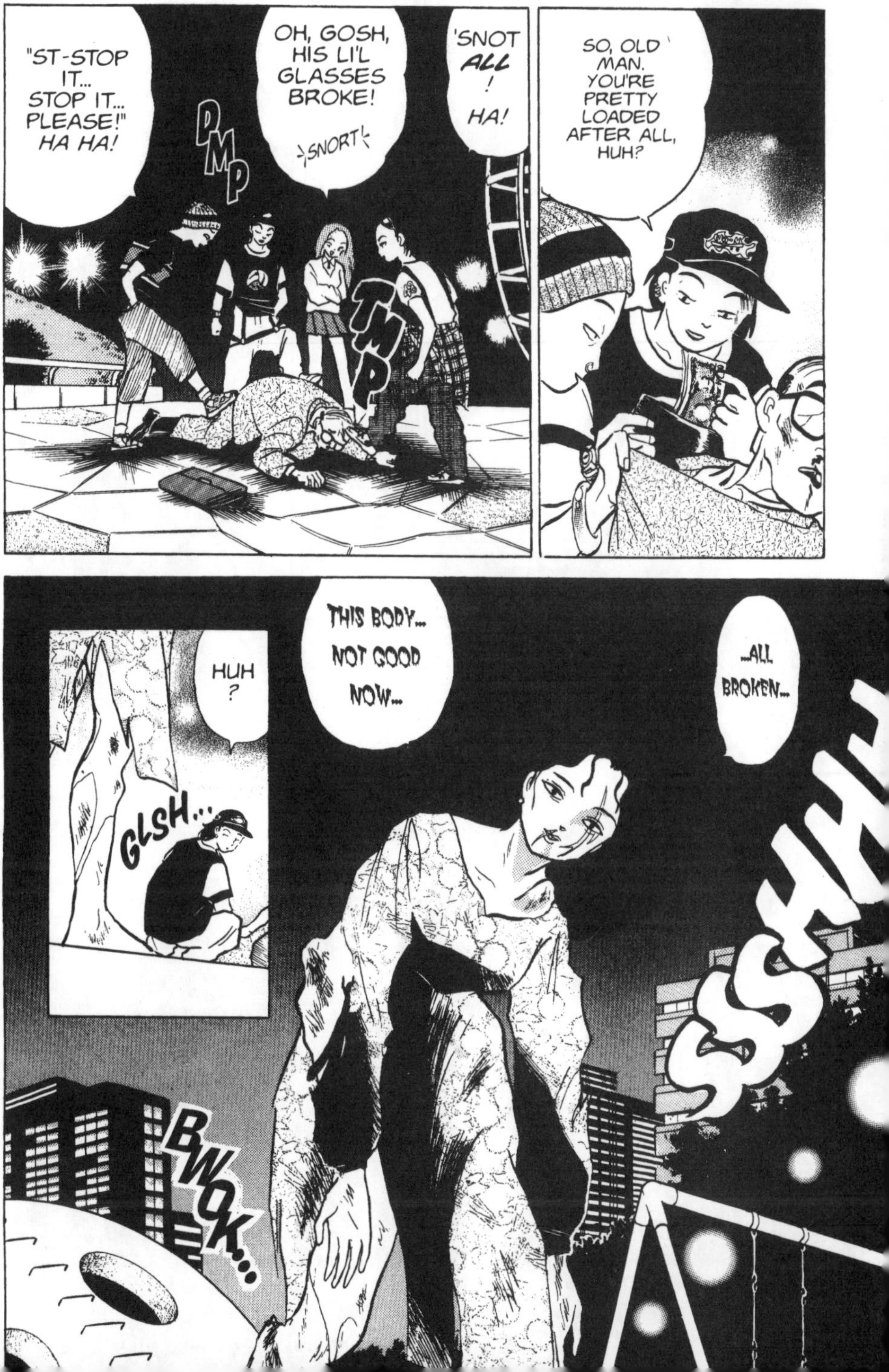
"ST-STOP IT... STOP IT... PLEASE!" HA HA!
DMP
OH, GOSH, HIS LI'L GLASSES BROKE!
SNORT
'SNOT ALL! HA!
TMP
SO, OLD MAN. YOU'RE PRETTY LOADED AFTER ALL, HUH?
HUH?
GLSH...
THIS BODY... NOT GOOD NOW...
...ALL BROKEN...
SSHH
BWOK...

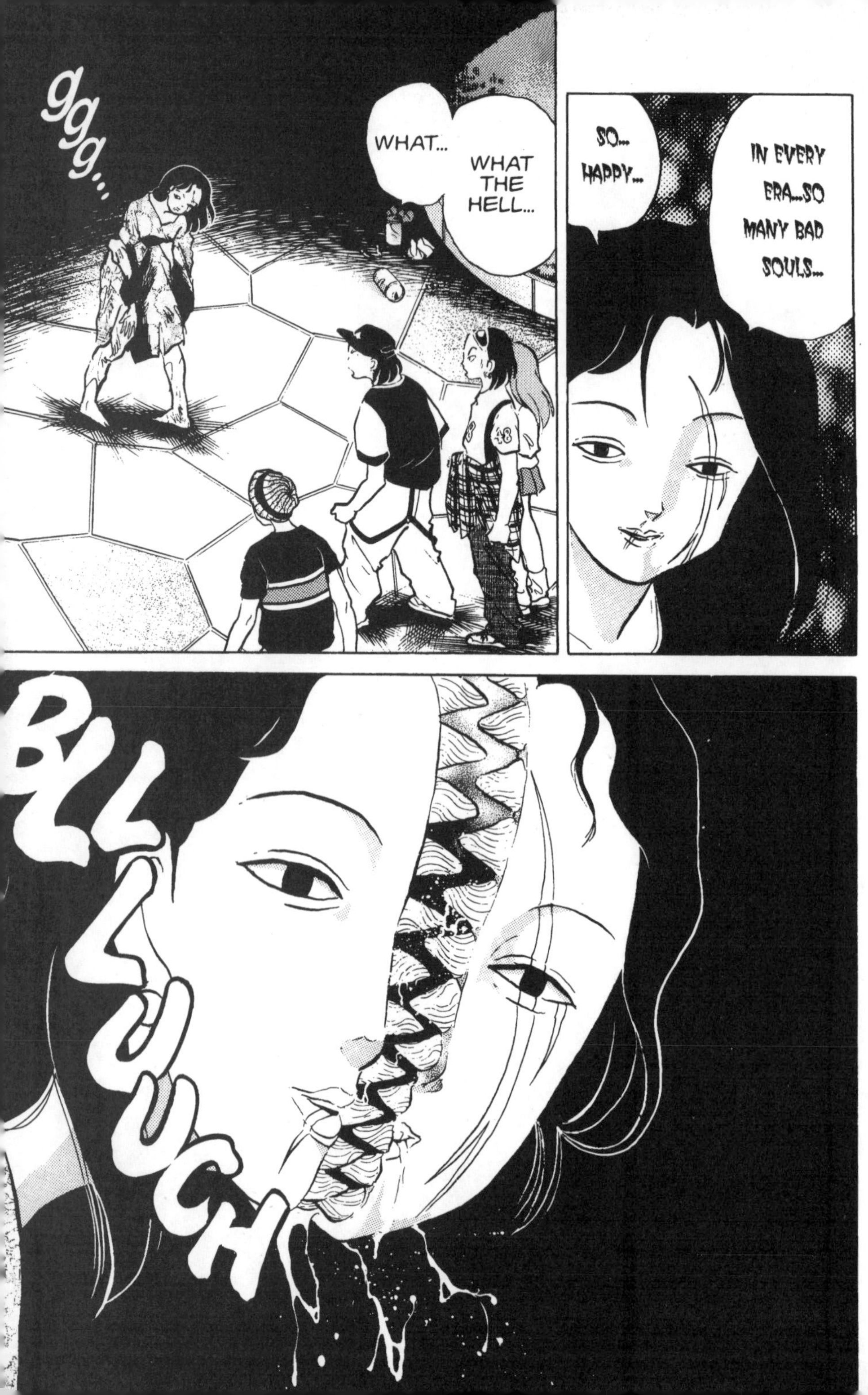
ggg...
WHAT...
WHAT THE HELL...
SO... HAPPY...
IN EVERY ERA...SO MANY BAD SOULS...
BLLUUCH!

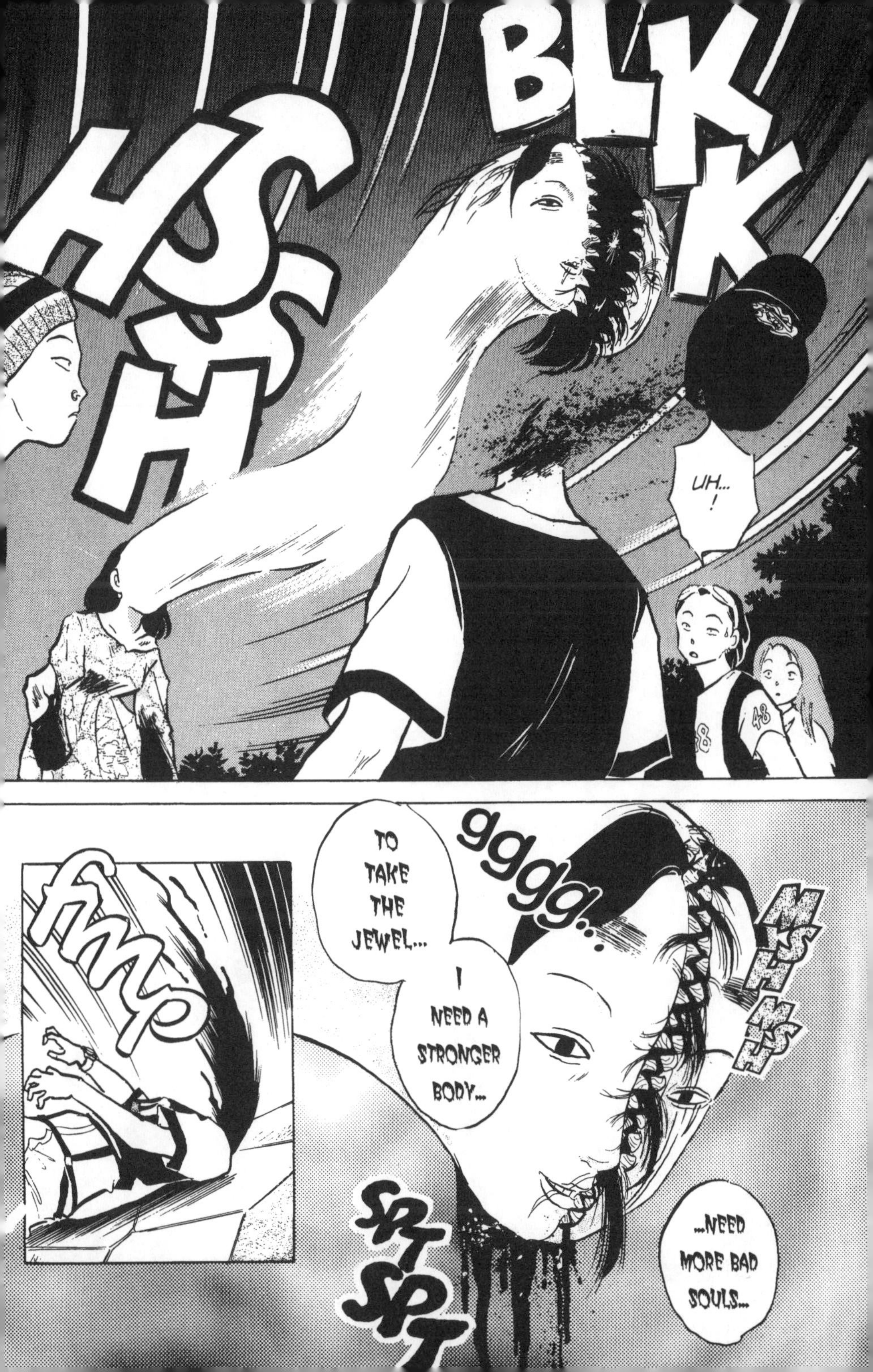
HSSH
BLK
UH... !
FMP
TO TAKE THE JEWEL...
ggggg...
I NEED A STRONGER BODY...
MSH MSH
SPT SPT
...NEED MORE BAD SOULS...

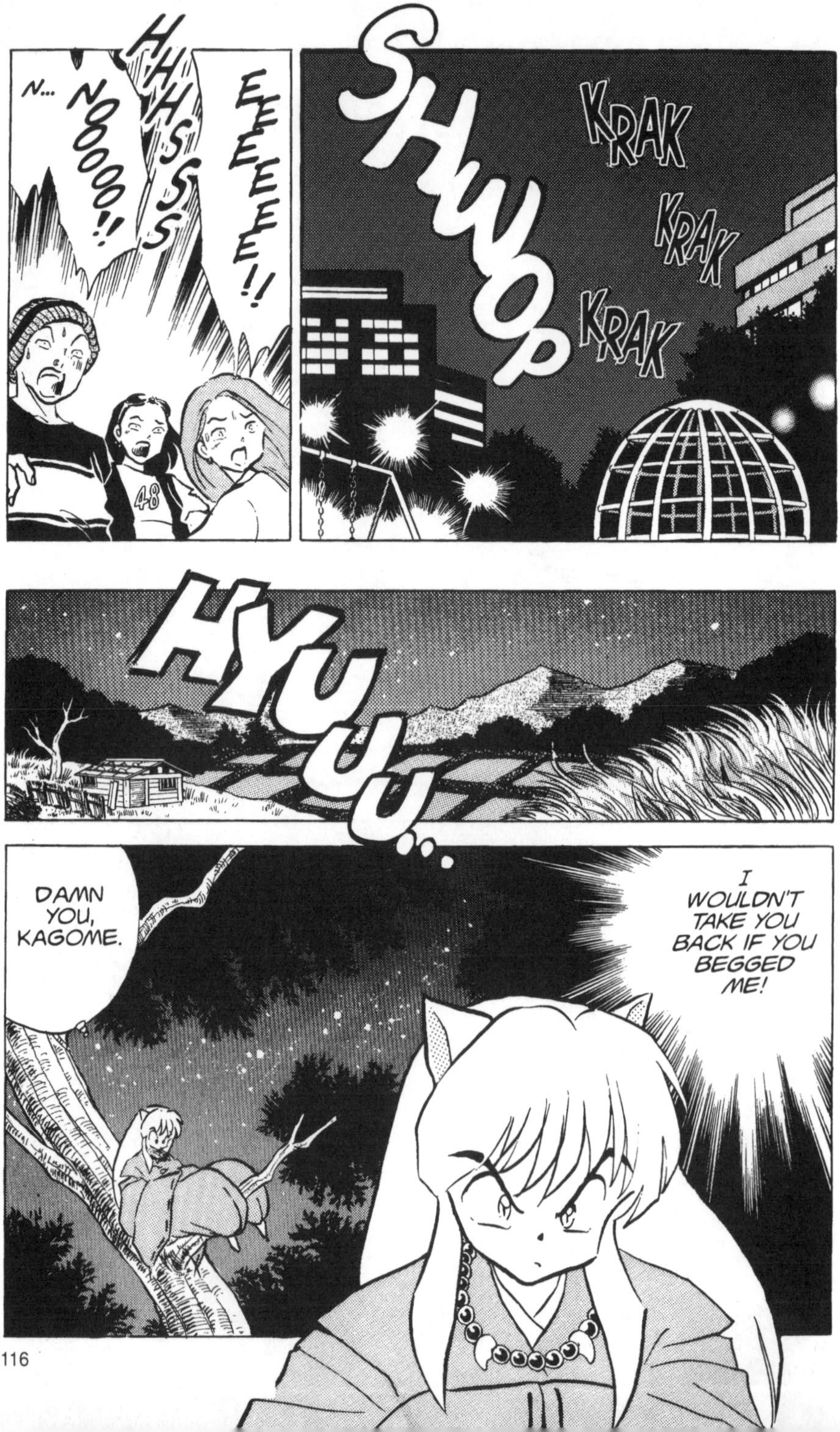
N...
NOOOOO!!
HHHSSSS
EEEEEEE!!
SHWOP
KRAK
KRAK
KRAK
HYUUUU...
DAMN YOU, KAGOME.
I WOULDN'T TAKE YOU BACK IF YOU BEGGED ME!

SCROLL SEVEN

FACE OFF

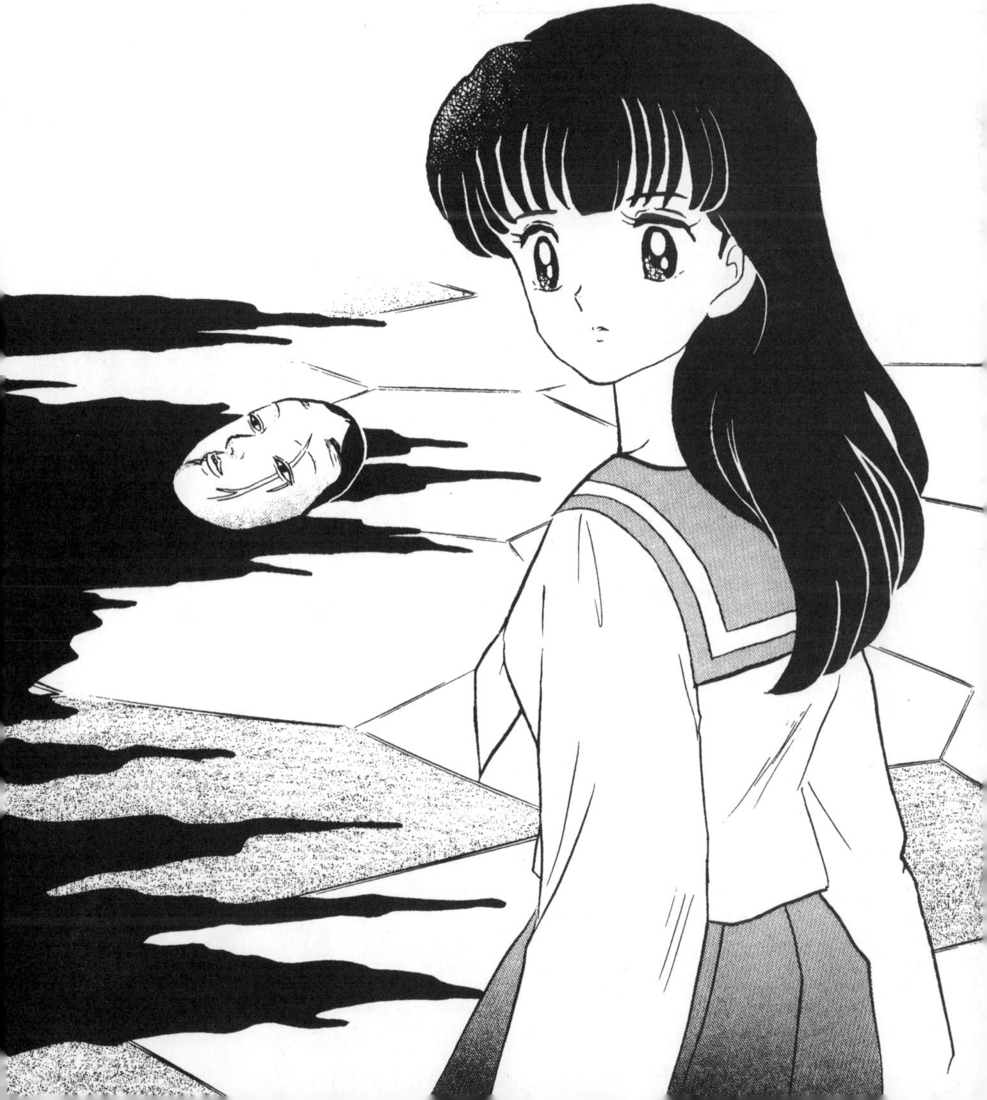

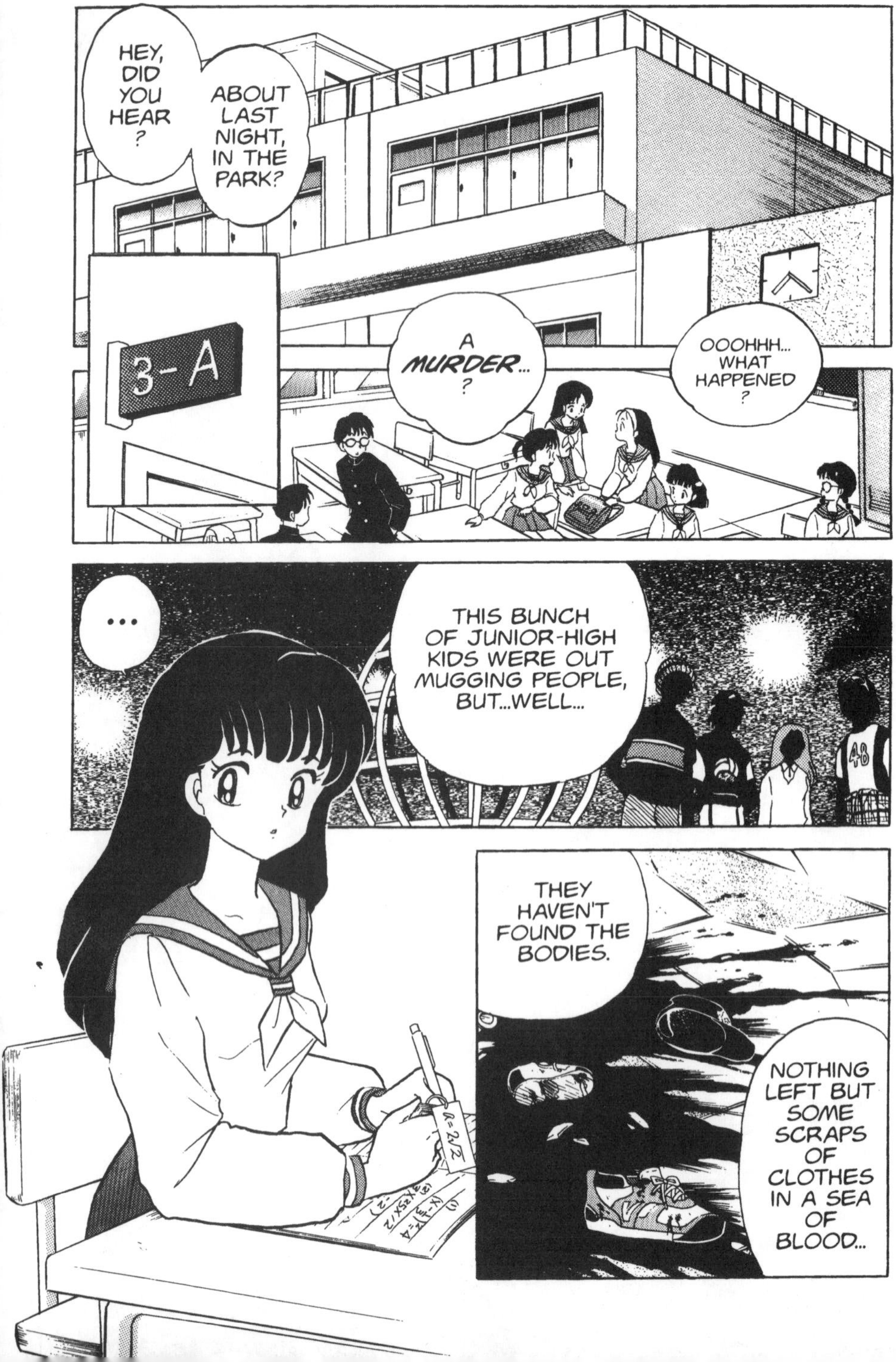
HEY, DID YOU HEAR?
ABOUT LAST NIGHT, IN THE PARK?
3-A
A MURDER...?
OOOHHH... WHAT HAPPENED?
...
THIS BUNCH OF JUNIOR-HIGH KIDS WERE OUT MUGGING PEOPLE, BUT...WELL...
THEY HAVEN'T FOUND THE BODIES.
NOTHING LEFT BUT SOME SCRAPS OF CLOTHES IN A SEA OF BLOOD...

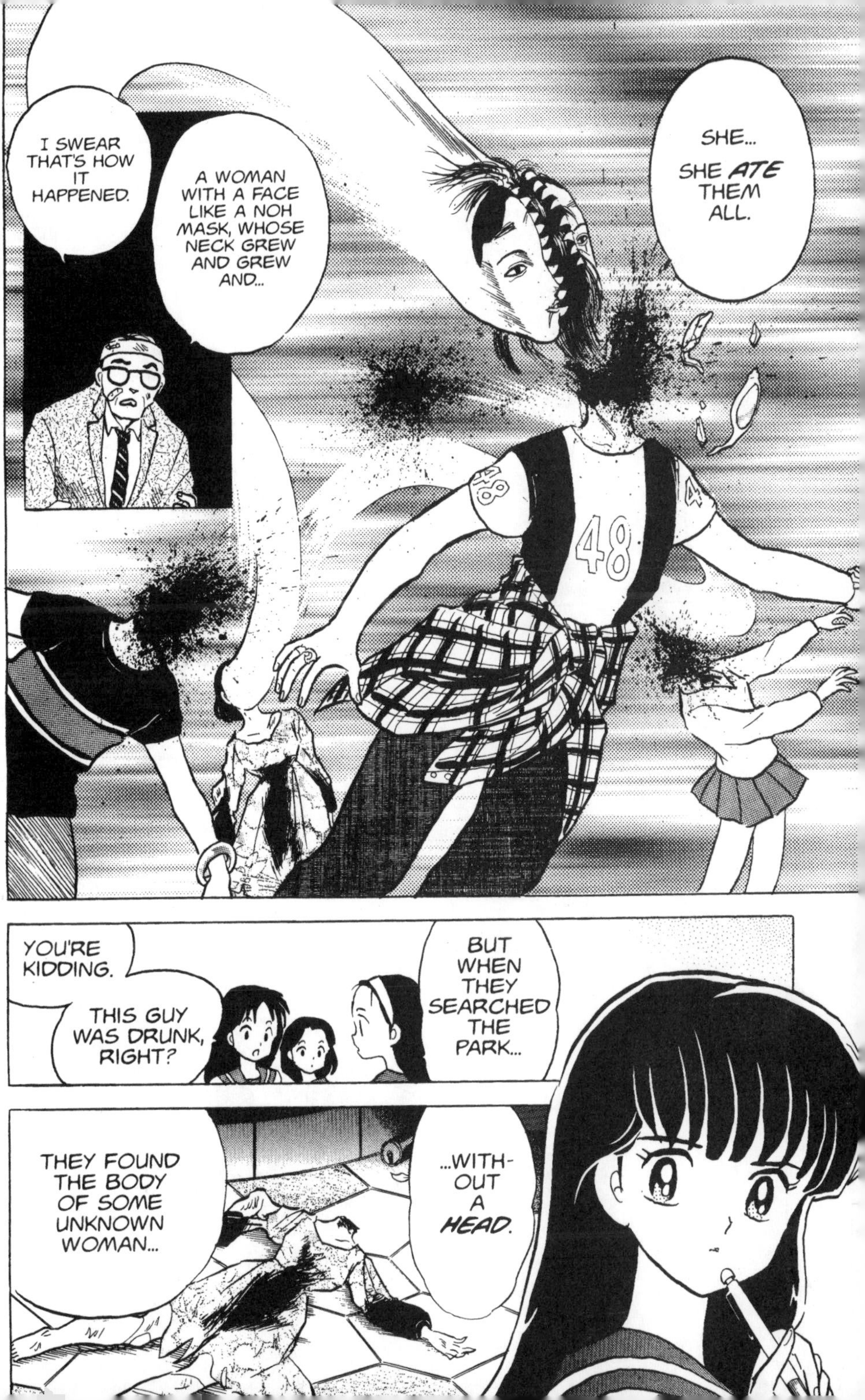
I SWEAR THAT'S HOW IT HAPPENED.
A WOMAN WITH A FACE LIKE A NOH MASK, WHOSE NECK GREW AND GREW AND...
SHE... SHE *ATE* THEM ALL.
48
48
YOU'RE KIDDING.
THIS GUY WAS DRUNK, RIGHT?
BUT WHEN THEY SEARCHED THE PARK...
THEY FOUND THE BODY OF SOME UNKNOWN WOMAN...
...WITH-OUT A *HEAD*.

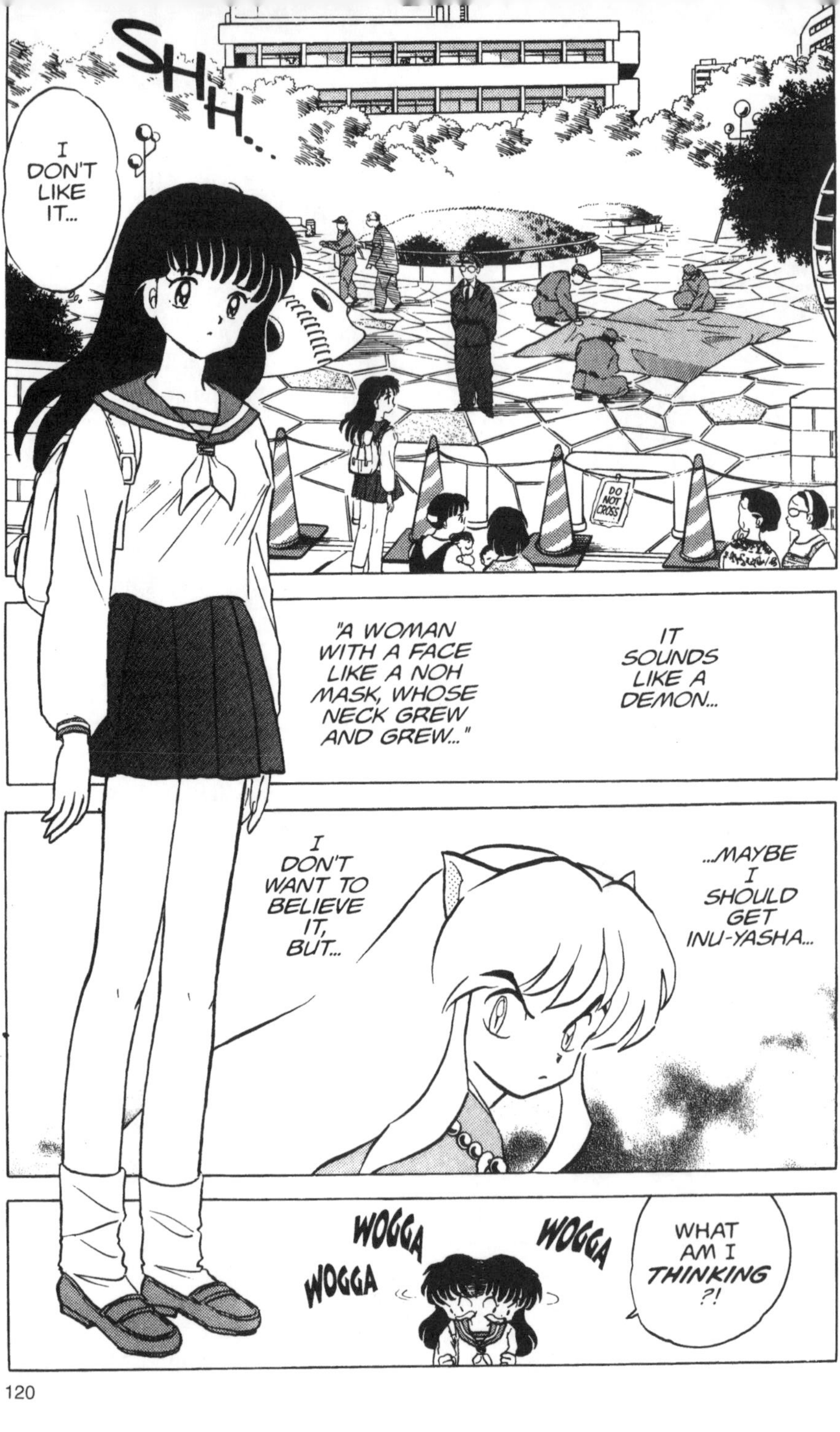
SHHH...
I DON'T LIKE IT...
DO NOT CROSS
"A WOMAN WITH A FACE LIKE A NOH MASK, WHOSE NECK GREW AND GREW..."
IT SOUNDS LIKE A DEMON...
I DON'T WANT TO BELIEVE IT, BUT...
...MAYBE I SHOULD GET INU-YASHA...
WOGGA
WOGGA
WOGGA
WHAT AM I *THINKING* ?!

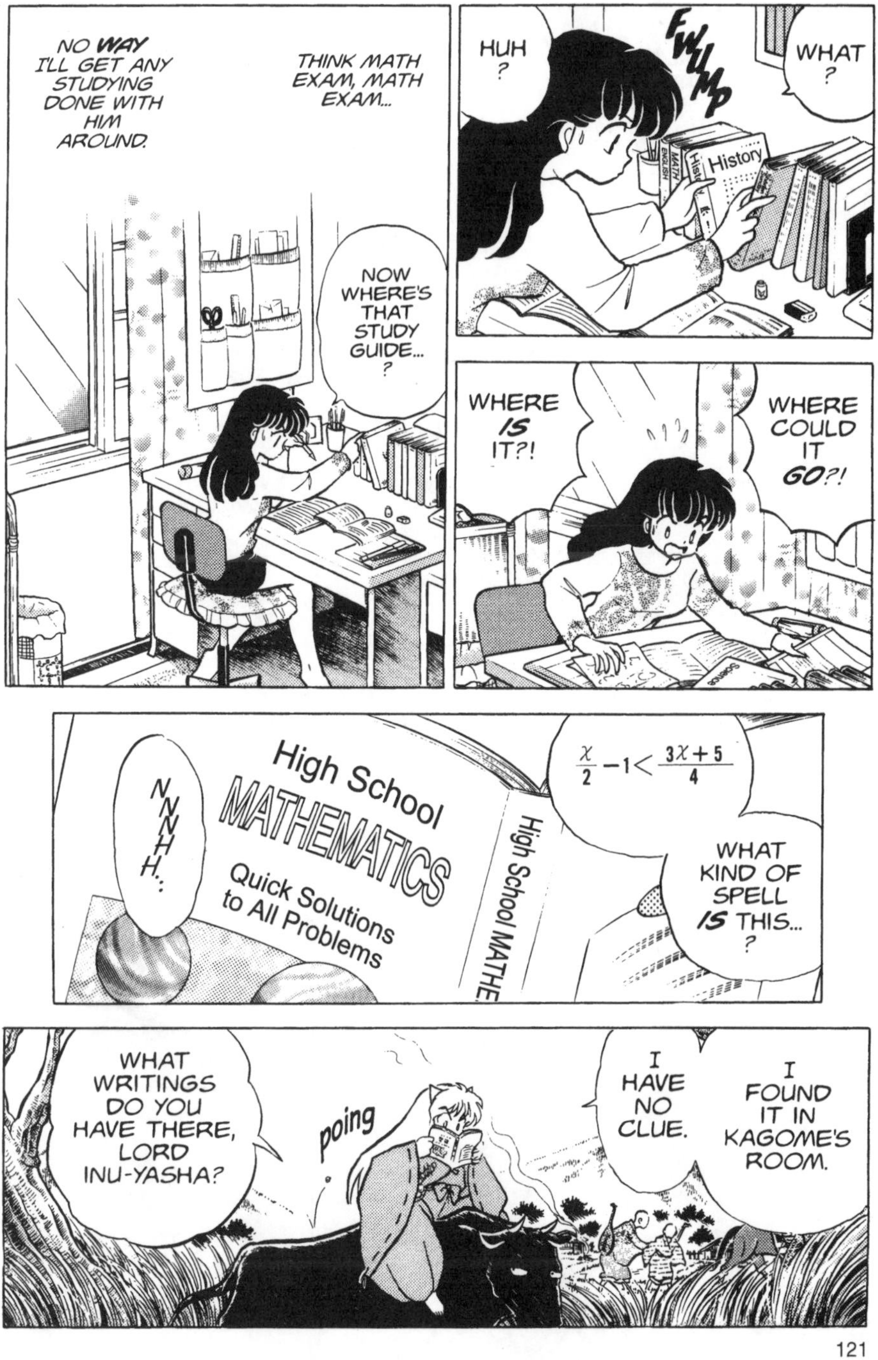
NO *WAY* I'LL GET ANY STUDYING DONE WITH HIM AROUND.
THINK MATH EXAM, MATH EXAM...
NOW WHERE'S THAT STUDY GUIDE... ?
HUH ?
FWUMP
WHAT ?
History
WHERE *IS* IT?!
WHERE COULD IT *GO*?!
NNNHH...
High School
MATHEMATICS
Quick Solutions to All Problems
High School MATHE
$\frac{x}{2}-1<\frac{3x+5}{4}$
WHAT KIND OF SPELL *IS* THIS... ?
WHAT WRITINGS DO YOU HAVE THERE, LORD INU-YASHA?
poing
I HAVE NO CLUE.
I FOUND IT IN KAGOME'S ROOM.

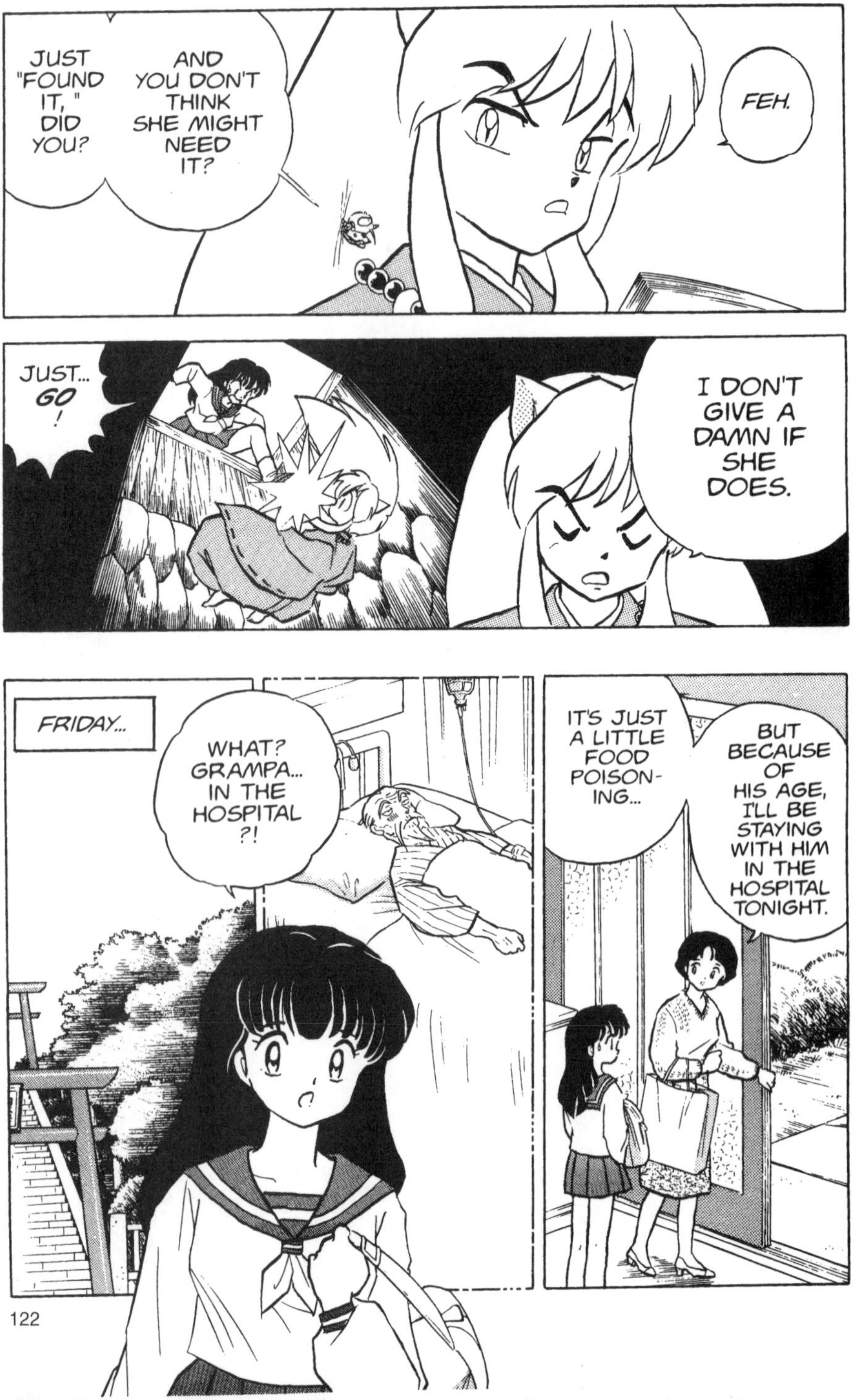
JUST "FOUND IT, " DID YOU?
AND YOU DON'T THINK SHE MIGHT NEED IT?
FEH.
JUST... GO!
I DON'T GIVE A DAMN IF SHE DOES.
FRIDAY...
WHAT? GRAMPA... IN THE HOSPITAL ?!
IT'S JUST A LITTLE FOOD POISON-ING...
BUT BECAUSE OF HIS AGE, I'LL BE STAYING WITH HIM IN THE HOSPITAL TONIGHT.

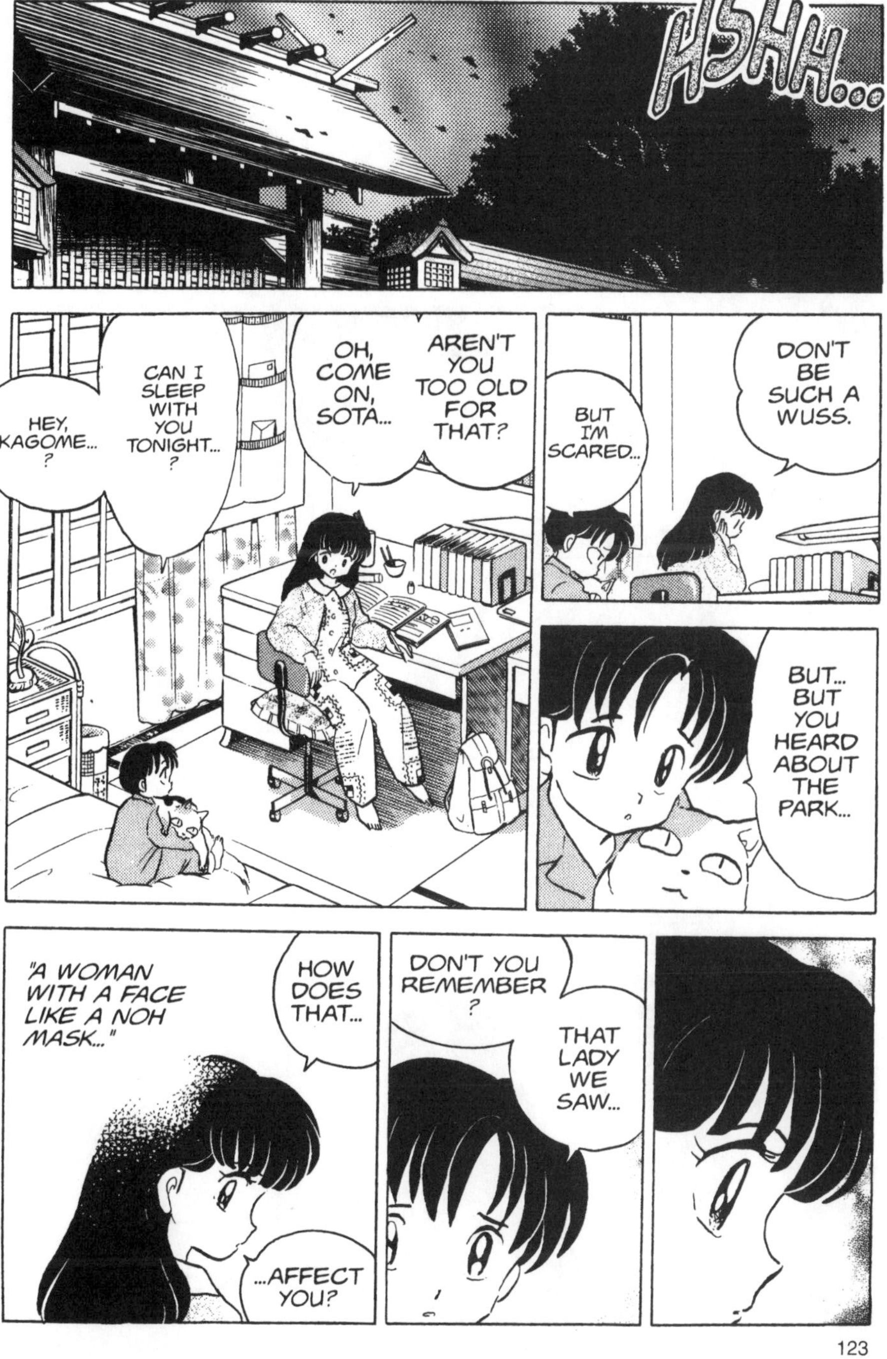
HSHH...
HEY, KAGOME...?
CAN I SLEEP WITH YOU TONIGHT...?
OH, COME ON, SOTA...
AREN'T YOU TOO OLD FOR THAT?
BUT I'M SCARED...
DON'T BE SUCH A WUSS.
BUT... BUT YOU HEARD ABOUT THE PARK...
"A WOMAN WITH A FACE LIKE A NOH MASK..."
HOW DOES THAT...
...AFFECT YOU?
DON'T YOU REMEMBER?
THAT LADY WE SAW...

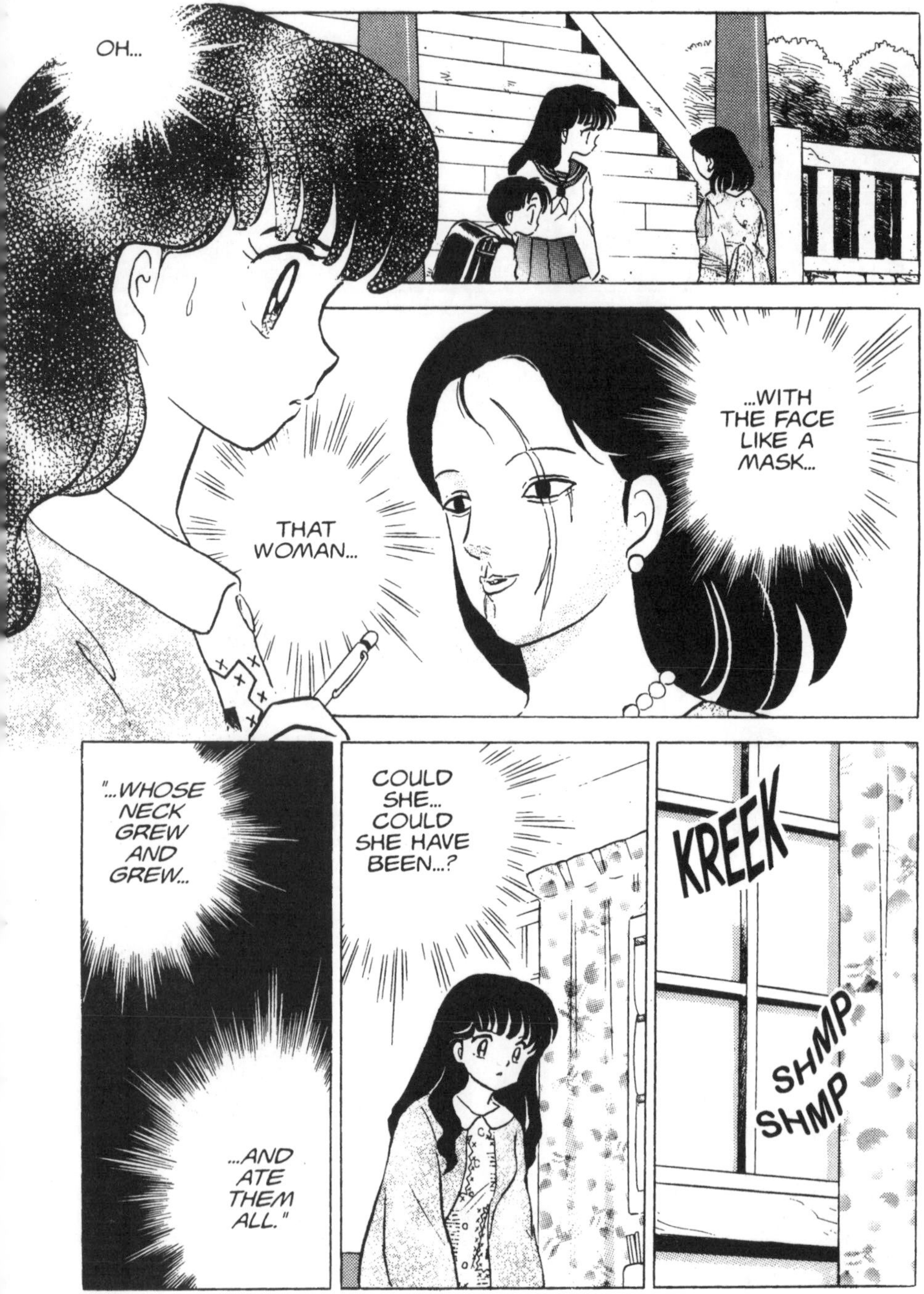
OH...
THAT WOMAN...
...WITH THE FACE LIKE A MASK...
"...WHOSE NECK GREW AND GREW...
...AND ATE THEM ALL."
COULD SHE... COULD SHE HAVE BEEN...?
KREEK
SHMP
SHMP

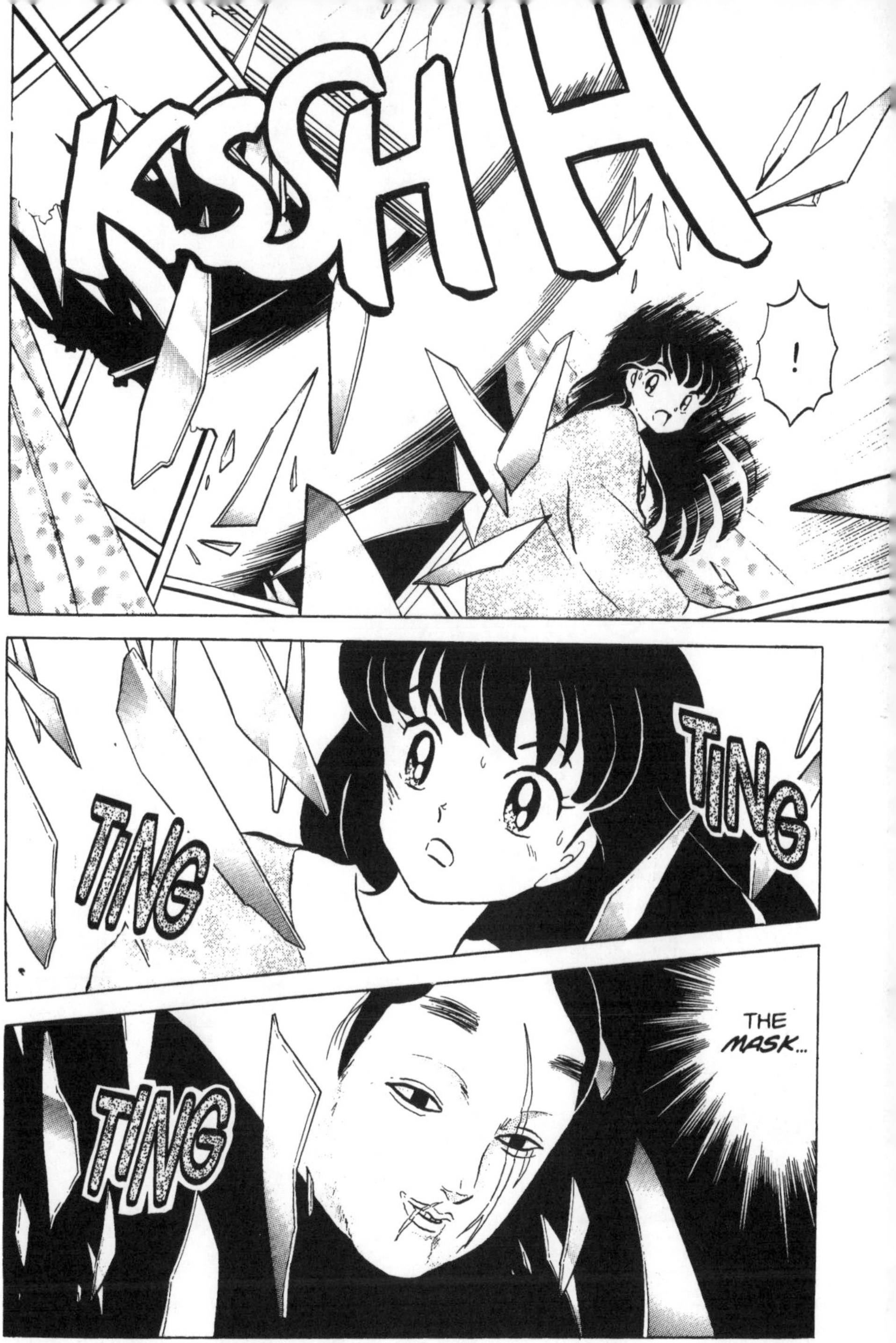
KSHH
!
TING
TING
TING
THE *MASK*...

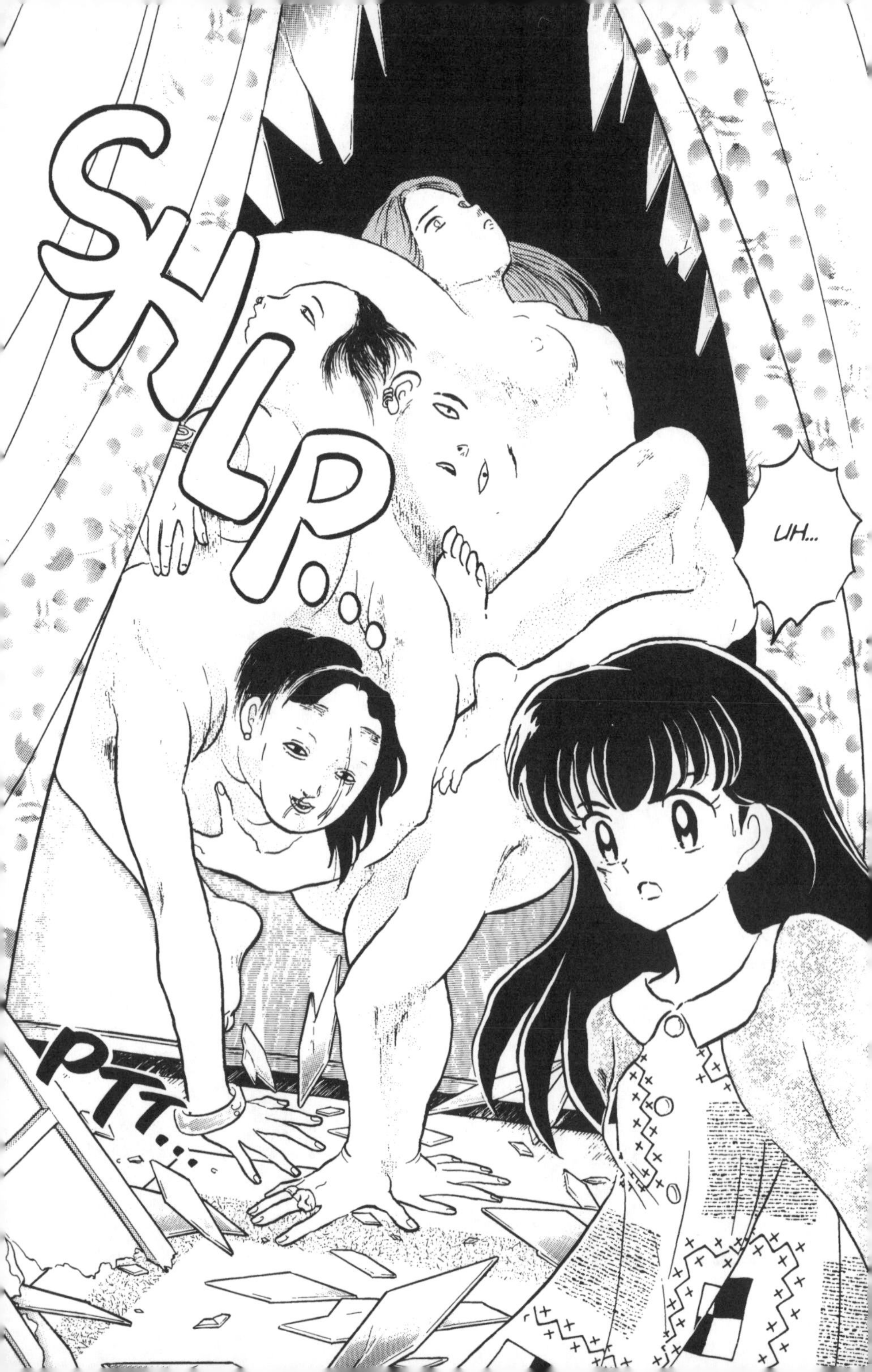
SHLP...
UH...
PTT...

NEED...

...A BETTER... BODY...

SHE...

SHE HAS A SHARD OF THE JEWEL...

GLINT

GIVE ME... THE SHARDS...

!

SHE KNOWS...

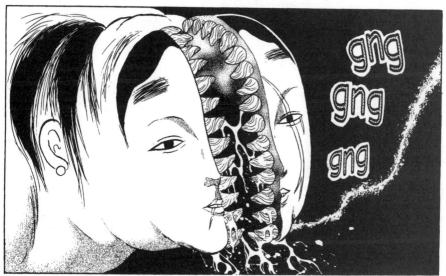

gng gng gng

127

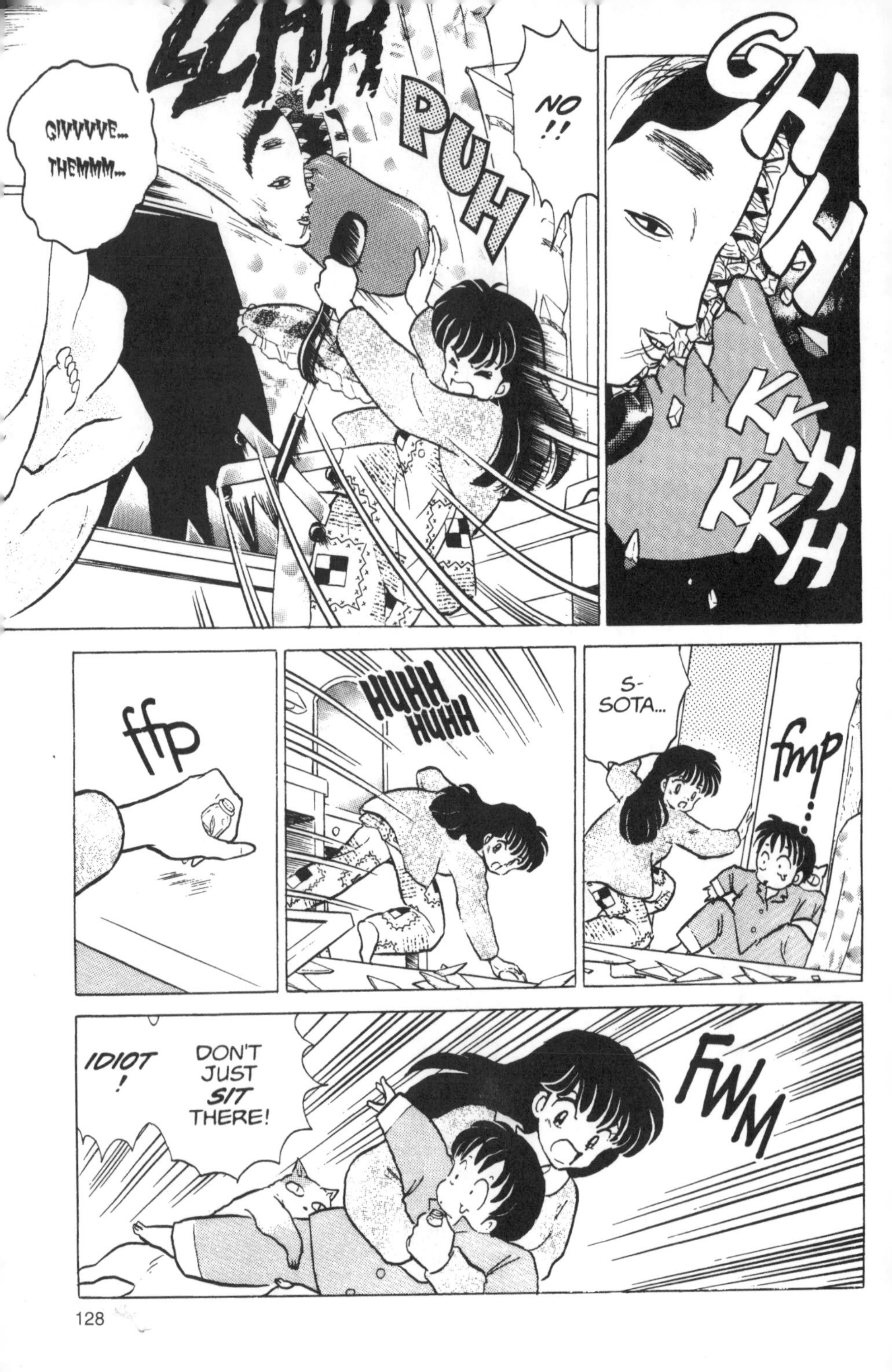
LCHH
GIVVVVE... THEMMM...
PUH
NO !!
GHHH
KKHH KKHH
ffp
HUHH HUHH
S- SOTA...
fmp...
IDIOT!
DON'T JUST SIT THERE!
FWM

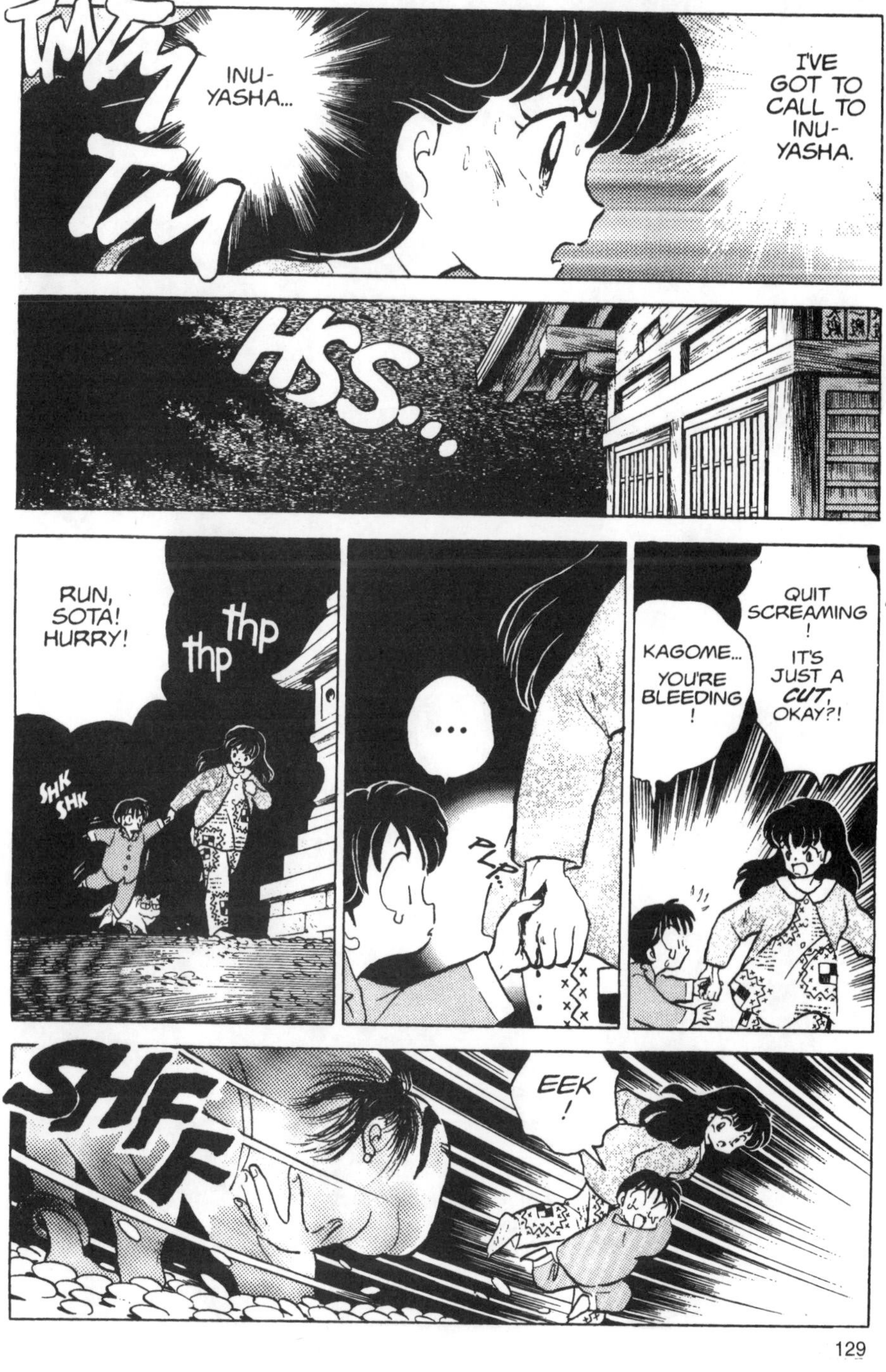
TMTMTM
INU-YASHA...
I'VE GOT TO CALL TO INU-YASHA.
HSS...
RUN, SOTA! HURRY!
thp thp
SHK SHK
...
PLP...
KAGOME... YOU'RE BLEEDING!
QUIT SCREAMING! IT'S JUST A *CUT*, OKAY?!
SHFF
EEK!

YAAA!

KA...
KA...
KAGOME...?

PLUP?

SOTA...

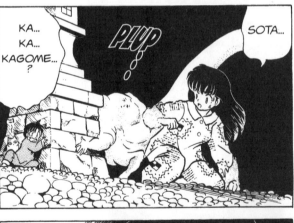

THAT
MONSTER
WANTS
THESE
SHARDS...

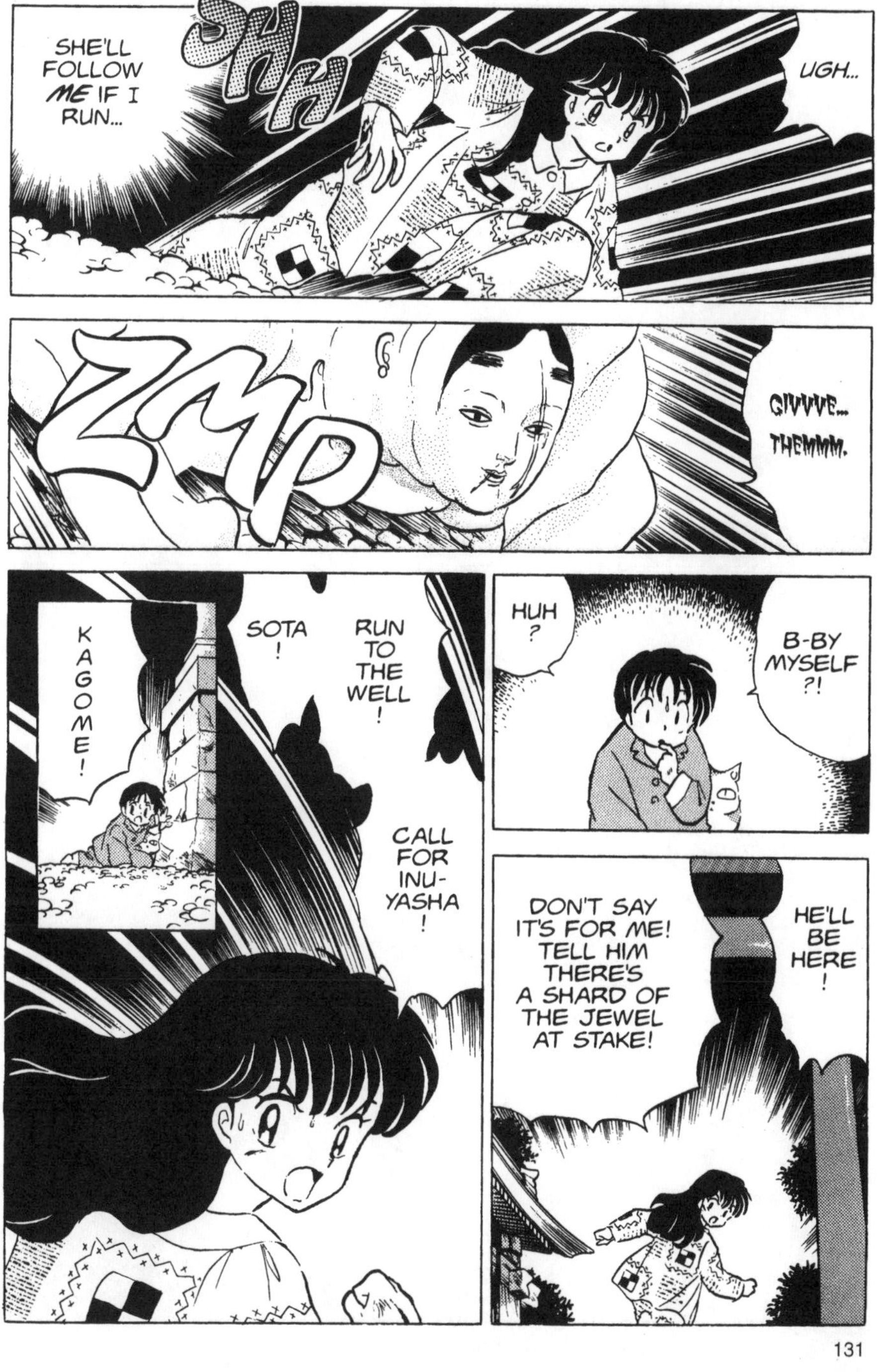
SHH
SHE'LL FOLLOW ME IF I RUN...
UGH...
ZMP
GIVVVE... THEMMM.
KAGOME!
SOTA!
RUN TO THE WELL!
CALL FOR INU-YASHA!
HUH?
B-BY MYSELF?!
DON'T SAY IT'S FOR ME! TELL HIM THERE'S A SHARD OF THE JEWEL AT STAKE!
HE'LL BE HERE!

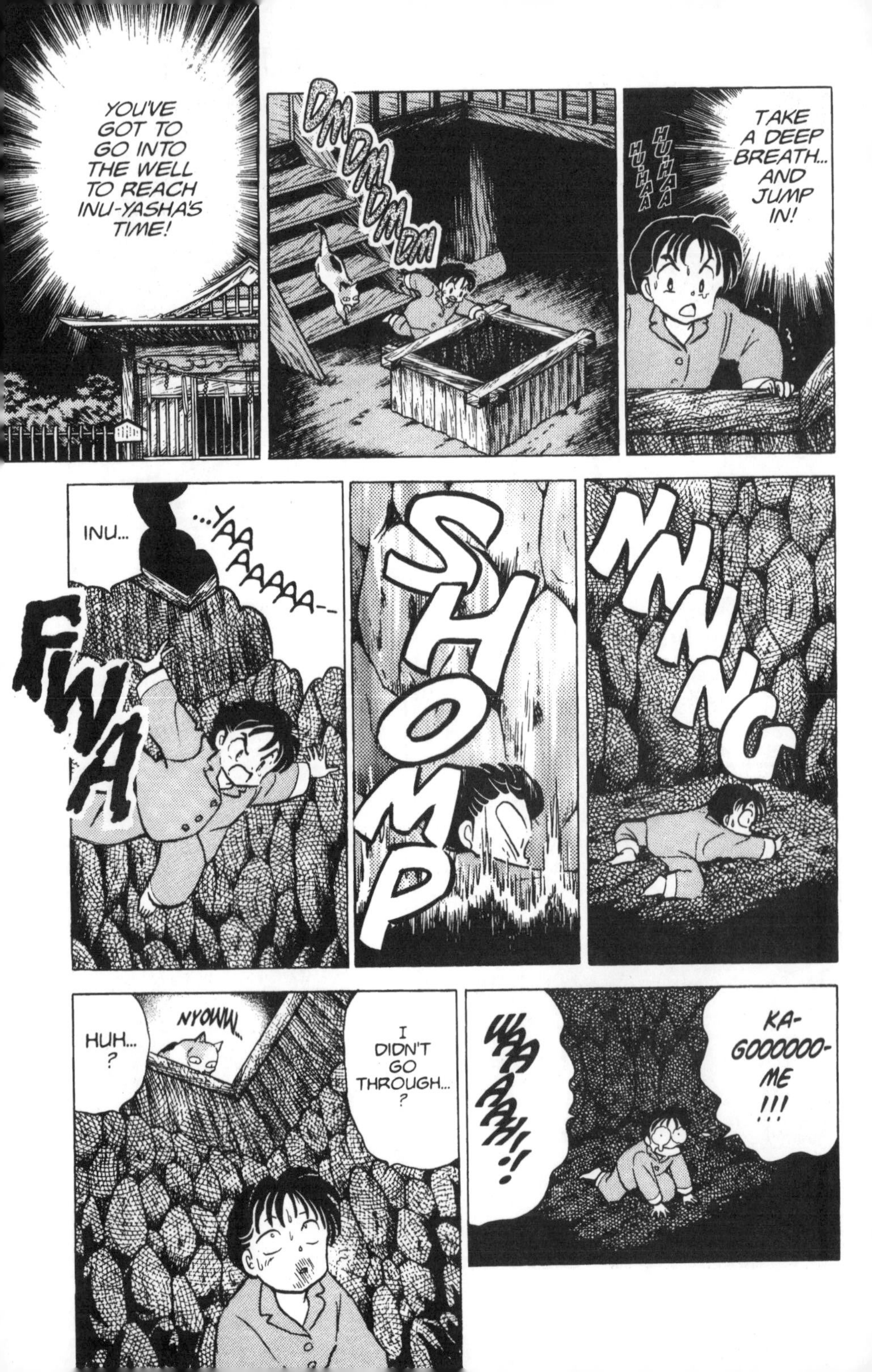
YOU'VE GOT TO GO INTO THE WELL TO REACH INU-YASHA'S TIME!
DMDMDMDM
HUHA HUHA
TAKE A DEEP BREATH... AND JUMP IN!
INU...
...YAAAAAAAAA--
FWA
SHOMP
NNNNG
HUH...?
NYOWW...
I DIDN'T GO THROUGH...?
WAAAAH!!
KA-GOOOOOO-ME!!!

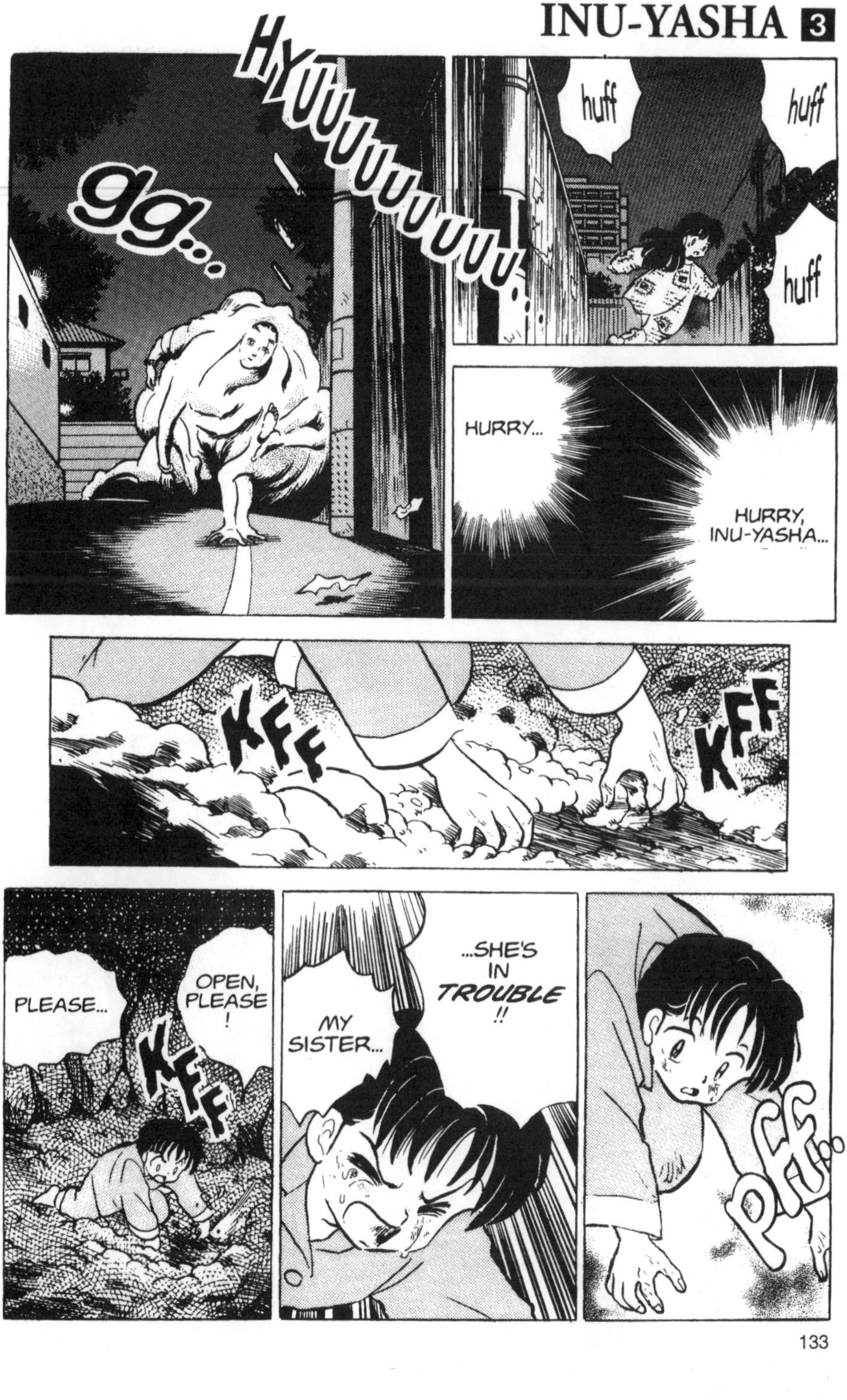
HYUUUUUUUUUUU...
gg...
huff
huff
huff
HURRY...
HURRY, INU-YASHA...
KFF
KFF
PLEASE...
OPEN, PLEASE!
KFF
MY SISTER...
...SHE'S IN TROUBLE!!
PFFooo

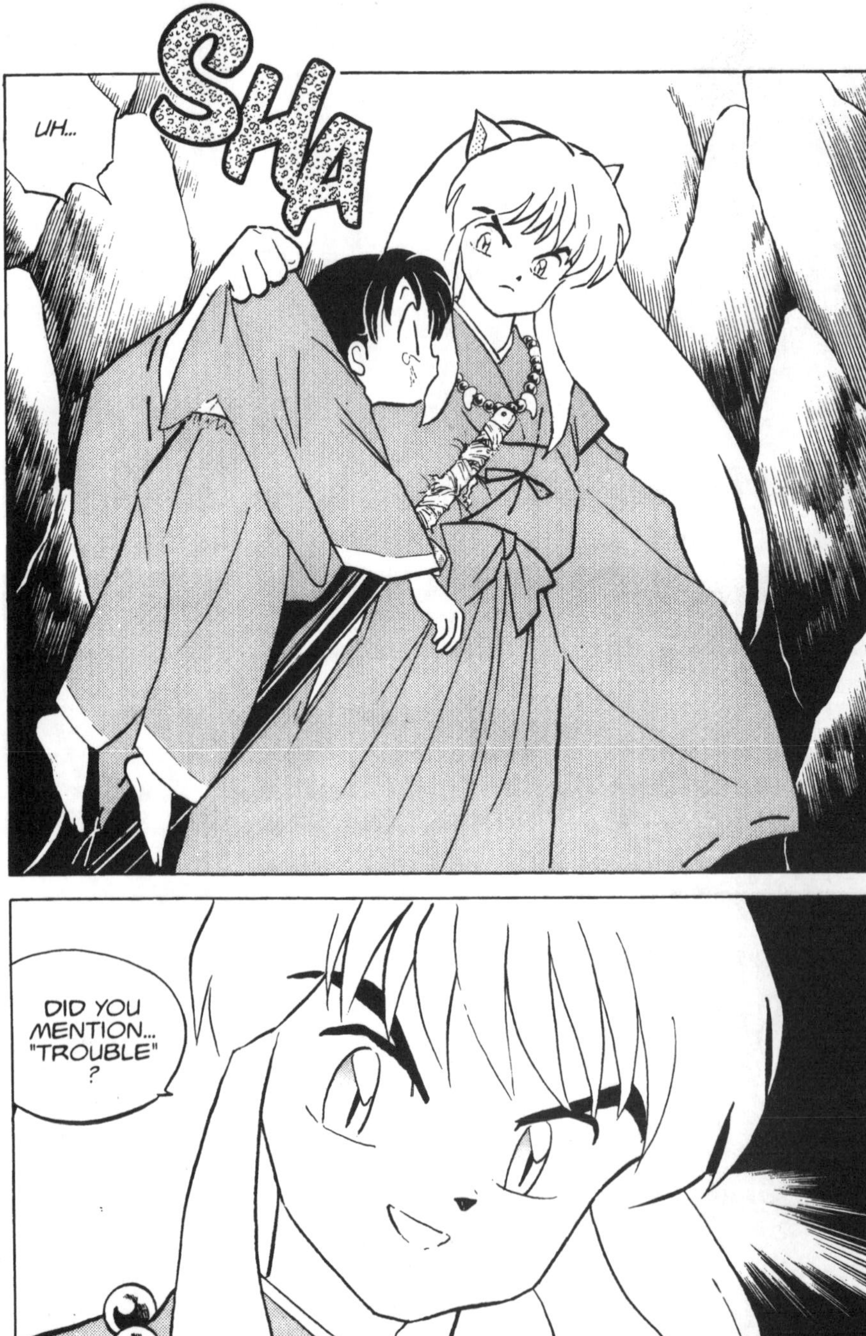
SHA
UH...
DID YOU MENTION... "TROUBLE" ?

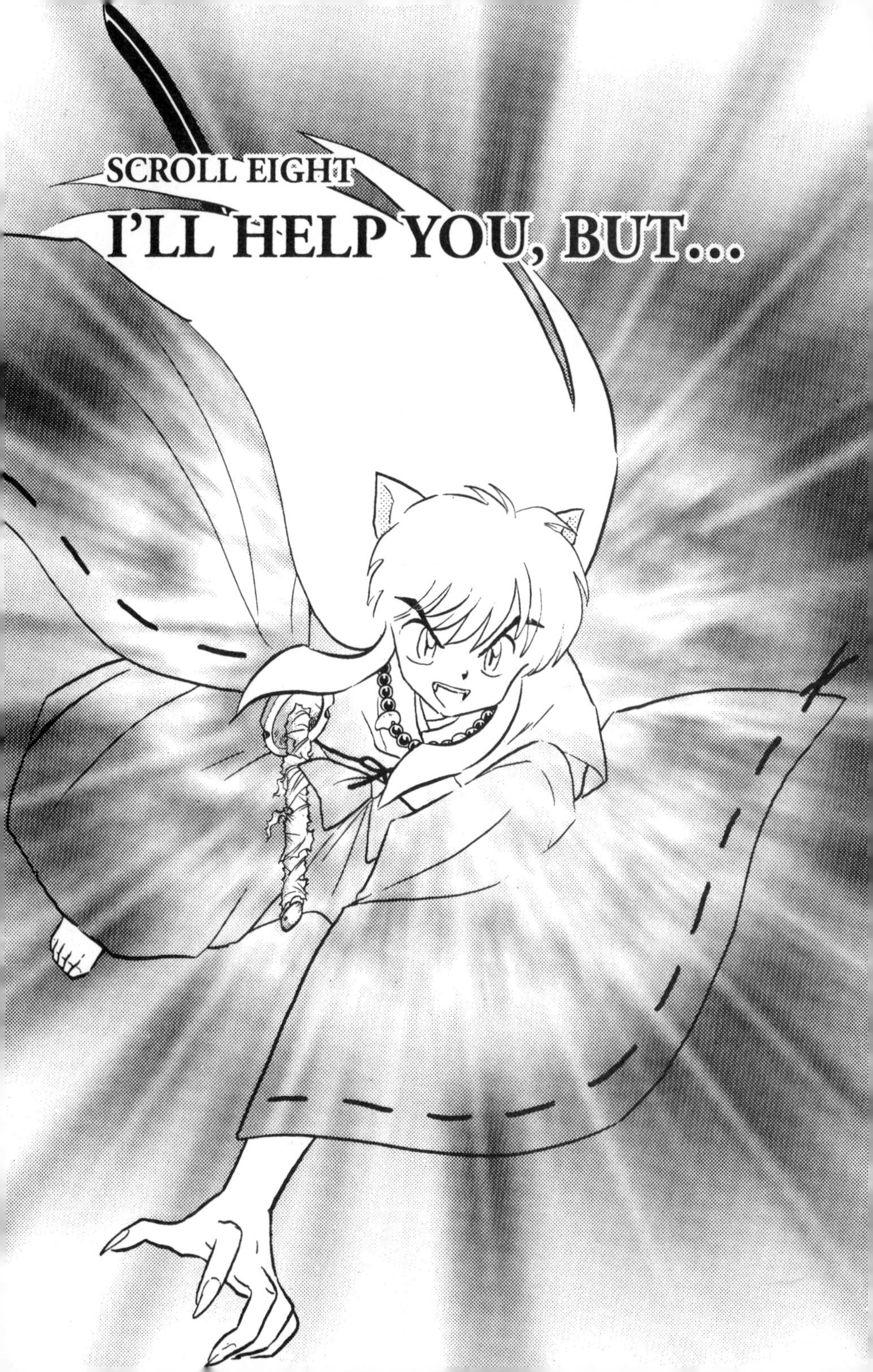
SCROLL EIGHT
I'LL HELP YOU, BUT...

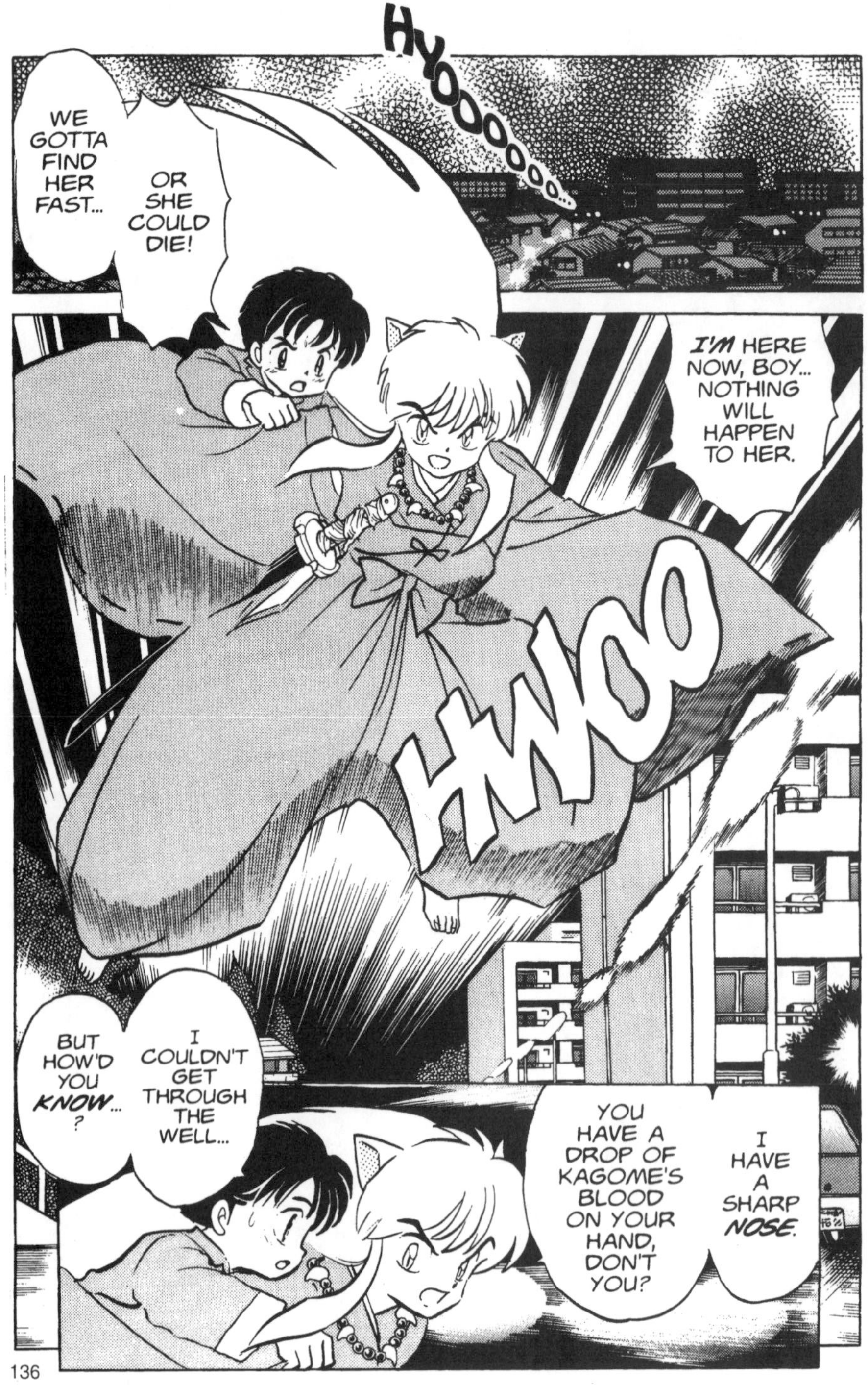
HYOOOOOOO...
WE GOTTA FIND HER FAST...
OR SHE COULD DIE!
I'M HERE NOW, BOY... NOTHING WILL HAPPEN TO HER.
HWOO
BUT HOW'D YOU KNOW...?
I COULDN'T GET THROUGH THE WELL...
YOU HAVE A DROP OF KAGOME'S BLOOD ON YOUR HAND, DON'T YOU?
I HAVE A SHARP NOSE.

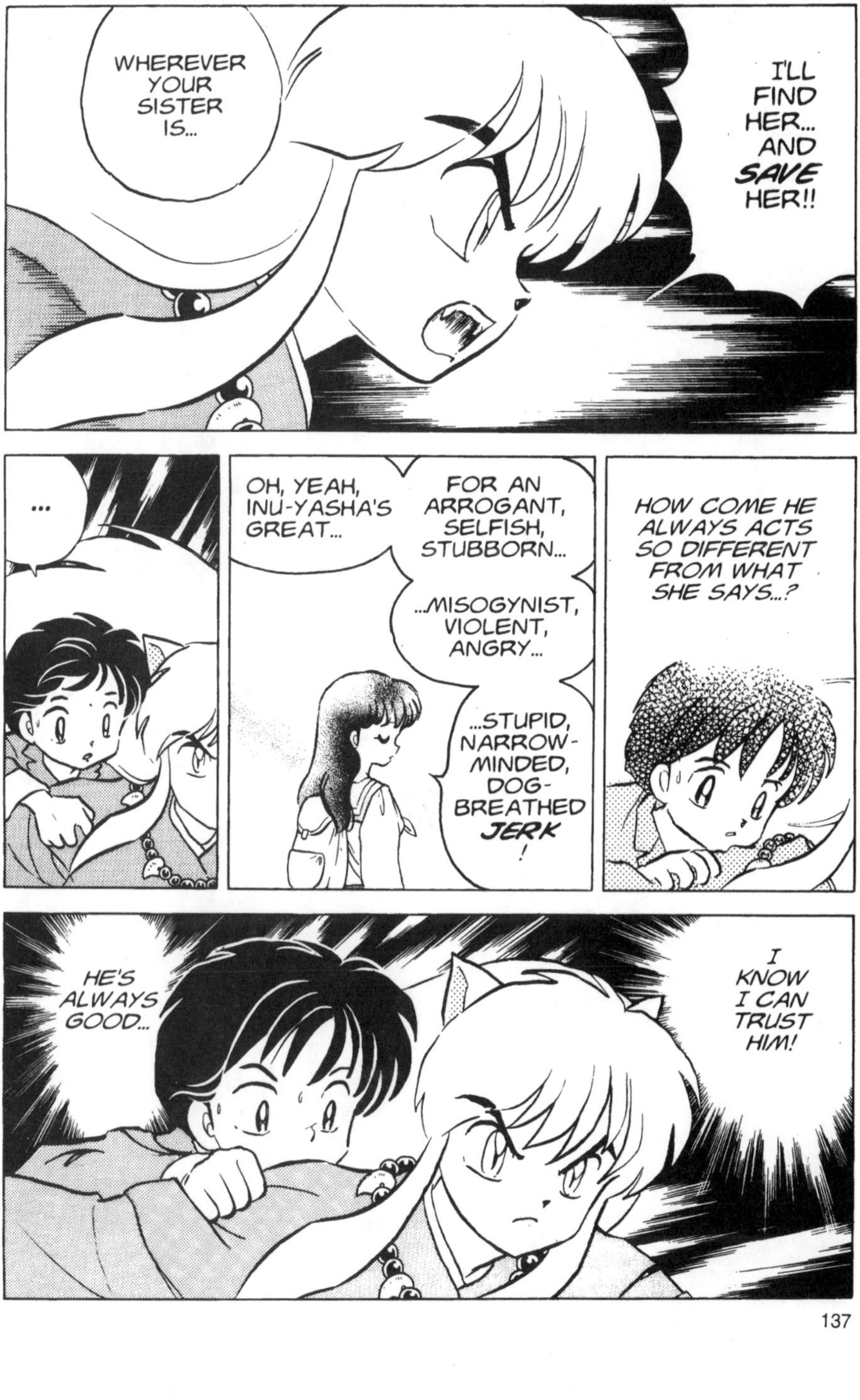
WHEREVER YOUR SISTER IS...
I'LL FIND HER... AND SAVE HER!!
...
OH, YEAH, INU-YASHA'S GREAT...
FOR AN ARROGANT, SELFISH, STUBBORN...
...MISOGYNIST, VIOLENT, ANGRY...
...STUPID, NARROW-MINDED, DOG-BREATHED JERK!
HOW COME HE ALWAYS ACTS SO DIFFERENT FROM WHAT SHE SAYS...?
HE'S ALWAYS GOOD...
I KNOW I CAN TRUST HIM!

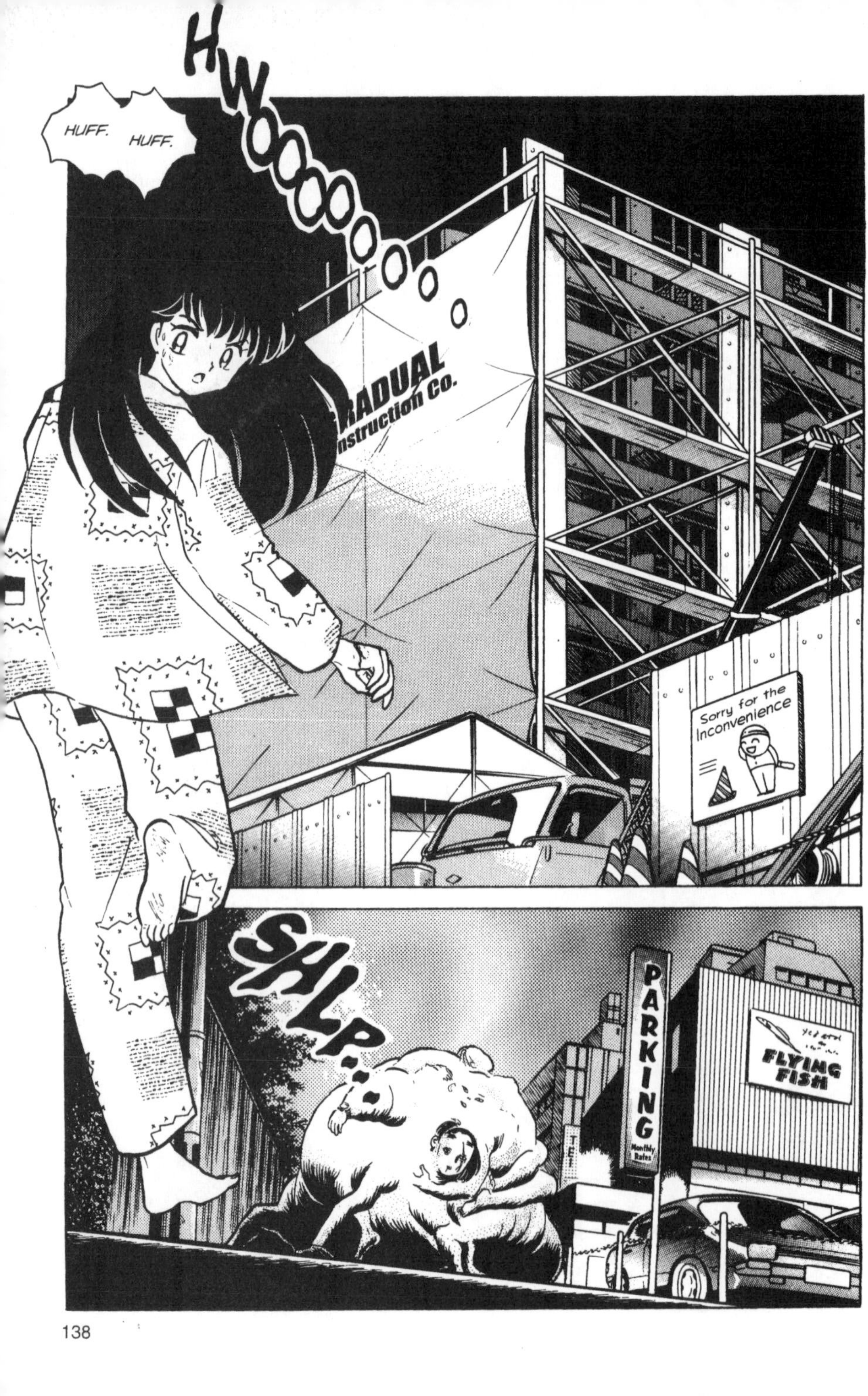
HUFF. HUFF.
HWOOOOOOOO
RADUAL
nstruction Co.
Sorry for the Inconvenience
SHLP...
PARKING
Monthly Rates
FLYING FISH

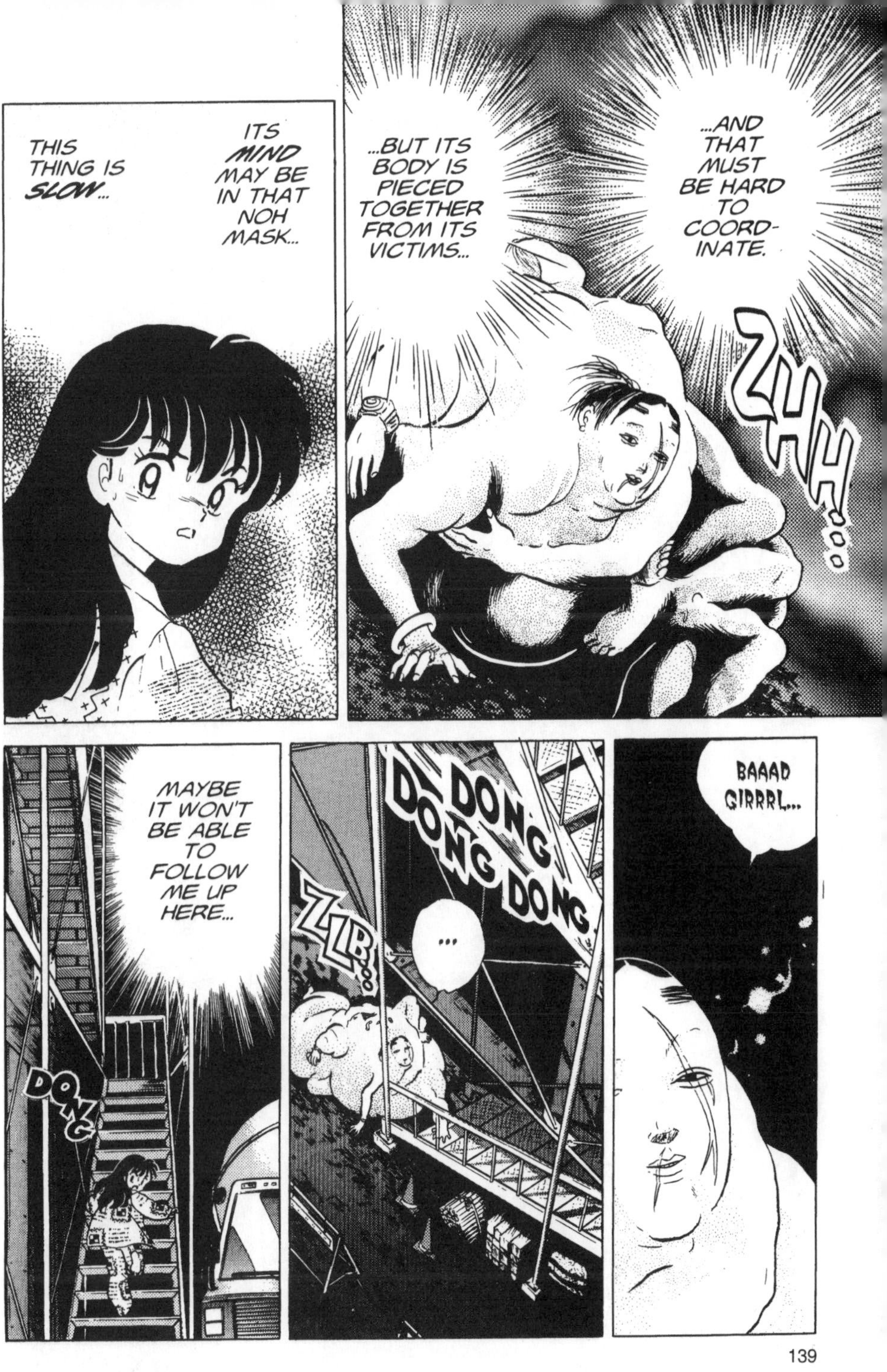
THIS THING IS SLOW...
ITS MIND MAY BE IN THAT NOH MASK...
...BUT ITS BODY IS PIECED TOGETHER FROM ITS VICTIMS...
...AND THAT MUST BE HARD TO COORD-INATE.
ZHH...
MAYBE IT WON'T BE ABLE TO FOLLOW ME UP HERE...
DONG
DONG DONG DONG DONG
ZLB...
...
BAAAD GIRRRL...

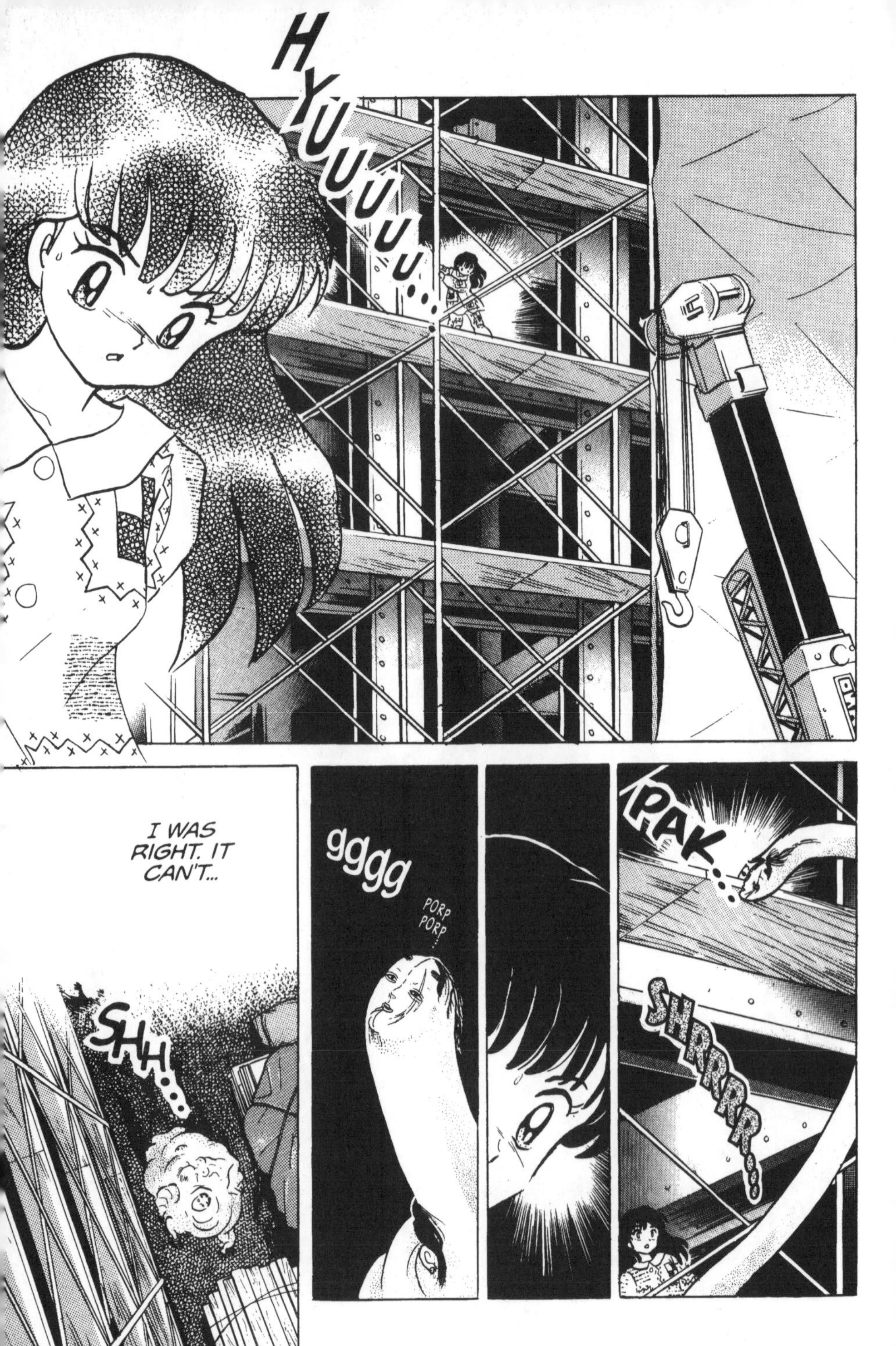
HYUUUUU...
I WAS RIGHT. IT CAN'T...
SHH...
gggg
PORP PORP
PAK...
SHRRRR...

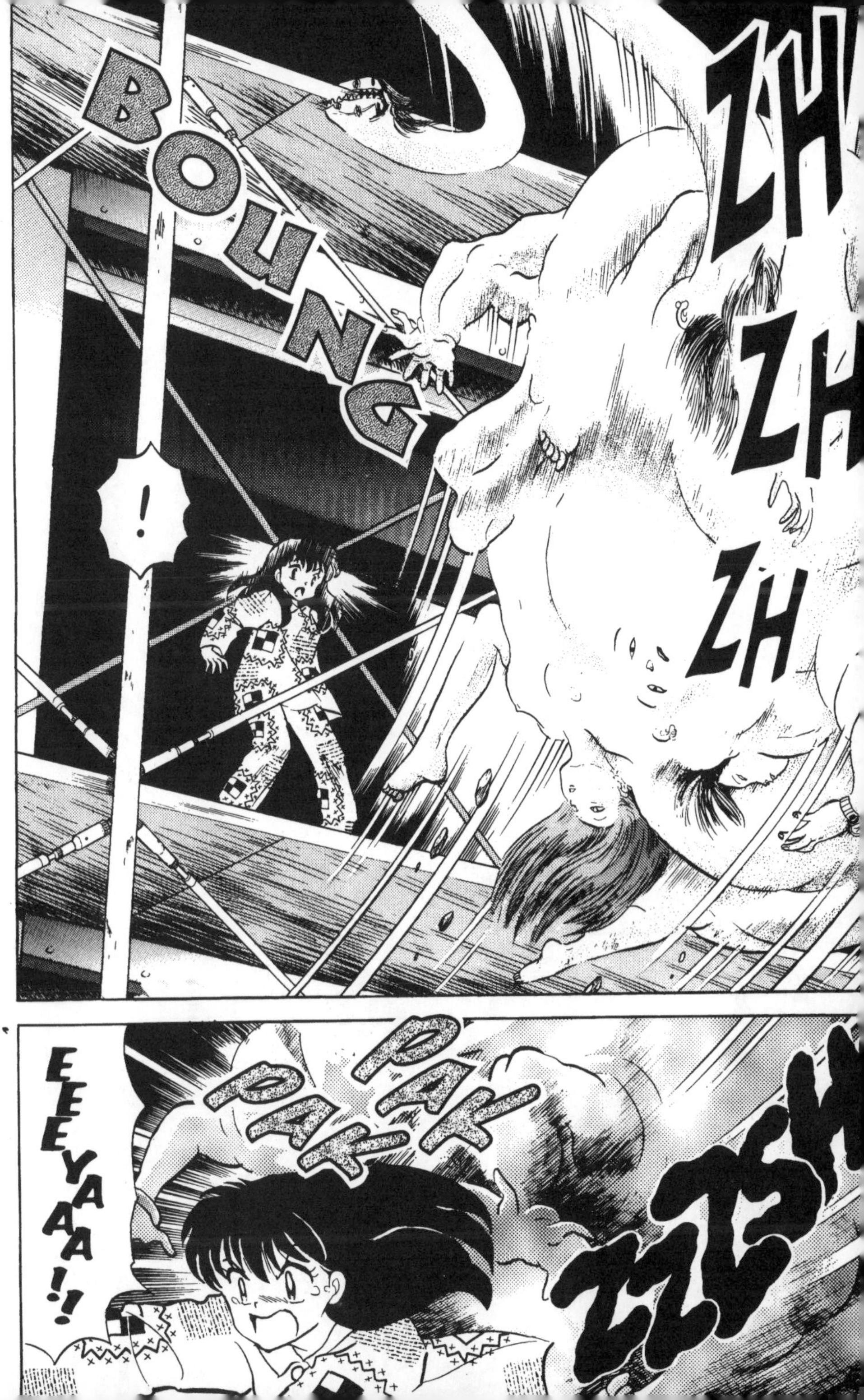
BOUNG
!
ZH
ZH
ZH
ZH
EEEEYAAAA!!
PAK
PAK
ZZZSH

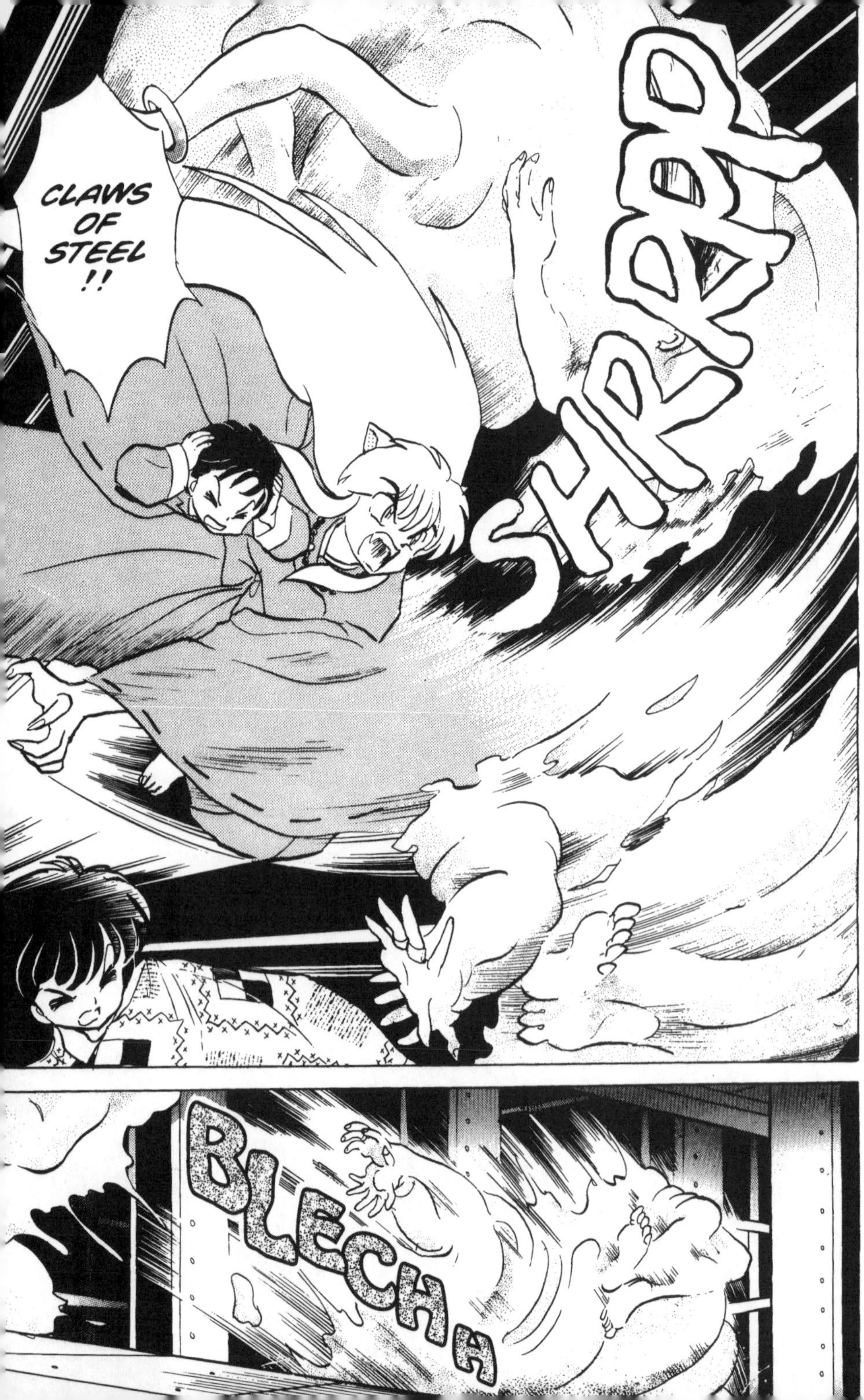
CLAWS OF STEEL !!
SHRRDD
BLECHA

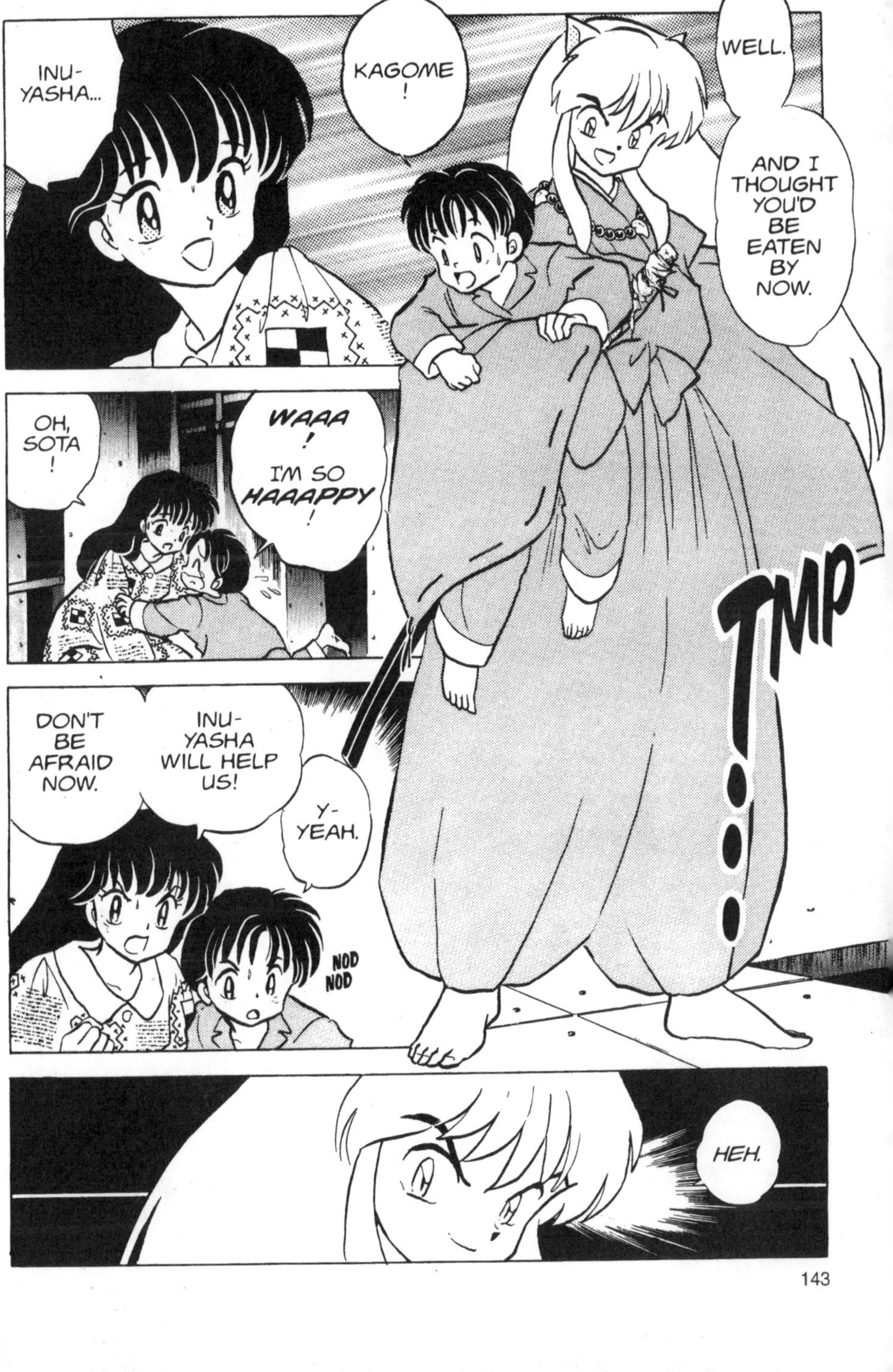
INU-YASHA...
KAGOME!
OH, SOTA!
WAAA! I'M SO HAAAPPY!
DON'T BE AFRAID NOW.
INU-YASHA WILL HELP US!
Y-YEAH.
NOD NOD
WELL.
AND I THOUGHT YOU'D BE EATEN BY NOW.
TMP...
HEH.

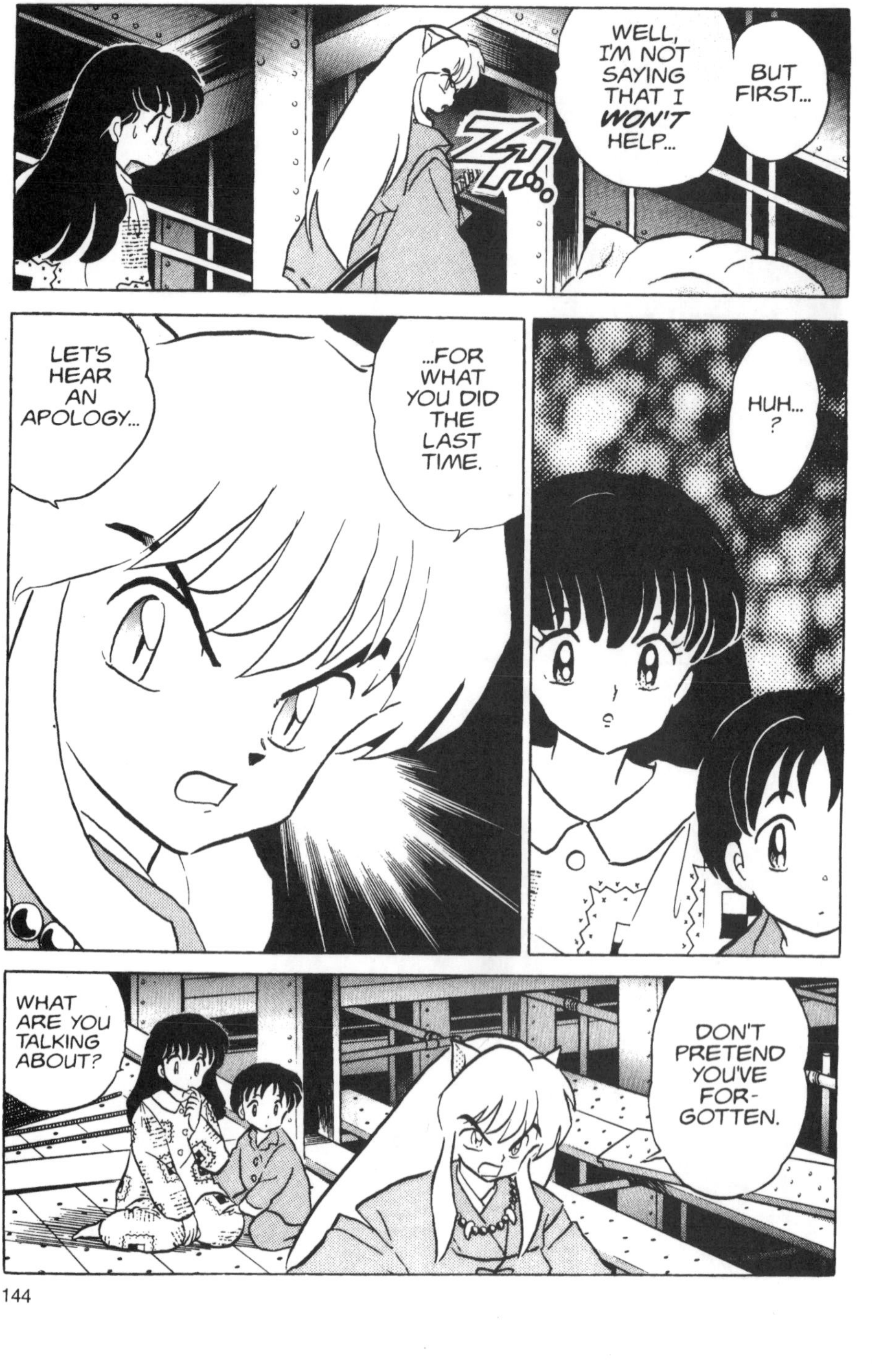
WELL, I'M NOT SAYING THAT I *WON'T* HELP...
ZH...
BUT FIRST...
LET'S HEAR AN APOLOGY...
...FOR WHAT YOU DID THE LAST TIME.
HUH...?
WHAT ARE YOU TALKING ABOUT?
DON'T PRETEND YOU'VE FOR-GOTTEN.

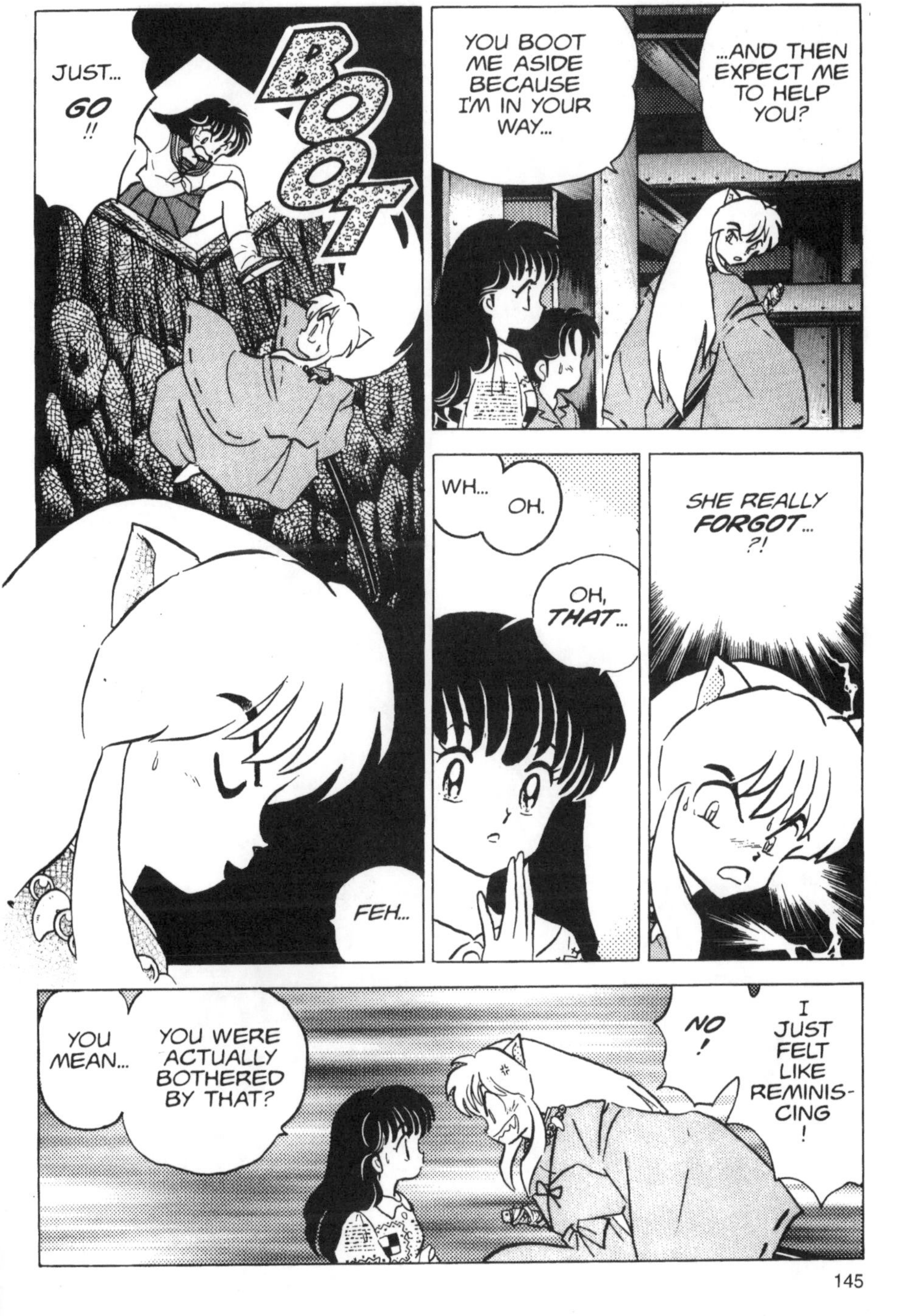
JUST... GO!!
BOOT
YOU BOOT ME ASIDE BECAUSE I'M IN YOUR WAY...
...AND THEN EXPECT ME TO HELP YOU?
WH... OH.
OH, THAT...
SHE REALLY FORGOT...?!
FEH...
YOU MEAN...
YOU WERE ACTUALLY BOTHERED BY THAT?
NO!
I JUST FELT LIKE REMINIS-CING!

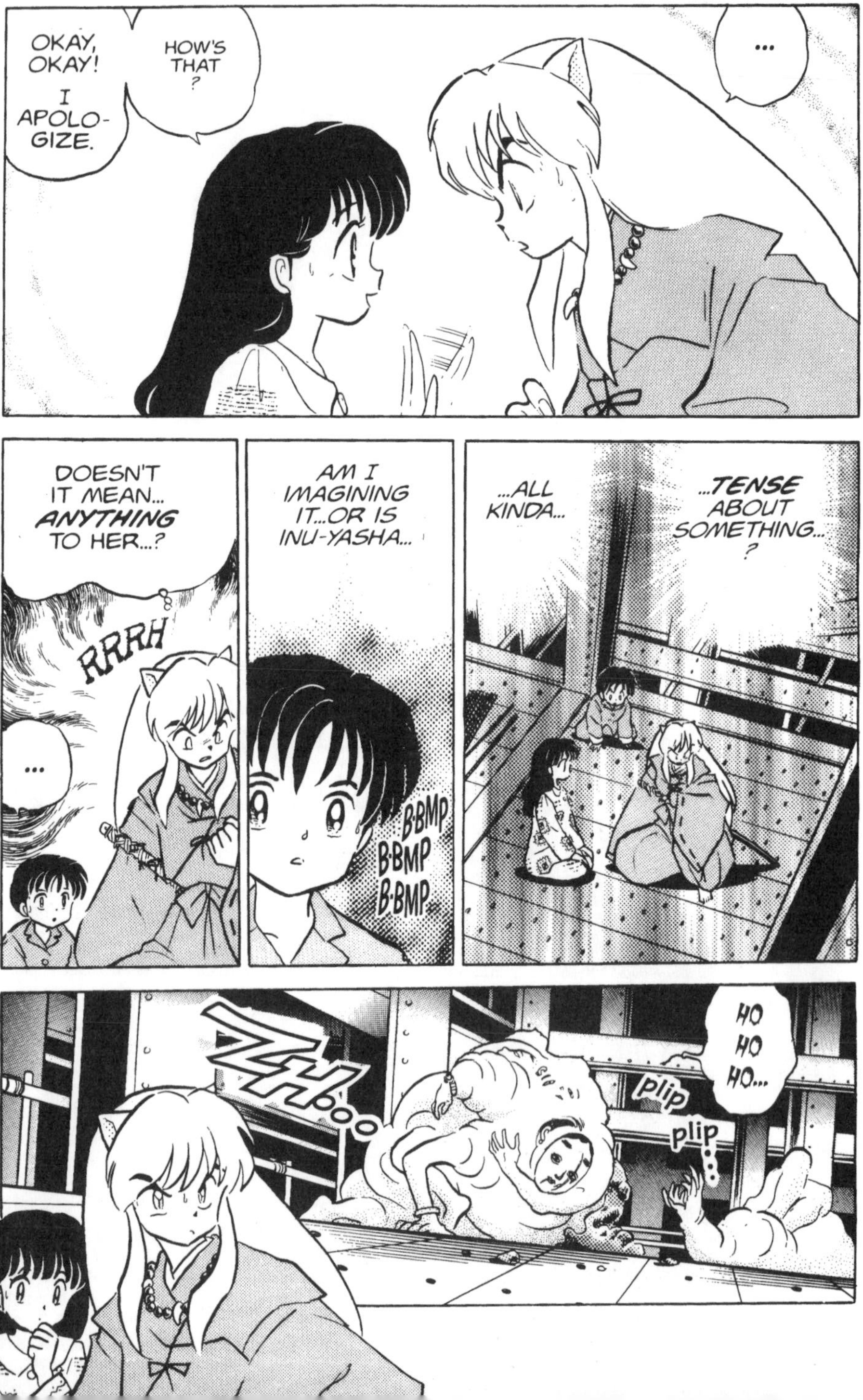
OKAY, OKAY! I APOLOGIZE.
HOW'S THAT?
...
DOESN'T IT MEAN... **ANYTHING** TO HER...?
RRRH
...
AM I IMAGINING IT...OR IS INU-YASHA...
B·BMP
B·BMP
B·BMP
...ALL KINDA...
...**TENSE** ABOUT SOMETHING...?
ZZH...
HO HO HO...
plip
plip...

YOU DAAARE...

...TO SPLIT MY PRETTY BODY...?

UGH.

AN UGLY ONE, AREN'T YOU?

WHAT KIND OF DEMON ARE YOU, EH?

ZHH

INU-YASHA!

ITS MIND IS IN THE NOH MASK...

AND IT HAS A SHARD OF THE SHIKON JEWEL IN ITS FORE-HEAD.

OH HO.

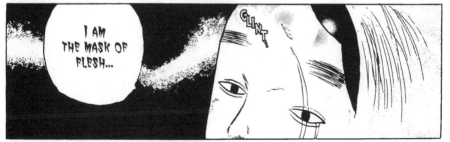

I AM THE MASK OF FLESH...

GLINT.

147

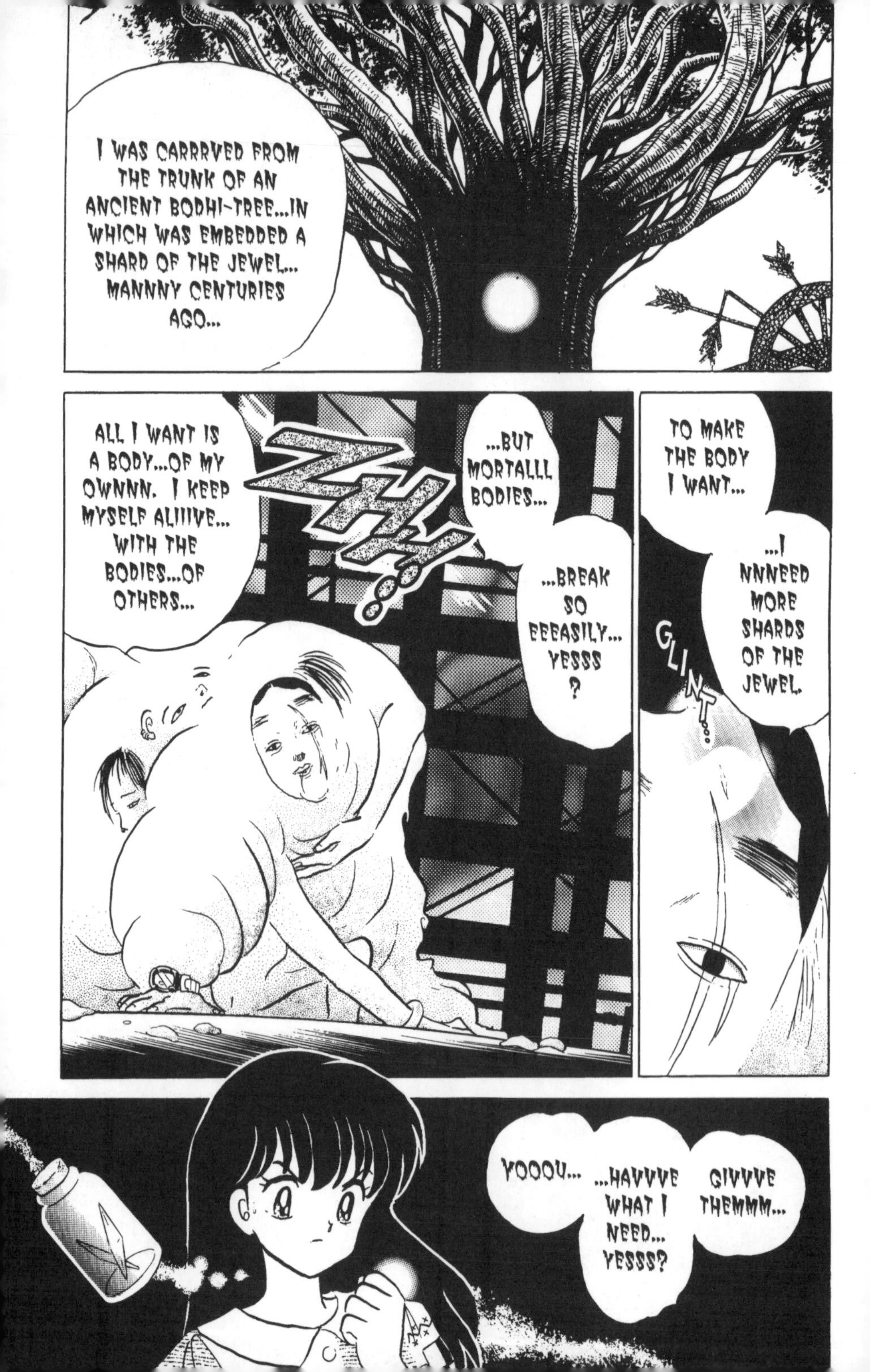

I WAS CARRRVED FROM THE TRUNK OF AN ANCIENT BODHI-TREE...IN WHICH WAS EMBEDDED A SHARD OF THE JEWEL... MANNNY CENTURIES AGO...
ALL I WANT IS A BODY...OF MY OWNNN. I KEEP MYSELF ALIIIVE... WITH THE BODIES...OF OTHERS...
ZZT..
...BUT MORTALLL BODIES...
...BREAK SO EEEASILY... YESSS ?
TO MAKE THE BODY I WANT...
...I NNNEED MORE SHARDS OF THE JEWEL.
GLINT..
YOOOU...
...HAVVVE WHAT I NEED... YESSS?
GIVVVE THEMMM...

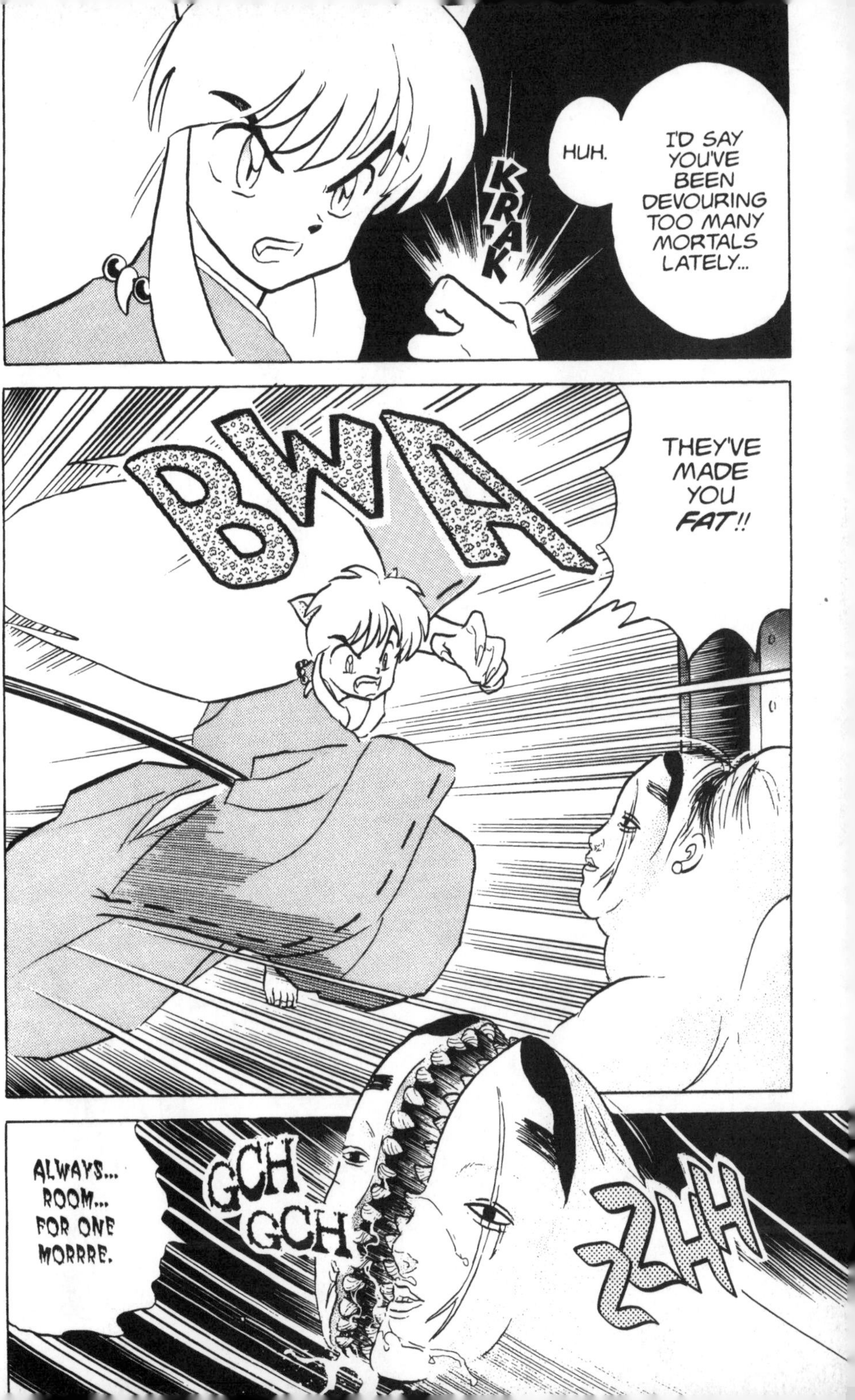
HUH.
I'D SAY YOU'VE BEEN DEVOURING TOO MANY MORTALS LATELY...
KRAK
BWA
THEY'VE MADE YOU FAT!!
ALWAYS... ROOM... FOR ONE MORRRE.
GCH GCH
ZHH

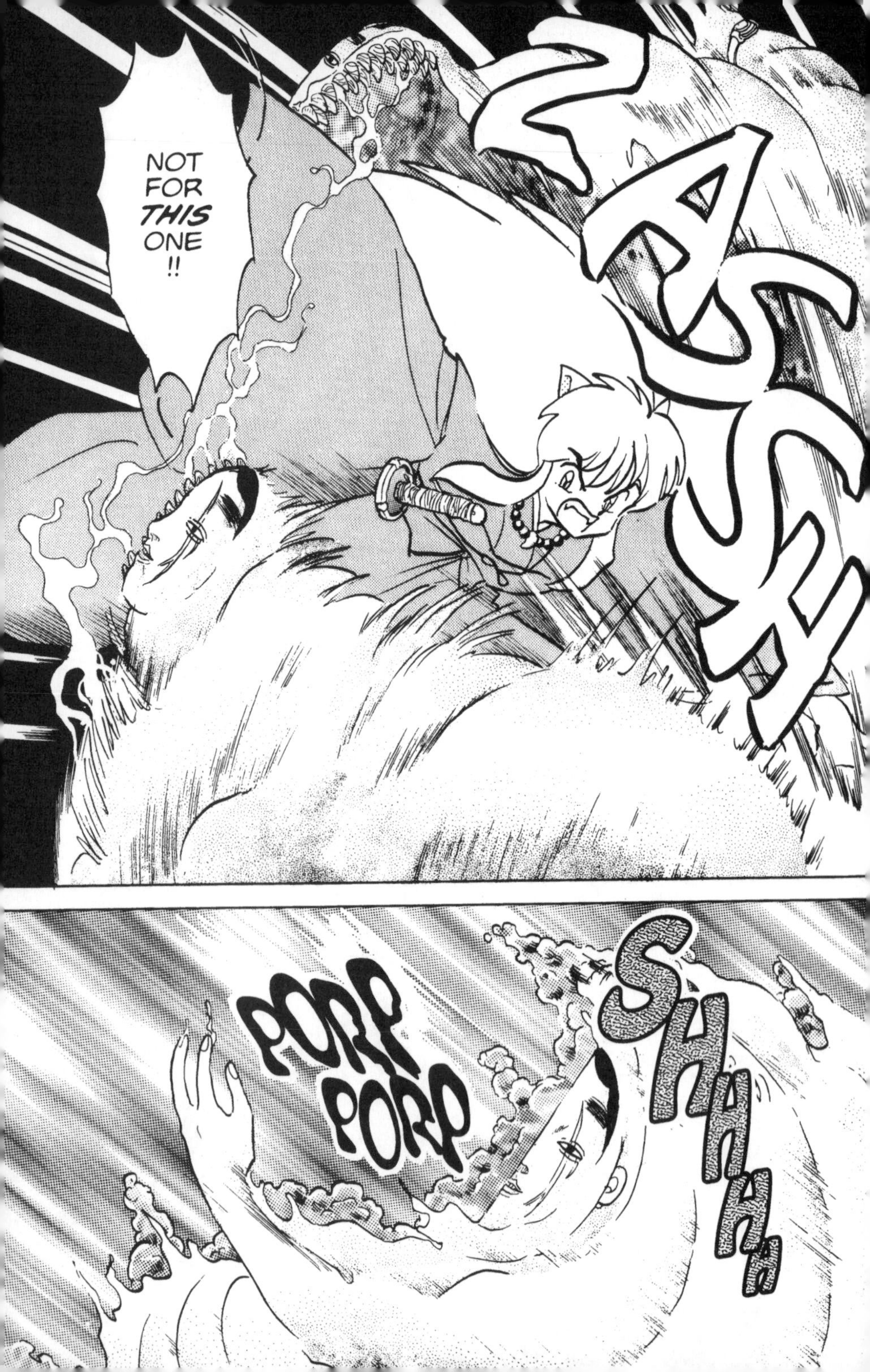
NOT FOR ***THIS*** ONE !!
ZASSH
POP POP
SHAAAA

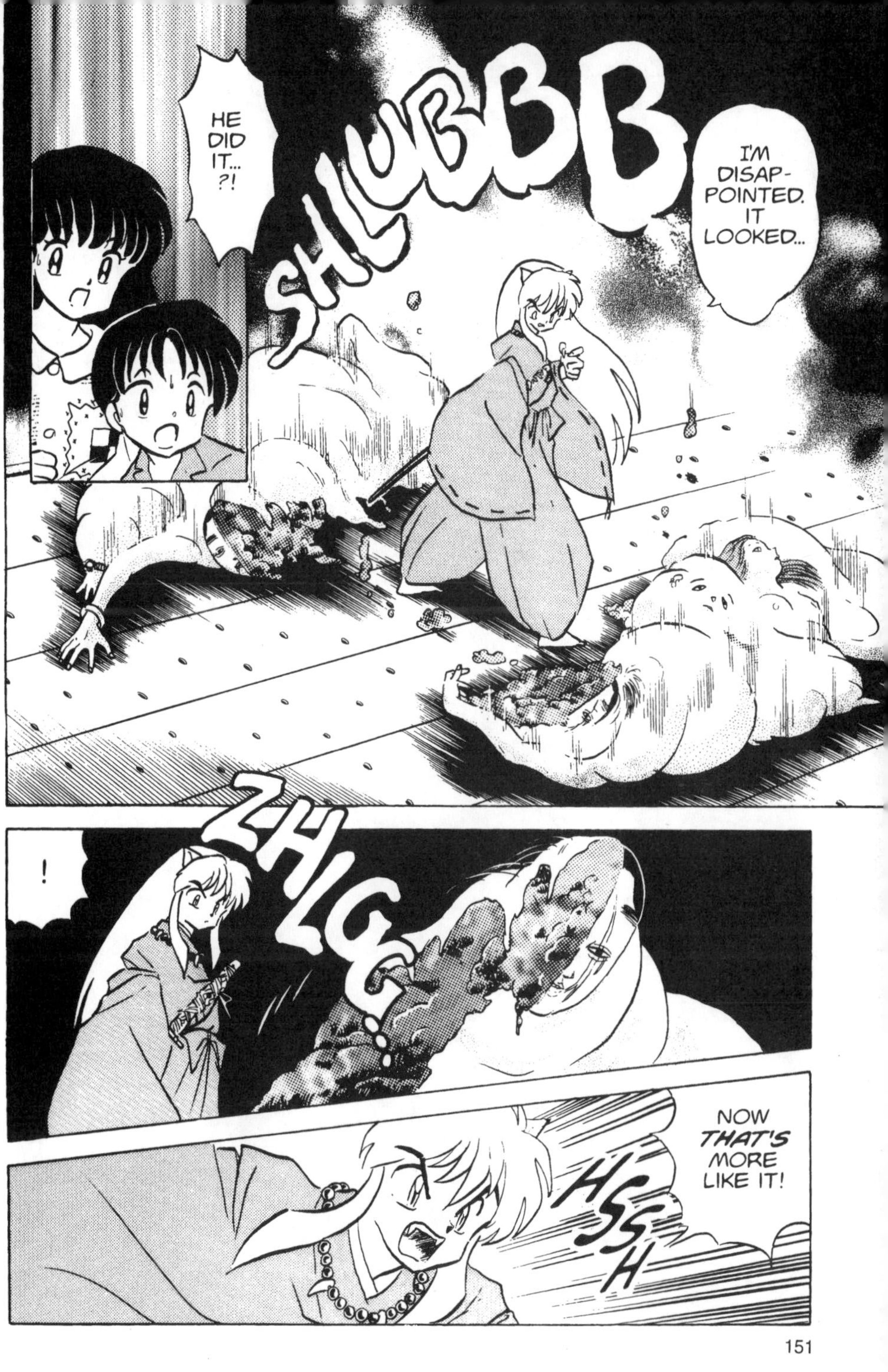
HE DID IT...?!
SHLUBBB
I'M DISAPPOINTED. IT LOOKED...
!
ZHLGG...
NOW *THAT'S* MORE LIKE IT!
HSSH

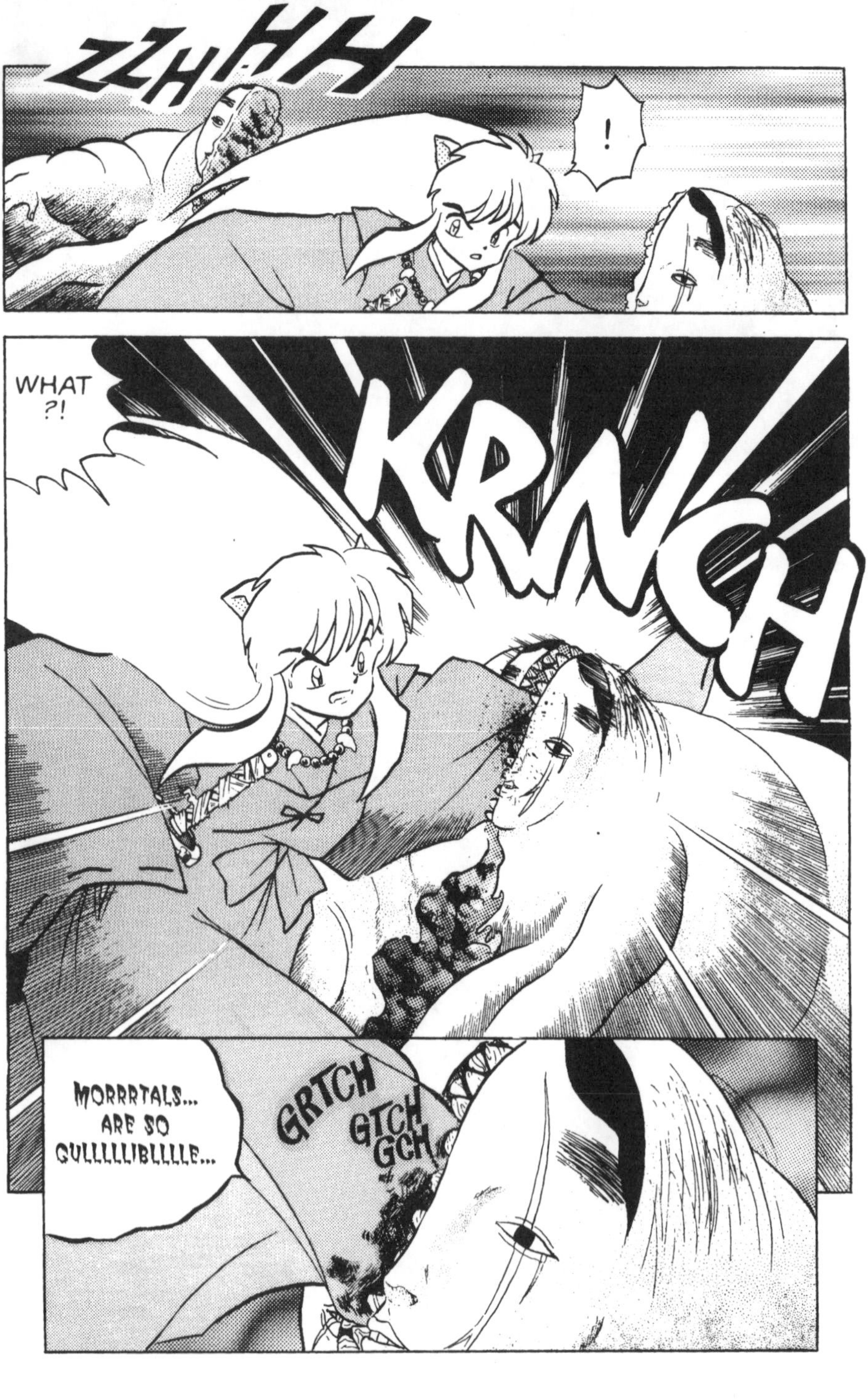
ZZHHH
!
WHAT ?!
KRNCH
MORRRTALS... ARE SO GULLLLLIBLLLLE...
GRTCH
GTCH GCH

SCROLL NINE

HALF A DEMON IS WORSE THAN ONE

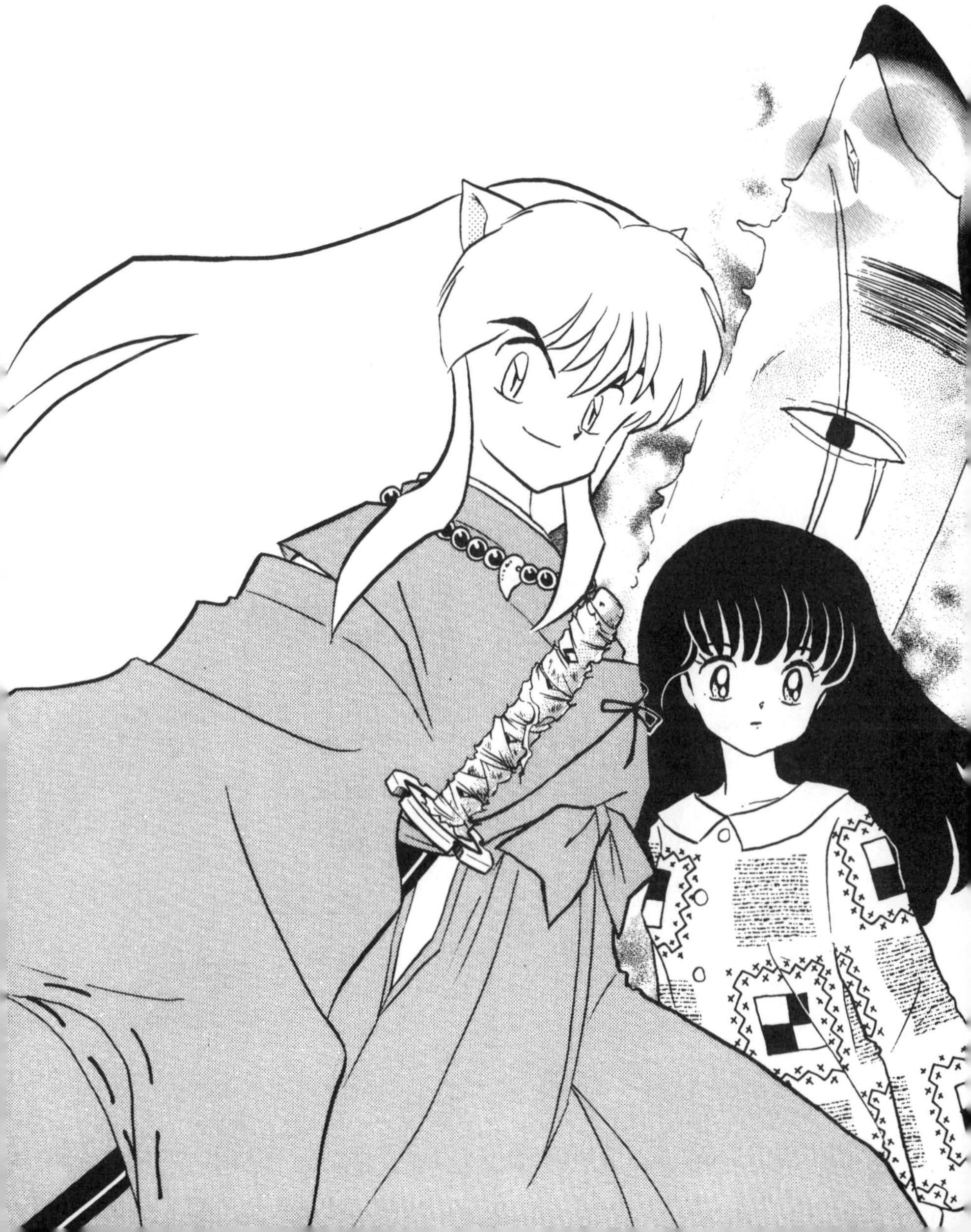

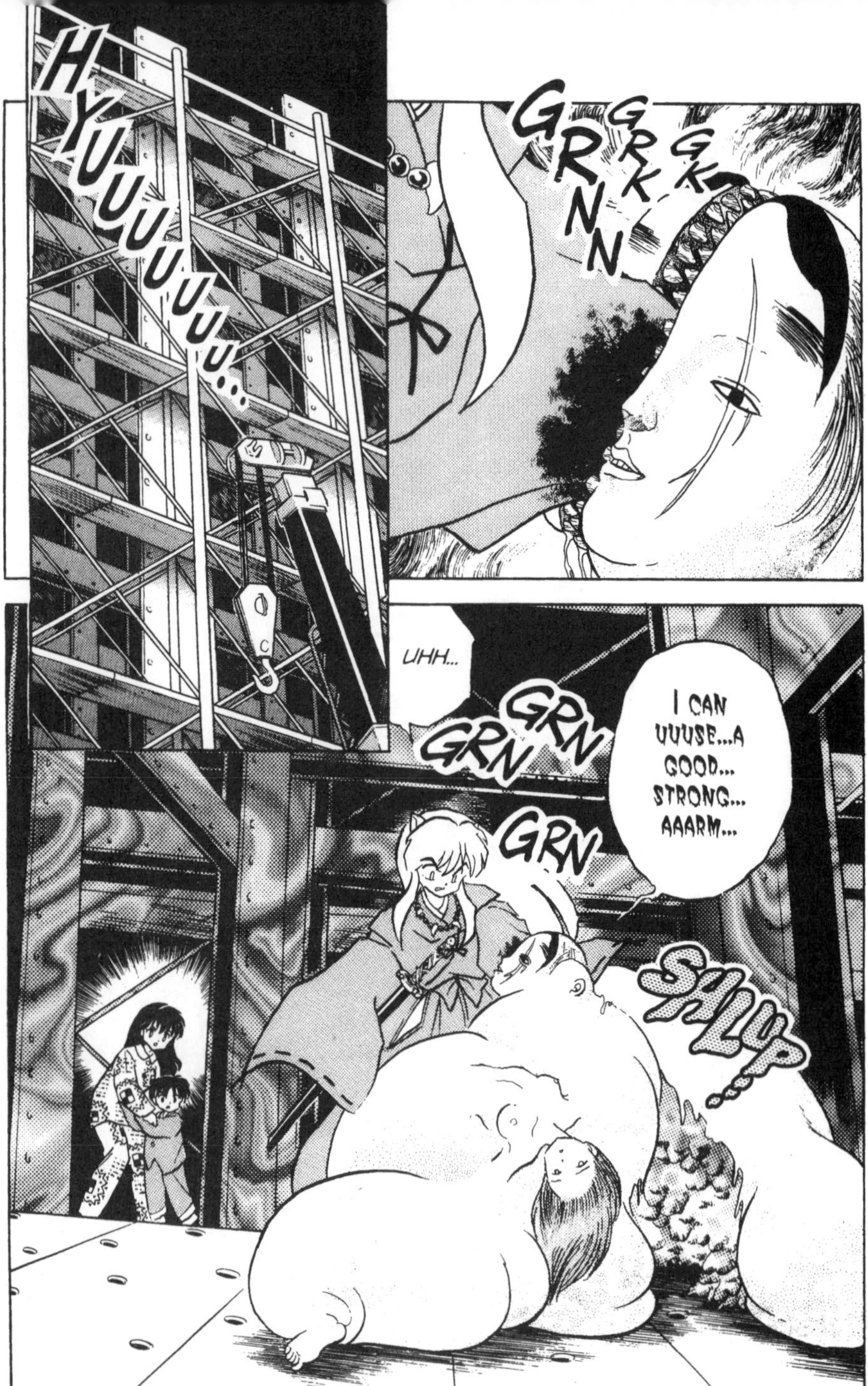
HYUUUUUUU...
GRNN
GRK
GK
UHH...
GRN
GRN
GRN
I CAN UUUSE...A GOOD... STRONG... AAARM...
SHLUP...

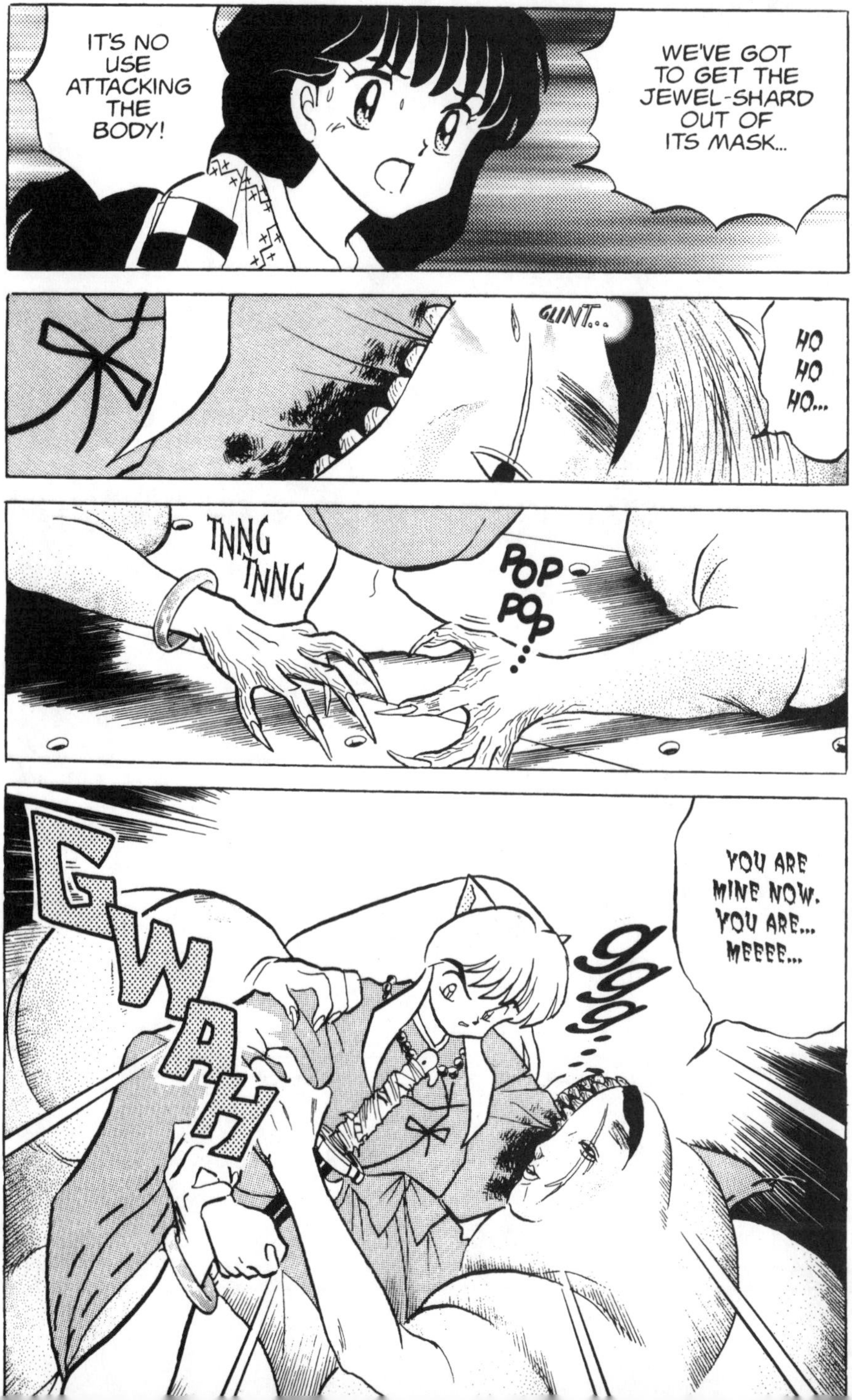
IT'S NO USE ATTACKING THE BODY!
WE'VE GOT TO GET THE JEWEL-SHARD OUT OF ITS MASK...
GLINT...
HO HO HO...
TNNG TNNG
POP POP...
GWAH
YOU ARE MINE NOW. YOU ARE... MEEEE...
ggg...

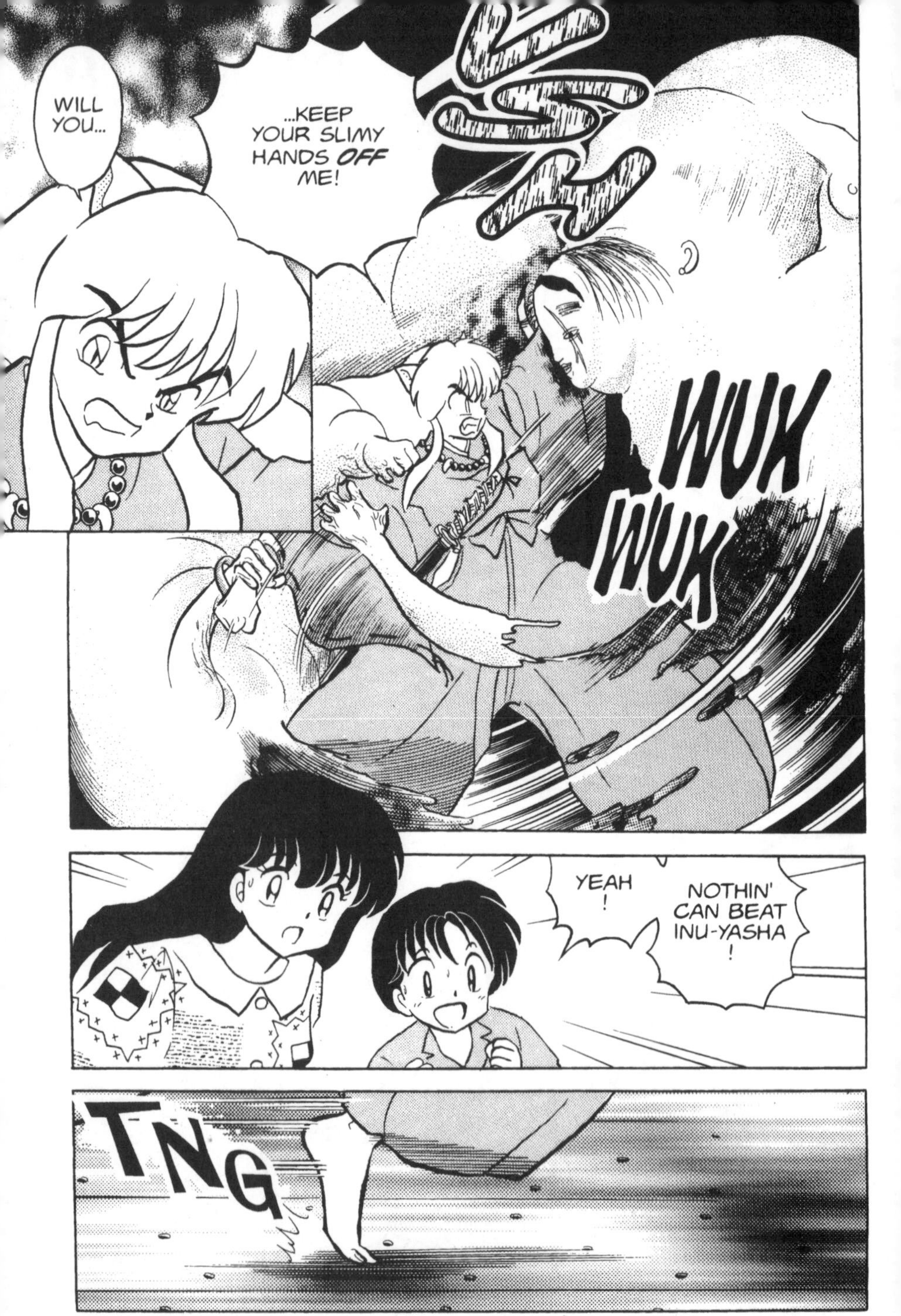
WILL YOU...
...KEEP YOUR SLIMY HANDS OFF ME!
WUX WUX
YEAH!
NOTHIN' CAN BEAT INU-YASHA!
TNG

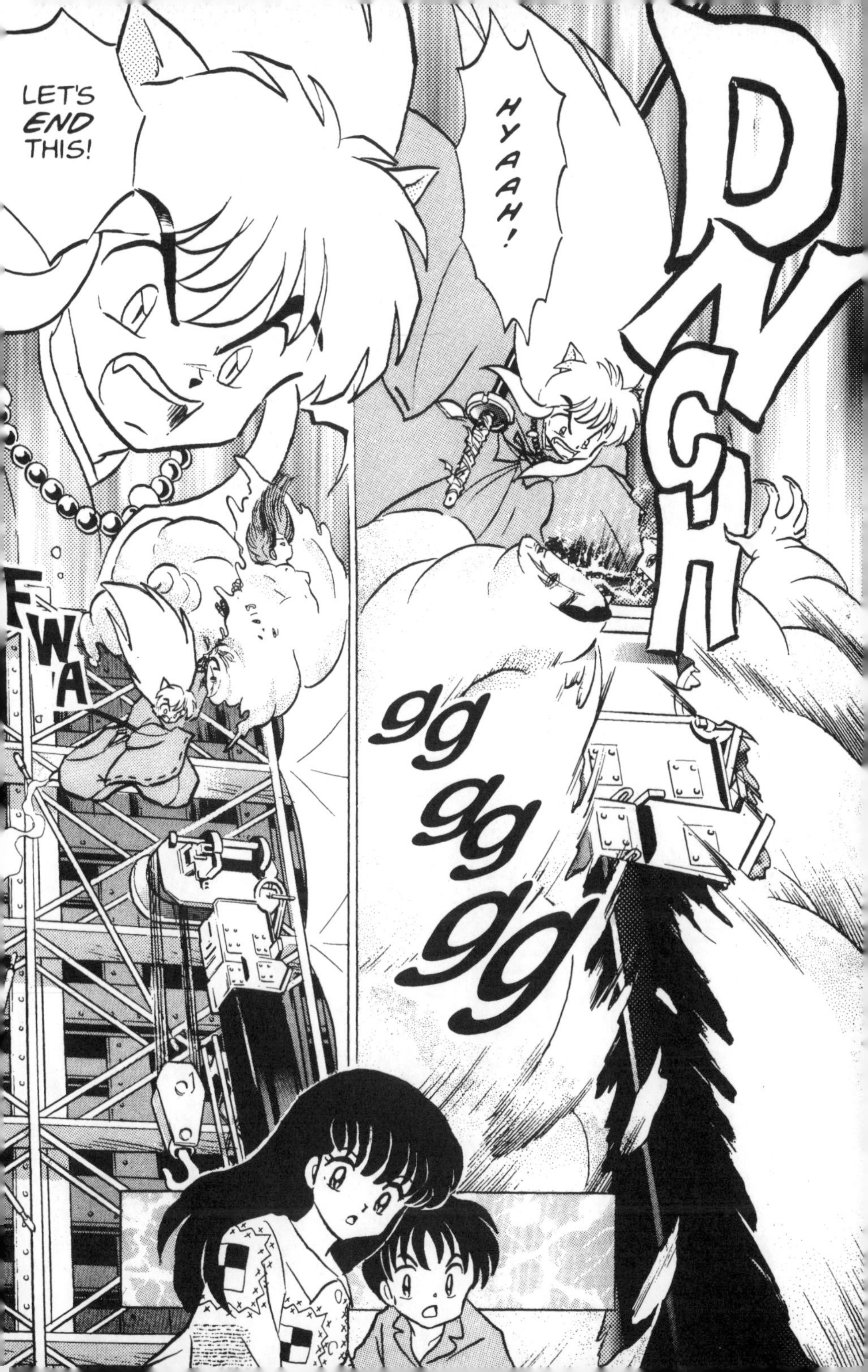

LET'S *END* THIS!
HYAAAH!
DNGNH
FWA
gg gg gg gg

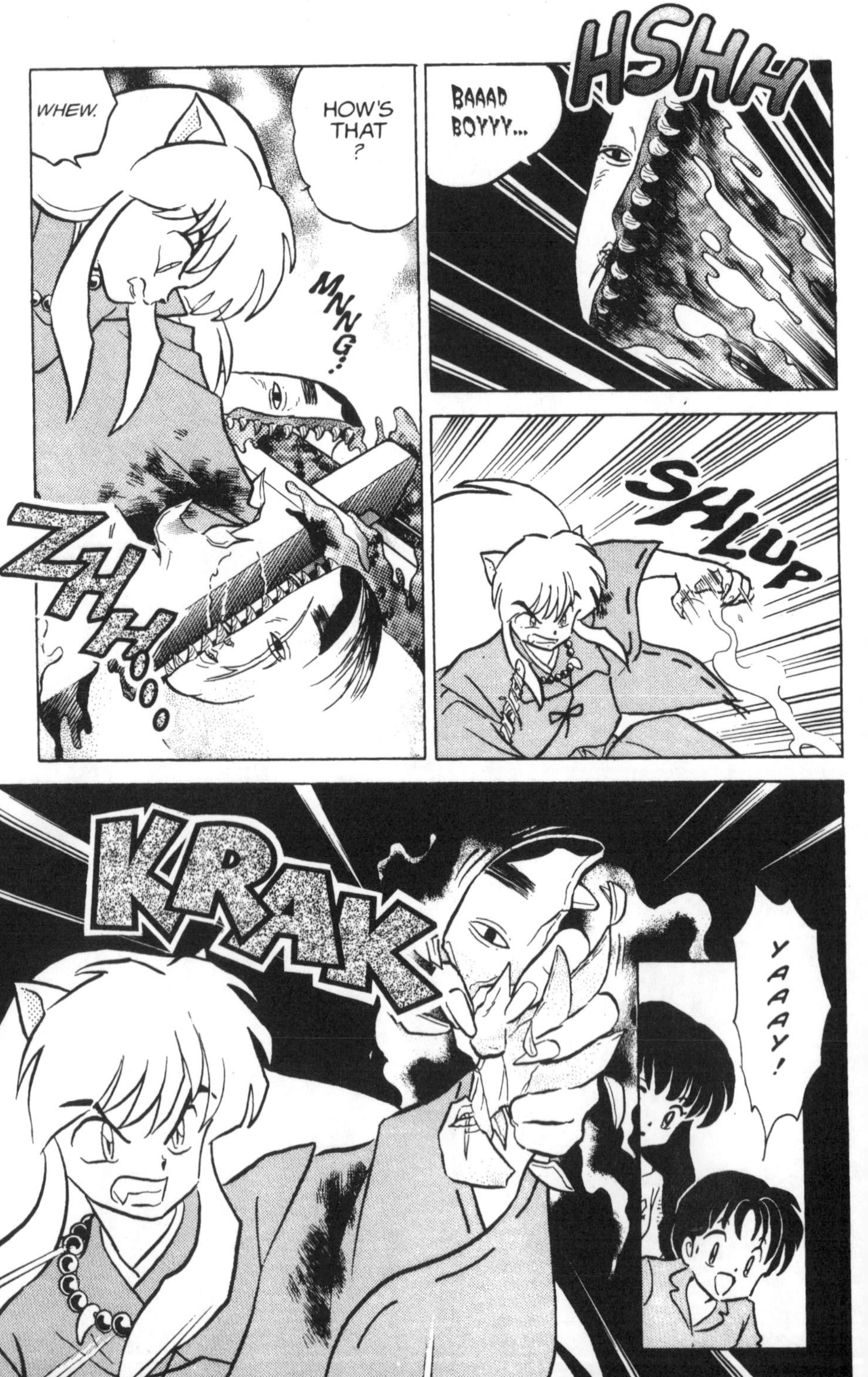
WHEW.
HOW'S THAT?
MNNG...
ZHH...
BAAAD BOYYY...
HSHH
SHLUP
KRAK
YAAAY!

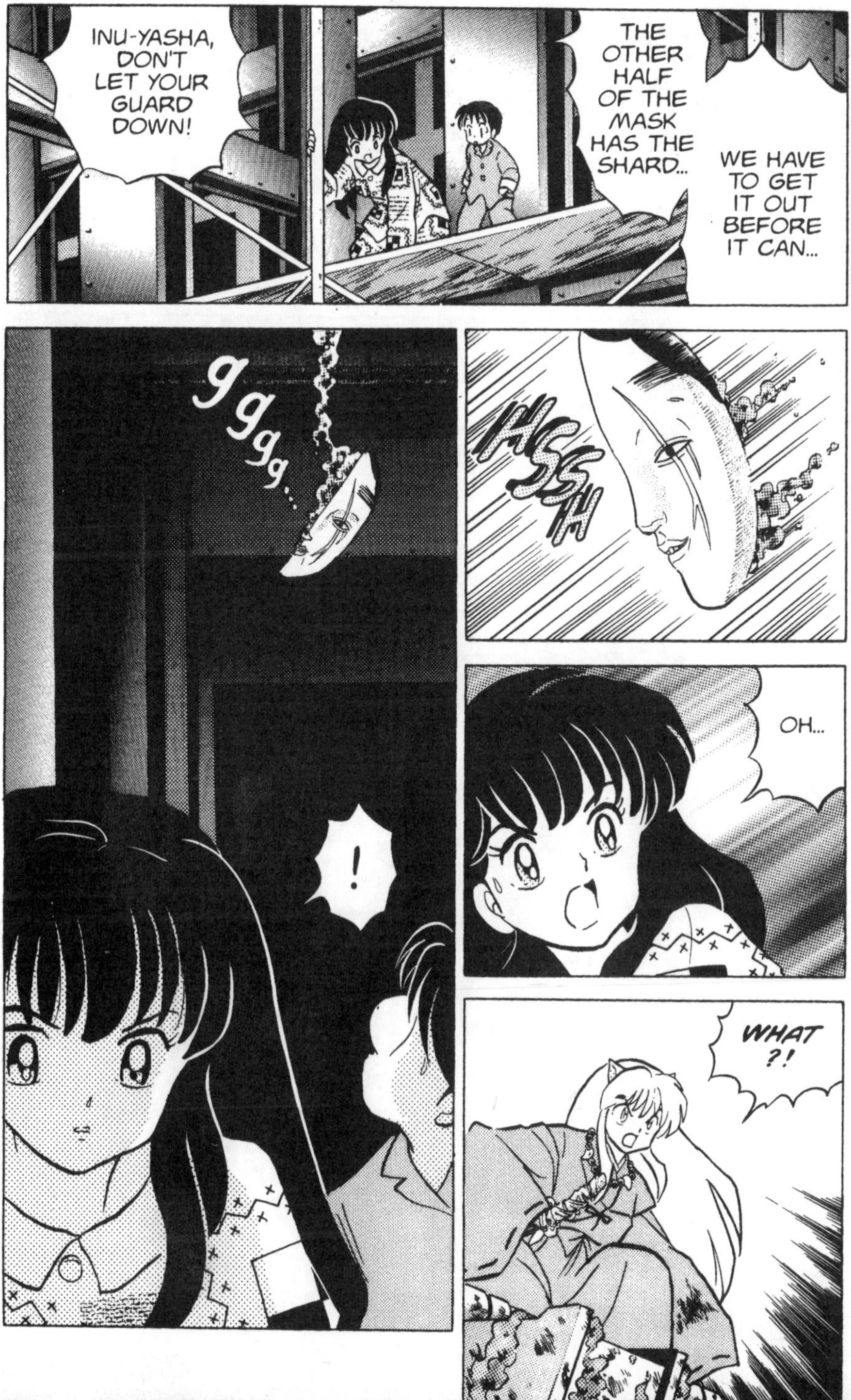
INU-YASHA, DON'T LET YOUR GUARD DOWN!
THE OTHER HALF OF THE MASK HAS THE SHARD...
WE HAVE TO GET IT OUT BEFORE IT CAN...
gggg...
!
HISSSH
OH...
WHAT?!

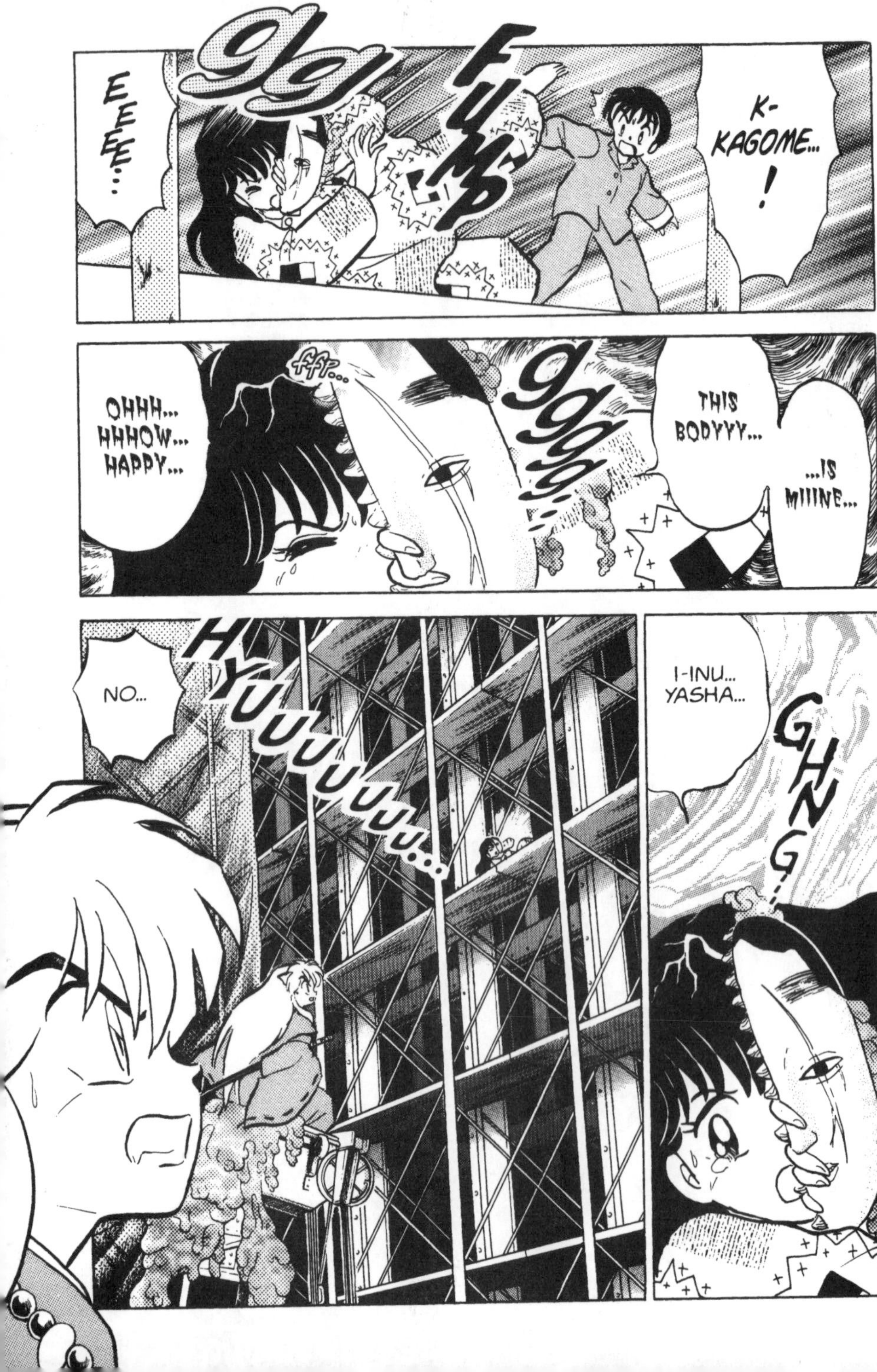
EEEEE...
FUMP
K-KAGOME... !
OHHH... HHHOW... HAPPY...
ffp...
gggg...
THIS BODYYY...
...IS MIIINE...
NO...
HYUUUUUUUU...
I-INU... YASHA...
GHNG...

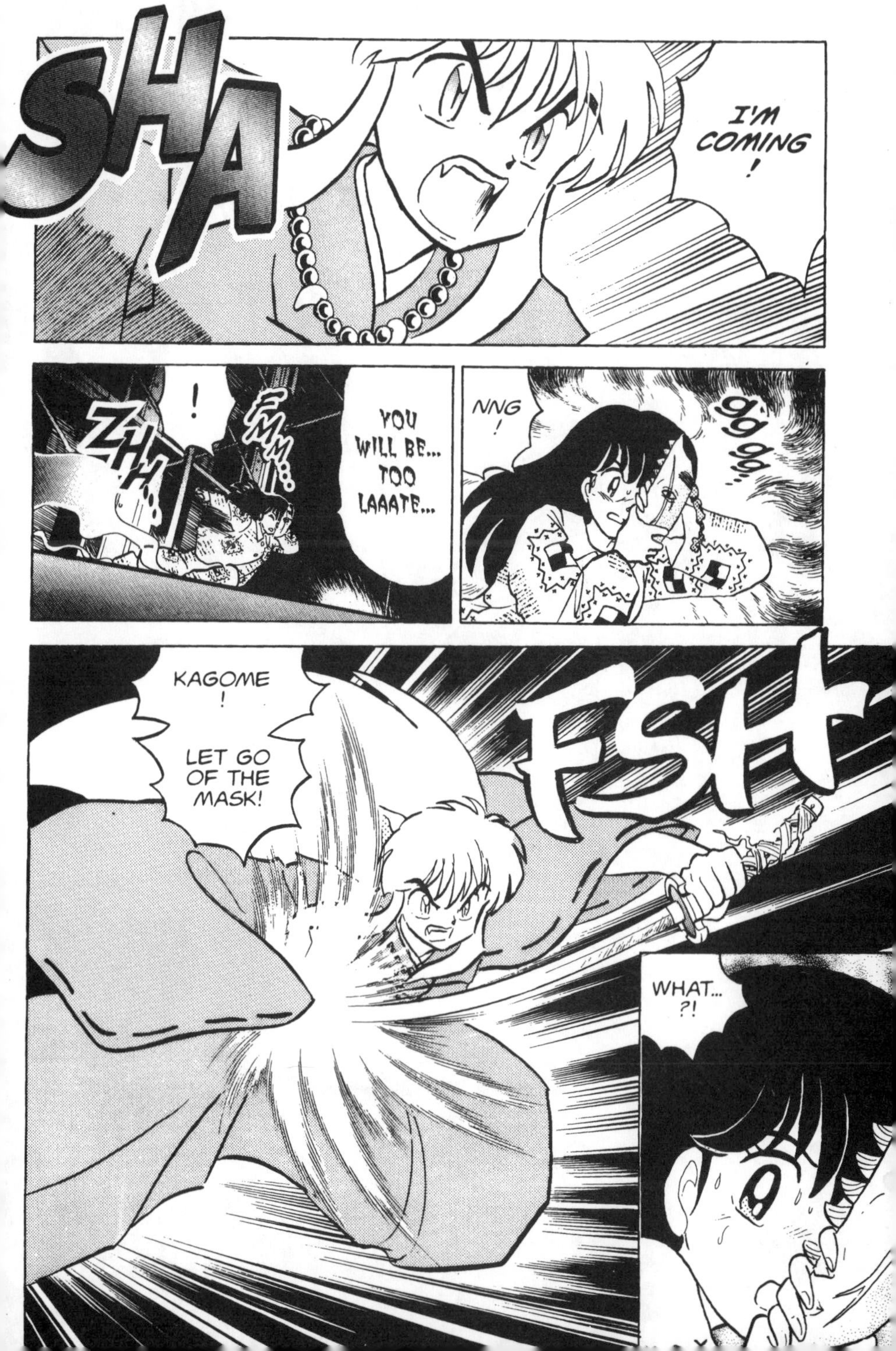
SHA
I'M COMING !
ZHH
!
FMM...
YOU WILL BE... TOO LAAATE...
NNG !
gg gg...
KAGOME !
LET GO OF THE MASK!
FSH
WHAT... ?!

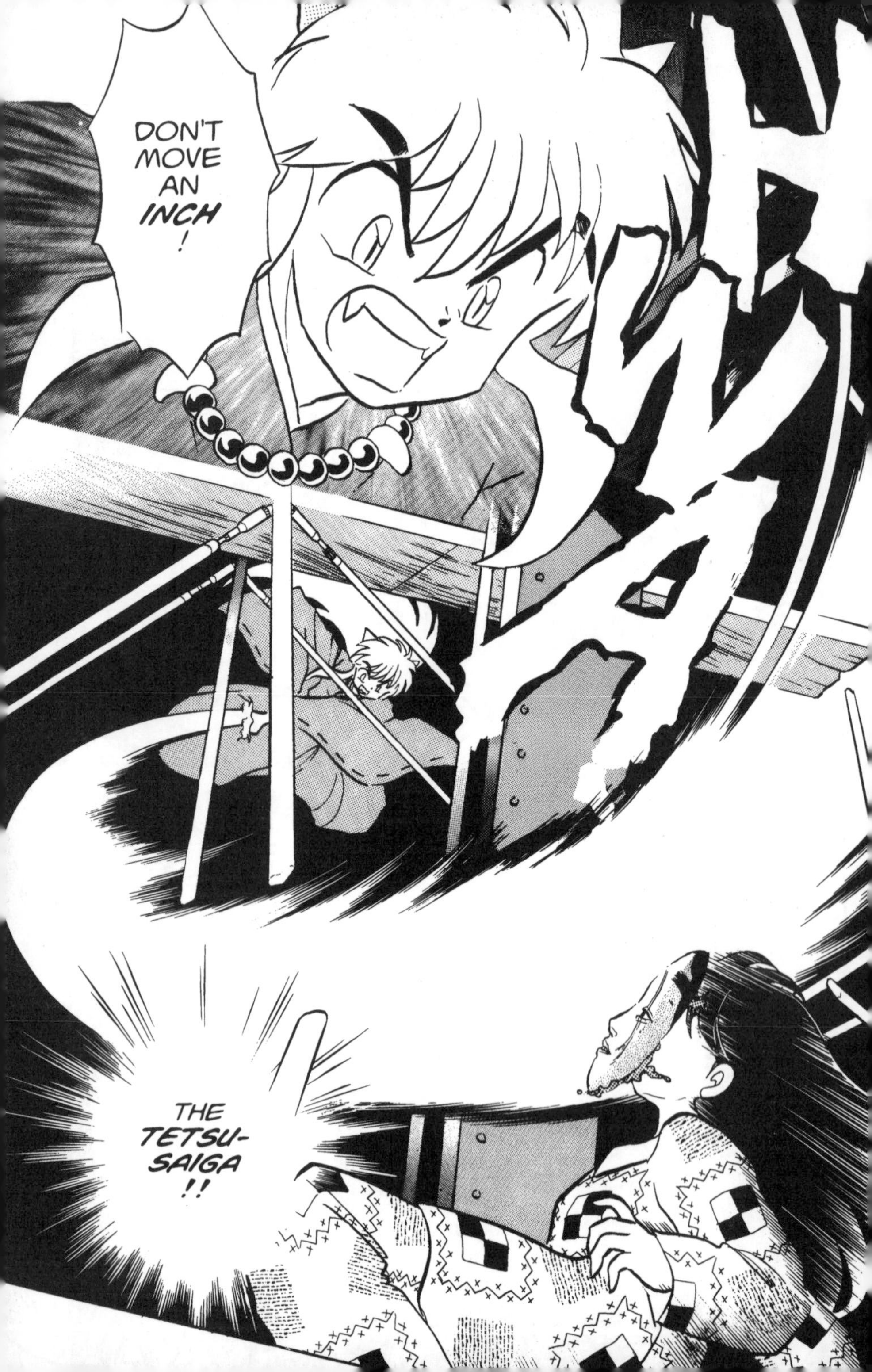
DON'T MOVE AN INCH!
THE TETSU-SAIGA!!

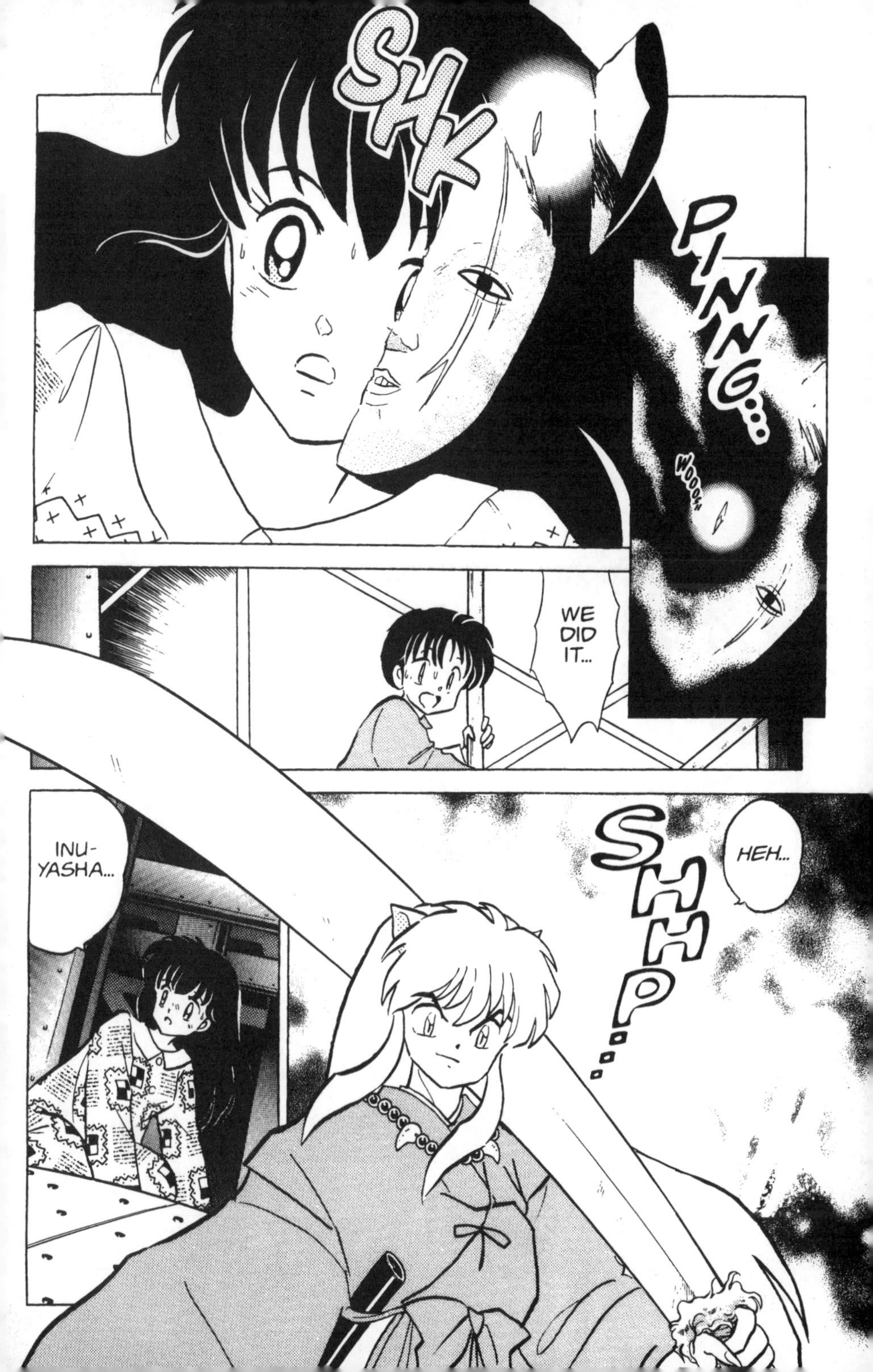
SHK
PINNG...
WOOOSH
WE DID IT...
INU-YASHA...
SHHP...
HEH...

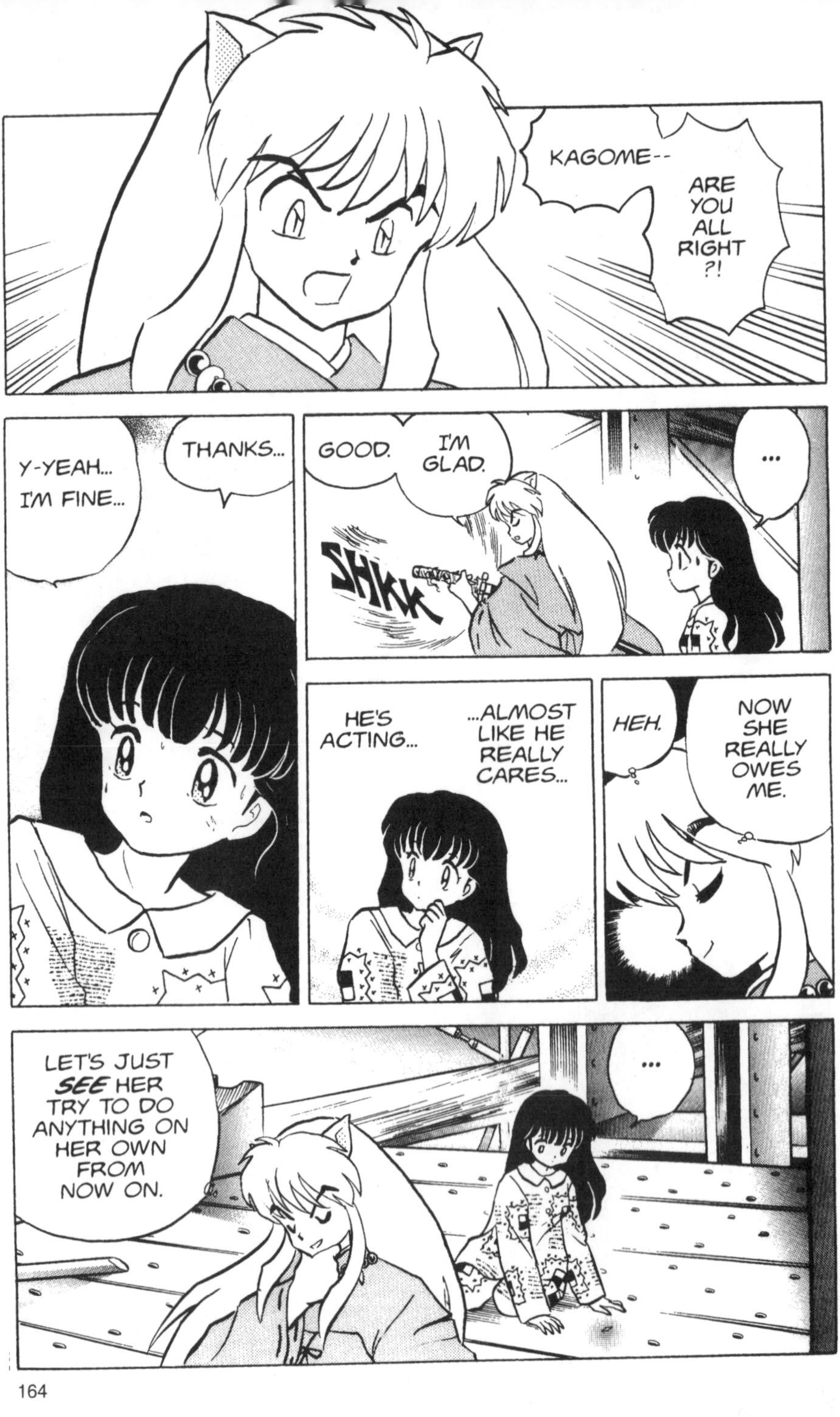
KAGOME--
ARE YOU ALL RIGHT ?!
Y-YEAH... I'M FINE...
THANKS...
GOOD.
I'M GLAD.
SHKK
...
HE'S ACTING...
...ALMOST LIKE HE REALLY CARES...
HEH.
NOW SHE REALLY OWES ME.
LET'S JUST *SEE* HER TRY TO DO ANYTHING ON HER OWN FROM NOW ON.
...

THE MASK...

IT SAID IT SURVIVED FOR CENTURIES...

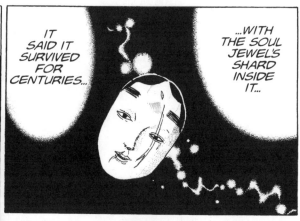

...WITH THE SOUL JEWEL'S SHARD INSIDE IT...

WHICH MEANS...

...OTHER SHARDS COULD HAVE SURVIVED TO THE PRESENT, TOO...

twee...

WHAT...?

MORNING...?

AAAA!!

gasp

MY MATH EXAM!!

BRRR

RRR

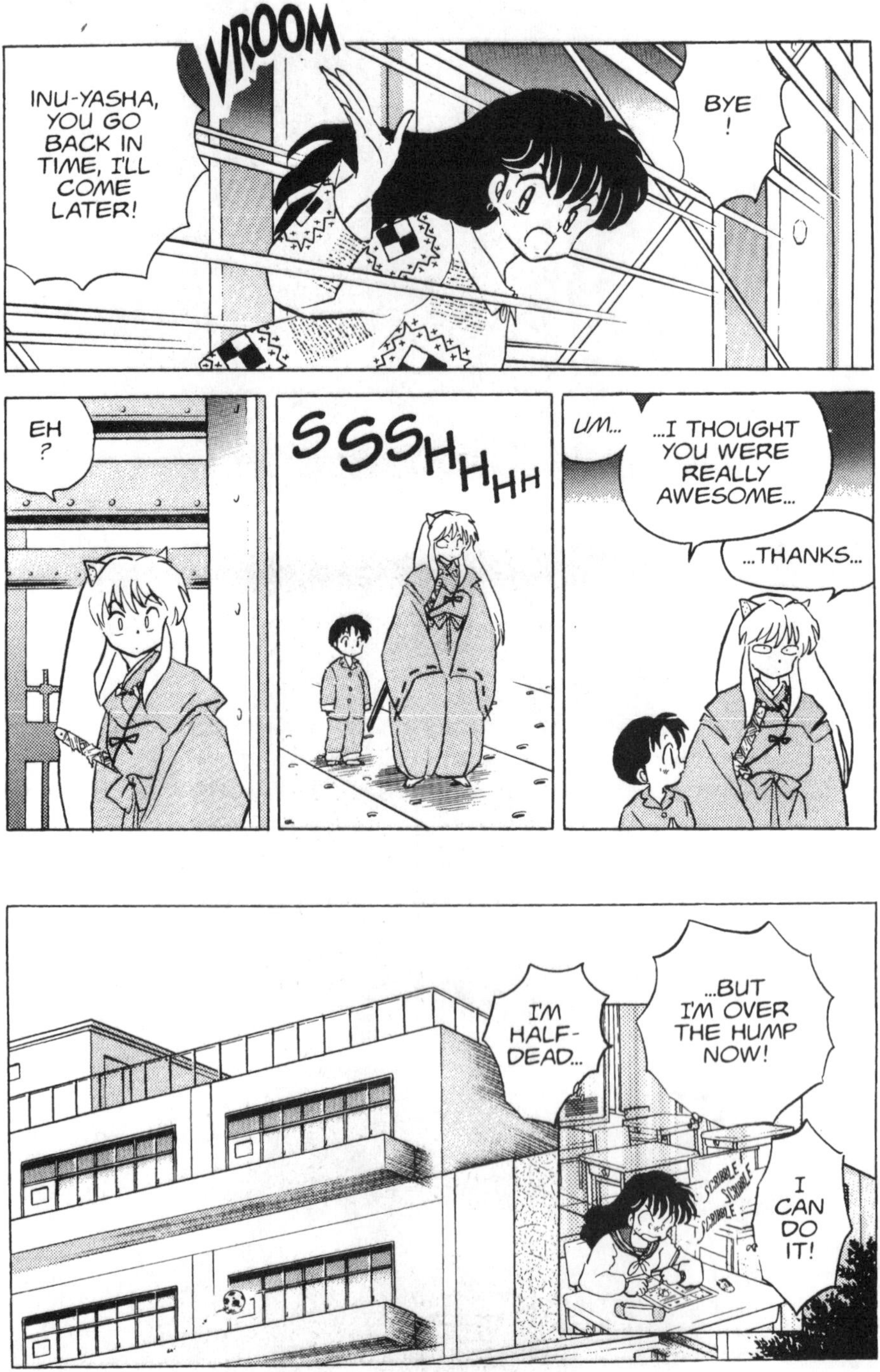
VROOM
INU-YASHA, YOU GO BACK IN TIME, I'LL COME LATER!
BYE!
EH?
SSSHHHHH
UM...
...I THOUGHT YOU WERE REALLY AWESOME...
...THANKS...
I'M HALF-DEAD...
...BUT I'M OVER THE HUMP NOW!
SCRIBBLE SCRIBBLE SCRIBBLE
I CAN DO IT!

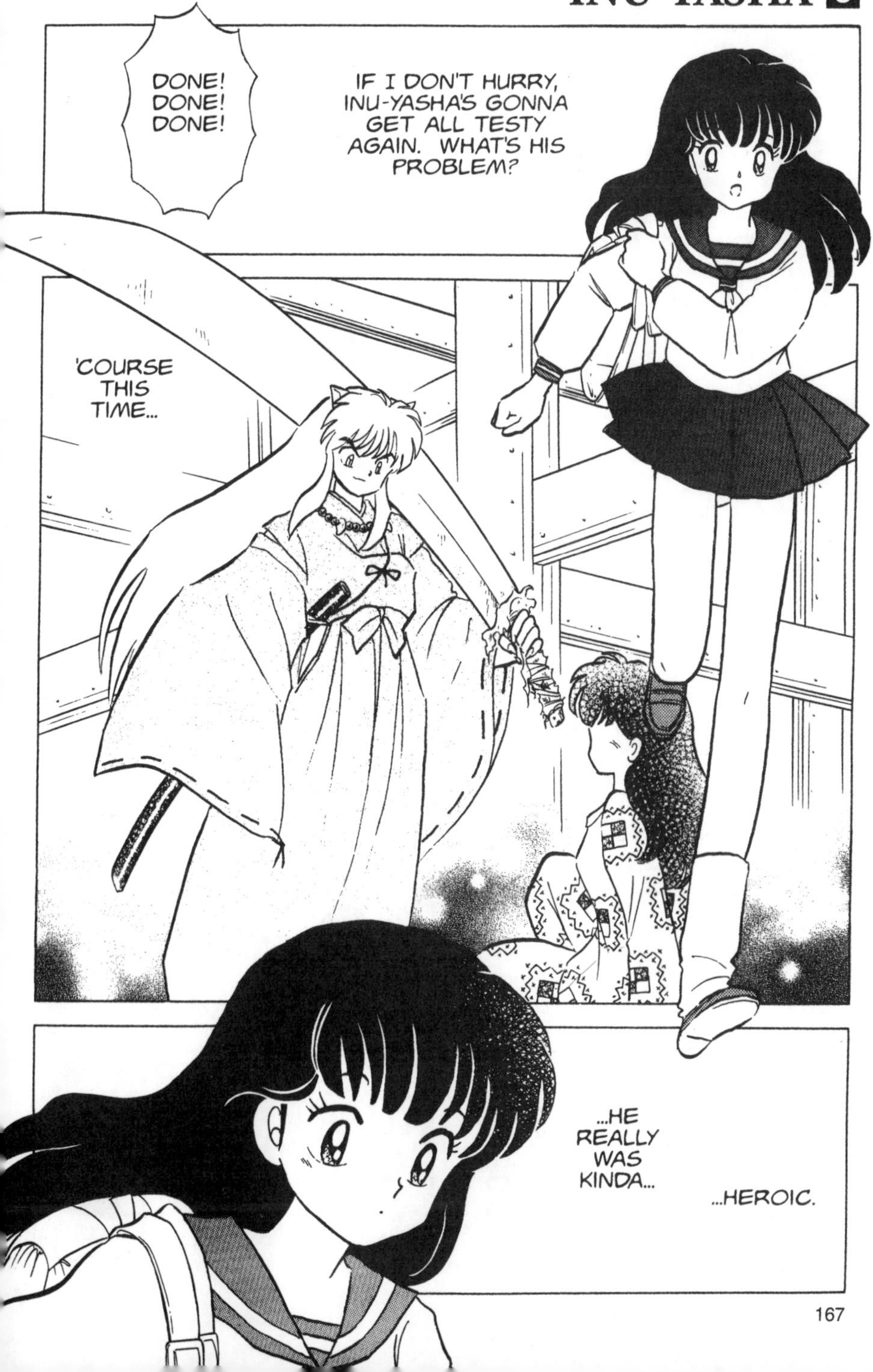
DONE! DONE! DONE!
IF I DON'T HURRY, INU-YASHA'S GONNA GET ALL TESTY AGAIN. WHAT'S HIS PROBLEM?
'COURSE THIS TIME...
...HE REALLY WAS KINDA...
...HEROIC.

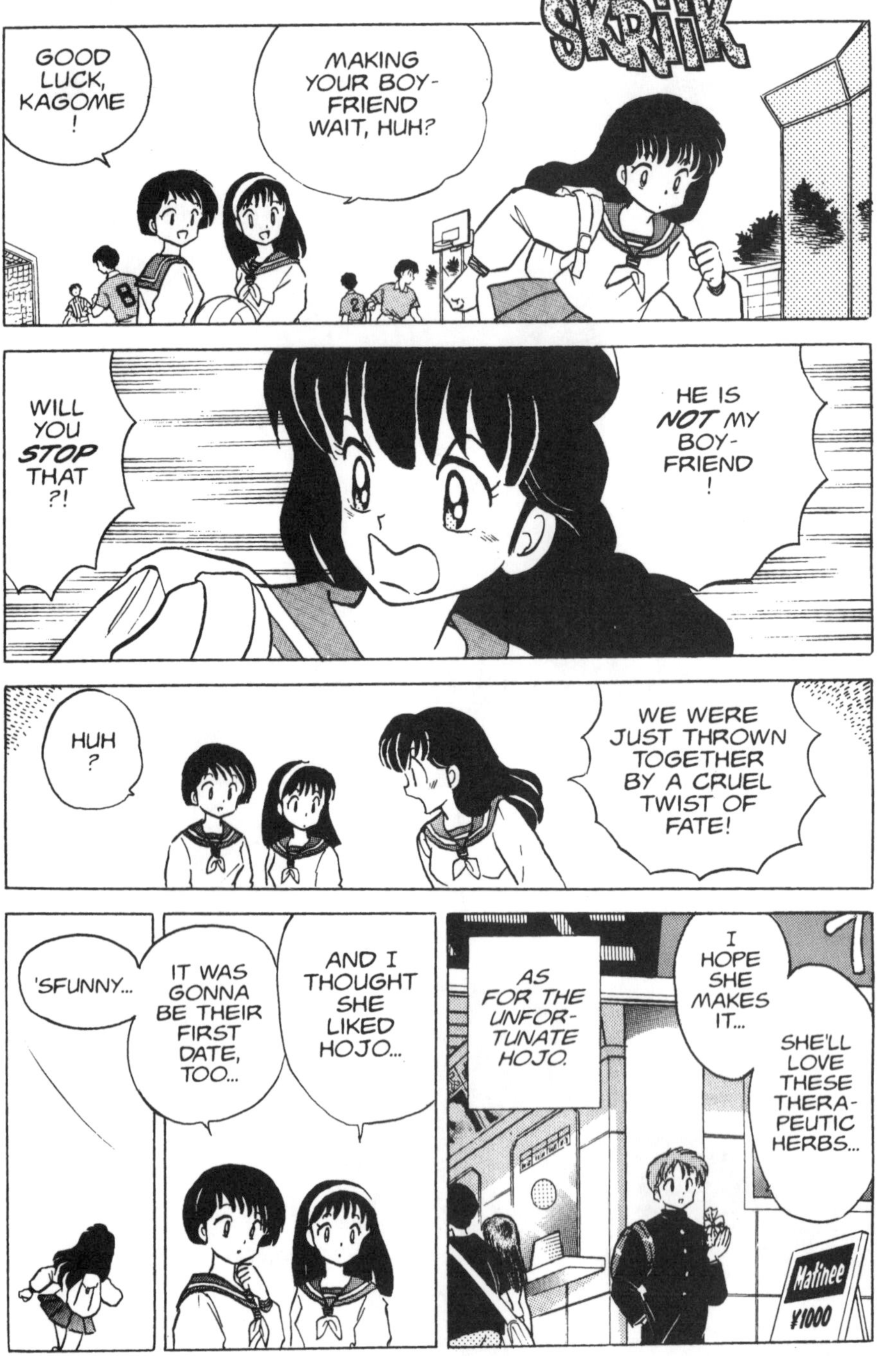
SKRIIK
GOOD LUCK, KAGOME!
MAKING YOUR BOY-FRIEND WAIT, HUH?
WILL YOU STOP THAT?!
HE IS NOT MY BOY-FRIEND!
HUH?
WE WERE JUST THROWN TOGETHER BY A CRUEL TWIST OF FATE!
'SFUNNY...
IT WAS GONNA BE THEIR FIRST DATE, TOO...
AND I THOUGHT SHE LIKED HOJO...
AS FOR THE UNFORTUNATE HOJO.
I HOPE SHE MAKES IT...
SHE'LL LOVE THESE THERAPEUTIC HERBS...
Matinee
¥1000

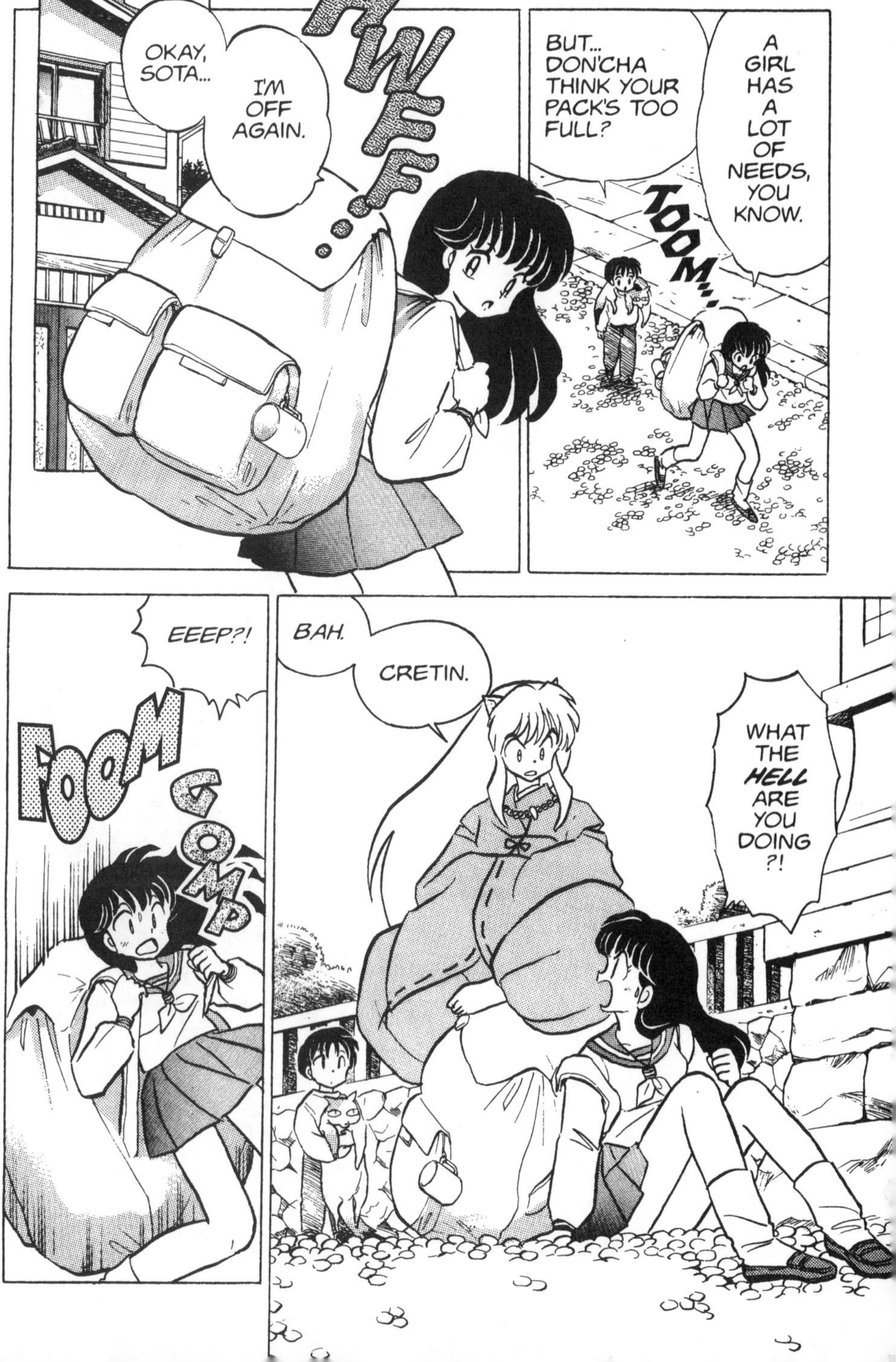
HWFF...
OKAY, SOTA...
I'M OFF AGAIN.
BUT... DON'CHA THINK YOUR PACK'S TOO FULL?
A GIRL HAS A LOT OF NEEDS, YOU KNOW.
TOOM...
EEEP?!
FOOM
GOMP
BAH.
CRETIN.
WHAT THE HELL ARE YOU DOING?!

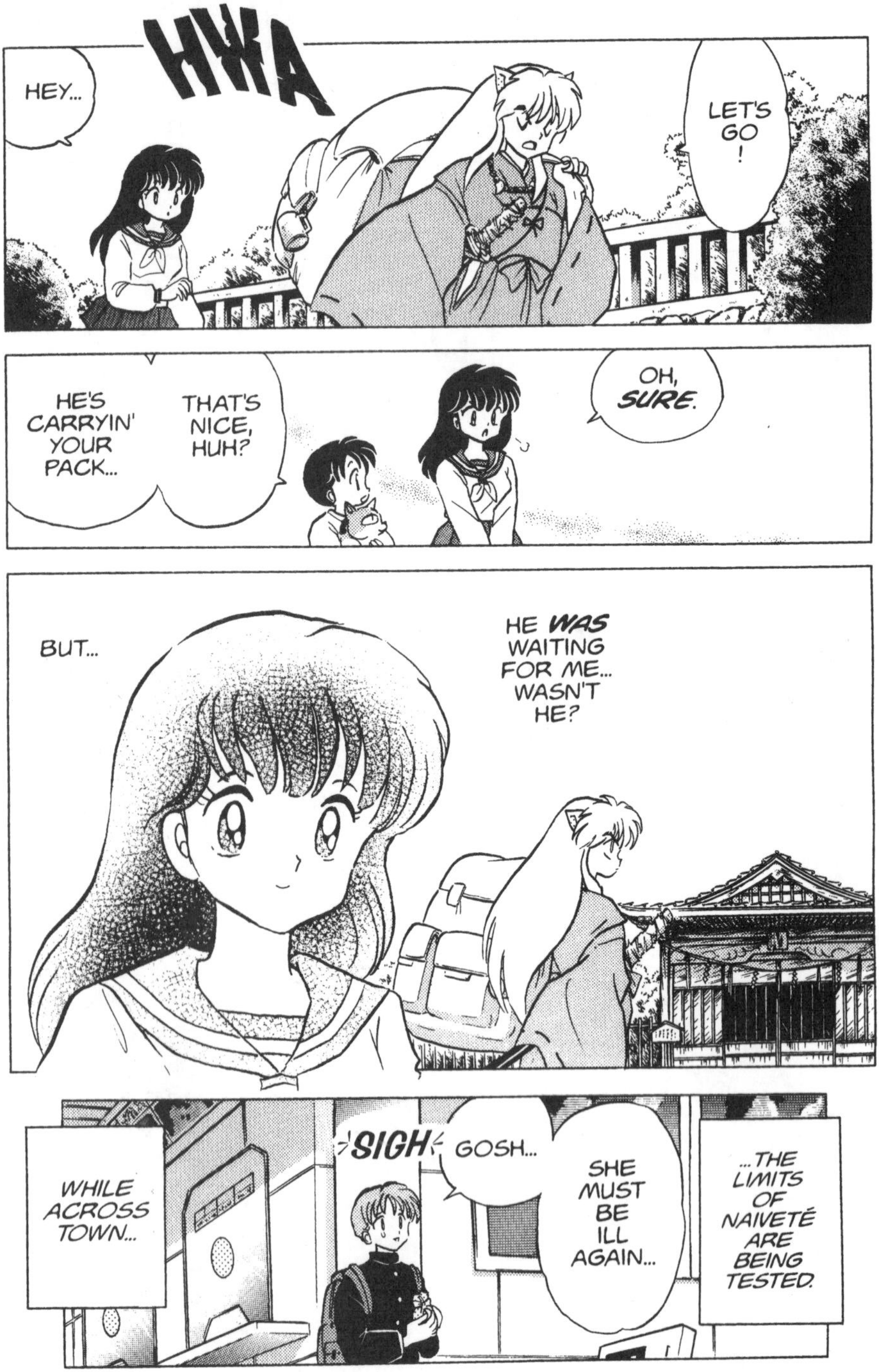
HEY...
HWA
LET'S GO!
HE'S CARRYIN' YOUR PACK...
THAT'S NICE, HUH?
OH, SURE.
BUT...
HE WAS WAITING FOR ME... WASN'T HE?
WHILE ACROSS TOWN...
SIGH
GOSH...
SHE MUST BE ILL AGAIN...
...THE LIMITS OF NAIVETÉ ARE BEING TESTED.

SCROLL TEN
FOXFIRE

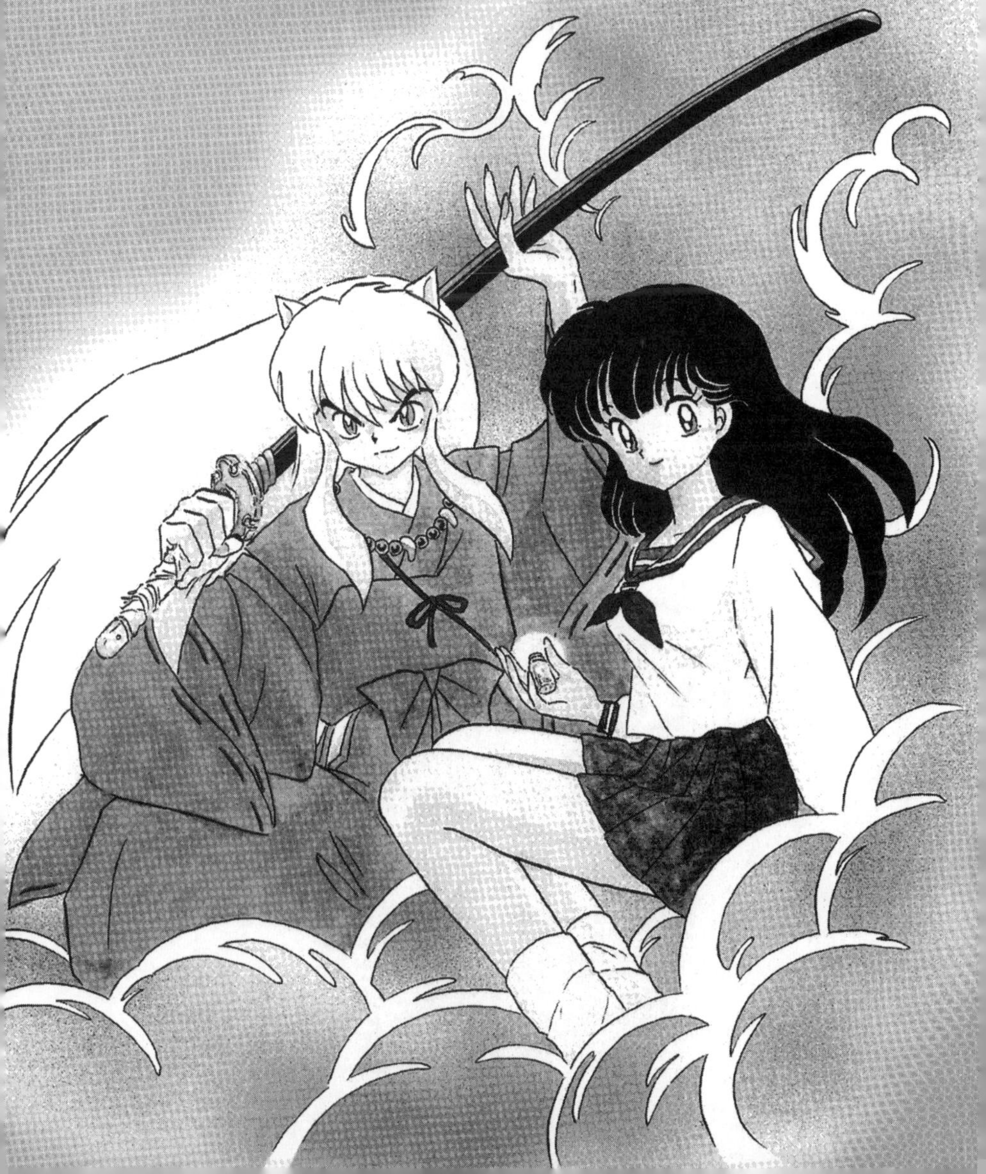

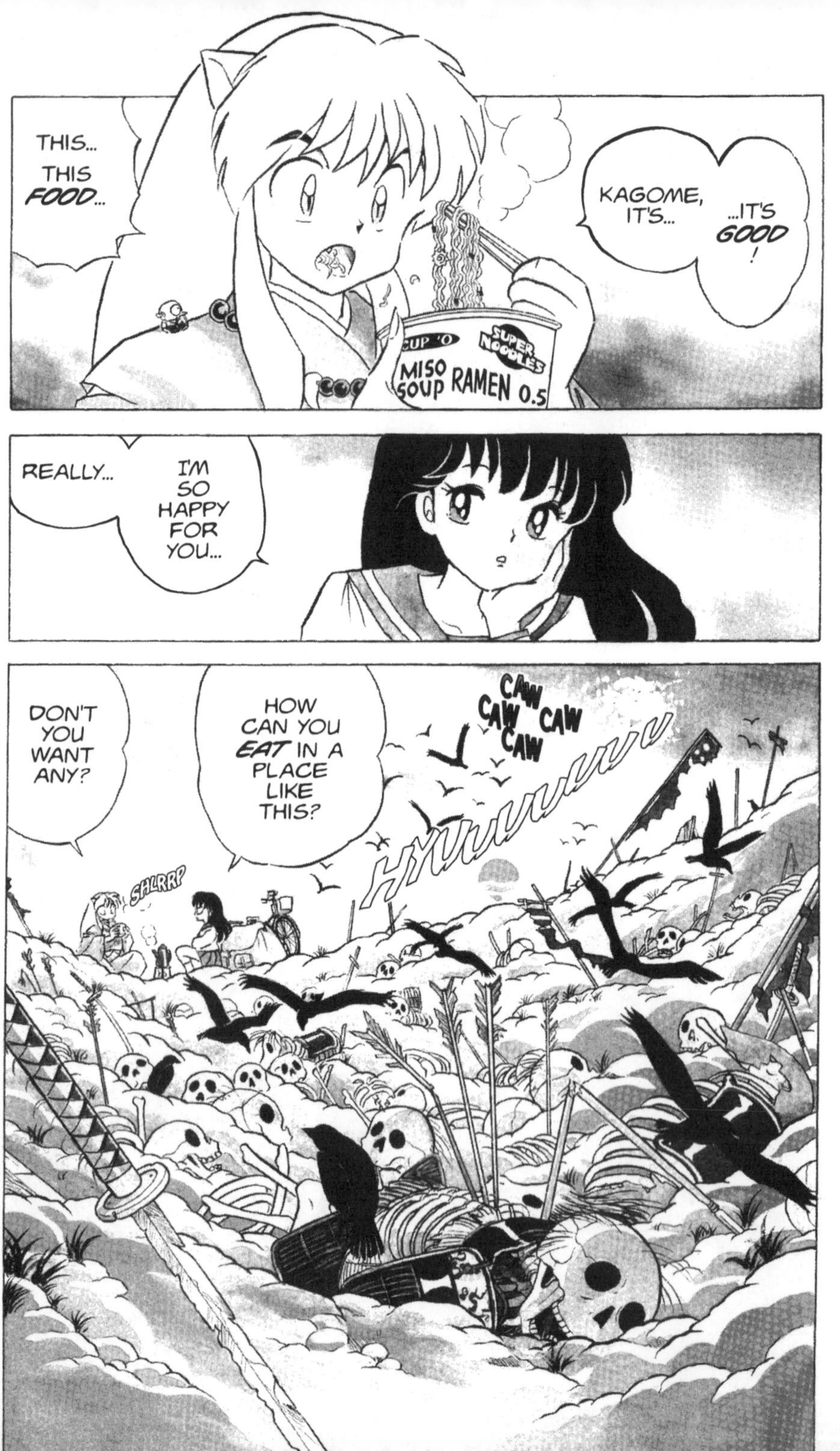
THIS... THIS *FOOD*...
KAGOME, IT'S...
...IT'S *GOOD*!
CUP 'O
SUPER NOODLES
MISO SOUP RAMEN 0.5
REALLY...
I'M SO HAPPY FOR YOU...
DON'T YOU WANT ANY?
HOW CAN YOU *EAT* IN A PLACE LIKE THIS?
CAW CAW CAW CAW
SHLRRP

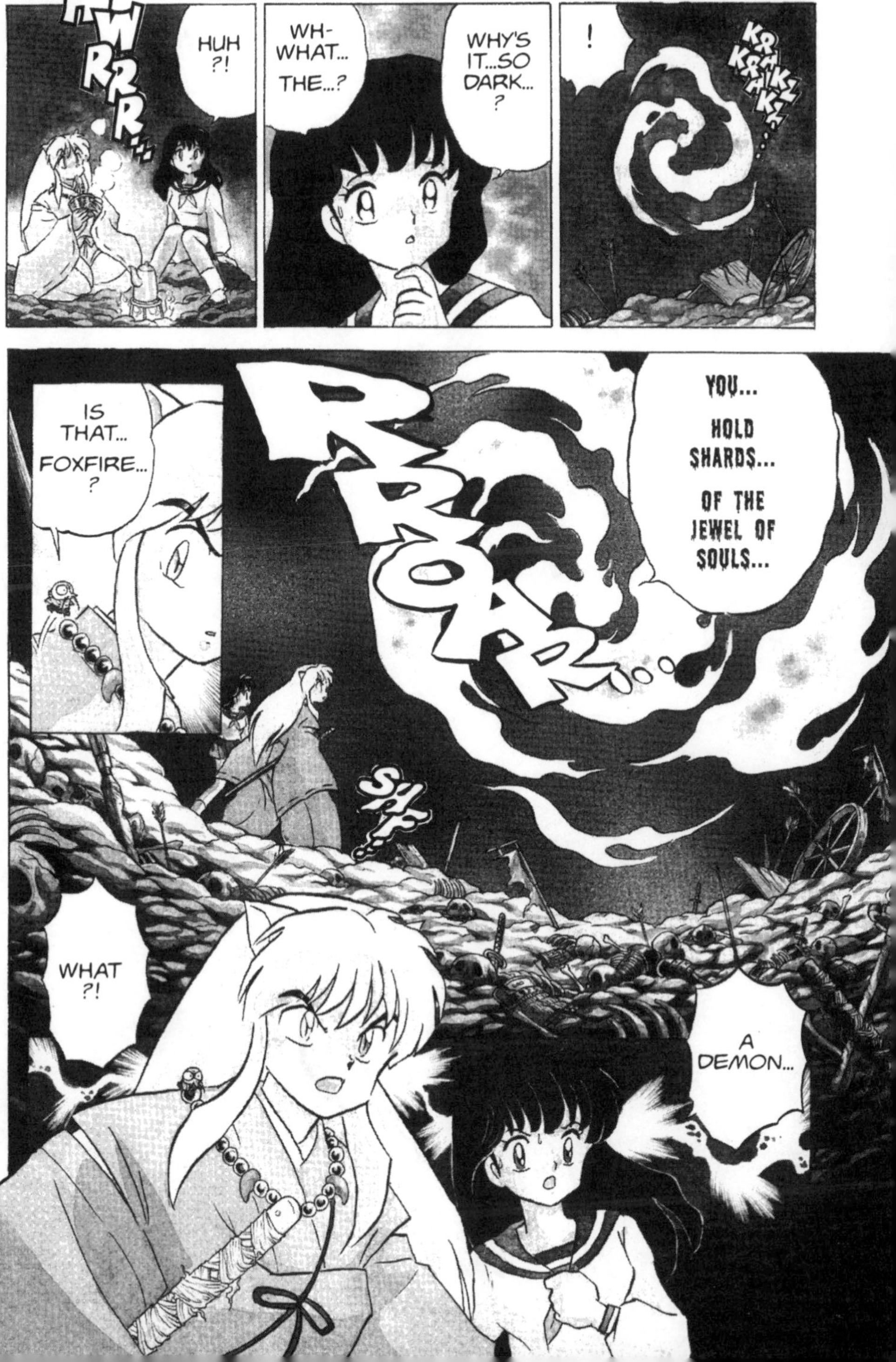
HWRRR...
HUH ?!
WH-WHAT... THE...?
WHY'S IT...SO DARK...?
!
KRAKAKAKA...
IS THAT... FOXFIRE...?
RROOAARR...
YOU... HOLD SHARDS... OF THE JEWEL OF SOULS...
SHF...
WHAT ?!
A DEMON...

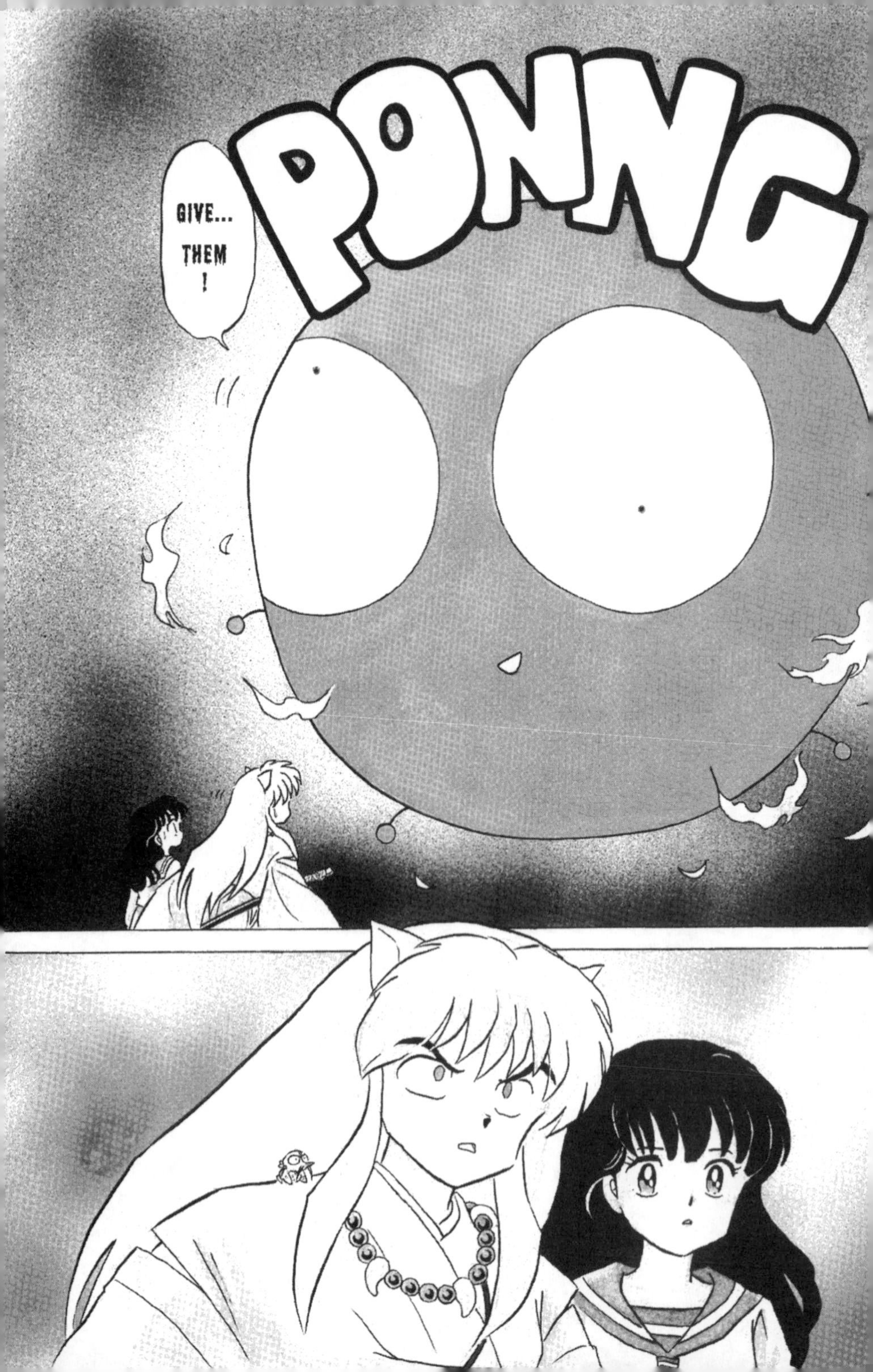
GIVE... THEM !
PONNG

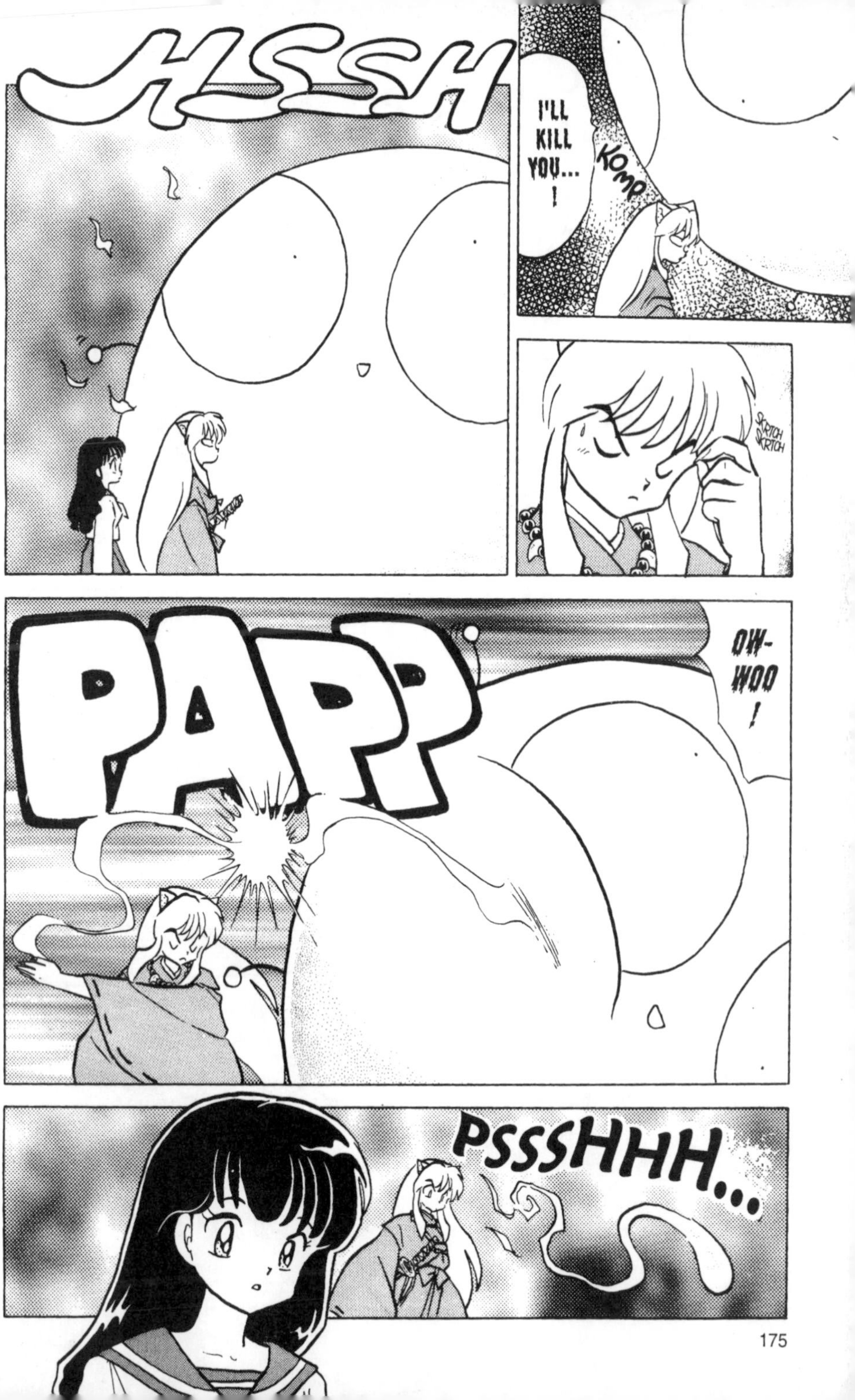
HSSH
I'LL KILL YOU...!
KOMP
SKRTCH SKRTCH
PAPP
OW-WOO!
PSSSHHH...

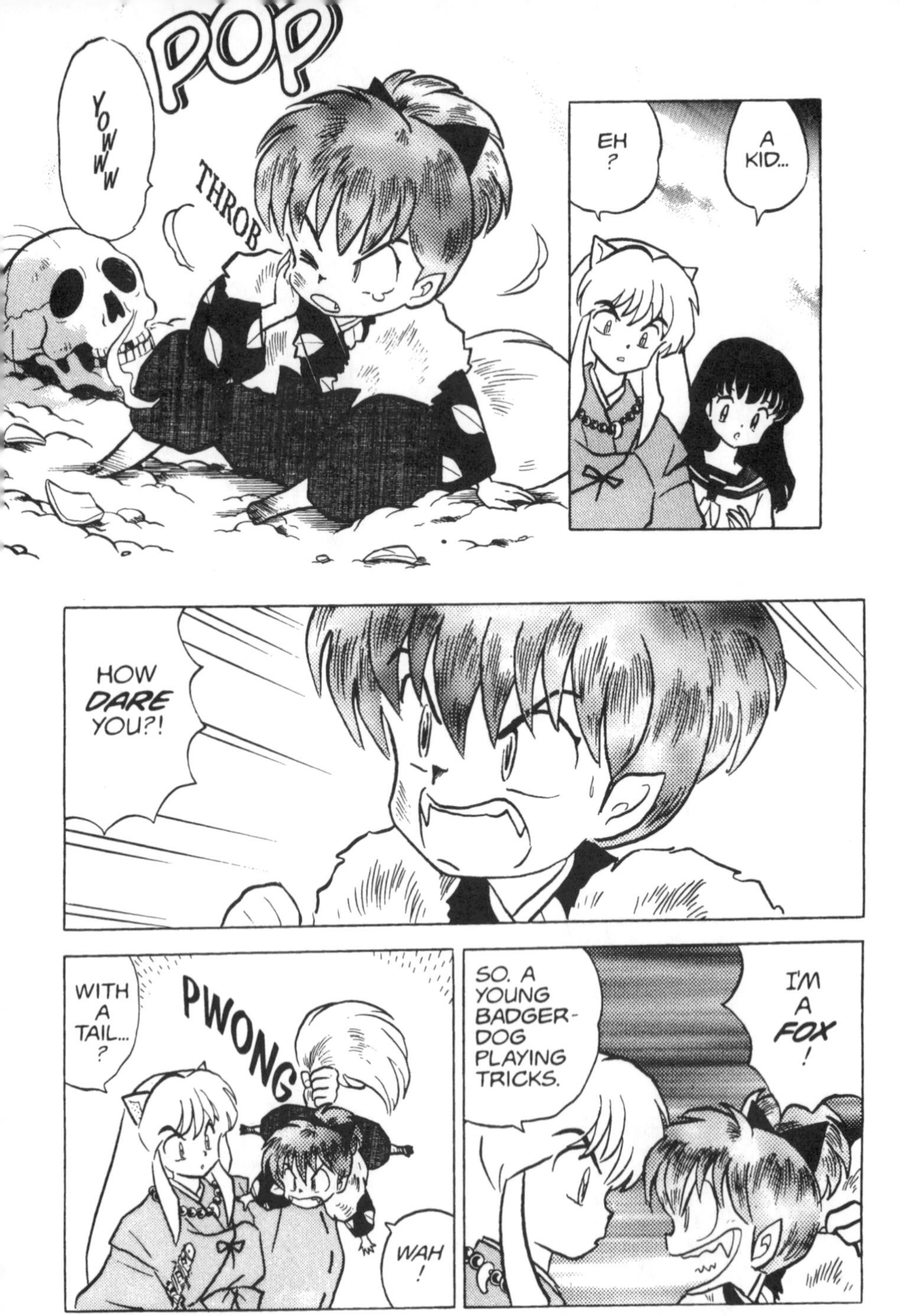
POP
YOWWWW
THROB
EH?
A KID...
HOW DARE YOU?!
WITH A TAIL...?
PWONG
WAH!
SO. A YOUNG BADGER-DOG PLAYING TRICKS.
I'M A FOX!

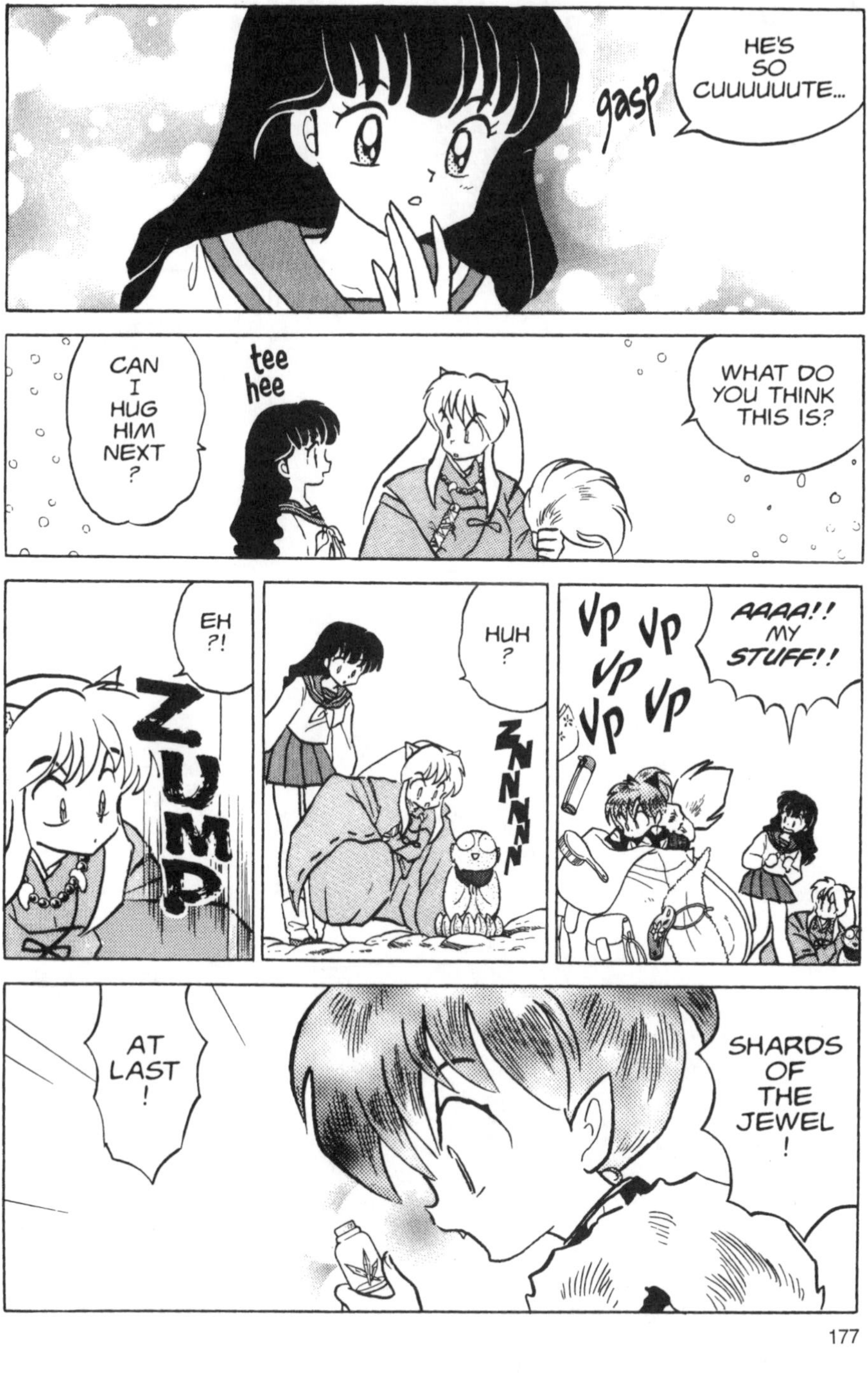
gasp
HE'S SO CUUUUUUTE...
CAN I HUG HIM NEXT?
tee hee
WHAT DO YOU THINK THIS IS?
EH?!
ZUMP
HUH?
ZNNNNN
VP VP VP VP VP VP
AAAA!! MY STUFF!!
AT LAST!
SHARDS OF THE JEWEL!

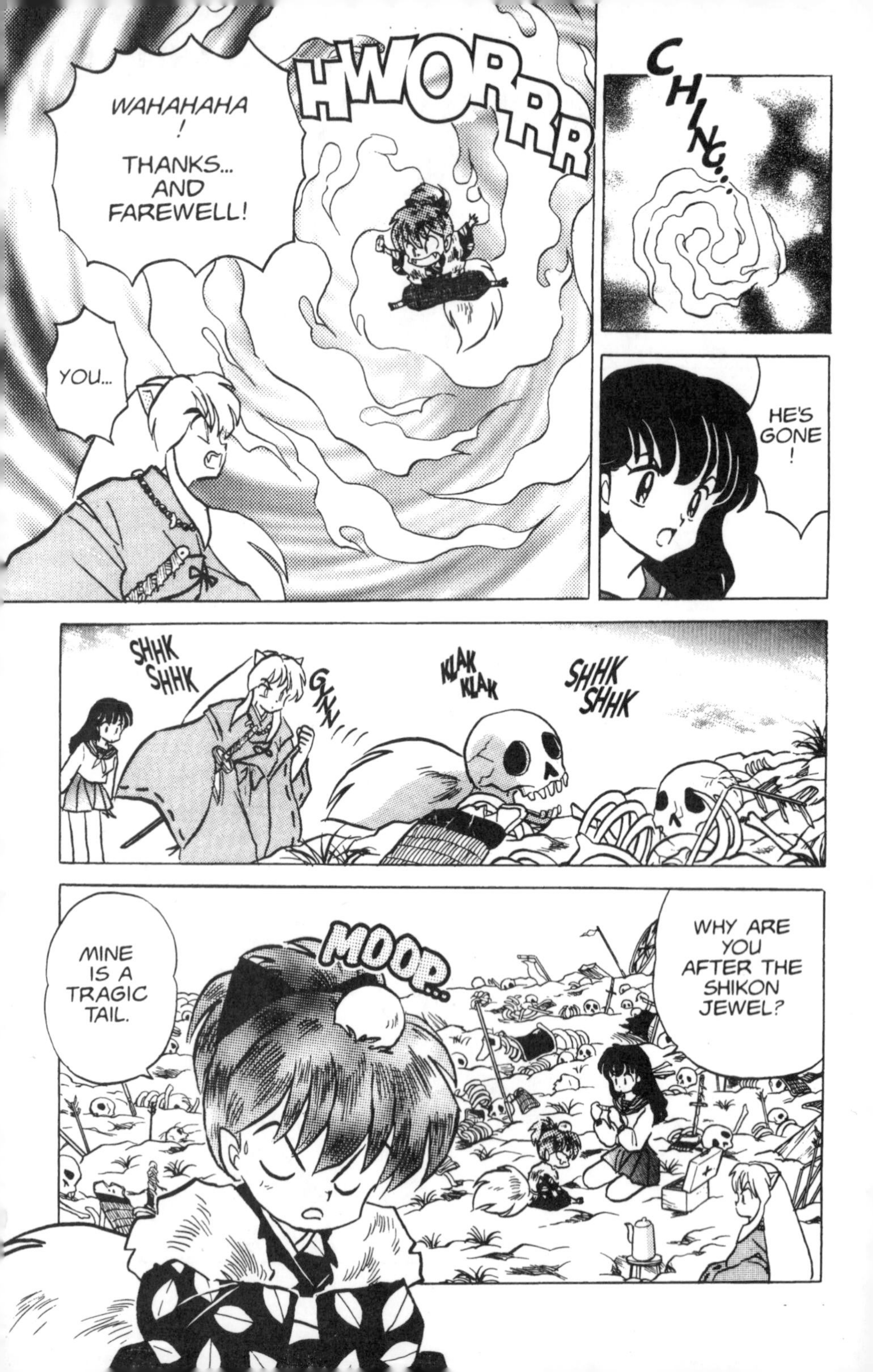
WAHAHAHA! THANKS... AND FAREWELL!
HWORRRR
YOU...
CHING...
HE'S GONE!
SHHK SHHK
GNN
KLAK KLAK
SHHK SHHK
MINE IS A TRAGIC TAIL.
MOOP...
WHY ARE YOU AFTER THE SHIKON JEWEL?

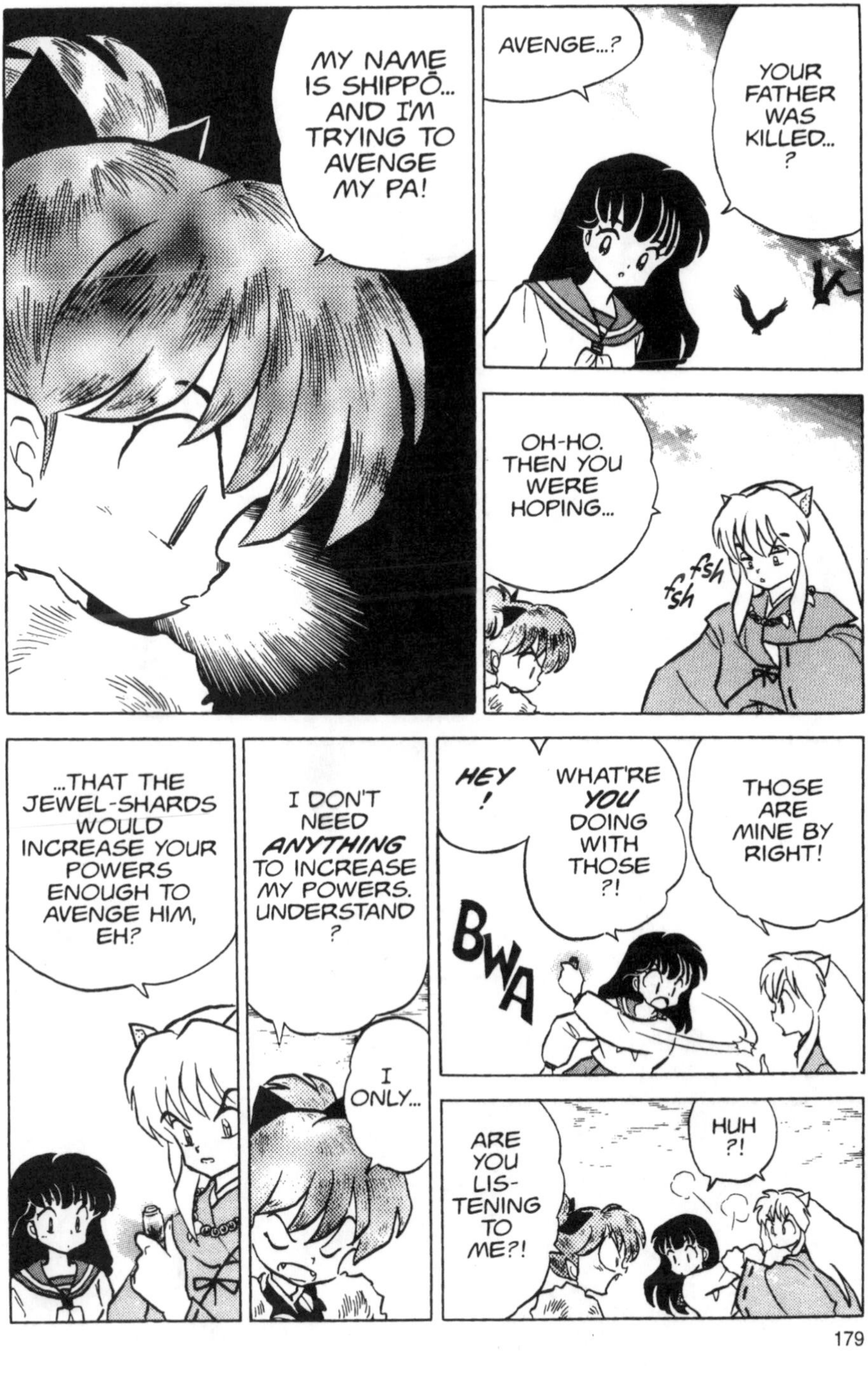
MY NAME IS SHIPPŌ... AND I'M TRYING TO AVENGE MY PA!
AVENGE...?
YOUR FATHER WAS KILLED...?
OH-HO. THEN YOU WERE HOPING...
fsh fsh
...THAT THE JEWEL-SHARDS WOULD INCREASE YOUR POWERS ENOUGH TO AVENGE HIM, EH?
I DON'T NEED ***ANYTHING*** TO INCREASE MY POWERS. UNDERSTAND?
I ONLY...
HEY!
WHAT'RE ***YOU*** DOING WITH THOSE?!
THOSE ARE MINE BY RIGHT!
BWA
ARE YOU LIS-TENING TO ME?!
HUH?!

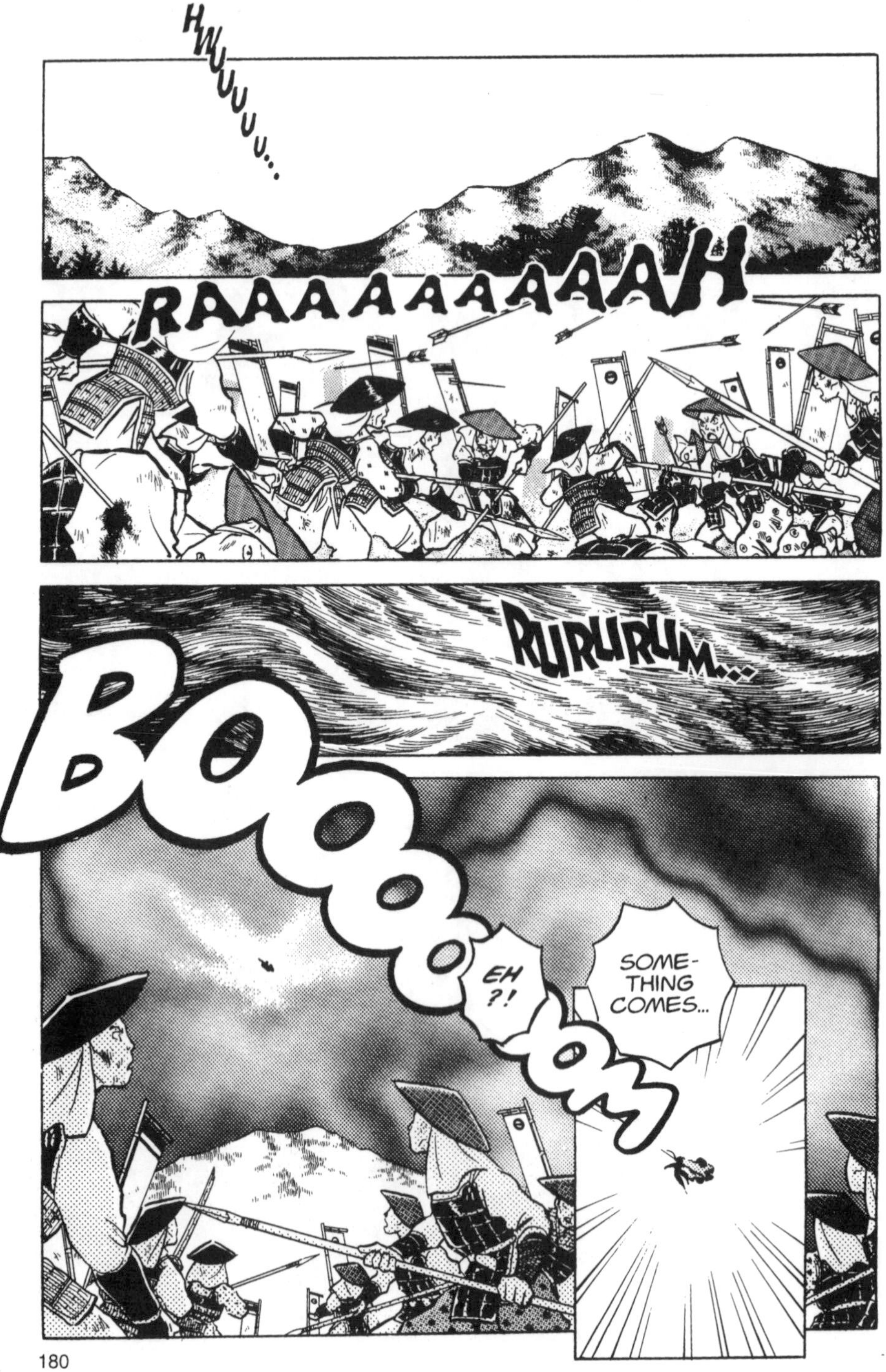
HWUUUUU...
RAAAAAAAAAH
RURURUM...
BOOOOOOM
EH ?!
SOME-THING COMES...

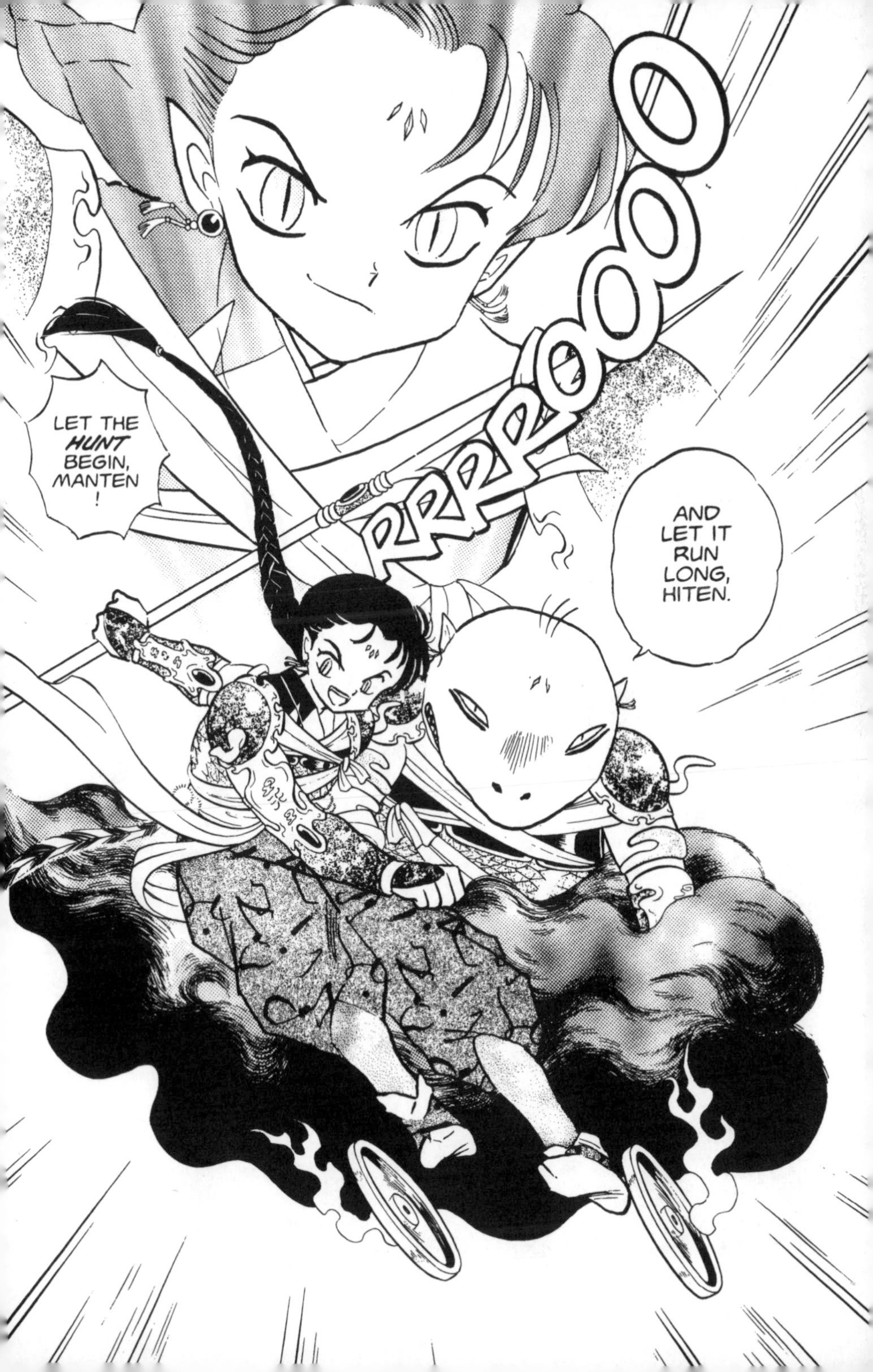
LET THE *HUNT* BEGIN, MANTEN !
RRRROOOOO
AND LET IT RUN LONG, HITEN.

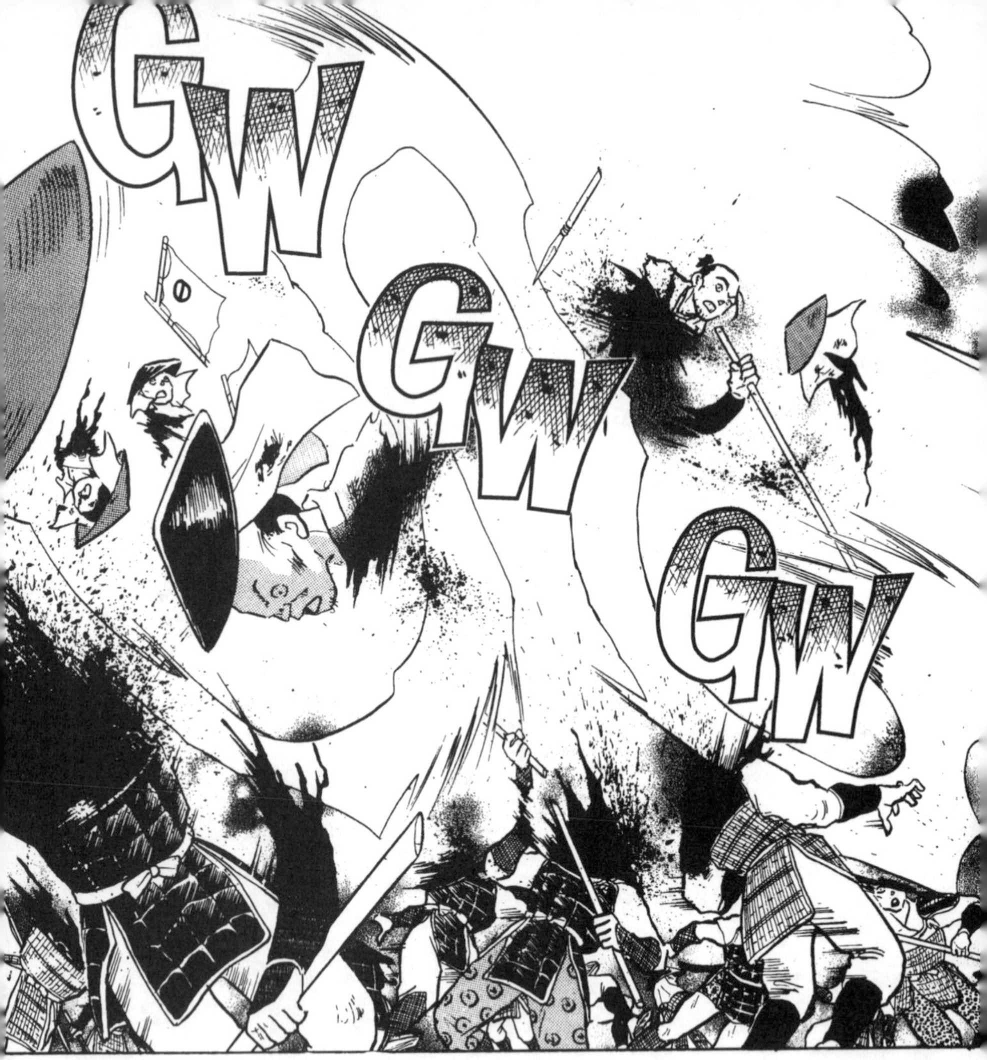
GW
GW
GW
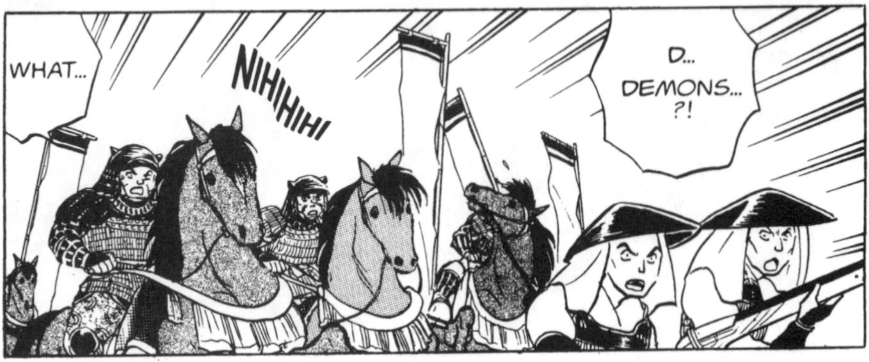
WHAT...
NIHIHIHI
D... DEMONS... ?!

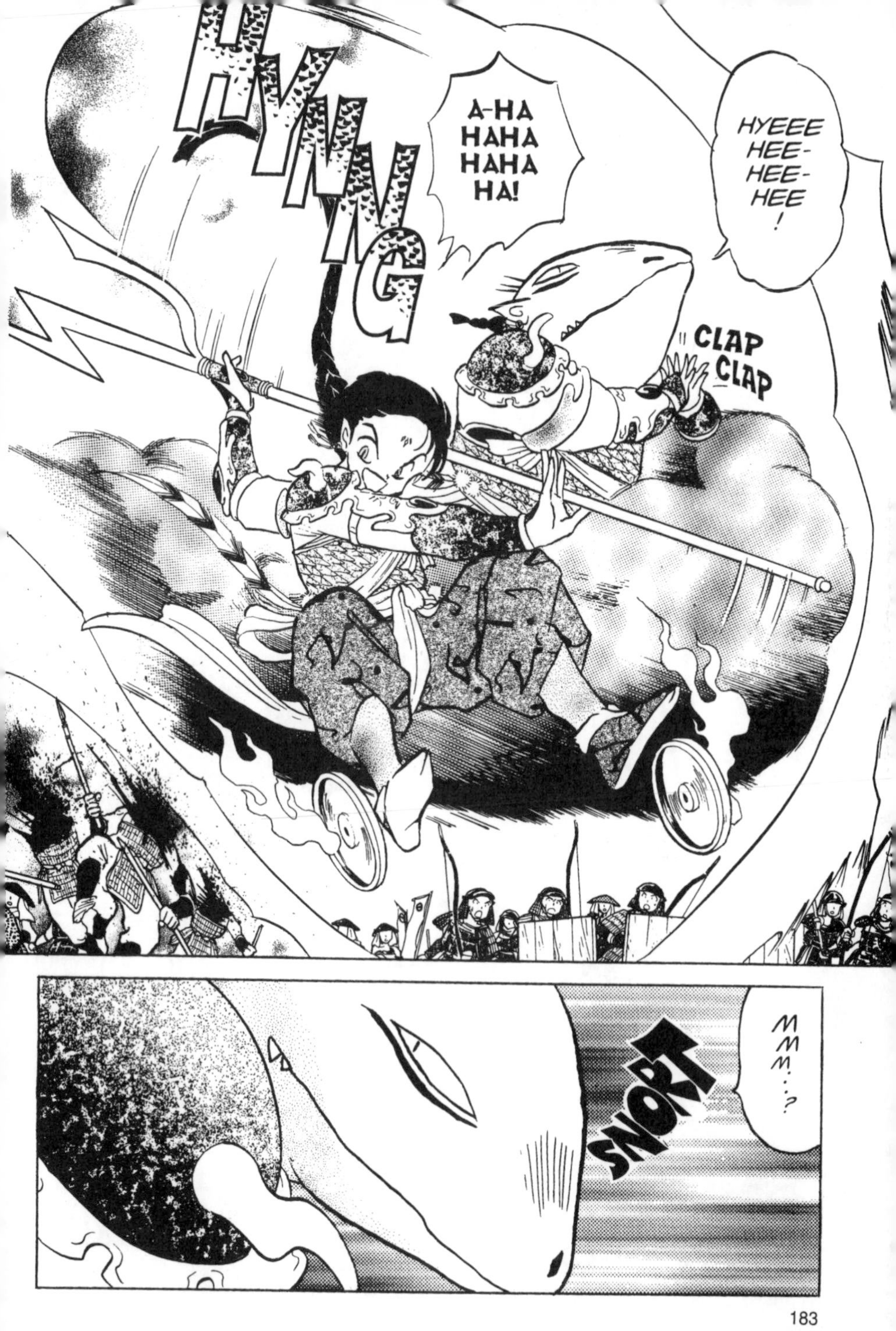
HYNNG
A-HA HAHA HAHA HA!
HYEEE HEE-HEE-HEE!
CLAP CLAP
SNORT
MMM...?

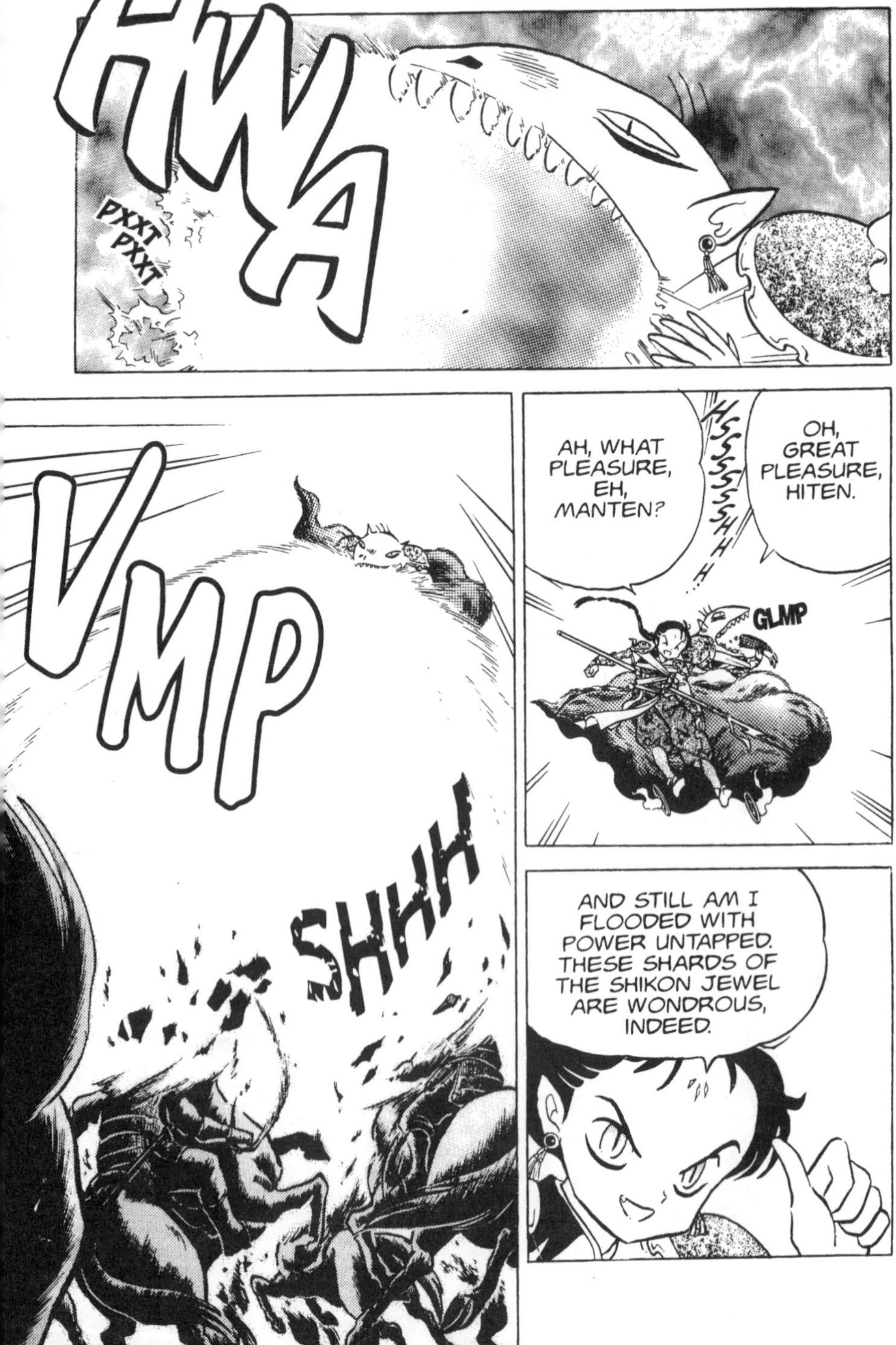
HWA
PXXT PXXT
VMP
SHHH
AH, WHAT PLEASURE, EH, MANTEN?
HSSSSSHH
OH, GREAT PLEASURE, HITEN.
GLMP
AND STILL AM I FLOODED WITH POWER UNTAPPED. THESE SHARDS OF THE SHIKON JEWEL ARE WONDROUS, INDEED.

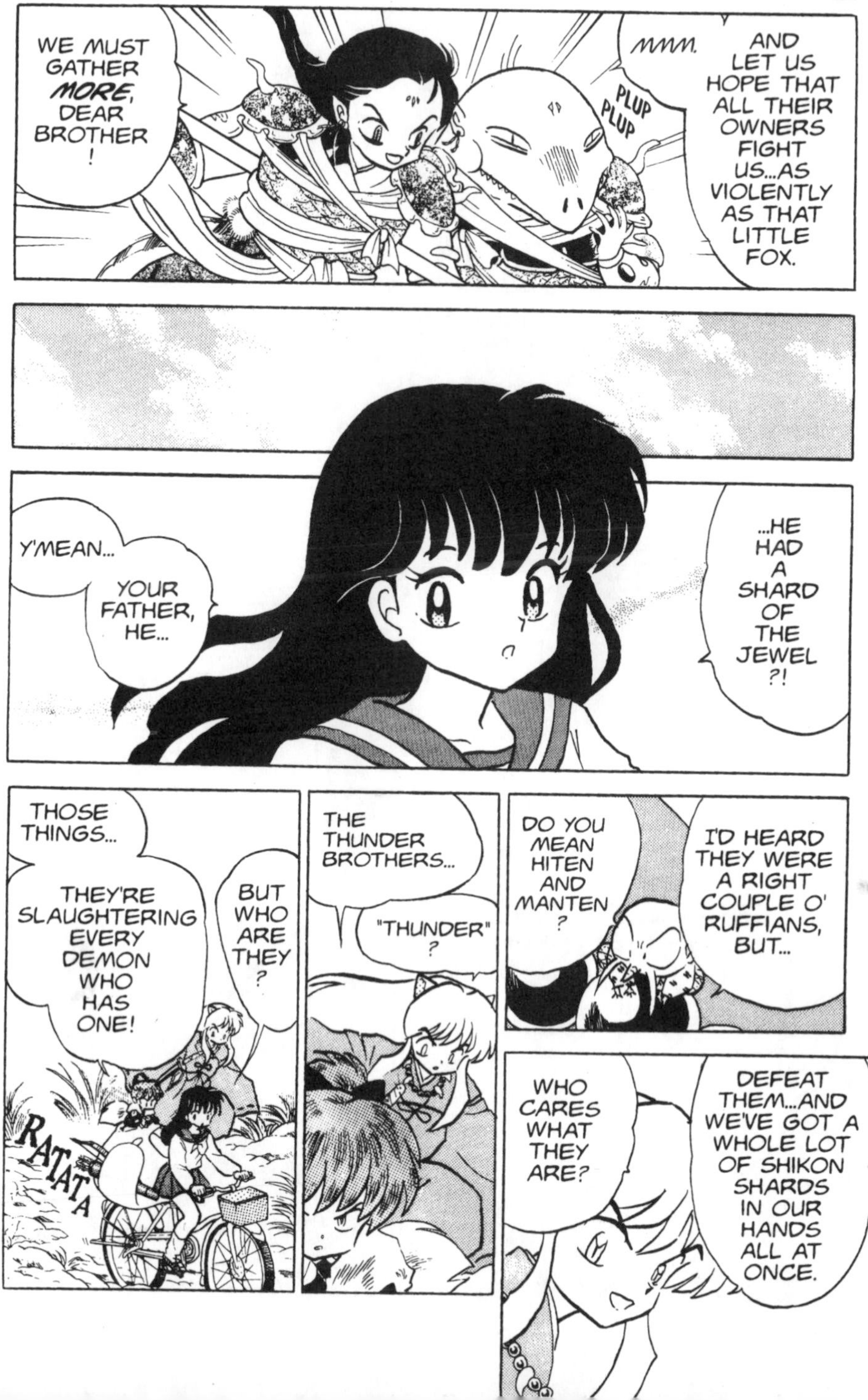
WE MUST GATHER MORE, DEAR BROTHER!
MMM.
AND LET US HOPE THAT ALL THEIR OWNERS FIGHT US...AS VIOLENTLY AS THAT LITTLE FOX.
PLUP PLUP
Y'MEAN...
YOUR FATHER, HE...
...HE HAD A SHARD OF THE JEWEL?!
THOSE THINGS...
THEY'RE SLAUGHTERING EVERY DEMON WHO HAS ONE!
BUT WHO ARE THEY?
RATATA
THE THUNDER BROTHERS...
"THUNDER"?
DO YOU MEAN HITEN AND MANTEN?
I'D HEARD THEY WERE A RIGHT COUPLE O' RUFFIANS, BUT...
WHO CARES WHAT THEY ARE?
DEFEAT THEM...AND WE'VE GOT A WHOLE LOT OF SHIKON SHARDS IN OUR HANDS ALL AT ONCE.

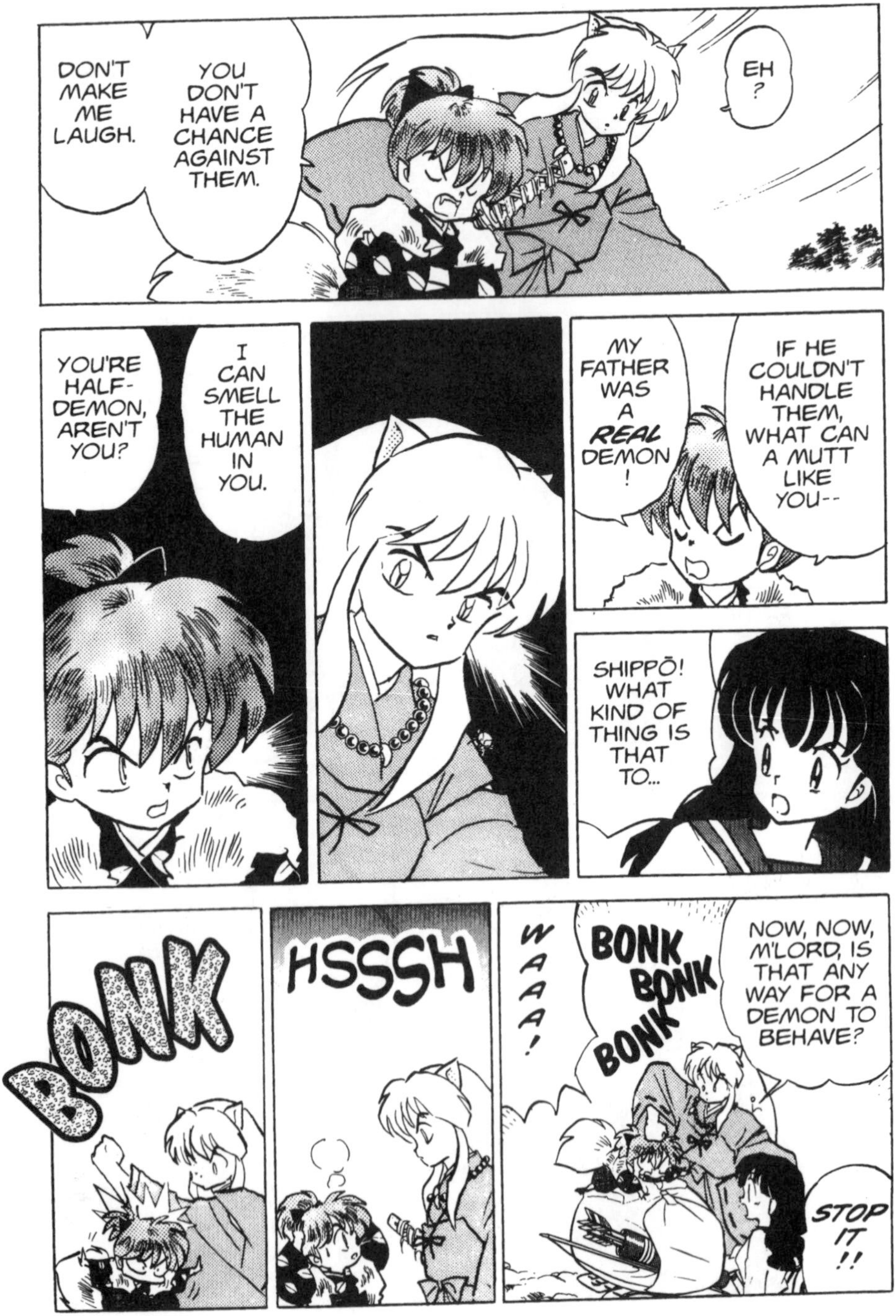

DON'T MAKE ME LAUGH.
YOU DON'T HAVE A CHANCE AGAINST THEM.
EH?
YOU'RE HALF-DEMON, AREN'T YOU?
I CAN SMELL THE HUMAN IN YOU.
MY FATHER WAS A REAL DEMON!
IF HE COULDN'T HANDLE THEM, WHAT CAN A MUTT LIKE YOU--
SHIPPŌ! WHAT KIND OF THING IS THAT TO...
BONK
HSSSH
WAAAA!
BONK BONK BONK BONK
NOW, NOW, M'LORD, IS THAT ANY WAY FOR A DEMON TO BEHAVE?
STOP IT!!

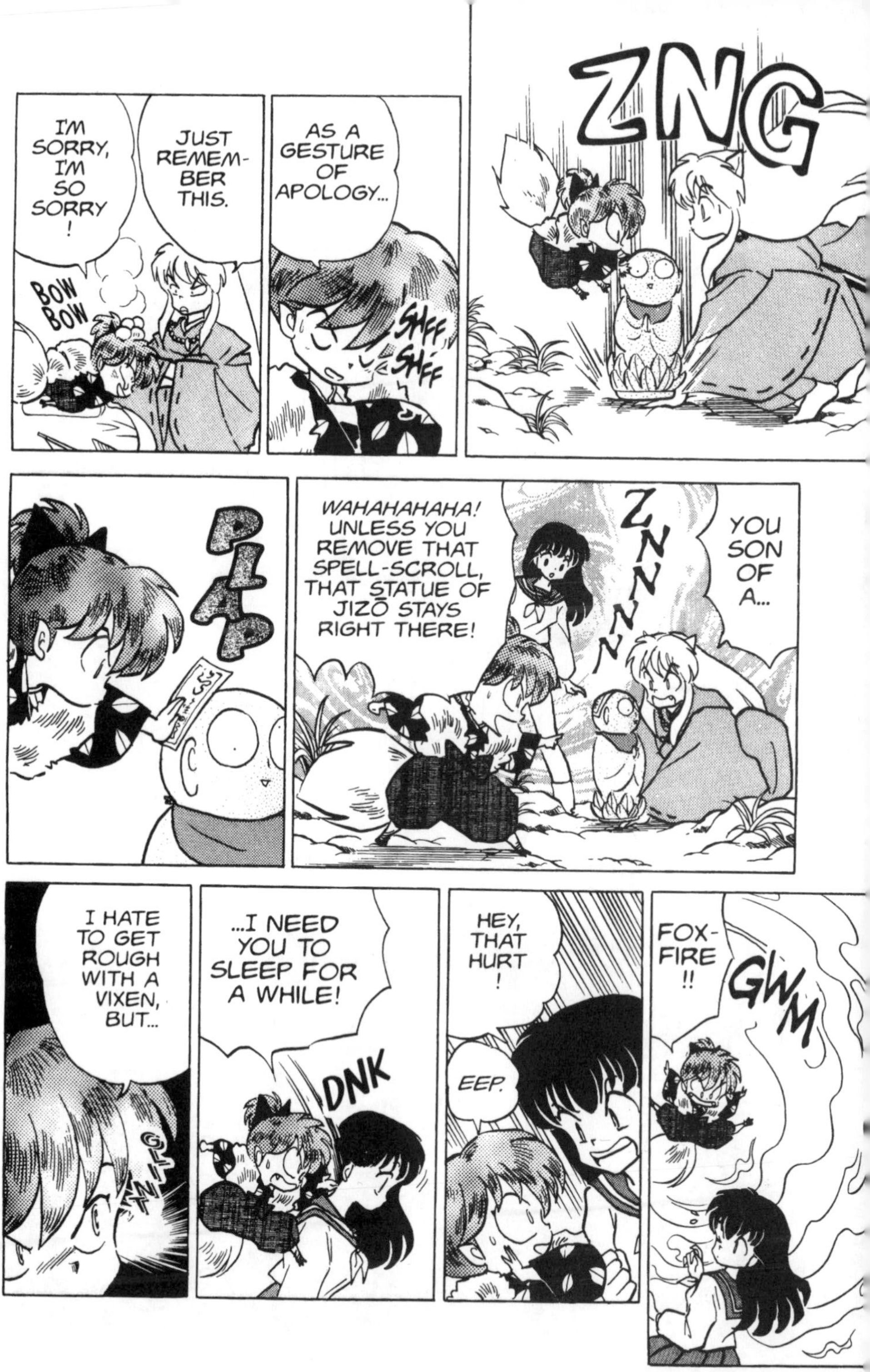
I'M SORRY, I'M SO SORRY!
JUST REMEMBER THIS.
BOW BOW
AS A GESTURE OF APOLOGY...
SHFF SHFF
ZNG
PLAP
WAHAHAHAHA! UNLESS YOU REMOVE THAT SPELL-SCROLL, THAT STATUE OF JIZŌ STAYS RIGHT THERE!
ZNNNN
YOU SON OF A...
I HATE TO GET ROUGH WITH A VIXEN, BUT...
GLINT
...I NEED YOU TO SLEEP FOR A WHILE!
DNK
HEY, THAT HURT!
EEP.
FOX-FIRE!!
GWM

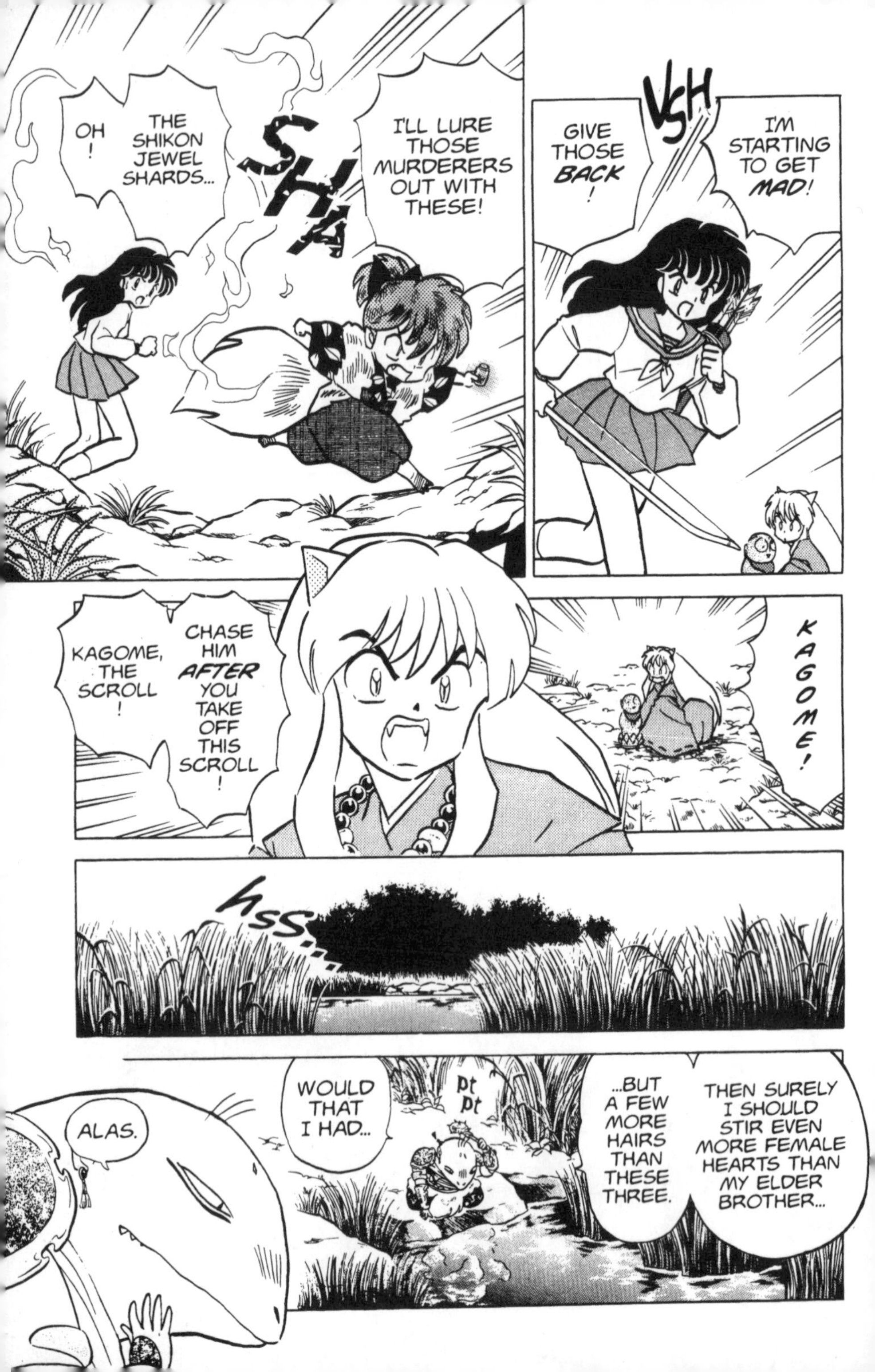
OH!
THE SHIKON JEWEL SHARDS...
SHA
I'LL LURE THOSE MURDERERS OUT WITH THESE!
GIVE THOSE BACK!
VSH
I'M STARTING TO GET MAD!
KAGOME, THE SCROLL!
CHASE HIM AFTER YOU TAKE OFF THIS SCROLL!
KAGOME!
hss...
ALAS.
WOULD THAT I HAD...
pt pt
...BUT A FEW MORE HAIRS THAN THESE THREE.
THEN SURELY I SHOULD STIR EVEN MORE FEMALE HEARTS THAN MY ELDER BROTHER...

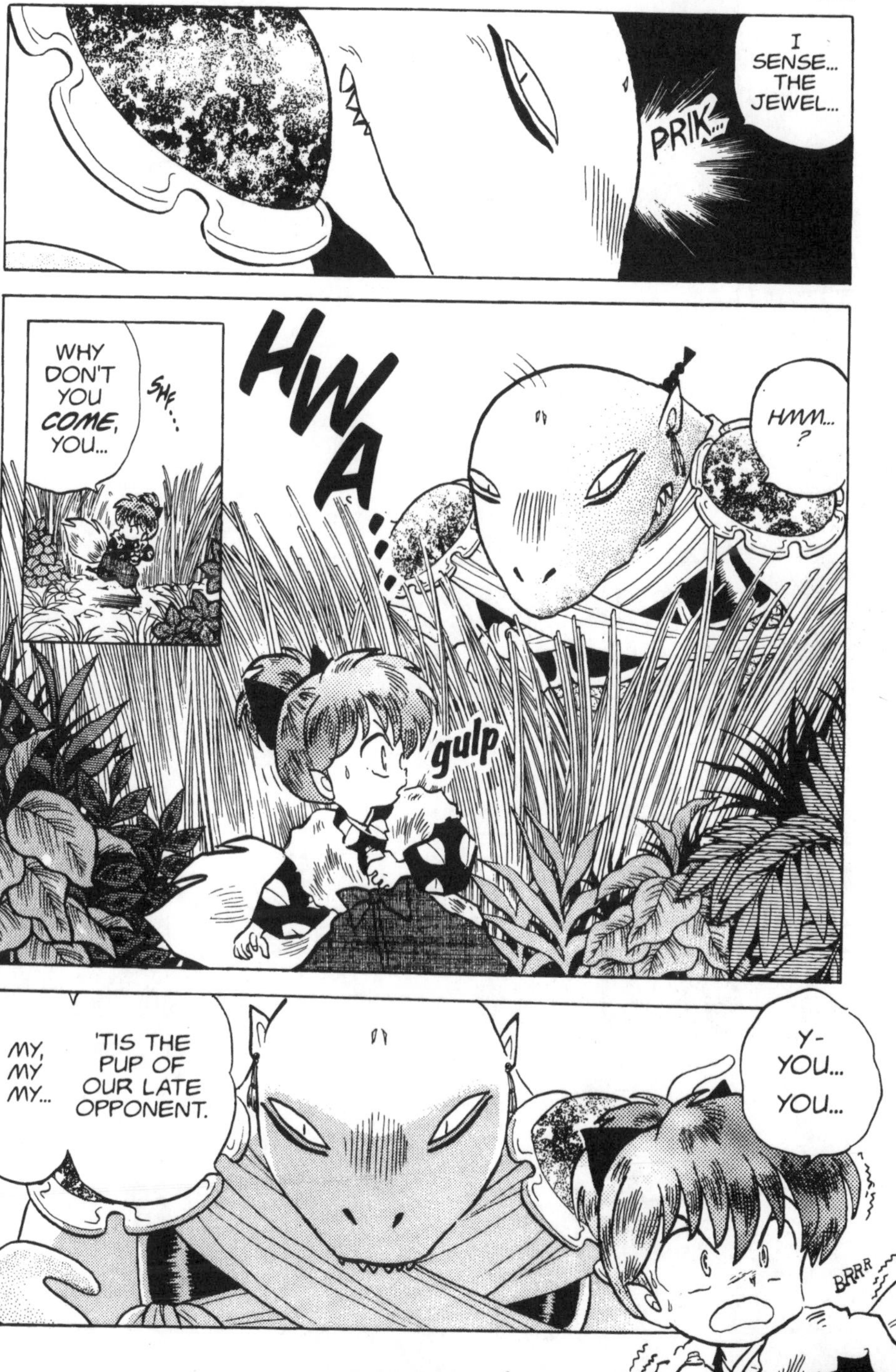
PRIK...
I SENSE... THE JEWEL...
WHY DON'T YOU *COME*, YOU...
SHF...
HWA...
HMM... ?
gulp
MY, MY MY...
'TIS THE PUP OF OUR LATE OPPONENT.
Y-YOU... YOU...
BRRR

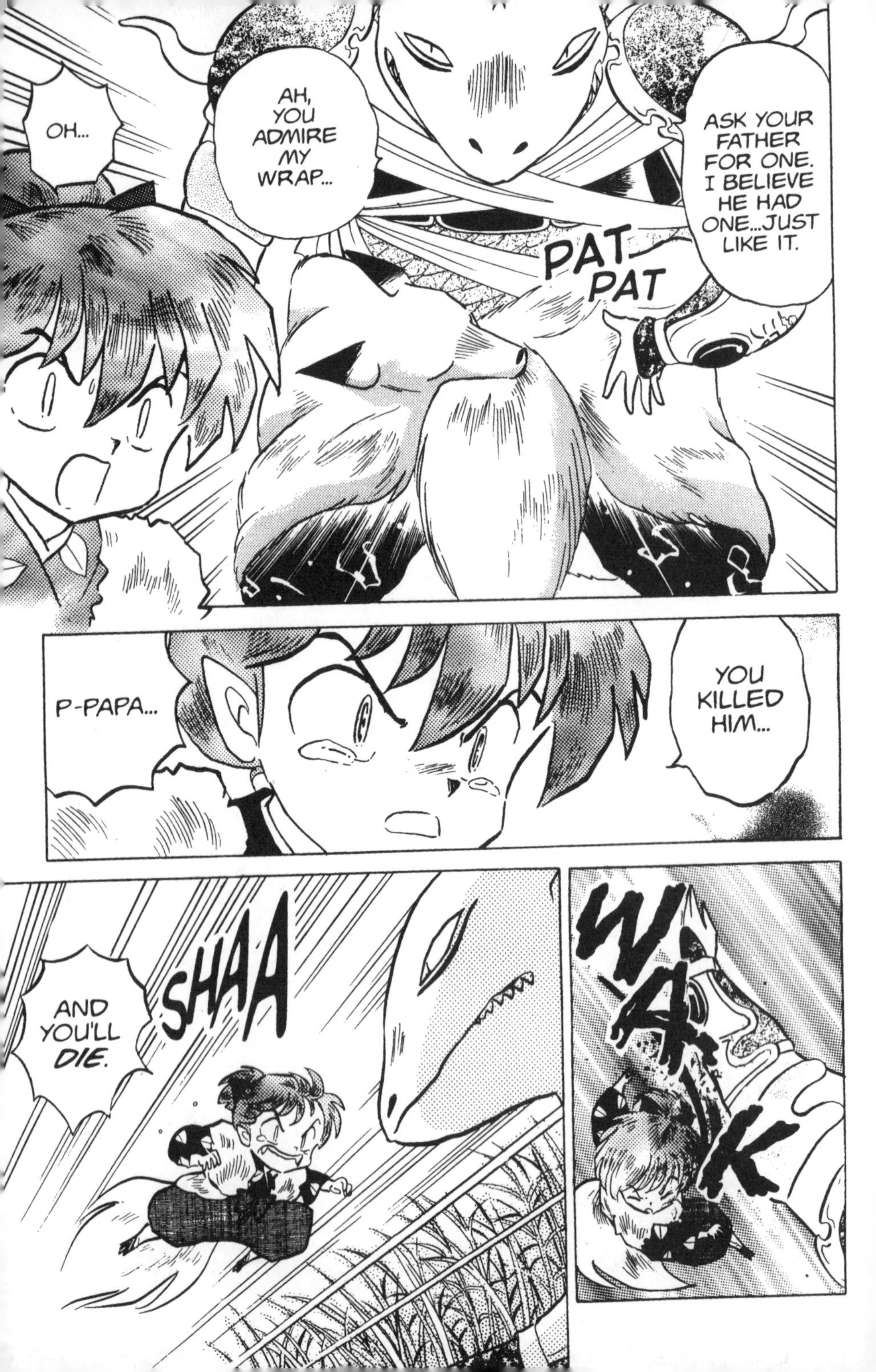
OH...
AH, YOU ADMIRE MY WRAP...
ASK YOUR FATHER FOR ONE. I BELIEVE HE HAD ONE...JUST LIKE IT.
PAT PAT
P-PAPA...
YOU KILLED HIM...
AND YOU'LL *DIE*.
SHAA
WAK

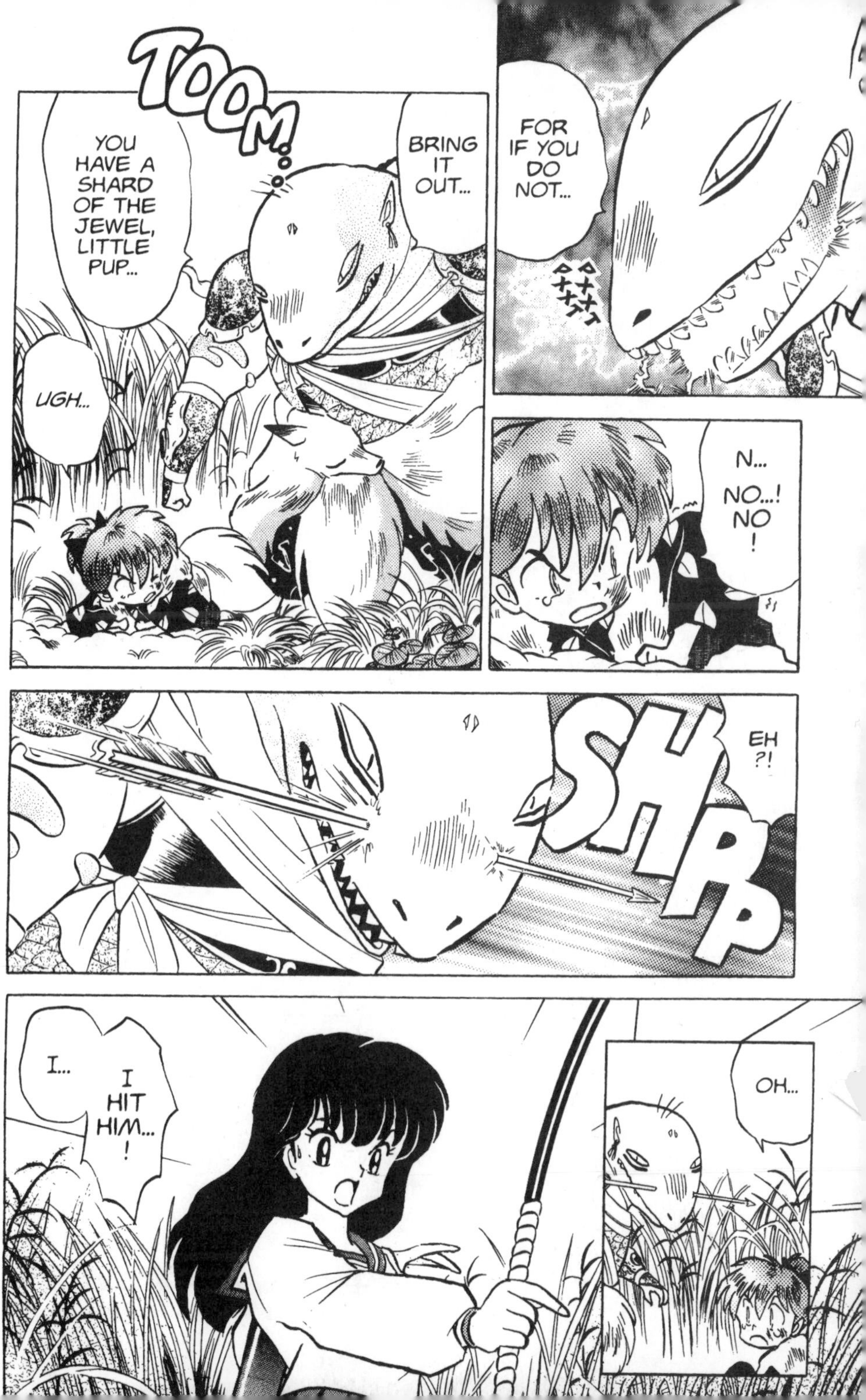
TOOM
YOU HAVE A SHARD OF THE JEWEL, LITTLE PUP...
BRING IT OUT...
UGH...
FOR IF YOU DO NOT...
N... NO...! NO!
SHPP
EH?!
I... I HIT HIM...!
OH...

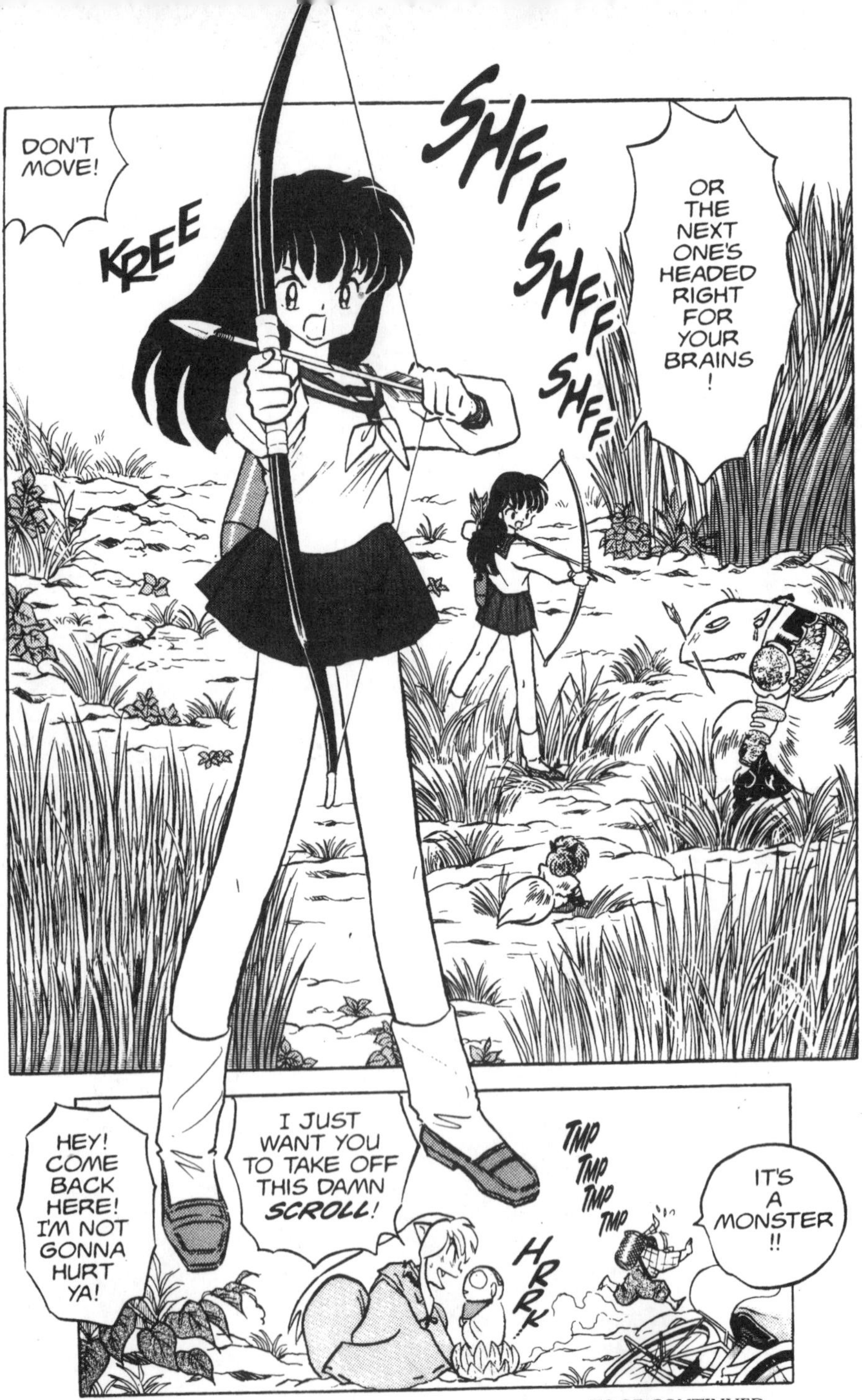
DON'T MOVE!
KREE
SHFF SHFF SHFF SHFF
OR THE NEXT ONE'S HEADED RIGHT FOR YOUR BRAINS!
HEY! COME BACK HERE! I'M NOT GONNA HURT YA!
I JUST WANT YOU TO TAKE OFF THIS DAMN *SCROLL*!
HRRK
TMP TMP TMP TMP
IT'S A MONSTER!!

TO BE CONTINUED…